Thomas Holland

and the Prophecy of Elfhaven

Book One

K. M. Doherty

Wizard's Mark Press

ISBN-13   978-0-9915720-3-8

1st Edition: March 2014
2nd Edition: June 2018
Book 1

Visit the website: www.ThomasHollandBooks.com
Visit us on Facebook: www.Facebook.com/KMDoherty.author
Tweet with the author on Twitter: @authorKMDoherty

Cover art by: Daniel Johnson of Squared Motion
www.squaredmotion.com

Map of Elfhaven by: K. M. Doherty

Here be
Dragons

The Northern Wastelands

Ruins of the
Wizards Council
Deltar
City of the Dwarves

Hidden Glen
of the
Wood Sprites

Enchanted Spring

Ruins of the
Library of Nalanda

Space Ship
crash site

X

Realm of the
Ogres

Portal
Opens

Elfhaven O

Magic Crystals

Tom captured
by Trolls/
Troll Encampment

Icebain Mountains

Floating City
O
of the
Lake Elves

The Deathly Bog

The Southern Plains
of Illusions

Tontiel Pass

Tontiel Mountains

Land of the
Trolls

Elfhaven
and enviorns

Kiloters
2   4   6   8   10

****

About the author

****

Bellchar is a critically acclaimed author in Elfhaven. That's in a parallel universe, for those of you who don't know. Obviously, Bellchar is a rock troll. As this is his first novel published on the planet Earth, and due to the fact that there appears to be strong and continued prejudice against rock trolls on this planet, Bellchar has wisely decided to publish on Earth using a "quill name." The author has chosen to write under the name of a human who befriended him some years back, K. M. Doherty. The two first met when, due to an unfortunate series of mishaps, Bellchar journeyed to the planet Earth. But that's another story…

Acknowledgements

I'd like to thank everyone who helped make this book possible. First off, thanks to my editor Katherine Mayfield, an award-winning author in her own right. Also thanks to my close friends and family for taking the time to read my draft and who gave important and thoughtful feedback: Mackenzie, Travis, Tim, Jan, Di, Geof, and Carlos. To my partner Lin for having the good sense to suggest I find a writers group early on. And that said, to the Great Bay Writers Group for their invaluable feedback on my first draft. And finally, I'm very grateful to Anne Mitchell for slogging through an early draft painstakingly editing it, line-by-line, yanking out comma's left and right with great abandon.

Contents

Prologue: Blend Elves and Dwarves, Trolls and Ogres, add a pinch of magic, stir

Tom shielded his eyes from the brilliant green light. A moment later the light faded. *Why is it suddenly so cold?* he wondered. As his eyes began to adjust to the darkness, the space before him flickered strangely. Battle cries rang out off to his left, immediately followed by the sound of intense fighting. A few seconds later the space flickered again and the sounds of fighting grew nearer.

"They're punching holes in the barrier. The battle's begun," cried a girl. But she was nothing like any girl that Tom had ever seen. She had dark brown almond-shaped eyes, long pointy ears and a beautiful thin face. As she turned toward him, her fear-filled eyes touched something deep within him.

"What are you waiting for? Come on, help me clear these rocks," yelled a short stocky lad with a rugged face, a squat bent nose, huge furry eyebrows and a large battle axe strapped across his back. Turning toward the voice, Tom saw a massive stone wall like ones he'd seen in pictures of medieval castles. He could just make out the outline of a tiny roughhewn wooden door, though it was mostly hidden by a large pile of rocks stacked against the castle wall. Tom ran over. Everyone stooped down and began frantically throwing rocks left and right, everyone except a taller boy dressed in a rich royal blue doublet with large gold buttons. The tall boy had the same odd facial features as the girl, but his shoulders were slumped forward dejectedly, and although he held a sword, the weapon pointed uselessly down at the ground.

"Devraj, git yer sorry elven hide over here and help us!" screamed the stocky lad to the tall boy with the sword. But Devraj, the tall boy, didn't move.

Suddenly a group of huge green hairless giants ran up, cursing and swinging massive wooden clubs at the kids. Just before the weapons smashed into them there was a loud "whomp" and blue sparks flew in every direction, lighting up the forest around them and sending the beast's clubs flying

1

backwards with tremendous force. The creatures cursed once more.

"The ogres have found us!" cried a young, freckle faced boy.

By now most of the stones were gone, so the stocky lad grabbed the door's ancient gnarled bone handle and pushed. Nothing happened. Slamming his shoulder against the door, he yelled, "Come on, don't just stand there, help me!" Tom, along with several others, ran up and pushed with everything they had, but it still wouldn't budge.

Devraj spoke flatly. "It's no use. I told you. It's sealed with fairy magic."

The beasts swung their clubs once more, and as before, blue sparks leapt outward and the clubs were thrown back violently.

"Avani, try yer magic," urged the stocky lad.

Sounding desperate, the girl named Avani replied, "I'll try, Goban." As she lowered her head and relaxed her shoulders, a brilliant glow sprang forth from the satchel that hung from her belt.

The ogres screamed once more. A moment later several different, coal-black creatures rushed up holding a strange blunt rod. These dark beasts were even taller than the ogres, and their skin had natural rocklike armor covering their bodies. Massive heads with no visible necks seemed glued to their upper chests, and their eyes, though dark as night, seethed with anger. The rod the monsters carried had skulls for handles and slowly pulsed with a dark orange glow.

"Hurry, Avani! The trolls have the magic battering ram. It's only a matter of time 'til they break through the barrier," cried Goban.

Avani chanted something beneath her breath, sweat forming on her brow. The light from her satchel glowed brighter. Tendrils of magical energy arced and twisted, then reached out and touched the door, but still the door stood fast.

Trolls slammed the sinister device right at Tom but it abruptly stopped, causing the area to flicker once more. There was a sizzling sound, accompanied by a bitter smelling smoke that burned Tom's eyes and nose. The space before them began to glow a deep blood red.

A magical barrier seemed to be protecting them, but it was steadily being *melted away by the monsters device. Suddenly, a long green ogre arm reached through the steaming hole and grabbed Tom by the throat. The ogre began to squeeze.*

Tom sat bolt upright in bed, his eyes open wide, sweat dripping off his forehead. It was dark out, but faint strands of moonlight filtered into his room through his window. From what he could make out as his eyes scanned his room in the dim light, everything looked just as it had before he'd fallen asleep. He glanced at his digital wall clock/calendar. It read 11:27 pm on Monday.

I must have been dreaming. It was only a dream. Tom let out a deep sigh. Then, turning to his right, his eyes fell upon his closet. The door stood open and an eerie green glow came from within. Before he could decide what to do, there was a crackling sound, and green sparks flew off in all directions. A moment later the light slowly faded, leaving only a faint wisp of smoke and a tangy metallic smell. Tom blinked, then pulled the covers up tight around his neck. He vowed he would remain awake for the rest of the night and he'd remember his strange nightmare. But within moments his eyelids grew heavy, and soon he was dreaming of sailing his sunfish on a small lake with a warm gentle breeze. The sun was shining and he could hear birds softly calling in the distance.

The next morning Tom did not remember his dream, nor the strange green light that had beckoned from his closet...

Chapter 1: Just a boy, his dog... and his robot

Maybe I should cleanup my room. Tom had to turn sideways to navigate between a large mound of clean clothes and an even larger mound of dirty ones. *Nah—I know exactly where everything is. If I cleaned it up, I'd never find anything.* Chuckling to himself he continued on past a pile of tools and electronic and mechanical do-dads. In the center of the pile stood his latest invention, his nearly completed robot Chloe. Ignoring her for the moment, he continued on heading purposefully toward his bookshelf.

Max, Tom's enormous furry slobbering Saint Bernard sat beside the robot, his eyes lazily following Tom's progress across the room.

This time I'm not going to trip, Tom assured himself, as he carefully stepped over a half disassembled electric piano. Unconsciously, he touched the lump on his head and felt the scab that still remained. "Ouch!" he said out loud. It had bled and bled. Mom had freaked! He smiled at the memory of her rushing about like a frightened chicken, scooping up rubbing alcohol and Band-Aids, a bowl of hot water and a clean washrag. It wasn't often he got to see his mom lose her cool.

Tom cocked his head sideways and stared at a lone sock which dangled forlornly from a nearby ceiling tile. *How did that get there? Oh, I bet it was when I hid my secret code translator module. Hmmm, I invented that months ago. But how did the sock get there?*

Lowering his gaze he stopped to study his reflection in a mirror. He was of average height, for a twelve year old, well almost thirteen, but lankier than most. Reaching up, he tried unsuccessfully to smooth out his thick dark brown hair which stuck out in several directions all at once. His hazel eyes sparkled as he studied himself critically.

My cheeks are two high. They make me look dorky. Shaking his head he walked the last few steps to his bookshelf then gazed admiringly upon his personal library. Well, he liked to think of it as his library, but actually it was just a single pine board shelf mounted on the wall about a foot above his dresser.

Before him on his shelf sat many books of various shapes and sizes. Some books stood upright; a tall book, followed by two short ones, then three tall books next to a medium one, etc... Here and there, a book leaned over at an odd angle, while still others were stacked sideways. As if that weren't precarious enough, there was a second layer of books stacked on top of the first, in much the same haphazard manner.

Where is it? Tom read the book titles in his mind: *How Things Work (Inventions That Changed the World)*; *Medieval Armor and Weaponry*; *Hang Gliding for Beginners*; *Snowboard Like a Pro*; *Quantum Physics for Dummies*; *The Inventions of Leonardo da Vinci*; *Programming Robots for Fun and Profit*; and *Robotic Control Systems*.

Gotcha! Reaching out his left hand, he grabbed the book titled *Programming Robots for Fun and Profit*, and with his right hand he carefully steadied the books above and to its right. Taking a deep breath he slowly slid the book out from the shelf. Once it was entirely free, he released his hand from the other books and froze...

In a strained whisper he counted, "One, two, three, four, five." Then he let out a deep sigh.

Walking back the same way he'd come, Tom opened the book and thumbed through it to a well-worn page on installing motors. Without taking his eyes off the page, he sat down, cross-legged, beside his robot. Max looked up at him and drooled. Holding the book open with his elbow, Tom reached under a robotics magazine and pulled out his walkie-talkie.

"Jim-Bob, this is Mastermind. Come in. Over," Tom glanced at his wrist, checking the time on his classic LEGOs Indiana Jones watch.

A brusque voice crackled over the walkie-talkie. "James here, what is it now?"

"I'm almost finished with Chloe! You've got to be here when I fire her up for the first time!"

"Why not just call me on the phone, like everybody else?"

"The walkie-talkies are more fun. Besides, this way we get to use our codenames," replied Tom knowingly.

Setting down the radio Tom read the first couple of paragraphs to himself, glancing occasionally at his robot.

A few moments later, James opened Tom's bedroom door. "Or you could yell out the window. I just live next door, you know." James was taller and even skinnier than Tom. He had blond hair that was neatly trimmed except for a stubborn clump near the back that refused to lie down. His face was covered with freckles, and when he smiled you could see a gap between his two rather large front teeth.

Tom continued to read the instructions and without looking up said, "James! Took you long enough. Hey, get me that servo from my desk. The one with the blue gear attached."

"Servo?" said James, raising an eyebrow.

"Motor," replied Tom flatly. "Servo/motor, same thing."

James stared at a large, nicely framed poster of an old movie hanging on the wall above Tom's bed. It was titled "L'Empire Contre Attaque," which was the French release version of the Star Wars movie "The Empire Strikes Back." Tom had told him before that this copy had been autographed by George Lucas himself, and was one of his mom's prized possessions. When Tom had originally begged her to let him hang it in his room, she'd said no. She was afraid he'd ruin it, but eventually she'd relented, saying he had to promise to guard it with his very life.

James carefully stepped over the junk piles as he plotted a course for Tom's dresser. "Your mom hasn't made you clean up your room yet?"

"I'm an inventor. She's a scientist. Scientists understand the creative minds of inventors. She says—" Tom cleared his throat, then continued in a high-pitched voice, "'Your room's your room. Do with it as you will,

6

but the mess must stay in your room!'" In his normal voice, he wistfully added, "I do have to help clean the rest of the house, though..." After a moment, he continued, "If you think my room's bad you should see Mom's study."

James looked skeptical.

"Where is your mom?"

"It's Tuesday. On Tuesdays she teaches wushu at the Chinese Martial Arts Academy. So each Tuesday Uncle Carlos, Dr. Carlos Mendoza that is, comes over and makes us dinner. He's in the kitchen now, cooking."

"Dr. Carlos Mendoza," repeated James solemnly.

"He's got a PhD. He works with mom at the lab. Everyone just calls him Carlos."

James thought for a moment. "Wushu? Is that the same as kung fu?"

"I think so." Tom furrowed his brow, concentrating. "Mom says kung fu really means working with intensity, with total focus, living in the moment. She said a person can do anything with kung fu, gardening, or serving tea, or—building a robot." Tom grinned, glancing sidelong at his friend. Then he frowned. "She even said I should do my homework using kung fu."

Still walking, James chuckled. Once he'd arrived safely at the dresser, he scanned the items lying about for the motor. To his left were wheels, sprockets, gears, rubber bands, even a hydraulic arm. To his right were assorted electrical parts: diodes, resisters, transistors, a disassembled cell phone, along with a half-eaten apple and a rubber frog. Tom had tried to explain to James the difference between diodes and resisters, but he just couldn't keep them straight, let alone all the other parts.

"Were the swords on the wall in the living room your mom's?"

"Yeah, she knows several sword and staff forms. She tried to teach me a staff form last year but—the thing was too long and heavy. I kept tripping over it and hitting myself in the back of the head."

"Is this the one?" asked James, holding up a large motor with red and black wires hanging off it.

"No, the one with the blue sprocket."

James spotted the motor over to his right. It had wires attached which protruded out from under the half-eaten apple. Grabbing the wires, he slowly pulled the servo out, making sure not to touch the slimy-looking apple. Retracing his steps he sat down beside his friend, holding the motor so Tom could bolt it on using an open-end wrench.

"You've been working on your robot for months. Aren't you getting bored?"

"Nah, even though this'll be the first time she's actually ever moved, I talk to her constantly. I can tell her anything... I guess I think of her like a real person, like a best friend." Tom glanced at James and hastily added, "Not as good a friend as you, of course."

Apparently James hadn't taken offence. "What are you going to do once you've finished her?"

"Mom's trying to get a waver so I can enter her in the regional FIRST Robotics Competition here in Chicago. It's only a couple of months away. Who knows, if we can get in and she wins, we'll be going to the nationals."

"A waver?"

"Yeah," began Tom. "Normally the competition is for teams of high school students, and the robots are built from special kits. So, technically I'm too young and I'm not part of a team, and I didn't start from a kit, but other than that..."

James raised his brow but changed the subject. "What kind of competition is it? Obviously not a beauty contest," he said, looking at the bare struts, greasy gears, oily motors, and coiled wires. The robot was large, maybe two feet wide by two feet long, with its main body standing a foot and a half tall. A tubular mast rose up from the center of the robot. The mast had a platform on top, about a foot above the robot's main body that sported two large LEDs along with motion and infrared detectors. It looked like something out of a low-budget version of a "Transformers" movie—a very low budget version.

"Is that a car battery? Does she need that much power?" asked James.

"Yeah, I ordered some high-capacity, quick-recharge batteries, made specifically for robots, but they haven't arrived yet. I found this one in the garage. The auto shop thought the battery was the problem with Mom's car; turned out to be something else. They wouldn't take the battery back, though. Mom was pissed."

Tom finished tightening the last nut, then connected the battery to the central processing unit.

"Now for the moment of truth!" Raising his arm flamboyantly, Tom flipped a switch on Chloe's left side. The LEDs lit up and started flashing as she ran through her internal diagnostics. A gentle whirring noise sounded for a second, then the LEDs both turned bright green.

James looked impressed.

"So far, so good," said Tom proudly, as he picked up the remote controller. It had a small keypad, an LCD display and a miniature joystick set right in the center. He typed in a command, and the robot immediately spun around and took off at full speed straight for them. Tom jumped sideways and James hurled himself behind a pile of clothes as the robot tore past them. Tom's eyes grew enormous as he frantically typed in commands, but Chloe just raced straight into his closet, crashing into a baseball bat and flipping over backwards. She made a loud, high-pitched scream as her caterpillar tracks spun wildly. As if in slow motion, the bat, with a baseball mitt perched atop it, fell sideways. The mitt slid off the bat, hitting a snowboard which tipped over, taking with it a large box of LEGOs and sending them flying in all directions. The last to go were some well-loved transformer toys. They all ended up in an enormous heap, right on top of Chloe. From what Tom could see of his robot underneath the pile of junk, she resembled a beetle on its back, trying desperately to right itself—without having much luck.

Chapter One

Max hid his head beneath his paws and whined.

Tom, took a deep breath, then walked over to his robot. Bending down, he flicked off her power switch. Chloe's platform on top rotated slightly. Her LEDs, looking like eyes, stared up at him. An instant later the light faded and the tracks spun down, then stopped.

Max cautiously peeked out from under his paws. Likewise, James slowly rose up from behind the clothes pile, a dirty sock draped across his head.

"Probably just a bug in the main processing loop," said Tom with a sigh. "I'll have her fixed by Thursday."

Still eyeing the robot suspiciously, James asked, "I thought you said the competition wasn't for another couple of months?"

"Thursday, after school, Mom promised to take me to her lab and show me around. I want to bring Chloe. The guys at the lab have been asking about her."

James peeled off the dirty sock in disgust. "What does your mom do at the lab anyway?" he asked, trying to take Tom's mind off Chloe's failed first run.

"She's a scientist. Something to do with parallel universes."

"Oh, yeah, that rubber-band-theory stuff, right?" said James.

"It's string theory, nuts for brains." Tom paused. "I don't really understand it. But—someday."

James turned and headed for the door. "I've gotta get home. Mom's taking me to a magic show at the Palmer House tonight. Hey, would you like to come?"

"No thanks. I don't believe in magic. It's just smoke and mirrors."

James shrugged. "Ok, well—have fun at the lab, if I don't see you before then."

Without turning, Tom replied, "Sure thing." Putting his hands in his pockets he stared down at his robot. "Chloe, Chloe, Chloe," he muttered.

Max came over, rubbed against Tom's leg and yawned.

Chapter 2: Tom and Chloe visit the lab

"Tom, have you finished your homework yet? It's time to go to the lab," said his mother, Juanita, running a brush through her long auburn hair one last time. She was in her mid-thirties, tall and slender, yet very fit, owing mostly to her martial arts practice rather than to her career as a scientist.

Struggling to get his arm through his favorite Chicago Cubs hoodie Tom said, "Yup, just need to throw on some sneakers." Sitting down, he tied the bright green laces on his new Converse and asked, "Mom, can I bring Chloe?"

"Oh, honey, I don't know. I didn't intend to stay that long."

"Oh, please!" begged Tom. "You won't even know she's there. Besides, you said yourself everyone wanted to see her, once she was finished."

Juanita hesitated. "Have you fixed that bug yet? The one that makes her charge off at full speed and crash into baseball bats?"

Tom visualized scientists running for cover as Chloe went on a rampage, notepads and supplies flying in all directions. Screams rang out as hot coffee spilled into sensitive equipment; sparks and smoke filled the air.

"Why are you smiling?" she asked.

"Oh—nothing," replied Tom hastily. "Yup! She's fine. She hasn't misbehaved since Tuesday! Besides, there're no baseball bats at the lab, right?"

Juanita tipped her head and glared sidelong at her son. Finally she smiled. "OK, but keep her out of everyone's way, and if I tell you to turn her off, you turn her off immediately, got it?"

"Check!" said Tom.

Juanita just shook her head.

After they'd loaded Chloe into his mom's SUV, they drove off toward the lab. On their way, Juanita asked her son what the problem had been with Chloe.

"There were actually two things," began Tom. "I'd set her default-speed parameter too high. So I backed that off a tad." He glanced sidelong at his mom, to make sure she understood. She nodded absently.

"Also, her main programming loop only checked for new commands after the last command had finished. I reprogrammed her to check for new commands, like *stop*, while the last one's still running." His mom didn't respond, so he assumed she got it.

Gazing out the window, Tom saw some boys playing basketball on a playground beside the road. A shot went wide, flying clear over the backboard. The other boys laughed. Tom felt sorry for the kid they were laughing at. Tom wasn't very good at sports himself. In fact, he was usually the last one chosen to be on a team.

"How many people work at the lab, Mom?"

"There are five scientists, including myself and your uncle Carlos."

"Is there any 'way-cool' equipment there?"

Juanita smiled, "Sure there's 'way-cool' equipment at the lab."

"Like what?"

She paused, "Like: computers, lab instruments, massive flat-screen computer displays, and best of all, a detector array grid."

"Can I see them?"

"Of course. I'll give you a tour as soon as we get there."

Tom leaned toward his mom and in a hushed tone asked, "Are there any—dangerous experiments?"

She chuckled. "No, I'm afraid our experiments are all quite tame. Mostly we just collect data, then slowly, painstakingly analyze that data to try and prove the existence of parallel universes."

Tom's shoulders slumped slightly. He sighed and turned to check on his robot. She was fine.

"What are you and Chloe going to do next?"

"Well, after she wins the local robotics competition, I'll enter her in the nationals. Once we win that, I want to write a book about it. I think I'll call it *From Diodes and Sprockets to the Nationals: A Humble Robot's Journey*."

Juanita smiled and nodded, but he suspected she wasn't really listening.

Glancing outside, Tom noticed they were crossing a small stream. A fisherman stood on the riverbank, fighting with a fish. It looked like the fish was winning.

"Will Uncle Carlos be there?"

"He has the day off. He's running some errands, but everyone else will be there." As they approached the entrance to Fermilab, she stopped and showed the guard her credentials.

"Good morning Ms. Holland," he said, smiling and waving her through. After a short drive to her teams new building near the Lederman Science Center, she parked the car in her private parking spot. Together they got Chloe out of the car and onto the pavement. From there, Tom used his controller to get her to follow them. As they approached the building Juanita placed her security badge against the reader by the door. The door automatically swung inward and they took a nearby elevator down three floors to the underground lab.

A massive security door stood before them. Once again Juanita placed her badge by the reader. A moment later the door hissed open revealing a long, well-lit hallway beyond. Tom maneuvered Chloe in first, then they followed her and the door hissed closed behind them. Tom left Chloe by the door.

As they walked down the long hall Juanita pointed to a door on her left. "That room houses our Cray main-frame computer, one of the fastest most powerful computers in the world. And behind that door on the right we have our own power generation station, capable of bringing online a hundred terajoules of power, though we've only ever used about half that much."

"Wow," said Tom, sounding impressed.

At the end of the hall, she placed her hand on the door knob but before she opened it she turned and said, "This is the control room. Most people call it command central, but I like to call it 'The Bridge.'"

"Can I bring Chloe?" blurted Tom.

"Of course," she said.

Tom turned back. Chloe was right where he'd left her at the far end of the hall. Pulling the controller from his pocket he glanced sidelong at his mom, and smiled. But instead of grabbing the joy stick he pressed a large red button, then lowered the controller. Chloe spun around and headed straight for them.

"Chloe can run autonomously?" said Juanita, with awe in her voice.

"For the FIRST competition, the robots have to do some simple tasks by themselves. Like on autopilot."

"Very impressive!" she said.

Tom's face lit up with a proud grin. "'Atta girl!" he said, as Chloe rolled to a stop in front of them. Tom reached down and patted her platform.

Chloe made a satisfied chirping noise.

Juanita rolled her eyes, then led them through the door and into a cavernous room. Everywhere Tom looked, there were large, brightly-lit computer screens. Some showed colorful graphs. Several had rows of numbers that were constantly changing on them. Still others displayed what could have been power levels. The scientists sat by their individual work stations. Everyone seemed excited about something.

"Here's where the rubber meets the road," she told her son. "It's the primary control room where we run experiments, and collect and analyze data. And over there, by the wall, we have our pride and joy: the detection array grid which makes all our research possible."

At the far end of the room stood a massive square framework, made up of four large round pipes per side, bolted securely to the floor. On the framework were mounted various instruments along with several strange alien-looking devices. These devices were black and about as long as Tom's arm and as wide as his fist. They had several shiny parallel disks radiating out from their centers. To Tom, they looked like some futuristic weapon. Massive power cables were attached to them and they were surrounded by a rat's nest of hundreds of individual sensor wires, patch cords, and computer cables. A soft hum emanated from the detector grid.

Tom's mouth fell open. *An inventor's paradise.*

"The data we collect from the array is analyzed by programs running on the main frame. It's a time-consuming process and would seem rather boring to most people, I'm sure. Nothing ever happens rapidly in the field of science."

Juanita turned toward her fellow scientists and raised her voice, "Everyone, I'd like you to meet my son Tom and his robot Chloe." The researchers got up and walked over to them.

"Tom, I'd like you to meet Sashi. She's from India and has been on our team since the beginning."

"I am most pleased to meet you," said Sashi with a warm smile and a nod.

"And this is Leroy."

"Hey, bro." Leroy smiled warmly as he shook Tom's hand.

"And last, but certainly not least, is Cheng."

Cheng clasped Tom's hand in his. "Tis a great honor to finally make your acquaintance—and Chloe's, of course."

They asked questions about his robot, and Tom was excited to show her off. After answering them all, he gave a quick demonstration of what Chloe could do. Everyone seemed honestly impressed, and said how fantastic it was to finally meet him. Smiling once more, they all headed back to work.

Turning, Tom stared again at the detection grid and the strange-looking devices attached to it. His mind wandered... He saw himself standing alone on a desolate planet; an army of alien mutants stood before him. They were green with long, muscular arms ending in deadly looking pincers. Slime dripped from their fangs as they slowly surrounded him. They paused for an instant, then, as one, they began to hobble straight for him. Tom was armed only with one of these strange-looking weapons from the detection grid. As the creatures neared, Tom swung the weapon up and fired. Pieces of green alien slime flew in all directions. Obviously they were no match for Tom and his "energy blaster..."

"Tom—Tom—Earth to Tom?" said his mom.

Tom wondered how long she'd been calling. "Oh, sorry... What are those energy blaster thingies?"

"Ah, a good question, and you're not too far off, actually. Those are powerful Temporal Field Distortion generators."

"Temporal—Field—Distortion generators?" repeated Tom.

"That's right. We call them TFD's for short," she began. "They kind of—well—stretch the space-time continuum. It makes the area we're interested in, the space inside the grid, thinner and more pliable; like when you help make pizza dough, and you keep stretching it. Understand?"

Tom squinted, "I guess so, sort of—"

"TFD's are what make this whole experiment possible, or at least economically feasible. They dramatically increase the flow of energy from one universe to the other—kind of like priming the pump. Once they're fired up, we use the sensors to try and detect minute amounts of energy leakage between our universe and another universe that's close by, relatively speaking, that is. In the early days of trying to prove the existence of parallel universes, or the multiverse as some like to call it, we used super-colliders to break up atoms and measure the energy difference, before and after the collision. If there was less after the collision, it would prove that some of the energy had escaped to another universe. These TFD's allow us to measure the inflow and outflow of energy much more accurately and use only a fraction of the power required to run a super-collider."

Juanita turned to one of her scientists. "Sashi, how are the readings shaping up this morning?"

"We've confirmed the entry and exit particle count and as before, it's greater than the simulations predict," replied Sashi.

"Strange, and there's been a steady rise in energy levels?" said Juanita absently.

"Yes, as you know, the first six months that we were monitoring, the rate of energy entering our universe remained fairly constant. This morning I was reviewing the logs and I noticed that three nights ago, Monday at exactly 11:27 pm, there was a sudden spike in the energy flow. It quickly fell back down but ever since it's been steadily increasing. And in the last few hours it's increased almost exponentially."

"What power setting are we currently running at?"

"Power is at 50 percent. We just upped it to that level last week," confirmed Sashi.

Juanita paused. "OK, let's try bumping it up to 60 percent. The simulations show favorable results at that level." Then turning to her son, she said, "Tom, you might find this interesting."

Sashi pushed a large slider lever up a few notches. "Power levels at 60 percent." At that moment there was a faint tremor accompanied by a crackling noise. "Particle transfer rate has multiplied—by a thousand percent!" Sashi glanced up at Juanita, looking shocked.

Everyone stopped what they were doing and turned to face them. Juanita glanced at each of them in turn, then asked, "Any idea what could be causing this?" No one spoke. After a moment's consideration, she continued, "Increase power to 75 percent."

Sashi hesitated, then turned back to her control panel. She moved the slider lever once more. "Power at 75 percent." Another stronger shudder occurred; this time accompanied by tiny green sparks that highlighted the edges of the detection grid, all the way to the floor.

"The model doesn't predict anything like this," blurted Cheng.

"I know we can't explain this... It's behaving far differently than anything we've seen before." Juanita paused. "But—we may not get another chance like this."

Suddenly she turned to face her son. "I'm not expecting any problems, honey, but I don't want to take any chances, either. Would you please go out and wait for me in the hall?"

"But, Mom!"

"No 'but Moms!' Now go!" Tom turned and took a couple of steps toward the door, then he stopped and glanced back. His mom faced the sensor panel; all eyes were on her. She let out a long sigh, then to Sashi said, "Increase to full power." Tom continued to watch.

"Wait!" cried Cheng, "this is way beyond any of the models' predictions. We're flying blind here. Shouldn't we power back down and analyze the data first? See if we can figure out what's wrong with our model? Then see what it predicts once we've fixed the model?"

Juanita paused. "Do we all agree that even at a hundred percent power we are way below the threshold that could tear a hole into another universe?" There were nods from all the scientists. "And do we also agree that this may be a singular event, that something in our universe, or in the other universe, is aligned in such a way that—whatever is happening, this may be a once-in-a-lifetime occurrence? If we don't act now, we may never get another chance." The scientists glanced nervously at one another.

"I won't go on without complete agreement. How many are in favor of raising the power to a hundred percent?"

Gradually, everyone except Cheng raised their hands. Cheng stared at his co-workers uneasily. One by one, his eyes met each of theirs, lingering longest on Juanita's. Finally he took a deep breath and slowly raised his hand.

"All right, then. We're all in agreement."

Sashi looked at Juanita, who gave her a slight nod. Glancing once more at her teammates, Sashi slowly turned back to her console. Using both hands this time, she pushed the lever all the way to the top. "Power levels at…" Before she could finish her statement there was a loud "whoomp." The sparks intensified; momentarily dancing around the edges of the detection grid, they swiftly expanded into a solid green sheet of light pouring from the whole space outlined by the sensor array. Slowly a blurry scene of another world appeared. After a moment, the image stabilized and the green light faded, except for a few traces around the edges of the grid. Alien-looking trees and shrubs came into focus. Their bark had deep furrows running parallel to each branch and trunk. Where the branches attached to the trunks, they were bigger and rounder, giving the eerie appearance of muscles. What made it look even stranger was the fact that, near the ends of the branches, many tiny twigs emerged in a fan pattern, resembling fingers. The twigs moved slightly, as if blown by a gentle breeze. At least—Tom hoped that was why they were moving...

Several scientists gasped.

"This should not be happening! These power levels are only a fraction of the energy needed to punch a hole into another universe!" Juanita paused, then as if to herself said, "Unless—unless there's something on the other side—something that's…" Sensing all eyes on her, waiting for her to decide what to do next, she said, "Quick, we don't know how long the portal will stay open. Let's send through some sensors; gather some data about the other world. We need temperature and barometric sensors, a gas sensor, a spectrometer, plus seismic and gravitational sensors."

"But we aren't prepared," blurted Cheng. "We'd need a mobile transport platform to carry the sensors over and to broadcast the results back."

Tom ran up behind his mom and pulled her sleeve.

"Can we rig up a radio onto each piece of equipment, then throw them through the portal?" asked Juanita.

Leroy responded, "We don't have enough radios and it would take too long to configure them all. Besides, they might be damaged by just throwing them through."

Once again Tom pulled on his mother's sleeve, "Mom?"

Juanita, still looking at the incredible alien scene before her, and with a hint of irritation in her voice said, "Not now, Tom. Can't you see this is critical?"

Then she noticed that the others were looking past her, so she followed their gaze. They were looking at Tom, who was pointing straight down— at Chloe.

"Leroy, you round up the sensors. I'll configure a radio to interface with them. Sashi, you figure out how to attach all this gear to the robot. Tom, you instruct Cheng on how to run Chloe." The team scrambled to accomplish their individual tasks and twenty frantic minutes later, they had completed the final tests. Chloe was heavy with the car battery and with all the new equipment attached to her, but with some effort, Cheng aimed her straight for the portal.

"We don't know whether the electromagnetic spectrum in the other universe, is compatible with ours, or even if the portal will pass the radio signals through. This is definitely a long shot, but it could advance scientific knowledge by a hundred years if we succeed. We have to try!" Juanita turned toward her son and her face assumed a serious look. Bending over she placed her hands on his shoulders and looked him straight in the eyes. "You realize we may not be able to bring Chloe back, don't you? We don't even know if we can control her once she's through the portal."

"That's OK, Mom. I understand." To his robot he said, "We're counting on you, Chloe." Then he nodded at Cheng.

Juanita smiled, kissing her son on the forehead, then turned back to the others. "OK, one small step for mankind..." Then to Cheng said,

"Punch it, Chewy!"

Cheng glanced sidelong at Juanita, shook his head, then typed in a command on the controller. Chloe took off fast—a little too fast—heading straight for the portal. Three feet, two feet, one foot away—even moving this fast, when Chloe reached the portal it seemed as if she slowly dissolved from front to back, then she disappeared entirely. For a tense couple of seconds everyone held their breath... Suddenly Chloe reappeared on the other side, moving fast, headed straight for a tree.

"Stop!" cried Tom. Cheng's fingers flew across the tiny keyboard. Nothing happened. Cheng typed again and again. At the last moment, Chloe slowed, then stopped just inches before hitting the tree.

Cheers rang out.

Juanita let out a deep sigh. "OK, do we have an uplink to the instruments?"

Leroy replied, "Carrier signal is strong, and... yes I'm receiving data from barometric and gas sensors... and yes, from the others as well. Barometric pressure at 30.1 inches of mercury; well within the normal range for Earth. Slightly higher oxygen levels and slightly lower carbon dioxide and nitrogen levels, but it looks remarkably similar to Earth's atmosphere!"

"What about seismic anomalies?"

"Only minor tremors, possibly active volcanoes on the planet, but none nearby."

"Temperature readings?"

"Reading 28 degrees Celsius, 301 degrees Kelvin, also Earth-like."

"Spectral analysis?" asked Juanita, barely contained excitement evident in her voice.

"Spectral analysis shows—mostly a semi-normal elemental breakdown but—there's something... They have the same number of protons and electrons as our atoms, but the atomic weight is different, implying they have a different number of neutrons. Thus their signature doesn't match any known elements... from our universe, that is."

"Interesting... Any idea if the differences would cause any problems for humans?"

"We'd need to do a thorough analysis to know for sure."

"Hmmm," said Juanita aloud. She thought for a moment. "As much as I'd like to, we can't risk sending someone through. At least not until we've done the analysis."

"But..." began Sashi, who was cut off immediately as another tremor rocked the building. This one was stronger than the last. Supplies began falling off shelves. The lights flickered.

"I'm losing the carrier signal!" yelled Leroy.

Juanita paused only a second. "Bring Chloe back."

Cheng typed in a command and Chloe turned around to face them. "She's responding sluggishly."

At that same instant there was a crackling sound and green sparks appeared at the edges of the grid. Smoke was coming from somewhere and Tom's eyes began to water.

"Hit the red button!" yelled Tom. Cheng hesitated, then slapped his hand down hard on the button. Chloe took off straight for the portal.

Juanita pointed and yelled, "Tom, get behind that cabinet!" She turned to the others. "Are we losing power?"

"No," shouted Sashi, "power is holding steady at a hundred percent."

"Then why..." but before Juanita could finish her thought, there was a loud "whoosh" and the green light surrounding the portal shrank to a single bright dot, which lazily danced around the center for a moment, then winked out with a soft "pop." All that remained was a wisp of smoke and the slight tangy odor of ozone.

Everyone just stared in shock. The last thing Tom remembered was seeing Chloe's LED "eyes" looking forlornly across the gulf at him. Now Chloe was stuck on the other side...

After a few moments, Juanita spoke, "Make sure we back up all the data. We'll be analyzing it for some time to come." She looked around the room at all the faces. Expressions of excitement, wonder, disappointment, triumph, and sadness were evident all around her. Finally her eyes settled on Tom as he stepped out from behind a cabinet. A tear ran down his cheek.

"Oh Tom," she hurried over and knelt down in front of him, placing her hands on his shoulders.

"Tom, I'm so sorry about Chloe. This was an amazing breakthrough, though. You know we couldn't have done it without her, right?"

"I know," began Tom, trying to choke back a tear, "it's just that—I guess—I didn't really expect to lose her."

"Oh, Tom." She lowered her gaze for a moment. "But you still have James, and Max, right? And there's always Uncle Carlos and me."

Tom wiped the remnants of the tear from his cheek and stood up tall. His mom grinned and ruffled his hair.

A slight smile crossed his face.

"Honey, would you mind if I stayed awhile and did some work? There's a lot to be done. I'll call Uncle Carlos and see if he can take you home."

"That's alright, Mom. I'd like to stay."

Juanita nodded, then stood and addressed her team. "Everyone, in case it hasn't sunk in yet: we've just made history here this evening. You should all feel proud of what you've accomplished. We weren't expecting or prepared for any of this. It took quick thinking and fast coordinated teamwork, but you pulled it off. And as a result, the world will never be the same."

As the team pondered her words, recognition dawned on their faces as they realized what they'd actually accomplished, and what that would mean for mankind.

Juanita looked from face to face. "I know it's late, but I'm sure you feel as eager to analyze this new data as I am." The scientists nodded enthusiastically.

"Great! Sashi, you verify that the instruments were still transmitting when the portal collapsed. Leroy, take a look at the data for the time period leading up to the portal opening. Say—the last hour or so. See if you can spot anything unusual. Cheng, go over the sensor readings we got back from the planet. Start working on a simulation to see if the planet could support human life. I'll take a look at our current model and try to figure out why it didn't predict this event." Before she could say another word, her team rushed off to tackle their individual assignments. Juanita glanced around the room—excitement shone brightly on everyone's faces. She smiled as she walked briskly to her workstation.

* * *

Chloe raced forward but the portal collapsed in a shower of green sparks before she could reach it. Speeding through the space where the portal had just been, she stopped at the edge of the clearing. Her platform slowly rotated around in a full circle. She let out a forlorn chirp. Suddenly the sound of footsteps thundered from off to her left. Chloe turned toward the sound. The crashing footfalls grew louder. Chloe backed up under cover of a large tree. A moment later a dark beast with huge muscles and natural rock-hard armor came crashing into the clearing, then abruptly stopped, its beady eyes scanning the area. Chloe stood still. The creature raised its head and sniffed the musty humid air, glancing right, then left. It took a step toward the robot. As it did, it brushed a small tree with its forearm. Twigs from the tree quickly wrapped around the beast's muscular arm, then seemed to tighten. Idly the creature snapped its arm away, uprooting the tree then flung it off without even looking. Sniffing the air once more, it quickly turned and stomped away. Chloe's platform rotated slightly, her LEDs pointing in the direction that the beast had gone. She made another weak chirp.

Chapter 3: Tom's birthday surprise

One week later, on Tom's birthday...

Juanita was frustrated. It had been nearly a week since the portal had opened and she and her team had put in long hours going over all the data. Juanita was the last one left at the lab, and she was lost in thought. For the hundredth time, she studied the data for something, anything that she might have missed. Finally, she put down her tablet, stretched, then rubbed her eyes. Glancing at her watch, she realized how late it had gotten.

"Tom!" she exclaimed. Hurriedly walking to the coat rack she put on her floor-length tailored wool coat, then reached for the light switch. As she did so, she noticed her reflection in the tall mirror beside her. Turning her body slightly to the right, then to the left, she smiled. It wasn't often that she noticed how nice she looked, and she loved the way the tailored coat showed off her slim figure, her curves in all the right places.

At that moment a slight tremor, almost too faint to feel, shook the building. Juanita, still adjusting her coat, stopped and slowly turned around. She took a step toward the detection grid; her head tipped slightly to one side. After a moment, she shook her head, smiled, and headed briskly back for the door. Flipping off the light switch she hurried from the building.

Unbeknownst to her, a moment later there was a cracking noise, and a few playful green sparks danced around the edges of the detection grid...

* * *

Arriving home, she closed the door behind her and smiled at her son. "Hi, honey!" She glanced at her brother Carlos, a tall muscular man,

25

ruggedly handsome with bright hazel eyes that radiated intelligence. However this evening, those same eyes just looked critically up at the clock on the wall. Carlos raised an eyebrow. She gave him a sheepish shrug. In the corner of the room Max raised his head and yawned.

"I'm just gonna change. I'll only be a minute," she said, as she walked to her bedroom and closed the door. Twenty minutes later the door opened and she walked back in dressed in a nice, floor-length dress, with matching patent leather high-heeled shoes.

"Hmm, you clean up pretty well, sis. You should dress up more often," remarked Carlos.

Juanita tipped her head sideways and scowled at her brother. "Thanks, it's a new dress. I bought it special for the occasion."

She faced her son. "Sorry I'm late, honey."

"That's OK, Mom. Carlos made me a root beer float, my favorite, and I've been telling him about the night the portal opened; the night we lost Chloe."

Juanita sighed and glanced sidelong at Carlos, "A root beer float, huh? Hope it doesn't spoil your appetite. So, ready to go to dinner, or would you prefer to open your presents first?"

Tom's eyes lit up. "Open my presents first, of course!"

She smiled and ruffled his hair. "OK, let's sit down."

They sat on the couch with Tom in the middle. Two presents sat conspicuously stacked on an end table beside the sofa.

"Which one do you want to open first?" she asked.

Tom's eyes fastened immediately on the biggest present. "Could I open Carlos's present first?"

Juanita gave her brother a knowing look. "Of course, dear."

Tom eagerly began tearing the wrapping paper from the bigger present. Max got up, shook himself and then slowly walked over. Colorful pictures of balloons and birthday candles flew in all directions and within seconds a plain brown box, with no markings on it, lay before him. Max sniffed and pawed at the scraps of wrapping paper as Tom quickly flipped open the lid.

Within, Tom found a hand-tooled leather belt with ten pockets of various sizes and shapes. Tom's eyes lit up. "Wow, the adventurer's belt I wanted!" Tom noticed that embossed into the belt itself were the large, bold letters "T. H.".

Carlos glanced at Juanita. "Look inside the pockets. I've added a few 'upgrades' along with the things that came with it."

Tom opened the largest pocket. Inside were four brand-new walkie-talkies. "These are high-quality units," said Carlos. "They're shock-resistant and waterproof down to 20 meters."

"Wow, four of them?" said Tom, a quizzical look on his face.

"I thought I'd get enough for you, James, and a couple of your other friends. Plus, there's some spare batteries in there, too."

"Awesome!" said Tom, eagerly opening the other pouches. Besides the spare batteries, he found fifty feet of ultra-strong thin wire; a miniature tool set, complete with screwdrivers, pliers, a file, and a tiny crescent wrench; a Swiss army knife; smoke bombs; a flare gun with several flares; a magnifying glass; and an LED headlamp with both red and white LEDs. But a huge smile burst upon Tom's face when he saw the last item: a pair of infrared night goggles.

Tom hugged his uncle. "Thanks, Uncle Carlos! This is great! The smoke bombs and goggles will be fun, but I'll probably use the knife the most!" Tom glanced sidelong at his mom who furrowed her brow and glared at Carlos.

Tom's uncle cleared his throat. "Ah—you've been good about using your old, miniature pocket knife safely, so I think it's time you graduated to a real knife. This one is *very* sharp, however, so be extra careful!" Carlos glanced at Juanita. She took a deep breath but said nothing.

"I will be," Tom assured him.

"One more thing: the flare gun is not a toy. You can only use it if there's a real emergency, like when you are out sailing your sunfish and you get into trouble, okay?"

"Got cha," said Tom excitedly. "Can we go now? I want to try some of these things out on our hike!"

"I'm afraid it's a little too late for a hike this evening," said his mom, fidgeting as she glanced at Carlos. "Tomorrow's Saturday—perhaps your uncle will take you for a hike in the morning."

Carlos smiled. "That'd be great. Where would you like to go?"

"How 'bout Timber Ridge?"

Carlos raised an eyebrow. "Timber Ridge? Isn't that the one with that high, narrow suspension bridge; the one that wobbles and bounces as you walk on it? I thought you were afraid of heights."

"I am. Heights scare the crap out of me."

"Tom!" scolded his mother.

"Oops, sorry Mom," said Tom, glancing sheepishly at his uncle.

Juanita glowered at Carlos once more. Conveniently avoiding her gaze, Carlos's eyes intently studied the ceiling.

Tom rushed on, "But there's another trail that goes around. So we don't have to take the bridge."

As Carlos's gaze returned to Tom, his eyes softened and a gentle smile spread across his face. "Maybe it would be good for you to cross that bridge. Sometimes we have to confront our fears if we're ever going to conquer them."

Tom shuddered. "I think I'll conquer my fears another day."

Carlos snorted, ruffling Tom's hair.

Smiling, Juanita cleared her throat. "There's another gift."

"Oh, yeah!" Tom grabbed the second present, the one from his mom. It was a smaller rectangular box, with the same birthday wrapping paper. Once again paper flew everywhere and within seconds Tom was holding up a blue-grey knit sweater vest. He blinked a couple of times, then turned it over and looked at the back.

"Thanks, Mom," he said, as he pulled the vest over his shirt, then hugged his mom. Juanita sighed, glancing over Tom's shoulder at her brother.

Carlos shrugged, then smiled back. "Shall we go in my car?"

As they stood up Tom strapped on his new adventurer's belt. Suddenly Juanita looked hurriedly around the room. "I'm afraid I left my computer, my tablet at the lab. Would you mind if we stopped on the way to the restaurant?"

Carlos scowled, pointing at his watch. Juanita nodded.

"I'd love to see the lab again!" said Tom enthusiastically, as he grabbed his hoodie and pulled it over him. "Come on Max."

Juanita locked the door and then they all headed for Carlos's Jeep Wrangler, just as James walked around the corner of the garage.

Tom smiled at his friend. "Hey, James. What's up?"

James bent down to pet Max. "Not much. Just came over to see what you got for your birthday."

Tom turned to his mom. "Can I show James my new adventurer's belt? He'll go bonkers."

"Sorry, we're running late. Maybe James could go on the hike with you and Carlos tomorrow."

Tom glanced at his uncle. "Can I give him a radio, at least?"

"Sure, they belong to you," he replied.

Tom walked over to James, reached into his belt and pulled out one of the walkie-talkies, handing it to his friend. Tom adopted a serious look. "This is a real-deal professional-type unit. Guard it with your life."

James took on an equally serious look, then nodded, but his eyes quickly lit up as he turned the device over in his hands. "Wow, it's way heavier than our old ones, thanks!"

Tom headed for the car, calling over his shoulder, "I'll show you the rest of my birthday stuff tomorrow."

"Great," replied James. "Oh, and—happy birthday."

"Thanks. See you tomorrow." Tom opened the passenger door and flipped the seat forward. Max jumped in back and lay down, bits of birthday wrapping paper stuck to his fur. Tom climbed in next to Max.

Carlos sat in the driver's seat, with Juanita beside him. She immediately pulled out her smart phone and began texting.

"Maybe on Sunday James and I can go to Harold Hall beach. It's just around the corner," said Tom.

His mom looked up from her phone. "What? Oh, we'll see."

Once they'd arrived at the lab, Juanita put away her phone and they all jumped out of the car, including Max.

"Oh, honey, I think you should leave Max in the car. We won't be that long."

"Ah, but Mom, Max'd love to see the lab. Besides, it's my birthday, remember?"

Juanita looked to Carlos for support, but Carlos just grinned. She gazed down at Max who stared back up at her with big, hopeful eyes. After a moment she sighed. "Well, I guess it is your birthday. Just make sure you keep him out of trouble, OK?"

"No problem-o," said Tom, grinning as he made a fist and pulled it in close to his chest.

Within minutes they entered the lab. Juanita found her tablet, sitting on the counter right where she'd left it. She flipped it on and touched the display. An app window opened, spreading to fill the screen and lighting up her face. Carlos cleared his throat and tapped his watch.

"I know, I know. Just give me two minutes," said Juanita, without looking up.

Tom walked over to a low table near the detection grid. On the table sat Chloe's controller. He picked it up and idly turned it over in his hands. He was thinking of that day a week ago, the day Chloe left for an adventure on another planet, the day she left without him.

Tom glanced around the room. Everything looked just like he remembered it.

Suddenly, a shudder passed through the building. Tom glanced at Max, then over at the sensor grid, just ten feet away. Telltale green sparks began to outline the array. Within seconds, there was a loud "whoomp" and green light filled the whole space within the grid. The portal had opened once more.

Juanita and Carlos ran for their workstations.

"Are you picking up anything from the sensors on Chloe?" cried Juanita.

"No, I'm not receiving the carrier signal," replied Carlos, his fingers flying across the keyboard.

"Are you monitoring the right frequency?"

Carlos looked up, "6950?"

"Correct," she replied. "Maybe Chloe ran out of power."

Tom whirled around to face them. "No, Chloe powers down after ten minutes if you don't send her a new command."

Suddenly Tom remembered the controller in his hands. "Wait a second!" Tom pointed the controller at the portal and hit the power switch, then watched for any sign of Chloe. "There she is!" he cried. "Her LEDs are lighting up. She's under that large tree, over there to the right." He typed in a command and Chloe spun around in a tight circle, then stopped. "Are you getting anything yet?" yelled Tom.

At that same instant, startled by the unexpected sight of movement, Max turned his head and spotted Chloe. The dog leapt to his feet. He barked twice, then ran straight for the robot. "No," cried Tom, running after Max, Chloe's controller still in hand.

Staring intently at his display Carlos replied, "Yes, I'm starting to receive data."

"NO! Tom, stop!" screamed Juanita, her tablet crashing to the floor as she raced after him.

Hearing the commotion, Carlos looked up from his console. Instantly taking in the dire scene he leapt to his feet and bolted after the others.

Everything happened in slow motion. Nearing the threshold Tom picked up speed and reached for Max. Juanita was right behind. Carlos was gaining fast. Another shudder shook the building. Max ran through the portal and disappeared.

Desperately Juanita yelled, "Tom stop!" The lights flickered. Green sparks began to form around the edges of the grid. Juanita strained, reaching for Tom's hoodie. Tom ran through the portal just as another, larger shudder shook the building. The gateway began to shrink. Juanita cried, "NO!" and leapt through the portal. One more second and Carlos would be there. Suddenly a blinding burst of green sparks flew in all directions, accompanied by a loud "whoomp."

Carlos slammed into the wall behind the detection grid and slid to the floor. He glanced up. One lone, green dot hovered above him. Slowly the dot faded away. Carlos stared in horror at the now blank wall. He reached for his nose and when he pulled his hand away, there was blood on it. Staring upward once more he vowed, "Somehow I'll find a way to bring you both back. I will bring you back."

Chapter 4: The prophecy begins...

It was dusk, and getting darker by the myntar. Bellchar, an enormous rock troll with heavy brow and jutting chin, moved cautiously in the shadows. As with any rock troll he stood at least ten feet tall, had an enormous head slumped way forward, no visible neck, fat stubby fingers at the end of long muscular arms and his whole body was covered in natural armor. This particular troll had a long deep scar running above his right eye. As he walked he kept a tree between himself and the elven city of Elfhaven, his dark eyes searching for any sign of an elven guard. At that moment, off to his right and about thirty paces away he spotted a lone sentry patrolling the outskirts of the city.

Keeping an eye on the elf, he hastily moved behind a small clump of trees. Snap! went a twig. He froze. The sentry turned toward the sound, paused, then began moving in Bellchar's direction. As the sentry approached the invisible magic barrier that protected the elven city, he craned his neck, raised his head, and sniffed the cool night air. Frowning, he glanced first left, then right.

Bellchar placed his hand on the rough bone hilt of his grimy rusted dagger, the hint of a smile crossing his stony features. Slowly, careful not to make a sound, he drew the dagger from its well-worn leather sheath. *I be in trouble if I kill da elf.* Phawta, his commander, had given him specific orders: "No kill elves. Just map der defenses; der strengths, der weaknesses. Dey must not know we here."

The sentry continued to walk straight toward Bellchar. There was a crackling sound and tiny blue sparks momentarily highlighted the elf's features as he passed through the barrier.

Lowering himself ever so slightly, Bellchar arched his back while flexing his powerful leg muscles, preparing to launch. He turned the blade parallel to the ground, tightened his grip on its hilt and allowed himself another slight smile. *Closer, a little closer.* Saliva dripped off Bellchar's brown, rotting teeth.

Suddenly there was a noise from beyond the barrier.

"Sanuu, what's wrong?" called a voice.

Sanuu, a tall slender elf and one of the head palace guards of Elfhaven, turned toward his friend and fellow guard saying, "Tappus, I thought I heard something, but..." Sanuu glanced back in the direction the noise had come from, his eyes sweeping the area one last time. "It, ah—it must have just been my nerves," he reasoned, "or perhaps it was that gremlin trying to get through the barrier again to cause some more mischief."

"Ha," laughed Tappus. "He's a pest, that one, for sure! Come on, it's almost end of shift. Let's head back for supper. Our replacements can deal with your gremlin! It'll give them something useful to do for a change."

Sanuu glanced back at the woods once more. "Guess you're right." Squinting, he took one last step in that direction, his keen elven eyes trying hard to pierce the hidden darkness. Finally, he turned and walked back through the barrier. The same crackling sound and blue aura once again highlighted his features. Then the two began walking back toward the gate in the city's outer wall.

* * *

Once the sounds of the sentry's footsteps had receded into total quiet, Bellchar slammed his dagger back into its sheath and stepped out from behind the trees. His blood-shot eyes seethed with anger as he walked up and touched the barrier. Sparks flew and Bellchar's hand was thrown back several inches. Unable to contain his rage any longer he bared his teeth, clenched his fist, reared back and threw a powerful punch at the barrier. There was a low pitched "whump" accompanied by a brilliant blue flash. Bellchar was hurled backwards ten feet where he landed hard with a thud, dust flying in all directions.

"Ouch!" groaned Bellchar, not moving. *Maybe Phawta right. Maybe me dumb.* Blinking dully for a couple of sectars, he slowly, stiffly rose to his feet. Cracking his neck left and right, he stooped and grabbed a small tree then effortlessly ripped it from the ground, roots and all. Carefully this time, he waved the tree in front of him as he approached the barrier. When the tree neared it, blue sparks arced across the gap. Bellchar inadvertently jumped back, hastily looking over his shoulder, an embarrassed look on his face. No one was there, of course, so he took a deep breath, drew himself up to his full height, and began walking beside the magic barrier, occasionally tapping the tree against it, watching for any tell-tale signs of weakness.

* * *

In a deep, guttural voice Phawta barked, "Fowlbreth! It be dark soon. Why we wait? Aren't da scouts back?"

"Dey back. All 'cept Bellchar," rasped Fowlbreth, drool dripping off his large jutting chin.

"Bellchar," spat Phawta, "will prob'ly foul dis up like last time."

"He be back soon," assured Fowlbreth.

"Hmmm," grumbled Phawta. "Once he back, we leave dis place. It stink of elves."

"Um—stinking elves," began Fowlbreth smiling, exposing two missing teeth. "Mission over. How 'bout we kill some *stinking elves* 'afore we leave?"

"No. We've orders."

"Ah, but troops 'r restless. They did good. Let em have der fun. No one miss a few scrawny elves?" whined Fowlbreth.

"NO! Soon we be up to our arses in slaughtered—" Phawta stopped mid-sentence at the sound of an unusual noise. They turned their heads

35

in unison and saw a strange green glow off to the left of the trail.

"What dat?" snorted Fowlbreth.

"If elven spies, you may get your wish, Fowlbreth." To the others, Phawta bellowed, "Find dat noise! If elf, kill him quick, 'afore he sounds an alarm."

Chapter 5: Adventure! Careful what you wish for...

Tom found himself standing in a small clearing, Chloe's controller in his hands. He turned back to see a shimmer where the portal was still visible. It emitted a snapping, crackling sound accompanied by a soft green glow. The daylight was starting to fade. Off to his right he saw Chloe; her LEDs were off.

That's odd. I just sent Chloe a command a moment ago. She's supposed to stay on for ten minutes before powering down.

It was a bit chilly and Tom was glad he had on his warm hoodie. He glanced around. *Where exactly am I?*

As he turned a full circle, he viewed the strangely shaped trees, with branches like witches' brooms and twigs resembling long, thin fingers. Huge leafy ferns covered the ground, similar to paintings he'd seen of prehistoric forests.

Tom walked over to examine one of the strange trees. A gentle breeze blew a branch against his elbow. Immediately, several twigs wrapped firmly around his arm. Tom leapt back and the twigs reluctantly let go.

Did that tree just grab me? Tom shuddered, backing quickly into the center of the clearing, he glanced around nervously.

I guess we're not in Kansas anymore Toto. Hey, speaking of Toto, where's Max? He was right in front of me when I went through the portal. At that moment he heard a dog bark off to his right.

Tom slipped Chloe's controller into a pouch on his belt and ran off toward the sound yelling, "Max! Come here, boy. We've got to get back through the portal before it closes."

As he ran around the bend into a slightly larger clearing, he stopped dead in his tracks.

There, just a few feet in front of him stood Max, attempting to hold off five enormous, grotesque-looking creatures. Each beast was easily four times Tom's height. They had dark hides with natural armor that looked as if large cobblestones had been glued all over their bodies. Their heads were large, hunched way forward and with no visible neck. Their faces had bulbous noses, small, dark, hollow eyes, jutting chins displaying huge lower teeth, and large flat ears near the back of their heads. They were clothed only in dirty, torn loin cloths, loosely tied around their mid-sections.

To Tom it seemed as if everything was happening in slow motion, but in truth, it was only a moment before he and Max were completely surrounded. Tom involuntarily stepped back.

Max leapt between Tom and the nearest beast, barking fiercely. The monster, keeping his eyes calmly on Tom and with a quick, easy backhand motion, swatted Max sending him flying over the heads of the other creatures. He landed hard with a thump and a whimper.

"Run Max!" cried Tom. "MAX RUN!" Max hesitated only an instant, then turned and ran through the woods. One of the monsters threw a pike which splintered a small tree right beside Max. Another beast started after him.

"STOP!" barked Phawta. "Let it go. It just his pet."

Fowlbreth grabbed Tom from behind and simultaneously drew a grimy dagger from his belt, rapidly raising it to Tom's throat. "Kin I kill da stinking elf?"

"NO—dat no elf." Phawta slowly walked around Tom, his nostrils flaring as he sniffed the strange, unfamiliar odor. "You stupid, Fowlbreth? Kain't you see da pathetic shriveled ears. Da beady little eyes, da large, ugly nose."

"Hey, I'm right here! And who are you calling *ugly* anyway?" shouted Tom, with mock courage. "Let me go or I'll have Uncle Carlos beat the crap out of you!"

"Well, well now, the pup has spirit!" laughed Phawta. Smiling, he leaned forward and asked, "What manner of creature be you? You no elf and yer too big for a gremlin. Besides, gremlins kain't talk."

Tom struggled desperately to back away from Phawta's horrid stench, but Fowlbreth's viselike grip held firm. "My name's Tom. I'm a boy, a human of course. What are you?"

"What am I?" laughed Phawta, standing upright again. Smiling broadly, he glanced back at his patrol. The others chuckled.

"What am I, you ask? You ain't from 'round here, is you boy?" More chuckles.

"Never seen a troll 'afore?" asked Phawta.

"Kain I kill da *huu-man* then?" pleaded Fowlbreth impatiently.

"Hmmmm," said Phawta, absently stroking his rocky chin. After a moment, he abruptly stopped smiling. Leaning in close once more, his dark and steely eyes boring right through Tom, he said, "No, I tink Sliembut may want to ask it some questions first." Standing, he turned to the others, "Den you kain kill it!" There was laughter all around.

But Tom didn't feel like laughing. He was worried about Max and more than a little worried about himself. *At least they hadn't found Chloe.*

* * *

Prince Devraj, a tall elven boy with sharp jawline and cheekbones, glanced around nervously, "I should never have let you talk me into taking you and your brother outside the city after dark. We are well beyond the barrier's protection."

"It wasn't dark when we left the city," stated Avani, casually flipping back her long, golden hair. She was tall for a thirteen year old, though thin, as were most elves. Plus she had a firmness to her stance, giving her a look of self-confidence; a look that clearly stated she was used to having her way. As she turned to face the prince, her large, almond-shaped eyes sparkled in the pale moonlight.

"Well, it's after dark now and we haven't found any of your—precious dancing crystals."

"They're 'singing' crystals, silly, not dancing crystals, and their beauty and magical powers make them well worth the risk," reasoned Avani. "Besides, they sing loudest just after sunset so it should be easier to find them."

The prince was also thin, yet taller, being two years Avani's elder, and his knitted brow and high rigid cheekbones made his face appear as if it were frozen in a perpetual frown. Which—indeed it was. He wore a rich royal-blue doublet with large golden buttons.

The prince scowled. "How would you know when they sing the loudest? I've never seen or heard a 'singing' crystal, have you? In fact, I've heard they're nothing but a myth. Just the stuff of legend; tales told to children so they'll go to sleep."

"Well, I've never actually seen one, but I know they're real. I can feel them." *They're calling to me, even now.* The sound was like nothing she could ever have imagined. A marvelous choir of pure and perfect singers, yet there was something else, some magical—pull; an attraction her mind could not easily resist.

"I've also been told that you don't find singing crystals, they find you," said the prince. "What's more, they only choose to help one person. One person, and one person only, for their entire lifetime. What makes you think you're so special that they would choose you?"

When Avani didn't respond, Devraj continued, "I agreed to help you search for ten myntars, but it's been nearly half an oort. I insist we head back now. There have been rumors of troll sightings within Elfhaven valley."

Avani snapped out of her semi-trance. "Trolls would be fools to come this close to the elven capital. Besides, it's a beautiful night and we haven't gone far. How 'bout just another five myntars? If we haven't found any crystals by then we can leave." Avani smiled devilishly. "Or would you prefer to come back tomorrow and try again?"

"No! I am Prince Devraj, heir to the throne and your elder. After all, I'm fifteen solar cycles while you're still but a child. You will do as I command."

"I'm thirteen and five months, practically an adult, and I'm perfectly capable of taking care of myself," said Avani sharply.

"And what of your eight-year-old brat of a brother, can he take care of himself?"

Kiran, Avani's freckle-faced younger brother, though obviously shorter than his sister, had the same self-confident stance as she, but there was also a mischievous glint in his eye. "Hey, I'm not a brat. Besides, I'm as brave as Avani is any day!" challenged Kiran.

"You aren't scared of a few—trolls, are you Devraj?" asked Avani with a wry grin.

"I'm no coward!" hissed Devraj. Clenching his teeth he let out a long, controlled breath. "All right, but just another five myntars, and not a sectar more!"

"Great!" she said, smiling as she squeezed Devraj's hand. Then she spun around and strode off.

Ten myntars later, just beyond a large rock outcropping, they found a beautiful stream with a small grove of unusual trees growing beside it. Their bark had silver flecks which sparkled in the moonlight, and an unmistakable odor of vanilla filled the air.

"Look!" exclaimed Avani. Over by a bend in the stream and beneath an overhanging fern, the ground shook slightly, then a small mound began to rise. Suddenly, like sparkling mushrooms, ten singing crystals pushed their way up above the surface. They pulsed with light: red, blue, green, and gold, alternating in intensity as if competing to see who would be noticed first. The crystals played a haunting melody which seemed to be coming from within Avani's mind.

The music is so beautiful. The sound seems to match the colors of the crystals, somehow. Their song continually changed and had a slightly hypnotic effect. Glancing over, she noticed Prince Devraj and her brother seemed transfixed, their eyes staring blankly ahead. Avani reached down and touched the nearest crystal. As she did so, its light grew brighter and it sang louder. Avani began to glow herself, but when she released the crystal the effect slowly faded.

The prince shook his head and blinked. "Come on, it's late, we have to go."

Avani slowly nodded. Reaching out, she tested several crystals, and finally chose three. Wiggling them free from the ground she shook off the loose dirt, then placed them in a leather satchel that hung from her belt. They made a soft, gentle musical chord and Avani sensed they were contented to be with her.

"Won't the sound attract trolls?" asked Kiran.

"No," she said, "only magical creatures, like elves, can hear them."

"OK, you've got your stupid crystals, now can we please—" Devraj was cut off as a large, woolly, slobbering creature broke free from the trees and ran headlong into the prince, knocking him over backwards. The beast barked at him urgently!

Lying on his backside, like an upside-down crab, Devraj scrambled to get away from the strange beast. As soon as it was off him the prince jumped to his feet and drew his sword.

"No!" cried Avani.

Kiran, oblivious to the tense scene around him said, "Awesome, what is that thing?" He took a step toward it.

The creature ran a few steps back the way he'd come, then turned and barked again.

"I think it's trying to tell us something," said Avani.

Devraj lowered his weapon slightly, but kept it pointed toward the beast.

It spun around in a tight circle, then ran a few steps farther away, turned and barked once more.

"I think it wants us to follow it," said Kiran, walking briskly toward it.

"Kiran, stop!" commanded the prince. "We don't know anything about this creature. It could be trying to lead us into a trap."

Avani relaxed her shoulders, tipped her head slightly toward the beast, and focused her mind. Kiran and Devraj watched her. After a moment, she said, "I sense urgency in the creature, but no malice or ill intent. I say we follow it and see where it leads."

"I am the prince, and the eldest. We will return to the city and let the guards know of this strange beast. They can decide what to do."

Suddenly the creature took off running with Kiran in hot pursuit. Avani turned to the prince and smiled. "Well, I guess the decision's been made for us." She pivoted smartly, then ran off after her brother.

Devraj yelled, "Wait! Stop!" Under his breath he screamed, "*aaaaahhhhhhh!*" His sword rang out as he slammed it into its sheath and dashed after the others.

* * *

For nearly ten myntars they'd been running deeper into the forest and farther away from the safety of the barrier, when Max finally slowed and then stopped. A thin mist had set in. Panting and with his tongue hanging out to one side, Max stared up at Kiran as he stopped beside him. Moments later Avani ran up, followed swiftly by Prince Devraj. Thirty paces ahead, through the fog and a thick forest of trees and bushes, they could just make out a campfire and the silhouettes of several trolls sitting beside it. The trolls were speaking, but they were too far away for the young elves to hear what they were saying.

"Looks as though there are only five or six; probably a scouting party," whispered the prince, "We must inform the guards and my father, King Dakshi."

Chapter Five

Avani studied the scene intently a moment longer, then nodded. "Agreed. Come on Kiran, let's head back before they notice us." She turned to leave.

"Wait!" whispered Kiran grabbing his sister's arm and pointing. "There's something tied to that tree over there, off to the right."

The two turned back to see what had caught Kiran's attention. After a moment Avani whispered, "He's right. Something—or someone—is tied up. We've got to get a closer look."

"What we've 'got to do' is go for help," hissed Devraj.

"Help from whom, the elven guards? What would we tell them? We need more information, so they'll know what to do," reasoned Avani, her eyes fixed intently on Devraj. When he didn't respond immediately, she hurried on, "Look, you and Kiran stay here and keep this creature quiet. I can be stealthier than either of you, so I'll sneak up close and see what's going on. Then I'll come right back and we can go tell the guards."

"I'm going with you!" said Kiran firmly, "I'm just as steely as you and you might need my help."

Avani furrowed her brow, hesitating. "Its 'stealthy,' and you should stay here where it's safe."

Kiran stood up tall—for an eight-year-old elf boy, that is—and crossed his arms defiantly. "If you go. I go!"

Avani glared at him in frustration and finally sighed, "Okay, but only if you're quiet, and if I say run, you run. Agreed?"

"Sure!" said her brother triumphantly.

"Then we'll all go," said Devraj, through clenched teeth. He knew full well he couldn't talk Avani out of anything once her mind was made up.

Avani turned and led the way silently through the underbrush. As they neared the clearing, they could hear the trolls arguing.

"I say kill da huu-man now! We hungry, he just slow us down," said a voice.

"Obey me, Fowlbreth! I said we take da boy to Sliembut for

questioning."

At this point, Avani and the others had reached the last row of trees before the clearing. They were about thirty paces to the right of the campfire. Directly in front of them there was indeed a boy tied to a small tree. But the boy was no elf child. He looked similar to an elf, but his face was all wrong. His ears were short and flat and his eyes were small and too close together. Plus his nose was round instead of pointy. He sat ten feet away, directly on the ground with a filthy rag tied across his mouth, and his hands were bound together behind the tree.

Just then Max started crawling toward the edge of the clearing. Kiran grabbed his collar at the last moment. Max let out a slight whimper. The prince grabbed the hilt of his sword and stared at the trolls. The elves held their breath. Luckily the trolls were still intent on their argument, oblivious to the noise that Max had made. Avani glanced back at the boy. He was now staring right at them, only his eyes looked much bigger.

Avani put her finger to her lips and mouthed the sound "shush." He seemed to understand and relaxed a little, glancing back to where the trolls stood arguing.

Avani turned toward Devraj whispering, "First I'll create a diversion by conjuring up a dragon. Then I—"

"Hold on. We are not attempting to rescue the boy. The plan was to get a closer look, then head back and tell the guards, remember? My father will decide what to do. If he chooses to attempt a rescue mission, it needs to be carefully thought out and planned. Besides, a troll patrol this far into elven territory is not good! There are bigger issues at stake here than just some scrawny—whatever he is."

At that moment, another troll entered the firelight, apparently returning from patrol. There was a quick recounting of events and what he'd learned.

"There isn't time. They're arguing whether to kill the boy or take him with them. Sounds like they intend to leave soon. If we go now, by the time we get back to Elfhaven the boy will likely be dead and the trolls will be long gone. So I'll conjure up a dragon and then—"

"You don't know how to conjure up a dragon," whispered Kiran, "and even if you could, it'd probably toast us as soon as you did."

Avani wrinkled up her nose at her brother, then turned to Devraj, "True I can't actually conjure up a *real* dragon, but these are just dumb trolls, remember? I can create the *illusion* of a dragon. It doesn't have to fool them for long, just a couple of myntars, by then we'll be gone."

"I'm the smallest and the steel—, stealthiest," said Kiran firmly, "so once Avani creates the dragon, I'll crawl over and untie the boy."

Avani stared at her brother, her eyes intently studying his face. Finally she said, "Okay," and then whispered to Devraj, "Once we have the boy we can make our retreat. You guard our rear," at which point Devraj raised an eyebrow and smiled slightly. Avani rolled her eyes.

"What?" whispered the prince with mock sincerity.

Avani continued, "You guard our FLANK as we make our escape. I'll hold the image of the dragon as long as I can. We probably won't get far before the image collapses, so we must be quiet and hope they don't notice the prisoner's gone, at least until we're far enough away, okay?"

Avani, Kiran and Max all gazed expectantly at Devraj. Glancing from one face to the next, he finally sighed. "All right, it appears we have no other choice. But if anything goes wrong, you two run for help while I try to hold off the trolls. Agreed?"

Avani and Kiran nodded. Max just drooled.

Glaring, Devraj pointed his finger at Avani and added, "And no changing the rules this time, do I have your word?"

"You have my word!" she whispered innocently.

The prince glanced once more at the boy tied to the tree, then back at the trolls. He drew his sword. "Summon your dragon!"

Chapter 6: Dragons and Elves and Trolls. Oh, my!

The fog had grown thicker and they could feel the heat being sucked from their bodies as if wrapped in a wet blanket. Avani sat in a lotus position, ignoring the mist and the cold. With her head held high and tipped slightly forward, her arms relaxed by her sides, she kept her eyelids almost closed. Reciting an ancient incantation, her lips moved ever so slightly. For almost a myntar nothing happened. Then the flap on her satchel bulged outward and a faint glow spilled forth. The glow brightened. A moment later, 60 feet away on the other side of the trolls, a blast of fire erupted, accompanied by a loud roar. With scales of stone and eyes of fire, a fierce dragon rose above the mist.

* * *

The argument raged on. "Kill the pup now!" demanded Fowlbreth. "Sliembut don't even hafta know! Besides da boy—" But his words were cut off by a thunderous roar and a blast of yellow fire. The trolls leapt back at the sight of a mighty dragon standing not 30 paces away.

"Grab weapons. Fan out. Slowly now! Don't spook it!" shouted Phawta. "Wait for my signal."

The dragon just stared at them, smoke wafting lazily from its flexing nostrils.

* * *

"Here, take my knife. It'll be quicker than untying him," said Devraj.

Kiran raised his brow. *Wow, the prince—being nice to me, what gives?* But all he said was, "Thanks."

Devraj glanced at the trolls, who were all looking the other way, staring at the dragon, then he nodded to Kiran. Feeling a little less brave than before, Kiran took a deep breath and turning the business side of the knife away from himself he bit down hard onto the blade. Slowly crawling out from the relative safety of the trees, the fog provided him a slight bit of cover.

As he crept the ten paces or so to the boy, he thought, *What was I thinking? Sounded like fun at the time. Don't look at the trolls. Don't look at the trolls. Just keep crawling. That's it... I can do this. Don't even THINK about looking at the trolls. I mean it. I really mean it!*

* * *

The knuckles on Devraj's sword hand turned white as he quickly glanced from the trolls, to the dragon, to Avani, to her brother, to the strange slobbering furry creature, then back again. *Why did I let Avani get me into this mess?* Kiran was now about halfway to the boy. The prince held his breath and idly placed his free hand on Avani's shoulder. The dragon quivered. Jerking back his hand, the dragon's image stabilized once more. Devraj let out a tense sigh.

* * *

"Look, da dragon," said Fowlbreth uncertainly, "it shakes. It afraid?"

"Stop!" cried Phawta, pausing to think. Then he snarled at Fowlbreth, "Dragons not know fear—Someting not right."

* * *

Tom held his breath as the strange child crossed the last few feet to where he was tied up. Once he'd arrived, the boy crawled behind him, so as to be out of sight from the trolls. Tom craned his neck to see. The boy grabbed a knife from his mouth and began cutting the ropes.

With shock Tom noticed the kid's strange features. Shorter and thinner than Tom, and probably younger, his face was taller than it was wide, even more so than a human, with long gently curving ears that ended in a point. His eyes were large and almond-shaped with warm, dark brown pupils, and unusually high cheekbones, almost no chin, a sharp, pointed nose and a mischievous-looking grin.

Finally the boy removed the filthy rag from Tom's mouth. Tom spat twice.

"Who are you? How did you know I was in trouble?" whispered Tom.

Kiran put his finger to his lips and whispered back, "I'm Kiran. A strange four-legged furry creature with long, floppy ears led us to you."

"Wow, good boy, Max! He's my dog—a Saint Bernard. Haven't you ever seen a dog before?"

From the edge of the trees, Tom could just make out the silhouette of another taller boy waving his arm emphatically, signaling them to hurry up and get back over there.

"OK, the ropes are free. Let's crawl to the others."

"Hey, how is it that you, and the trolls for that matter, can speak English?" asked Tom, rubbing his sore wrists.

"English? Oh, Is that your language? Don't you have magic where you're from?" whispered Kiran, shocked.

"Well—no, actually—we don't," replied Tom.

"Wow, strange. Come on follow me. We'll explain later. "

"What about the dragon?" asked Tom, nervously eyeing the huge monster on the other side of the trolls.

"Don't worry, it's my sister's."

A strange look came over Tom's face as he crawled after Kiran.

* * *

Once they'd reached the relative safety of the trees, Tom was greeted with a face full of licks from Max. "Stop Max, enough!" whispered Tom as he stood up stiffly, stretching his sore arms and legs.

"This is Prince Devraj and my sister Avani," said Kiran.

Why does she look so familiar? They all do, for that matter. And that name—Avani... Tom shook his head. "Hi, my name's Tom. Thanks for saving me, by the way."

"We have no time for idle chit-chat," said Devraj sharply. Careful not to touch Avani this time, he bent over and whispered in her ear, "We have the boy; time to depart." He offered his hand, palm up. Still chanting, she took his hand and rose unsteadily to her feet. The strain was evident as sweat ran down her forehead.

Kiran led the way, followed by Tom with Max at his side. Next came Avani, head slightly down, still chanting softly. Lastly strode the prince, his sword in hand; he kept glancing over his shoulder as they ran through the thickening fog.

A few moments later Devraj rasped, "Pick up the pace Kiran! We're at least ten myntars from the barrier."

But instead of hurrying, Kiran stopped abruptly, causing the others to nearly collide with him as they screeched to a halt.

"What are you doing, Kiran?" hissed Devraj in frustration.

His hand shook as Kiran slowly pointed straight ahead. There, ten feet in front of them, rising from the mist, was a spectral form. A ghost visage, made entirely of mist, now stood before them. Ragged wisps floated down from what appeared to be its arms. The prince hesitated only a second then ran to meet it, swinging his sword in a high arc. But an instant before the blade reached the apparition, the phantom dissolved back into the fog. There was a "whooshing" sound as Devraj's sword sliced only through air, leaving swirls of mist in its wake.

"Run," screamed Devraj, no longer concerned about stealth.

* * *

The trolls were now in position and cautiously approached the winged demon from all sides. The dragon's image shook once more.

"Someting fishy," said Phawta, scowling. The image shook again, then seemed to fade in and out. "Attack!" commanded Phawta. The trolls charged at full speed, weapons raised high, battle cries ringing. Suddenly there was a small "pop," and the dragon disappeared entirely. Unable to stop, Bellchar ran straight through the now-absent image, colliding headlong into Fowlbreth, causing them both to fall over backwards. The others barely stopped in time.

Bellchar raised his head and blinked. Commander Phawta cursed under his breath. "Bellchar, Fowlbreth, get up, you fools!" Glancing over to where the captive had been imprisoned, Phawta saw only cut ropes littering the ground. His powerful muscles flexed as if ready to explode. "Quiet! Someone helped da prisoner escape. Listen!"

Bellchar and Fowlbreth clumsily picked themselves up. Fowlbreth gave Bellchar an angry look. Bellchar just shrugged. They all listened intently.

"I hear someting, over dere." Fowlbreth pointed toward the barrier.

"After dem! Kill da elves. Leave da boy." Hissing through clenched teeth Phawta added, "I—want—da Huu-man—alive."

* * *

As Tom passed the spot where the apparition had been, the hairs on the back of his neck stood on end. Glancing over his shoulder as he ran, Tom saw the wraith rise up from the mist once more, turn toward him, and stare. Tom shuddered, turned back and ran faster.

After running for nearly ten minutes the prince called out, "They're coming! Stop over there behind those bushes to the left." Once they'd hidden themselves Devraj continued, "They'll be here any myntar. I will stand and fight. You three make a run for it. Alert the guards and bring help."

"No, wait, I have an idea!" said Tom, pulling out a couple of the walkie-talkies from his adventurer's belt. He turned them both on low volume, handed one to Avani, and spoke into the other one. "I got these for my birthday." His voice immediately sprang from her walkie-talkie.

Devraj jumped back, startled. "What kind of sorcery is this?"

"It's just a walkie-talkie. No radios here either?" said Tom. "Never mind." He cranked the volume up to full on both units and handed one to Devraj, saying, "Throw this as far away from us as you can."

Devraj looked uncertain for a moment, then his eyes brightened with understanding. He set down his sword and hefted the radio in his palm, then wound up, leaned back and threw the radio far into the night.

Tom cupped his hand around his radio, and began to speak.

* * *

"Wait! Listen," cried Fowlbreth. "I hear someting!" The trolls all stopped and listened.

Far off to their right they heard a voice. "What? A bunch of dumb, ugly trolls, can't even catch a few scrawny kids?"

From between Phawta's pursed lips came the words, "Kill—dem! Kill dem all..."

* * *

"What was that thing, that thing that rose up from the mist?" asked Tom, breathing hard as they ran.

"A mist wraith. No time to explain. Continue talking to the trolls," urged Devraj, "it will keep them distracted."

By now the fog had thickened and it was getting hard to see the path in front of their eyes. Tom ran on, but it was difficult running and holding the radio with one hand while he cupped the other hand around his mouth. Tom's eyes began to water from the fog. "Losers! Why you're nothin' but a bunch of sissies. And ugly, did you fall out of the ugly tree when you was little, or did your momma just throw you out?" Suddenly there was a crunching, crackling sound... Then, only static...

"I think they found the radio," said Tom.

"I can hear them heading this way again. The barrier has to be nearby." Devraj strained to see through the trees in the dim light. "There it is! A hundred paces up ahead." He glanced over his shoulder. "They're gaining on us. Run faster!"

As they picked up speed Avani tripped and fell. Tom stopped but the fog was so thick he couldn't see where she'd fallen. Running back, Tom found her in a heap just beyond a small log. He quickly helped her to her feet. She was shaking and he could tell she was exhausted. As he lifted her their eyes met for the first time. Avani had the same warm, almond-shaped eyes as her brother, and she smiled as she looked up at him. Tom couldn't help staring into her beautiful eyes.

Devraj turned toward them and scowled. "Come on, run!" he yelled.

As Tom passed Devraj, almost dragging Avani along, the prince shot him a menacing look. The mist was now so thick that they could no longer see the path. To make matters worse, it was almost pitch black as they ran through the underbrush. Branches and tall ferns slapped them in the face and across their chests. Twigs wrapped around their arms, causing them to have to jerk free. Tom was nearly exhausted. Finally, when they were just 50 paces from the barrier, Kiran yelled out for help. A guard heard him and sounded the alarm. The kids raced on. The trolls were only thirty feet behind them, and gaining fast. Suddenly twenty well-armed elven guards ran through the barrier and formed a protective shield around the kids as they ran through the barrier to safety. A few more steps and they were through the main gate of Elfhaven's outer defensive wall. Breathing in gasps, Avani collapsed once more.

The elven guards raised their swords and drew back their bows threateningly. The trolls slowed, then stopped. Even twenty elven guards were no match for six rock trolls. But at a word from the apparent troll leader, the trolls backed slowly away, their eyes, seething with rage, locked on the elven guards until, like wraiths themselves, they dissolved into the darkness, the mist, and were gone.

Chapter 7: Mom, lost but not forgotten

It was dark as Juanita lifted herself up from her hands and knees, where she'd landed after leaping through the portal. As she did so, her senses were assaulted by all the strange alien sights, sounds and smells.

Idly brushing dirt off herself, she called, "Tom—Tom are you there?" Spinning around at the sound of static crackling behind her, she saw the portal collapse to a single green dot, then wink out of existence.

She tried again. "Tom—can you hear me?" Still no answer.

I was right behind him. Where could he have gone so quickly, and wasn't it daylight when I entered the portal? Studying the ground for clues, she squinted, then bent down and brushed away a leaf. *Dog prints. Max!* And there, off to her right, footprints, heading in the same direction. Juanita stood up and ran. As she rounded the first bend she entered a small clearing. There were footprints all around and many of them were huge. *Bigfoot?* she wondered, smiling at the absurd notion, despite her worry. Studying the ground carefully, her smile vanished when she spotted signs of a struggle. Bending over, she noticed a pair of tracks led toward a large tree near the edge of the clearing, and there was another set of smaller tracks, Tom's sneakers. She ran to the spot where the tracks ended. Pieces of rope lay discarded beside the tree trunk. She picked one up. It had been freshly cut.

She called again, "Tom, Tom if you can hear me, please answer." But only silence greeted her ears. Walking swiftly around the clearing she thought, *There are so many prints, I can't tell which way Tom went.* It looked to her like the larger tracks went off to her right, so she followed them. On her third step one of her high heels got stuck between two exposed tree roots. Trying to free herself, she jerked her foot hard and the heel snapped off. Lifting up the shoe, she gazed on the now-flat heel. With a deep sigh she removed the other shoe and slammed it against the

55

nearest tree. This heel broke loose with a crack, flying off into the surrounding forest.

So much for my beautiful new shoes. Well, at least now they're practical. Putting the now heelless shoes back on, she continued on her way. Around the first bend the trail opened into another, slightly larger clearing.

Still too many prints. And they seem to be all over the place. Either it was a gathering of some sort—or a struggle.

She took a deep breath to calm herself. *I just need to treat this like any other scientific problem*, she realized. Her mind began methodically studying the available data for a pattern. In doing so she noticed that a group of prints led off to her left, so once again she followed them.

After several long minutes the prints started getting closer together, as if the group had slowed down, then stopped as the prints milled around in one area. One trail left the spot, heading off in a different direction. Juanita turned to follow, but stopped as she noticed moonlight glinting off a shiny surface. Something had been smashed deep into the soil beneath a huge foot print. She bent down and picked up the shattered object, and as she did so she drew in a sharp breath. *One of Tom's radios.* Dropping the pieces, she ran as fast as she could.

Chapter 8: Safe, at least for the moment

The children were just inside the outer wall of the elven city of Elfhaven. A moon was rising to the west, providing a faint light. Prince Devraj ran to Avani and knelt down beside her. "Are you all right?"

"Yes, thanks to Tom's quick thinking and his magic talking devices!"

"They aren't magic…" began Tom.

Devraj shot him a stern look, then turned back to Avani. "No, I meant because you collapsed, you're obviously exhausted; anyway, nice job with the dragon!"

"Yeah, that smoke coming out its nose was sweet!" added Kiran.

"Smoke? But I didn't—, oh, the crystals. I could tell they were boosting my magic. I couldn't have held out that long without em."

"Your Highness," said Sanuu as he and Tappus rushed up, "your father, King Dakshi…" Sanuu had to take a couple of deep breaths.

"Yes, yes, get on with it," snapped the prince.

Sanuu glanced sidelong at Tappus, then rushed on, "Your father desires to speak with you. He says it's urgent."

The prince turned back to Avani and softened his tone. "Will you be all right, Avani?"

"Yes, I'm feeling much better. You run along and have some fun with daddy."

Devraj seemed caught off guard by the remark but managed, "Um—all right. I'll check in on you later."

"Oh, and I think they'd say yes anyway, but—if Prince Devraj were to request that our grandparents host Tom—I'm sure it would smooth the way…" said Avani, an expectant look in her eyes.

The prince glared at Tom, and clenching his teeth, he turned to Sanuu and said, "Make sure she gets home safely, and tell their grandparents that I hereby request they provide Tom with lodging, at least temporarily."

Sanuu tipped his head. "Yes, your Highness." The prince sprinted off toward the castle with Tappus and several other guards in tow.

"Is anyone going to help me up, or do you expect me to lie here all evening?" asked Avani. Tom hurriedly grabbed one arm as Sanuu grasped the other and they began lifting her to her feet. As they did, Sanuu's eyes met Tom's for the first time, his sharp elven eyes rapidly studying Tom's strange facial features. Immediately Sanuu dropped Avani and drew his sword. Avani pushed herself back up and quickly stepped between them, pressing her back firmly against Tom.

"It's all right. He's a friend. He saved our lives. Sanuu, put down your sword!" commanded Avani, rubbing her elbow and brushing dirt from her hair.

Wearing the stern mask of an elven warrior, Sanuu glanced from Tom to Avani, then back. Tom felt as if he was being held prisoner by Sanuu's fierce stare. Finally Sanuu relaxed his shoulders. Still keeping a wary eye on Tom, he slowly sheathed his weapon.

Avani turned to face Tom.

"Thanks." Tom released the breath he didn't realize he'd been holding. "That's twice you've saved my life today."

"You were never in any real danger this time. Sanuu was just protecting us. Besides, you saved our lives earlier," she said, smiling.

"But you saved me once before that, so now I owe you one," reasoned Tom.

"Hey, I saved his life, too. Don't I get any credit?" piped in Kiran. The other two laughed. Even Sanuu seemed to be resisting the urge to smile.

They began walking toward the city. In the moonlight Tom could just make out the silhouettes of buildings in the distance and a castle beyond them. The castle had high turrets at each corner, plus there was a tall spire in the center, near the back. Surrounding the castle was an even higher wall than the one they'd just passed through. The structures grew closer and closer until finally they turned right and headed down a street lined with small wooden homes. Soft warm candlelight radiated from the windows and the smell of wood smoke filled the air. There weren't many people out at this hour but Tom saw an old woman bringing in her laundry, the sheets shining white in the now-bright moonlight. As they passed by, she glanced up at them and her jaw fell open. Absently, she reached out and pulled a clothespin off the line, dropping the tunic to the ground without even noticing. Kiran snickered. Next they saw a tall boy, bringing home a basket of fresh-baked flatbreads from the now closed market. He turned his gaze on them and walked right into a hanging sign advertising dried lizard cakes, causing him to fall over backwards. That proved too much for Tom as both he and Kiran burst out laughing.

"I guess you don't get many humans and their giant, furry, slobbering pets around here, do you?" Tom asked, trying hard to stop laughing. They looked at Max who slobbered, as if on cue. Kiran and Tom broke up laughing once more.

"OK, OK," said Avani, holding back a snicker herself. "We don't want people to think we're laughing at them, do we?" Tom glanced at Kiran and they almost cracked up again.

"You're right," agreed Tom, rubbing a tear from his eye and trying hard not to think about the stir they were causing. "So, to change the subject, Devraj said that thing we saw in the forest, the thing that was sort of there and sort of not there was a mist wraith. What are they?"

"You saw a mist wraith, this close to Elfhaven?" said Sanuu, in shock.

Avani nodded. "That was the first one I've ever seen. We were lucky. They usually travel in packs."

"Yes, but what exactly are they?" persisted Tom, glancing from Avani to Sanuu to Kiran.

"I'm not really sure. We know they're magical beings, and they appear only when there's fog." Avani paused. "There's an old tale that every elven child knows by heart. I'm not sure whether it's true or if it's just a story told around campfires to scare children. It goes like this: There's a hunting party, far from home. They'd gotten lost and wandered unknowingly into the forbidden forest when suddenly a strange dense fog arose. Soon afterwards one of them let out a blood-curdling scream. Immediately the others turned in his direction. There, standing where the hunter had been, was a mist wraith. They ran to the spot but by the time they got there the wraith was gone, as was the hunter. All that remained were a few scraps of blood soaked clothing, but they never found his body..."

After a solemn moment of silence, Tom said, "I've been meaning to ask you. How is it that you can speak English? Kiran said something about magic."

"I can't speak—ah—your…English is it? Kiran's right. It's the magic. It allows everyone to understand each other. I can understand trolls and ogres, and they can understand me. But in actuality, their languages are quite different from ours. We suspect that even gremlins have a language, and just pretend not to understand us. Your—ah—English gets translated for us, in our minds, just as Elvish is translated automatically for you."

"Wow! That's pretty handy!" said Tom.

"I guess so. I never really thought about it. So, obviously it's different on your world?" she asked.

"Yes, for the most part each country has its own language. If we want to communicate with others we have to take years of foreign language classes in school!"

Avani looked shocked. "Wow, what a pain!"

"Tell me about it," agreed Tom. "I was lucky, though. I grew up in a bilingual family. I can speak both English and Spanish." He thought for a moment. "Mom says that several wars have been fought just because the two sides misunderstood each other. You obviously wouldn't have any of those problems."

"No, but we have other reasons to go to war…" Avani fell silent for a moment, then continued, "Let's take a shortcut." They rounded a corner, turning right down a small, dimly lit, dusty alley that soon opened up into an area of quaint, modest yet well-kept cottages. As Tom looked at one of the homes, he got the creepy feeling it was watching him. What's more, the buildings were expanding and contracting slightly, as if they were—breathing. The hairs stood up on the back of Tom's neck.

"Avani, are the houses—alive?"

"Well, everything in our world is infused with magic; trees, animals and yes, even buildings. So I suppose you could say they're alive."

Tom shuddered as he glanced sidelong from house to house.

"Hmm, I never thought much about that, either," admitted Avani.

Kiran bent down and scratched Max behind his ears, ignoring the conversation

Kiran and Max sure seem to have taken a liking to each other. Tom smiled.

As they rounded another corner they came upon a tall man, leaning on a gnarled garden hoe. He was dressed in dusty gray robes, his hood pulled down low about his shoulders; his face was partly masked in shadow.

"Good meeting, Kiran, Avani!" offered the stranger in a traditional elven greeting. He nodded at Sanuu.

"Well met, Lorin!" responded Kiran appropriately.

"And who is your new friend?" asked Lorin.

"This is Tom, Thomas Holland. He's from the planet Earth!"

Lorin leaned forward, paused, then muttered, "The prophecy."

Tom, Avani, and Kiran spoke in unison. "What?"

Lorin blinked. "Sorry, forgive the ramblings of an old fool. Where were we—oh yes, the planet Earth, is it? Well then, welcome to Elfhaven, Thomas Holland of the planet Earth! If you don't mind me asking, how did you come to be here on our world?"

"My mom's a scientist, back on Earth. Her team opened a portal to your universe, to your world. Max here ran through the portal. I tried to stop him."

Chapter Eight

Lorin gazed off into the distance. "There are ancient legends of gateways to other worlds."

Tom fidgeted uneasily. "I really need to get to the portal. I have to get back to Earth, to mom and Uncle Carlos. They'll be worried."

Lorin rubbed his chin thoughtfully. "If the legends be true, these—portals as you call them, only open but for a brief time. The one you sojourned through will be long closed by now. I'm afraid you're stuck here in Elfhaven, at least until another portal opens."

Tom's head dropped. He stared at his feet.

"Where are you all headed?" asked Lorin, changing the subject.

"We're taking Tom to meet our grandparents. Hopefully he can stay with us!" replied Kiran.

Lorin's gaze focused on Tom. "We shall meet again, Thomas Holland."

From what Tom could see of Lorin's eyes, masked deep in shadow as they were, they seemed to peer right through him, as if Lorin could read his mind.

"Sure—sure thing," said Tom nervously.

"Give my regards to your grandparents." Lorin waved goodbye stiffly and they continued on their way.

"We will," replied Kiran, over his shoulder.

* * *

Lorin watched the backs of the children recede into the distance. Idly rubbing his chin, he pondered, *A boy from another world—from the planet Earth. What does it mean? And now, of all times...* He furrowed his brow, watching them until they'd turned the corner and were lost from sight, and still he stared. Finally he turned and hobbled away, using his hoe as a cane.

* * *

Tom walked on, trying unsuccessfully to keep his mind off the breathing houses that surrounded him. "How is it that you hang out with a prince, anyway? Are you some sort of princess?"

Avani giggled. "No, I'm no princess." She glanced at Tom, then continued. "Dad was the last in a long line of—well it's like a secret society. They're called—" Avani corrected herself, "They *were* called 'The Keepers of the Light'. Dad held an important position in the elven court, with rooms and servants at the castle. He was one of the king's most trusted confidants."

"You keep saying *was*, past tense," observed Tom, watching her closely as they walked.

"My dad was killed in the last troll uprising, about a year ago." Avani glanced over at her brother but he seemed totally absorbed with Max.

"Oh, I'm sorry," said Tom awkwardly. He paused. "So—do you live at the castle?"

"I used to, when father was alive. Once he died, Kiran and I moved in with our grandparents. The king wants me to move back, though; he says I have to—" Avani switched to as deep and regal a voice as she could muster, "*You must—assume—the full duties as 'The Keeper.'*" Both Tom and Avani chuckled as she switched back to her own voice: "...at least once I'm of age; when I turn fifteen."

"Don't you want to live in the castle? Live the life of a rich noble? Fancy clothes; servants waiting on you hand and foot?"

"No way!" she cried. Avani glanced at Sanuu, who pretended not to be listening. "That's way too boring and pompous for me."

Tom thought he saw a smirk cross Sanuu's face, but before he could tell for certain, Sanuu turned away.

Avani changed the subject. "Um, I'm sure you can stay at Nadda and Nanni's with us, especially since the prince is requesting it."

"Nadda and Nanni?" asked Tom. "Are they your grandparents?"

"Those are the names everyone uses for their grandparents," said

Avani.

Tom thought for a moment. "Does your mom live with your grandparents?"

Avani lowered her voice. "Mom died in childbirth with Kiran." She glanced over at her brother once more, but he was holding a stick, playing tug-o-war with Max. It appeared Max was winning.

"Oh, that's awful!" said Tom, embarrassed again.

After a slight pause Avani continued in a brighter tone, "What about your parents?"

"I never knew my dad. He took off when I was two. Mom doesn't talk about him. From what I overheard Mom and Uncle Carlos say when they thought I was asleep, it sounded as if dad drank a lot."

Avani glanced sidelong at Tom and nodded. "Ah, he loved his ale too much. And what of your mother, you said you needed to get back to her?"

Tom perked up at the question. "She's great! She's a prominent scientist, a theoretical physicist actually, at Fermilab; the same place where my uncle works."

"Go on," said Avani, a puzzled look on her face.

"For some reason a memory just popped into my head: it's from a couple of years ago. Mom let me tag along and listen to one of her guest lectures at MIT. It was on parallel universes. That's what most of her research deals with."

Tom thought back, trying to remember exactly what she had said:

"... One of the important tenets of string theory, or at least one branch of string theory, doesn't just call for the *possibility* of parallel universes, it demands their existence! And, what's more, the underlying physics that we all know and love, and take for granted—string theory postulates that that *too* will be different! In most universes the constants that we use to calculate the effects of physical properties will not be the same as ours.

For instance, Planck's Constant—"

"I'm sorry, Tom," interrupted Avani apologetically, "but I don't understand."

Tom frowned, absently kicking a pebble, "I guess what Mom's lecture was really about," he said, pausing to choose his words carefully, "was that string theory predicts that lots of universes exist—universes that have worlds like yours and mine. Each universe would be governed by different laws of physics and because of those differences, strange things would happen. Things that people from our world at least, would call magic."

"Magic?" said Avani brightly. "Can you give some examples?"

Tom cocked his head slightly, "I remember a student asking Mom what types of things they might observe on worlds with different physics than ours. She gave several examples, but the following ones stuck in my head: creating matter from energy; turning things invisible; making objects hover in midair, things like that. That's when one of the students made a joke about magic. The whole class broke up laughing but once the laughter died down, Mom said he was absolutely right. She said things we all take for granted on our world, like smart phones, computers, and microwave ovens would all seem like magic to our great grandparents. She asked the students if it was too much of a stretch for them to imagine that a slight change in the laws of physics could very well bring about all manner of wondrous possibilities, things we might describe as—magic."

Avani hesitated. "I don't know about 'smart phones,' or any of that other stuff, but I do know that here in Elfhaven we can use magic to create things, or to make things disappear. We can even make them rise up and float in mid-air. Well, at least the wizards of old could do those things. A few of us still can, at least—we can do some of those things..." Avani trailed off, wistfully.

They walked on for a couple of moments before Avani continued,

"Did she say anything more about journeying to other worlds?"

Hmm. He remembered part of a conversation he'd had with his mom after her lecture…

"Do you think we can ever travel to another parallel world, Mom?"

"Travel to another world *within* a parallel universe, you mean? It's not too likely. Not within our lifetime anyway—though our lab has made incredible advancements in the field lately! It was just five years ago that the first measurements were made confirming that energy was *leaking* out of our universe and into another. We have since confirmed the existence of at least one other parallel universe that's close by—well, relatively speaking, that is. But this project has cost us over a billion dollars and uses an enormous amount of energy. To get enough power to actually cross over to a parallel universe would require a hundred times that much power."

"Wow," said Tom, fascinated. He pushed the subject still further. "Isn't there any other way to cross over?"

His mom glanced at him, smiled, and ruffled his hair, "The universes are always in motion. If the two were to collide at a spot, it might provide a portal from one to the other. Oh—and there is one more possibility— someone, or something—from the other universe," she paused for effect, "could open a portal to us!"

Tom's eyes had opened wide…

Walking along the hard-packed dirt road of the elven city, Tom finished his tale, and once again glanced over at Avani expectantly.

"Wow, that's exciting, what I could understand of it anyway. Your mom sounds nice and very smart; an amazing wizard."

Tom laughed. "She's no wizard—at least not like you think of wizards."

"Where's your mom now?"

"Back on Earth. She was there when I ran through the portal. She's probably worried sick about me. I'm going to be in big trouble when I get home—if I ever do get home, that is…"

They walked on in silence for a time. Finally Avani asked, "Those magical talking, walking devices you had…"

"Walkie-talkies," corrected Tom.

"You said you got them for your birthday. When was that?" she asked.

"Actually," replied Tom. "It's today."

Avani smiled brightly. "Today's your awakening-day? Happy awakening-day, Thomas!"

Blushing, Tom added, "We call it a birthday."

"I figured that much out for myself," she said smugly.

Chapter 9: Mom, so close, and yet...

Juanita had been running for nearly half an hour, but it was hard to see in the dark forest. The moonlight had vanished, swallowed up by a strange fog and the dense canopy of leaves above. Because of this, and to follow the footprints she was forced to slow to a walk and several times she had to backtrack when she lost the trail. Suddenly she heard voices up ahead. Hiding behind a tree, she slowly stuck her head out to see what was going on.

"We almost had dem," said a deep guttural voice.

"Da elven guards saved dem. Why we not fight? Dos scrawny elves no match for us," said another.

"We've orders. Besides, we too late. Dey went tru da barrier. You know we kain't go tru da barrier," said a third voice. Angry grunts and growls followed.

The creatures were hard to make out in the dim light, but Juanita could tell they were huge and covered with some tough-looking natural armor. There was no sign of Tom. Suddenly the beasts started moving—straight for her. Whipping her head back behind the tree, she scanned the area for a place to hide. A clump of thick bushes stood off to her left. With the fog and the cover of darkness, she crawled over to the shrubs and disappeared beneath them. The ground shook as the heavy footfalls of the massive beasts grew near. Juanita held her breath. The footsteps suddenly stopped.

"What dat smell?" said a voice.

"Smell like Huu-man," said another.

Juanita shifted her head slightly and peered out from under the leaves in front of her. A humongous black clawed foot stood not two feet from her. One of the giants sniffed the air.

A commanding voice replied, "It just da boy. He came dis way, 'member? Keep movin'. We must reach Sliembut afore daybreak."

"Da army here tomorrow. Why not wait for dem?"

"Sliembut said report now!"

Juanita shifted slightly so she could see their faces through the leaves.

The nearest monster sniffed the air once more, then frowned. The others started moving away again. Finally he snorted and stomped off after them.

Juanita sighed. *Tom wasn't with them. He must've escaped. He must be somewhere up ahead. They mentioned something about a barrier.* After the beasts' footsteps had receded into the distance, she crawled out from her hiding place, stood up, and began walking in the direction that the creatures had come from. Soon she heard still more voices so she hid behind another tree.

"It was lucky the children made it here when they did. Another few sectars and the trolls would've had them," said a clearly well-educated voice.

"I hate to think what the trolls would have done to them, if they'd gotten hold of them," said another.

"Well, they're safe now. Safe within the barrier."

"Did you see that odd-looking child? He's no elf."

"Strange events have begun, and there'll be stranger ones, before this is over, mark my words. Anyway, the king will know what to do with the boy."

Juanita slowly peered around the tree. These men were fully clothed and much smaller than the giant beasts, and they were armed with swords and bows. Soldiers, she assumed. From this distance they looked like long eared thinner versions of humans. The guards stood gazing in the direction the other creatures had gone. *Trolls. That's what these soldiers called them.* Juanita mulled the name over in her head as she silently crept off to her left, hoping to get around the guards. Once she was far enough away, she glanced back. The soldiers still stared off into the forest. A high rough stone wall stood up ahead, with an open gateway to her left. It was hard to see in the dark but she could just make out a grassy field beyond the gate. Juanita took a deep breath and prepared to sprint for the wall but at that moment she heard a sound behind her. She spun around, squinting in the darkness, but saw nothing. Taking a step backwards, toward the wall, there was a sudden tingling on her back. Once again she whipped around, facing the wall, but there was nothing there. Cautiously she raised her hand. When her arm was half extended, blue sparks appeared around her fingertips. She pulled back her hand.

That was odd. Slowly she raised her hand once more. This time when the tiny lightning bolts appeared she held her ground, then pushed her hand completely through.

Interesting feeling. Like nothing I've ever felt before. Not exactly unpleasant. In fact, it feels warm and soothing. Strange... She withdrew her hand back once more.

Could this be the barrier the soldiers spoke of? Only one way to find out. She took another deep breath and glanced off to her right, making sure the guards were still facing the other way, then braced herself for the sprint to the wall. But before she could move, someone grabbed her from behind and yanked her back, spinning her around to face them. It was another troll. She gasped, but managed to hit the creature hard with her fist. The troll didn't budge. Instead, the beast slapped a huge stony hand across her mouth, and whipping her around, clamped her body tightly to his. An elven guard heard the commotion and ran toward them. The troll dragged Juanita back deeper into the forest.

In a muffled attempt to cry for help she screamed, "Mmhelph hheellph." A rusty dagger instantly appeared at her throat. Juanita fell silent. Two elven guards ran up and stopped about ten feet away. They took a step forward, their features highlighted in that same strange blue aura; another step and they were through.

"Did you hear that?" asked an elf.

"I heard something. See anything?" replied the other.

"No, it's too dark. Listen…"

After a long pause. "I don't hear anything. Probably just some animal."

"Could it be one of the trolls we confronted earlier?"

"Nah. They're long gone, the cowards, Didn't you see how quickly they backed down when they saw they were outnumbered?" The guard chuckled.

Juanita felt the troll's muscles flex as he tightened his grip.

"Something wasn't right," argued the other elf. "Trolls don't usually back down from a fight."

The first guard laughed. "They're losing their nerve."

The beast tightened his grip still further; it was getting hard to breathe.

"Well, in any case, there's no one here now. Let's head back to the gate." A moment later the guards turned and walked away, muttering as they went. Once they had passed through gate, the troll eased his grip somewhat and in a quick, fluid motion swung Juanita up over his shoulder, as if she were weightless. He glanced around, then loped off at an easy pace, back in the direction she'd originally come from.

* * *

For what seemed like hours, Juanita had endured the torturous jarring, riding on the bony shoulder of the beast, plus she was getting chilled from her skirt constantly flapping about.

What would my mother say? In her head she heard her mother's voice, *Always wear clean underwear. You never know when you'll be on a strange planet, in an unknown universe, carried by a monstrous beast with your skirts flapping around like Marilyn Monroe.* She might have smiled, were it not for the dire circumstances. What made it even worse though, was that the creature smelled like rotten fish.

Thankfully, soon afterwards the troll began to slow down, then finally stopped. Grasping her wrist firmly, the troll dropped Juanita to her feet beside him. A group of trolls stood nearby.

"Bellchar, der you are. We tot you lost again," several trolls chuckled. "What dis?"

"Phawta, I not lost. I saw dis ting run for da city. I follow. Bellchar capture warrior princess." The troll puffed out his chest proudly.

Phawta, apparently the one in charge, squinted, leaning in for a closer view. "She no look like elven warrior princess to me." Extending a huge gnarled black finger he poked her, as if testing to see if she was real. Phawta sniffed. "Who you be?"

Juanita tried to step toward Phawta but Bellchar held her back. She shot Bellchar a stern look. "My name's Juanita Holland. I'm from the planet Earth. I'm looking for my son Tom, have you seen him?"

The leader raised his brow and mumbled, "Da boy brought his mother?" Several trolls snickered.

"You've seen Tom? Where is he? What have you done with him?"

"We were, ah—protecting da boy—helping him," said Phawta, glancing sidelong at his friends. "We try to find way to get him home, but a pack of cut-throat elves capture him. Take him prisoner. Back to Elfhaven," spat Phawta, "'tis da name dey call der filthy stink-hole of a city."

Juanita struggled against Bellchar's vise-hard grip. "I've got to find my son. Please let me go. I won't trouble you any longer."

"Oh, I like to let you go, I really would." The trolls chuckled. "But I'm afraid I must take you to Sliembut first. I sure he help you find your son, once he question you proper-like." Phawta smiled broadly, exposing two missing teeth. More snickers all around.

Juanita took a deep breath and appeared to relax, but suddenly she turned toward Bellchar, slamming her foot down hard on his big toe. Instantly she ran up his leg and kicked off from his chest, arching over backwards. Her momentum carried her in a tight circle, twisting

Bellchar's hand at a sharp angle. Bellchar cried out, let go of her wrist and grabbed his injured thumb. She kicked his knee, somersaulted between his legs and came up running. For a moment the other trolls just stared at each other, then they broke up laughing.

"See, I told you she warrior princess," said Bellchar, rubbing his thumb.

"After her, you fool," yelled Phawta. "Fowlbreth, go wid Bellchar, make sure you find her. Bring her back." The two trolls stared at each other, then ran off into the forest.

Chapter 10: A home away from home

"Hello, Nanni, Nadda. We brought a friend home. He needs a place to stay. Prince Devraj suggested he might stay with us, at least for a while. Is that okay?" Avani leaned forward, a pleading look in her eyes.

From the doorway Nadda, the children's grandfather, glanced at the guard.

"It's true, sir," began Sanuu. "The prince requested you consider letting him stay with you, at least for the time being." Sanuu bowed his head, pivoted smartly on one heel, then ran off toward the castle.

Tom studied Nanni, their grandmother, standing in the doorway beside her husband. She was short and round with a warm smile and deep laugh wrinkles around her eyes. Nadda was also rotund with sparse hair, giant hands, and a mischievous twinkle in his eyes.

The smiles immediately disappeared from Avani's grandparents' faces, however, as they turned to regard Tom. After a brief pause they stared at each other. "What—," began Nadda, obviously not wanting to offend but also not quite sure how to put it, "what is he?"

Kiran knelt and untied his shoes. "He's a huu-man and it's his awakening-day," he said matter-of-factly. "He's from another world. Oh—and this is his pet. The creature's called a 'Max' and his name is Saint Bernard."

Max barked.

"Tom saved our lives today, it's kind of a long story," added Avani hastily.

"No, he's a Saint Bernard and his *name* is Max," corrected Tom, but no one was listening.

"Oh, child!" cried Nanni. "Come in and sit right down and tell us all about it!"

Everyone entered the house and moved quickly into the tiny living room. Handmade curtains, in cheerful colors with neat flowing curves surrounded each window and many small paintings, hung at various heights, dotted the walls. The room was dimly lit by several strategically placed candles. Wax had dripped down their sides and puddled on the window sills and on the top of an old, rickety desk cluttered with papers. A small fireplace graced one wall and its logs had burned down to a soft, warm glow of red embers. Nanni and the kids sat down on a well-worn couch and two equally worn overstuffed chairs. Nadda went into the kitchen and made a fresh pot of tea. Once it had finished brewing, he served them each the steaming, fragrant beverage in tiny ornate tea cups as Avani told an abbreviated version of their tale. She left out some unimportant details, like why they were outside the barrier alone at night in the first place...

Nadda again went to the kitchen, saying he could hear them from there. After the story had been told and retold, with Nadda occasionally calling for clarifications from the other room, all the questions were finally answered to their grandparents' satisfaction. Nanni went upstairs and made up a bed in the spare bedroom for Tom. Still puttering in the kitchen, Nadda absentmindedly hummed a strange yet somehow comforting melody as Nanni descended the stairs and joined the others in the living room. Moments later, Nadda entered the room wearing an apron and carrying a steaming dish shaped like a small pie.

"Tom, we'd like to officially welcome you to Elfhaven and into our home! It's an old elfish tradition on awakening-day to celebrate the occasion with a special treat: a grub and mud pie with a delicious slug-slime meringue topping. What's more, as is the custom here in Elfhaven, we let the awakening-day boy, or girl, eat the whole thing themselves!" With obvious pride, Nadda smiled and held out the pie for Tom to take. Things appeared to be wriggling around on top. A look of pure horror enveloped Tom's face.

Kiran couldn't take it any longer and broke into uproarious laughter;

followed immediately by Avani. Their grandparents were not far behind.

"Now see what you've done," chided Nadda, choking back tears of laughter himself, "you've spoiled the joke, Kiran!" They laughed all the harder.

Nadda took off his apron and held it up along with the pie. "Here Nanni, take this mess to the kitchen and bring back the real cake!" Tom felt only slightly less anxious.

Still chuckling, Nanni took the apron and the pie and headed for the kitchen. A few moments later she returned with a more traditional-looking one-layer cake slathered with vanilla-colored frosting. It hosted several candles of varying sizes. The candles shone brightly but not from a flame. These candles glowed from within, each having their own unique color.

Tom cautiously sniffed the cake.

"Beautiful candles. Are they magical?" he asked, a hint of awe in his voice. Avani nodded.

After they'd all finished eating their slice of birthday cake, and of course a second piece for good measure, the grandparents put the kids to bed. Nadda showed Tom the bedroom he'd be sleeping in, as well as where the tiny washroom was, just down the hall. Tom asked about Max. Nadda said they would make him a nice warm bed by the fire.

"What shall I call you two?" asked Tom.

"Um, why don't you just call us Nadda and Nanni? That's what Kiran and Avani's friends call us. Besides, it's easier than trying to pronounce our elven names." Nadda winked, then he left the room, closing the door behind him.

Tom paused, then tentatively called out, "Good night!" But no one answered him.

Just down the hall Nanni was tucking Kiran in. Two stuffed animals lay close beside him, one on his right side, one on his left. "What's the stuffed dragon for?" she asked.

"Protection, in case a troll comes out of the closet."

Nanni glanced at the closet with a knowing look. "Ah, and what's the stuffed gremlin for, then?"

"Backup!" replied Kiran.

Nanni laughed all the way down the hall.

Once downstairs Nanni stared at her husband and in a hushed tone asked, "Do you think the kids know about the prophecy?"

In an equally hushed tone Nadda replied, "No, it's no longer taught in schools these days. Only us old folk would remember."

"What do you think, Nadda, could the boy be the one—the one from the prophecy?"

Nadda gazed up the stairs thoughtfully. "I hope not." Turning back to his wife he added, "I hope not for his sake."

Chapter 11: A tale of two kings

When Tom came downstairs the next morning, everyone was already seated at the breakfast table. Between Kiran and Nadda was an extra chair and table setting. Kiran smiled and slid the chair out for Tom. Over in the corner Max was eagerly wolfing down some food that had been set out for him. Max's food looked suspiciously like the slug-slime-topped pie from the previous evening. Tom shuddered.

"Good morning, Thomas. Hope you slept well," said Nanni.

Accepting the proffered chair from Kiran, Tom sat down. "Fine, thanks. What's for breakfast? Or maybe after last night, I shouldn't ask."

Nadda chuckled. Everyone else dug in, ignoring Tom's comment.

"After breakfast," began Avani, "I thought we'd give you a tour of Elfhaven. I think you'll enjoy it, especially since you say you don't have magic where you're from."

"That'd be great! Where do we start?" asked Tom eagerly.

"Now you three just be mindful," warned Nanni. "News of our strange visitor has surely spread throughout the kingdom like wildfire. There'll likely be loads of gawkers lining the streets. You just pay them no mind! You hear?"

"We'll be fine," Avani reassured her.

After breakfast, once the kids had finished washing, drying and putting away the dishes, Kiran went upstairs to change. Tom strapped on his adventurer's belt, then glanced up at the wall. "Is that a painting of you and your dad?"

Avani walked over and carefully lifted the picture off the wall, then brought it back and handed it to Tom.

"Yes, that's dad and me, and the baby's Kiran. He was one and I was six when that was painted. Kiran was obviously an ugly baby."

Tom snorted, then hastily glanced around to make sure Kiran wasn't there. "What's that thing your dad's holding?"

Avani hesitated, then dashed upstairs. After a couple of minutes Tom heard footsteps loudly pounding back downstairs. When she entered the room, she was holding a silver box that matched the one in the painting.

"It's all I have left from father. I keep it hidden in a locked chest in my closet." Avani handed it to Tom.

It felt cold to the touch and seemed out of place somehow. It was a perfect cube, about six inches per side and made of a dull, silver-gray metal. Tom flipped it over. On the back side, three colored buttons softly pulsed with light: red, green, and blue. Just below the buttons were three levers. Each lever was also colored, but the colors didn't match the button colors. The lever colors were cyan, magenta, and yellow. Tom rolled the cube back over. He had failed to notice it before, but on the top of the cube was a symbol etched into its surface. The symbol consisted of three squares equally spaced around a small circle in the middle. Squiggly lines stood between the circle and each of the squares. There were no other markings on the object.

"It belonged to dad. He was the last of an ancient order called 'The Keepers of the Light.' He told me that we guard an important secret, and that one day he would pass that secret on to me. I asked dad to open the box. He just laughed and said no, but he went on to say that the secret is bigger than just the box. Unfortunately, dad died before he had a chance to tell me the whole story, or even how to open the box. I think it contains something important, but I've never been able to open it."

"It's an odd-looking metal," said Tom, mesmerized by the strange artifact. Besides the feeling of cold, his fingers tingled where they touched the cube as if tiny electrical currents were pulsing through its surface.

"After my father's death, we had the dwarf master smiths take a look at it. They tried to open it, every way they knew how, but in the end, they didn't put a single scratch on it. In fact, they couldn't even identify what type of metal it was made of."

"Odd. And these levers—" began Tom, trying unsuccessfully to move them, "they seem to be stuck."

"Yes, they don't move. I don't know what they're for."

They must be used to unlock the thing somehow. Tom stared intently at the object trying to see the solution in his mind. "Your father didn't say anything more?"

"Well, I don't know if they're related but—he used to tell me a poem, over and over again at bedtime. I've often wondered if it had something to do with the box."

"What's the poem?"

"Let's see—the poem was titled 'A Riddle Within.' Avani cleared her throat. "Oh, colorful life—No, that's not right..." she furrowed her brow, concentrating, then said:

"Add the colors of life, to point the way;

Up, up I say, the levers shall sway;

Just when you thought, the riddle be solved;

Out pops another, to test your resolve;

Of nicknames past, the key to a key;

Sweetness springs release, as known were thee."

"Yes that's it!" she said confidently.

"Hmmm," Tom replied, analyzing the riddle in his mind. "Since the poem mentions colors and levers; it's gotta be giving us clues on how to open the box."

"Perhaps, but in any case, we don't have time to work on it now." Avani took the cube and placed it on the mantle. "I'll put it away when we come back. It's getting late; let's get going." Avani cupped her hands around her mouth and yelled, "Kiran! We're about to leave without you!"

Kiran sprinted downstairs and rushed to slip on his comfortable-looking green moccasins.

"Come on, Max, if there're gonna be gawkers, we might as well give them their money's worth!" said Tom. Max got up, stretched, and shook himself vigorously, sending slobber flying in all directions, then walked over to Tom.

"Bye, Nanni, Nadda! We'll be back by supper time," called Avani. Not waiting for a reply, she grabbed her cloak and closed the door behind them.

They started out heading eastward toward the center of town. Here the streets were made of smooth, hard, sunbaked clay and the rich smell of warm soil after a hot summer's rain filled Tom's nostrils. The smell somehow made him feel happy. Hundreds of tiny, flat, black-and-white tiles were laid out in geometric patterns to form walkways on both sides of the street. To Tom, the patterns appeared Middle Eastern in style.

Small yellow-green trees were planted in large holes in the walkways. They looked similar to the trees Tom had seen in the woods the day before, having the same gnarly bark and finger-thin twigs on the ends of each branch, but they didn't seem nearly as scary in town.

Just beyond the walkways stood small, neat and orderly wooden homes, with thatched grass roofs and cute little windows sporting crisscrossed braces in each one. They reminded Tom of hobbit homes in the shire, or at least what he imagined hobbit homes might look like.

Wisps of smoke gently rose from stone chimneys on several of the structures. In his mind's eye, Tom imagined all sorts of flavorful breads and pastries baking on open hearths within. The whole scene would have been awesome, had it not been for the fact that the homes expanded and contracted slightly, giving Tom the unnerving feeling that the building were watching him.

After walking ten blocks or so, Tom noticed the buildings had transitioned from homes to shops. Once again, the street was made of clay, but now the intricate tile walkways had been replaced by larger, rougher cobblestone sidewalks. There were still trees, but they were smaller than before, and although the buildings had the same alpine look, the windows were now much larger. Most of the shops had false fronts on their roofs—presumably, to make them appear taller and more impressive, like scenes he'd seen in old western movies. These shops stretched on for blocks and blocks.

As he walked, Tom realized that if he didn't stare at the buildings, the buildings didn't seem to stare at him. *That's a relief—that is, if I could just stop staring at em.*

People came and went from the stores, carrying groceries, clothing or other supplies. A few openly stared and pointed, but most pretended not to notice them, glancing back and whispering only after they'd passed by.

"That store makes the best sweetbreads," said Kiran, pointing across the street, "and that one over there is my favorite shop in town! If you go in late in the day and pretend to be shopping, the owner will give you a sweet sugar dumpling filled with warm squamberry filling. They're awesome!"

Avani faced Tom and they shared a knowing look, aware that the shop owner knew exactly what Kiran was there for: the treat!

At that moment, a guard came running around the corner, tripped over Max, and collided with Avani. She fell headlong into Tom's arms, nearly knocking him over. Their faces only an inch apart; their eyes wide with surprise.

"Awkward!" said Kiran, grinning.

But before the two could separate, Prince Devraj ran around the corner, saw the two in an embrace and with thinly veiled anger evident in his voice yelled, "Avani!" The two scrambled apart. Avani looked embarrassed and guilty all at the same time.

"I went by your home." The prince glared at Tom, his eyes shooting daggers. "Your grandparents said you took Thomas on a tour of Elfhaven."

Devraj shifted his gaze to Avani. "My father wants to speak with you, with all of us. He wants to hear, in our own words, what we saw and heard yesterday at the troll encampment. Follow the guard back to the palace at once."

Hastily glancing at each other, they all fell in step behind the guard. Tom, last in line, began to follow the others but the prince stopped him with a firm hand against his chest. Devraj paused, waiting 'til the others were out of earshot. "Perhaps I've not made myself clear, but Avani and I are pledged to be united. We will perform the ceremony as soon as she comes of age, when she's fifteen."

"But, the guard…" protested Tom.

"No excuses!" spat Devraj. "Keep your hands and eyes off her, do I make myself clear?"

Tom's voice cracked slightly as he uttered the word, "Perfectly."

* * *

On their way to the castle the prince ran up to lead the way. Tom and Max trailed behind. Tom still felt shaken by his encounter with Prince Devraj.

It wasn't my fault. I'm not trying to steal his girl. I don't care for Avani, not in that way—do I? Tom wasn't sure what he felt. He'd never had a girlfriend. *Can't we just be friends? Is that a crime? Why do girls always cause such trouble!*

At that moment Tom passed through the castle's main gates. The royal stables were to his left; glancing over he saw Lorin standing there. Tom slowed and began to wave but Lorin was deep in conversation with someone. The fellow was short and wore a dark brown hooded cloak drawn over his head, similar to Lorin's. An ornately carved, silver hilt of a sword peeked out from the stranger's cloak. As if sensing Tom's gaze, the figure adjusted his cloak, covering the sword's hilt. His head slowly rotated to regard Tom. Beneath the hood two fiery yellow eyes glowed ominously. Tom shuddered as he turned back and ran to catch up with the others. A moment later he glanced over his shoulder but the stranger was gone. Lorin, however, seemed to be following him...

* * *

After passing the stables, a large armory came into view on Tom's right. Two well-armed guards stood on either side of a large roughhewn wooden door.

As the kids climbed the thirty-odd steps that led to the Hall of Kings, they passed through a massive arched doorway. Tom guessed it was over twenty feet tall and almost as wide. On either side of him, long hallways disappeared into the distance with many doorways lining the inner walls. Elves were coming and going, briskly walking through the doorways on seemingly important business. As they approached the main hall ahead, a throng of people hoping to hear their tale tried to follow them inside, but were blocked by the palace guards.

Tom glanced back; he thought he saw Lorin slip inside as a guard helped an elderly woman pick up something she'd dropped. A moment later Tom checked again, but there was no sign of Lorin.

As they entered the hall, Tom noticed two ornate, hand-carved green doors that were swung open wide to each side. The center of each door had an enormous relief of an elephant carved into its surface. He stared at it for a moment, then caught up with the others.

Tom turned to Avani. "You have elephants in Elfhaven?"

"What's an elephant?" she replied.

"The doors—they have carvings of elephants on em."

Avani glanced back, then smiled. "Those are just mythical beasts. They don't really exist." Tom stared at her, but said nothing.

The room was well-lit by several colossal windows, each sporting arched tops that matched the curve of the doorway. Giant lanterns angled out from the walls on massive posts, adding to the brightness of the hall. The ceiling seemed to stretch upwards forever. Massive marble columns, spaced some twenty feet apart, lined each wall. A lofty platform, or dais, stood at the far end of the hall. Upon the dais, a tall, slender elf with a soft, yet wise-looking face sat on a crystal throne. He wore bright crimson and ivory-colored flowing robes, and held a golden staff. The head of the staff was fashioned to look like the talons of some mighty bird of prey, holding what appeared to be the largest emerald Tom had ever seen. To the elf's right stood a shorter, stalky, muscular fellow with bushy eyebrows and a full neatly-trimmed beard. His face bore a stern look, yet there was a mischievous twinkle in his eyes. He wore a simple brown tunic, a wide leather belt, and highly polished leather boots topped with fur. Slung over his broad shoulder was a huge axe, a leather thong wrapped tightly around its handle. An enormous belt buckle that sparkled of gold and silver and had some sort of crest emblazoned on it, adorned the belt.

Maybe this planet has professional wrestling, too? Tom smiled at the thought. Two rows of elven guards in formal attire marked the last twenty feet before the throne. Tom tried to make eye contact with several of the guards but they wouldn't look at him. Instead they remained perfectly still, staring straight ahead. Behind the guards were seated many elves in colorful, blousy costumes. Tom assumed they were nobles in the king's court. At five paces from the platform the prince stopped; they all followed suit.

Tom gazed around in awe at all the fascinating sights, but when he glanced at Avani and Kiran, he noticed they were standing rigid, their jaws tight, their gaze down.

"Father," began the prince, "I give you Thomas Holland and his creature, uh—his Max, Saint Bernard."

Max barked twice. Murmurs spread throughout the hall as everyone gazed in wonder at this strange creature. The king studied Max with a raised eyebrow.

"Of course you know Avani, last of the 'Keepers of the Light' and her brother Kiran. Tom, this is my father, his Royal Highness, Ruler of all the elves of Elfhaven province, King Dakshi."

"Well met," said the king, gazing down intently at Tom.

"Thanks," began Tom, shifting his weight awkwardly from foot to foot. "Ah, er, your Majesty?"

The king smiled as he stood up. He motioned for the stocky person on the dais to come stand beside him. "This is my closest friend, a master smith in his own right, and the leader of the sovereign nation of the dwarves, King Abban."

The dwarf king tipped his head toward Tom in acknowledgment. Then, glancing down and to his right, and in a deep booming voice said, "Tom, I'd like you to meet my son, Goban." There was a slight commotion: Tom heard what sounded like a rattling of pans; someone's voice said, "excuse me"; and lastly came a startled woman's gasp. Finally, a short but very stout dwarf lad wriggled out from between two guards. He had a flat square face with an equally flat pudgy nose that bent off slightly to the right at the tip. But it was his enormous bushy eyebrows that really caught Tom's attention. The boy straightened himself up, puffed out his chest, and with an exaggerated swagger, sauntered right up to Tom. Grasping Tom's hand in his, he vigorously shook it.

"Holla! I hear you's represents Earth, dog. Well, I represents Daltar!" Goban pointed at Tom's Converse sneakers. "Hey, those kicks are tight."

Tom just blinked. "Are you—speaking—Hip Hop?"

"Rumor has it that you's an inventor. That's old school, dude, but hey, I got mad skills, too! I can tell we'll be homies. Maybe we could hang at my crib sometime, yo?"

"Ah, sure—whatever you say." Tom, not exactly sure what he'd just agreed to, glanced sidelong at Avani.

She just shrugged.

Tom stared at the dwarf lad once more, *I've seen him somewhere before. But how could I? And that name—Goban…*

King Dakshi leaned sideways toward his friend Abban, covered his mouth, and whispered, "I know it's been awhile since I've seen your son. But, why does he now speak so strangely?"

"He thinks it makes him sound *cool*. His friends seem to concur," confided King Abban, then he added, "He gets it from his mother."

Dakshi nodded with a knowing look.

"One of the reasons I summoned you here today," resumed King Dakshi, his voice once again clear and strong, "was to hear, from your own lips, what exactly transpired yesterday with the troll encounter. Avani, if you please."

Avani took a small step forward, cleared her throat, then began her tale starting at the troll encampment, but the king immediately stopped her, asking her to go back to the point where they first left the barrier, and to speak louder. She squirmed and glanced nervously at the Prince, but Devraj just stared straight ahead.

Avani began again, louder this time. She told the story of searching for and finally finding the singing crystals. She then described Max's arrival and his insistence that they follow him. At that, the king leaned forward, gazing at Max with newfound respect in his eyes. Max just stared up at the king with his big brown eyes, his tongue hanging out to one side.

Avani continued telling the story of finding the troll encampment and of Kiran spotting Tom tied to a tree. Glancing sidelong at the prince once more, she hastily related her argument with Devraj about whether to go for help or not.

"Stop!" commanded the king. Then, glaring at his son he said, "Devraj, why didn't you insist on going for help?"

The prince cleared his throat, "Father, er—your Majesty, Avani reasoned that Tom would be dead before help arrived."

"And what made you believe that to be true?"

"We overheard the trolls speaking. They were waiting for a scout to return from patrol. Their leader said that once the scout was back they would leave. There was an argument whether to kill the boy then, or to bring him with them when they left. In either case we would have lost the chance to save him."

The king paused, then returned his attention to Avani. "Proceed with your tale."

Avani again glanced at the now scowling Devraj, then quickly went on to chronicle their daring rescue of Tom using her magic and Kiran's bravery.

A shocked look passed over the king's face. "I didn't realize your magical prowess was so great."

"I—I think it must've been the crystals. They seemed to be amplifying my power, sire." Avani reached into her satchel and pulled forth the three magic singing crystals, holding them high in the air for all to see. Even in the well-lit hall, the crystals glowed brightly at her touch. A moment later Avani began to glow herself, and as before Tom heard a beautiful melody playing in his mind. Murmurs spread throughout the crowd, jaws dropped at the sight of the legendary crystals. From the expressions on their faces, Tom could tell that everyone was hearing the magical sounds, too.

Whispers of awe sounded. "Avani—is the chosen one..."

The king, his brow still raised and conscious of the crowd's reaction, stared at Avani intently.

Suddenly uncomfortable with the king's scrutiny, she hurriedly stuffed the crystals back into her satchel.

"And what of master Kiran?" began the king. "Were you not afraid, attempting such a daring rescue?"

"I was scared spitless, your Highness! I almost peed my pants," replied Kiran. Laughter erupted from the crowd. Kiran's face turned red. The king smiled, waiting for the laughter to die down.

"Continue," said the king, nodding to Avani. She resumed her tale, relating the hectic journey back to safety, and highlighting Devraj's bravery in facing the mist wraith, at which point the slightest hint of a smile crossed the king's face. Avani next touted Tom's brilliant plan involving the use of his magic talking devices.

"Wait!" boomed King Dakshi. He turned to Tom. "Do you have these mysterious talismans with you?"

"Yes, sir, er—sire," replied Tom awkwardly.

"Could we see a demonstration of them?" asked the king.

"Of course, your Highness." Tom fumbled around, searching for the pocket that contained the radios. Pulling out two he stepped forward, reached up and handed one to the king.

"You turn this knob like so." Tom stepped back, twisting his own on/volume knob to the right. A firm click resounded, followed by the sound of static. "Now turn yours on, your Majesty."

The king reached for the knob, holding the device far out at arm's length. Slowly he turned the knob 'til it clicked; a red light gleamed confirmation. The king's shoulders relaxed slightly and he let out an almost imperceptible sigh.

"To talk, you put the radio near your mouth and press and hold this button here. Then you just talk; simple as pie, right?" Tom pressed the button, held the device to his mouth, and using his best truckers' accent said, "Breaker, breaker one-nine, this is Thomas Holland comin' atcha from Elfhaven castle. How's the weather up there on yon dais, your Majesty, over?" As if in slow motion, several things happened at once. The king jumped back, dropping the radio. The whole crowd of nobles gasped and leapt to their feet. At the same time King Abban deftly, in one smooth, well-practiced motion, swung his battle axe off his shoulder, bringing it up over his head, poised to deal a deadly blow to the seemingly demon possessed device.

"Stop!" cried Tom, his voice ringing out from the radio, now lying face up on the dais floor. The room fell deathly silent, all eyes focused on the possessed talisman. Tom, still pressing the talk button, spoke into the device once more. "It's just a radio. It's just relaying my words. See, I'm over here, speaking the same words into my radio. That's it. Look over here." Tom waved his hand above his head. The king lightly touched the handle of his friends battle axe. The dwarf relaxed his grip on his axe a little as King Dakshi bent down and cautiously picked up the radio.

"See," said Tom through the walkie-talkie, "it's just a harmless device." Murmurs spread amongst the crowd.

"Now you try," coaxed Tom. "Just press the button and talk."

The king glanced at his friend Abban, then slowly raised the radio to his mouth. He took a deep breath, pressed the button, and yelled the words, "Tom, are you there?"

Ouch! Tom scrunched up his face and plugged his ear. Then pressing his own "talk" button he said, "Yes I'm here and—you don't need to shout, your Highness." Hints of laughter echoed in the chamber but were quickly cut short as the king gave a stern look, his eyes sweeping the hall.

"What do you think? Pretty sick, huh?" said Tom, then he hastily added, "er—sire."

The king stepped to the edge of the dais, leaned down and handed the radio back to Tom, "These devices could be invaluable in the upcoming war. I could keep in touch with my generals instantly, instead of sending out messengers. Could we perhaps, borrow these—walking talk-ease?"

Walkie-talkies, thought Tom, but he just said, "Sure thing, and a— while you're at it, you might like to borrow my flare gun and a couple of flares as well." Tom found the gun and removed it along with two flares. "You load it like this, then point it up into the sky. When you pull the trigger it fires a rocket high in the air, then it bursts into a brilliant point of light. You can see it for several minutes and from miles away. Obviously I can't demonstrate it in here. Oh, and—one flare is white, the other red."

"Several minutes?" said the king, a puzzled look on his face.

"I think it's a measurement of time. Like a myntar, only different, your highness," piped up Kiran.

The king nodded, then glanced at his friend Abban. The dwarf relaxed completely, replacing his battle axe on his shoulder. King Dakshi motioned to one of his palace guards who then walked over to Tom. Tom handed him the two remaining radios, plus the flare gun and flares.

"Thank you, Thomas Holland. We are in your debt," said the king. "Avani, please go on with your tale."

Avani finished her story with Kiran's cry for help and the bravery of the elven guard that had saved them all.

Once it was over Avani stepped back with her friends. The king gazed down at his hands, absently stroking his large gold signet ring with its equally large emerald stone. Then he raised himself up to his full height and his eyes surveyed the crowd, finally settling on Tom.

"Tom, you've arrived during grave times," stated the king sadly. "For many years we have lived peacefully with the troll and ogre nations. Not a friendly relationship, mind you, but one in which both sides mutually agreed to ignore the other. About a yara ago, however, something changed. Without provocation the trolls attacked. At that time the barrier was strong and we were able to defend ourselves. But things have gotten worse. Dark forces are amassing against us. In years past, mist wraiths were only seen deep in the haunted forest and the forbidden swamp. Yet you've seen one here in Elfhaven valley, and there've been other sightings. Worst of all, something has stirred the trolls up to a frenzy, and they are out for blood: elven blood."

Once again the king's eyes swept the hall and in a louder voice he continued, "Everyone, many rumors are flying about. You are my trusted advisors, my court, my military strategists. You need to know the following information. That's why I called you all to this meeting here today, instead of having it in private. However, I must ask you all not to reveal what I'm about to tell you to anyone. As you will soon understand, this knowledge might start a panic here in Elfhaven, and the last thing we need right now is panic." As King Dakshi's gaze swept the hall, several people glanced uneasily at each other, then slowly nodded to the king.

"The timing of the upcoming war with the trolls could not be worse. As you all know the magic of our world has been weakening for some time. What you may not know, however, is the magical barrier that has protected our people for hundreds of years is also failing. Our scholars believe we may have only days left before it fails altogether; perhaps a week at most." Startled gasps filled the hall. Many of the nobles' faces went white with horror. Even some of the stoic guards broke down and stared at one another, their mouths agape.

"Quiet. Quiet!" shouted the king. Once the fear-filled murmurs had died down he resumed, "We believe that the barrier's magical power is controlled from within the Citadel. For hundreds of years, the care of the Citadel was entrusted to the Keepers of the Light, and to them alone. Unfortunately the secret of how to enter the Citadel, and of what lies within, died with Avani and Kiran's father, Pavak Dutta." The king gazed upon Avani and Kiran with a look of compassion and sadness.

"Up to this point our best scholars have been unable to open the Citadel. You now understand why this news mustn't get out to the general populace." Murmurs echoed around the hall.

The king gazed down at Tom once more. "We expect the trolls who captured you were an advance scouting party, sent here to gain information about our defenses, our weaknesses."

Then to everyone he added, "Moments before this meeting, our scouts reported seeing several thousand troll warriors gathering about thirty kiloters away, just beyond the Trontiel Mountains. The pass through those mountains is narrow and rocky. Even so, the bulk of the troll army could reach the outskirts of Elfhaven valley within a day or two. But already a platoon of a couple hundred trolls, just today, was spotted setting up camp near where Tom was held captive."

"Your Majesty," interrupted Kiran. Avani shook her head and shot her brother a look that could kill a ghost.

"Go on," said the king, a hint of annoyance in his voice.

"Can't you ask for help? Isn't there someone who will help us?"

King Dakshi's eyes flashed to King Abban, then he replied, "I've sent a desperate plea to my cousin in the south, King Bharat, ruler of the lake elves, asking for troops. But he has his own problems... I fear that even if he does send help, it will be too little and too late."

"Sire?" began Tom.

King Dakshi, unaccustomed to being interrupted, let alone twice in a row, furrowed his brow, "Yes, Thomas?"

"I came to your world accidentally. I was trying to keep Max from running through a portal; a portal from another world, another universe; my world, Earth. I know this must sound strange, but I have to get home. My mom and my uncle will be worried sick. Can you help me get back to Earth?"

King Dakshi paused. "Tis' not strange at all, Tom. There are legends of gateways to other worlds, legends which spoke of these thresholds opening often. However, no one has heard of a gateway opening in yaras, not 'til the one that brought you here, that is."

"Maybe the one I came through is still open. Can't we at least go see?"

The king frowned. "I am afraid it is too dangerous, what with the impending war." He rubbed his chin idly, then glanced at King Abban. "The legends indicate that these thresholds did not remain open long, but I give you my word that after the war is over, assuming we are still alive, that is, I will send a scouting party to see if your gateway yet exists."

Tom nodded; a tear trickled down his cheek. Avani noticed, reached over and gently squeezed his hand. The action did not go unnoticed by Devraj, however.

The king sighed. "And now for the final reason I brought you all here today. Besides learning exactly what happened yesterday, on your encounter with the trolls, I have a punishment that needs to be administered."

A fierce look came over the king's face. "You children were out beyond the barrier, after dark and without protection. Worse, you left without telling anyone where you'd gone. You repeatedly made choices that put yourselves in danger. When you learned of the enemy patrol you should have immediately reported your findings. That knowledge may prove critical to the very survival of Elfhaven. Yet you chose to risk yourselves and thus all of Elfhaven, for the unlikely chance that you could rescue Tom."

Avani glanced at the prince but once again he remained motionless.

The king continued, "Don't get me wrong, we are all glad that Tom is safe with us here today, but that does not excuse the grave errors in judgment that you all made."

Handing his staff to a guard, the king picked up a scroll from the arm of his throne. Its spindles were large, ornate golden knobs and the parchment looked dark and crisp. Rolling open the scroll he began to read, "A two-phase sentence will now be imposed on the following subjects: Avani Dutta, Kiran Dutta, Prince Devraj…"

"But sire—" began Devraj.

"Silence!" commanded his father.

Kiran and Avani stood rigidly, and Tom could tell they were holding their breath.

Affixing his gaze on the scroll once more, the king continued, "Each day, precisely at four o'clock in the morning and for two oorts henceforth, you three will do hard manual labor by cleaning the royal stables. Have I made myself clear?" asked the king, rolling up his scroll.

Devraj opened his mouth to speak but the king shot him such a sharp look that the prince closed his mouth, though his eyes burned with fury.

Hmm, an "oort" must be like an Earth hour. Tom raised his hand. The king, unaccustomed to this gesture, tipped his head to one side. "Yes, Tom?"

Straightening himself up, Tom took a deep breath. "If my friends are being punished for rescuing me then I want to share their punishment."

The king raised an eyebrow. "You have done nothing wrong. In fact, you are helping us with the use of your magical devices. I do not wish to punish you, Tom. Do you understand this?"

Tom nodded.

"And you would still take punishment with your friends?"

"I would."

The king paused. "So be it. I hereby sentence Thomas Holland to the same punishment as the others."

King Dakshi set down the heavy scroll and retrieved his staff. "And now for the second half of this decree; which, in accordance with Tom's wishes, he will also be sentenced to." The king's eyes met Tom's, his gaze so sharp that Tom had to turn away. Glancing at Kiran, a defiant look covered his face. Avani's face, however, was white as a ghost.

The king softened his manner and voice somewhat. "As all of us here today know, we, as a people, have gotten lax. We have lost most of our magical abilities, when they are needed most. Of course, we have our excuses: for centuries we had the wizards to protect us, so we did not feel the need of our own magic; the Citadel is not magnifying the magic as it once did; there has not been a real need for magic since the War of the Wizards; the books on magic were all destroyed in that same war; and on, and on. Still, we have no one to blame but ourselves. As I said, we have become soft, lazy, focused on our individual petty troubles, and not on the greater good of all elf kind, nay, the greater good of all who inhabit this world! We were once a mighty and powerful race, and at the same time we felt an obligation as stewards of our world. We strove to do what was best for the whole world, not just for elf kind, or worse yet, for our own individual kingdoms.

"To many, it may seem too late to make a difference, what with the imminent threat of war and the probable collapse of the barrier. But I say we have to start sometime. Months ago I discreetly sent seekers far and wide and they were able to locate someone with a vast knowledge of magic. He is a proficient practitioner who has agreed to teach the young here in Elfhaven valley. As of tomorrow, I hereby declare that the first school of magic, since the great schools from the age of the wizards, is now open!" With a wry smile, he added, "It will be called Gremlin Tower after the crafty, ingenious little critters that constantly seem to outsmart us. The old granary tower on the east side of town will be used as its first campus."

Once again the king adopted a stern look. "Returning to the matter of punishment, regarding your lack of good judgment yesterday—I've decided to send you all to magic school."

"School? Uhhhggg!" cried Kiran in disgust.

"Shush!" Avani slapped her hand over Kiran's mouth. She turned to her brother and whispered, "This will probably get you out of doing some of your chores at home." Kiran's eyelids rose slightly. She went on to say, "Besides, it'll be fun!"

The king pretended not to notice their exchange and continued, "Each day, after you've finished your morning duties at the stables, you will attend magic classes."

"At school you will be joined by others—children who show promise with respect to their magical abilities." Turning toward King Abban, King Dakshi said, "Of course it's your decision, but I think it would be a good idea if your son Goban would attend the school as well." King Dakshi paused, searching for a tactful way to put this: "Although dwarf kind has, in the past, shown little interest in—or aptitude—for magic, I think it would be a good experience for him. Through understanding our ways and culture, it might strengthen the bonds between our two races."

"Agreed," said King Abban, apparently taking no insult. His son Goban glanced up in surprise but before he could complain, King Dakshi went on, "Excellent! School will begin tomorrow morning promptly at

7:00 AM. Make sure you are on time and bring blank parchment along with writing quills and ink. Dismissed!"

King Dakshi turned back to discuss important matters with King Abban.

* * *

Tom watched as people began leaving the hall, talking hurriedly amongst themselves, fear in their voices.

Once most of the crowd had left, Prince Devraj strode up and stood below his father. "Sire," he began. The prince stared at King Abban, till the dwarf turned and walked a few paces away.

"Father, I must protest. The punishment is severe and far beneath my station. The heir to the throne should not be seen shoveling $%^&."

"Devraj!" snapped the king, "your language is inappropriate for an heir to the throne."

"Sorry, father. The *heir to the throne* shouldn't be seen shoveling *manure...*" hissed the prince. When the king didn't respond, Devraj hurried on, "Besides, I am older and have important responsibilities, especially with the upcoming war. I haven't time for menial tasks or for being sent off to public school like some—commoner."

"Avani is not a 'commoner.' As you said, she's the Keeper of the Light and someday she will be your bride. And when the day comes, when you assume the throne, she will be queen of the realm. And like it or not, Tom is definitely not common either." The king paused while Devraj fumed.

King Dakshi pulled himself up to his full height. "Truth be told, I am most disappointed in you, my son. As you said, you are the eldest. You are a prince and you represent the crown. The people expect great leadership from you and as you pointed out, one day you will be king. Yesterday you failed me. You failed yourself. You failed the kingdom. The knowledge of the troll scouting party is critical. Not only might we have lost that information, we might have lost you! Or worse, you could have been taken as a hostage, did you even think of that? No, yesterday you acted as a child. So starting tomorrow, you will be treated as a child."

"But father, it was not my—"

"Enough! Do as you are told."

The prince strained to contain his anger, his eyes locked with the king's in a battle of wills. Finally, Devraj pivoted and stormed from the hall.

King Abban walked back to his friend. Together they watched the prince leave. Abban placed his hand on Dakshi's shoulder. "Remember, he's still but a child."

"I know," conceded Dakshi wistfully, "but I fear circumstances may force him to grow up faster than we might wish." He paused. "I hope he is up to the challenge."

"He was not always this—strong-willed," said the dwarf king, more as a statement of fact than a question.

"Pig-headed, you mean," said Dakshi flatly. "His mother died at a traitor's hand when the boy was but eight years old. For some reason Devraj blames himself. He feels he should have prevented it, he should have saved her somehow. Of course there was nothing he could have done, but I think it damaged his self-confidence. As a result, he overcompensates by being quick to anger."

"Well, he is definitely headstrong and arrogant, but he showed great courage in the woods last night," reasoned Abban, meeting his friends' gaze head-on.

"They all did, along with ingenuity. But I could not tell them that. They still have much to learn." The king's gaze drifted over to follow his son's path. "One day soon, these kids may be our only hope…"

"Perhaps you should consider giving your son more responsibility. You could put him in command of one of your archer brigades in the upcoming war," suggested Abban.

King Dakshi took a deep breath, but said nothing. Finally he turned toward his friend. "There's one last bit of business I must discuss with you. I must ask you for a favor, a big one. I must ask for the support of the dwarf army."

"Ah—that," began Abban. "I wondered when you'd broach the subject." The dwarf king paused. "You know we're close friends and allies. We'll supply the elven army with the finest dwarf blades, bows, arrows and maces. As you well know, the quality of dwarf weaponry is unsurpassed. However, as I'm sure you've guessed, the dwarf high council is at odds over the situation. Many on the council rightly point out that the trolls are upset with the elves, not with the dwarves. If we join the fight, then we will likely incur the wrath of the trolls. Our cities would surely fall prey to their attacks."

"You know as well as I that once the troll army has destroyed Elfhaven, with their newfound confidence the trolls will turn their attention to overthrowing the dwarves. Together we stand a chance, slim as it may be, of beating them. Divided..." Dakshi allowed the unanswered question to linger in the air.

"You are correct as always, my friend. You know I'm on your side. Let me see what I can do to convince the council of elders." King Abban smiled, touching the hilt of his axe. "I'll knock some sense into em." Dakshi snorted, then smiled, in spite of the dire circumstances.

Chapter 12: Try, try again

The fog had lifted and the trolls were gaining on Juanita. She had bought some time by wading into a shallow brook and following it downstream for a few hundred yards. That had thrown her pursuers off her trail for a while, but somehow they'd figured out where she'd gone.

They'll be here any minute. Where can I hide? Frantically she searched the forest around her.

That log, over to the left. Maybe I can hide behind it. Sprinting to the log, she laid down and leaned in tight against it. The log sagged from her weight.

It's rotted. She peered at the end of the log.

It's also hollow. Scrambling around, she wriggled her way into the damp, moldy, smelly space. It was a tight fit. She barely could breathe as she desperately inched her way forward. Strange multi-colored mushrooms that glowed in the dark lined the sides. Her head suddenly came to rest against a solid part of the fallen tree. She couldn't turn around to look back, but it felt like her feet were sticking out. Desperately she tried to pull them in, but there just wasn't room. A moment later she heard voices and she recognized them.

"You lost her, fool!" yelled the troll named Fowlbreth.

"You mean, we—lost her," replied Bellchar. One of the trolls stepped up onto the log. The log began to sag. Juanita took a deep breath and using her back, pushed up with all her might.

From atop the log Fowlbreth continued, "No. Twas you dat lost her."

"She tricky dat one. She hurt my tum," complained Bellchar.

"Oh, did da little girl hurt poor Bellchar?"

Juanita turned blue and her muscles began shaking uncontrollably. Just then a creature resembling a slug started slithering up her arm, leaving a glowing green trail of slime in its wake.

"You tink you funny," spat Bellchar. "Come, we find her or we both dead."

The slug crawled under her sleeve, heading up her arm. Juanita choked back a scream.

Suddenly the weight lifted from the log and Juanita involuntarily gasped for breath, then froze, listening intently for any sign she'd been discovered, but all she heard was the muffled sound of receding footsteps. After waiting an agonizing couple of minutes, without hearing any further noise, she painstakingly wiggled her way back out.

Ugh. She pulled her blouse off her right shoulder and flipped away the slug. *That was disgusting.* Bending over she shook her long auburn hair, sending bits of glowing mushroom flying in all directions. Then letting out a deep sigh she dusted off as much dirt as she could from her once-pretty dress.

Surveying the ground around the fallen log, she could see which way the trolls had gone, so she turned and began walking in the opposite direction.

It was hard to get her bearings in the dim light. She'd been walking for a couple of minutes when, as she passed a large gnarled tree, a huge hand reached out and grabbed her arm.

"Just where might you be going?" asked a deep resonant voice. She whirled around, expecting to see one of her troll pursuers, but her eyes were greeted by a bizarre sight. There, standing before her, was a giant, fat, hairless creature with large ears, a jutting jaw, small beady eyes, huge rippling muscles, and a faint green tinge.

"What? First trolls and now Shrek? Give me a break."

"My pleasure," replied the creature as he raised his club and brought it down squarely upon her head.

Chapter 13: Tom's tour de force

Once the kids left the castle, they resumed their tour of the city, walking back the way they'd come earlier. After ten blocks or so the space on the right opened into a large grassy area with a few shrubs and some ornamental trees. In the center of the square was a circular raised platform, maybe ten feet across.

"This is Bandipur Park," began Avani, turning into the commons and heading for the platform. "It's very old. In the center, that's a magical fountain. It was created thousands of years ago by our ancestors, with the help of wood sprites." As they approached Tom could see it was filled with water and looked like a kids wading pond back home, except for the statues of sea monsters gazing up at him from just below the water's surface…

Kiran spoke up, "When it was working water used to rise up and take on the shape of some old dude. Then he'd start talking. You could see his mouth move and everything. Plus he'd speak to you. It sounded strange though, sorta gurgling and faraway like."

"Some old dude?" said Tom.

Avani glanced at her brother and shook her head. "The water would take on the appearance of a king or sage or wizard from the past."

Kiran leaned in close to Tom and in a quiet tone said, "The cool thing was, when you walked around it, the guy's eyes would follow you. It was fun to come here late at night with friends. Very spooky!"

Tom glanced at Avani. "You said it used to work. When did it stop?"

"When I was young it always worked perfectly, but a week and a half ago, it began to fail. The next day, it stopped altogether. What's more, at the same time this fountain quit working, magical devices all over town started running erratically or stopped entirely."

A week and a half ago, Tom paused, thinking. *That's about when the portal first opened. About the time I lost Chloe.* He felt a sudden pang of sadness remembering the fateful night that had started it all.

I should never have chased Max through the portal. Now I've lost Mom. Will I ever see her again? Will I ever get back to Earth… Tom stared blankly at the fountain.

Avani turned and walked away saying, "Come on; I'll show you the library next. You're going to love this!"

The library was only a couple of blocks away and off to their right. It was a massive stone structure, which Tom thought was unusual in itself, since he'd seen only wooden buildings so far; but it also had large stone columns out front. The columns had pictures of elves in heroic poses etched into their surface all the way around. One such scene depicted an elf standing beside a dead dragon, holding a spear. Another showed an elf crossing a raging river on a tiny raft. A third portrayed several valiant elves in full battle armor courageously fighting off a horde of ferocious trolls. To Tom, the columns gave the library a dignified, official look. As the kids began to ascend the broad stairs leading to the main entrance, a couple of boys about Tom's age came bounding down the steps toward them.

"Hey, Malak, Chatur!" called Avani, nodding to each one in turn.

"Hey, Avani, Kiran. Is this your new alien friend?" asked Chatur excitedly.

"She said hi to me first, knucklehead," said Malak. "That means I get to talk first. Hey, Avani, Kiran!"

"Where does it say that you get to talk first just because your name's called first, huh?" challenged Chatur.

Malak frowned. "Everyone knows that. Everyone who has at least one brain cell, that is!"

Chatur grasped Malak in a headlock and threw him to the ground, where they rolled around fighting on the cold, hard steps.

"Boys," said Avani with mock disgust. Since they didn't respond immediately she tried again, louder this time, "Boys! Could you two juveniles stop fighting long enough so that I can introduce you to my new friend?" Turning to Tom she asked, "Where're you from again?"

"Earth. The planet Earth. It's—it's in a parallel universe," said Tom, realizing how strange that sounded.

The two boys picked themselves up and dusted themselves off. "That hurt," said Malak, out of the corner of his mouth.

"It's supposed to hurt when you get your butt whooped!" replied Chatur.

"Enough, children!" cried Avani, then she leaned close to Tom and whispered, "They constantly argue, and over the stupidest things." Turning back, and in her normal voice said, "Tom, I'd like you to meet my infantile friends Chatur," Tom shook Chatur's hand, who grinned and gave a sidelong glance at Malak, "and his best friend Malak." Malak shook Tom's hand vigorously.

"And this is Saint Bernard, he's a Max," added Kiran, not wanting to be left out.

"His *name* is Max, actually," said Tom, frowning, but they were all staring at Max.

"Does it bite? Can it talk? Does it have claws? Is it full grown? Is it male or female?" asked Malak and Chatur in a rapid-fire barrage of questions.

"No, no, no, yes, male," Tom fired back.

"It only bites obnoxious Elvin brats," said Kiran flatly.

As one, Malak and Chatur sneered at Kiran.

Chatur bent down and shook Max's paw warmly. "Any friend of the alien Tom is a friend of mine."

Max licked his hand and slobbered. Everyone laughed.

"Are you going to the library?" asked Malak.

"Of course they're going to the library, doofus," said Chatur, gazing disgustedly at the dog slobber on his hand.

"Can we tag along?" asked Malak, ignoring Chatur's insult for once.

"No! You just came from the library and besides, we've got lots more to show Tom and you'll only slow us down," said Avani firmly.

"Ah, but you won't even know we're here," pleaded Malak.

Avani chuckled. "Fat chance of that. No, you run along home. You'll get to see Tom tomorrow, I promise."

Chatur's and Malak's shoulders slumped forward dejectedly.

As the two turned and walked off down the street, Tom asked Avani, "You said they always fight like that?"

"Yes, ever since they were little." Avani shook her head. "The way they fight you'd think they were brothers, but they're just good friends." Then she added, "But don't even think about fighting one unless you can best them both. Believe it or not they're fiercely loyal to one another."

As the pair walked away, Tom saw Chatur wipe dog slobber onto Malak's sleeve. Malak punched Chatur in the shoulder. "You'd never know it to look at them," said Tom. For some reason they reminded Tom of his best friend James. *I wonder if I'll ever get to see him again?*

Avani shrugged, then turned and continued up the library steps. Tom followed her.

Ahead, an intricate carving of an old steam locomotive adorned the library's gigantic red wooden door. Tom raised his brow. "What's that?"

"That picture? It's just an artist's whimsical rendition of a machine from the future. Come on; wait 'til you see what's inside." As they walked toward the door, Tom couldn't take his eyes off the carving of the steam engine.

At that moment, Kiran bolted past them, running up the last few steps. Struggling, he opened the massive door and entered the library.

They followed him in. The scene was breathtaking: The library had a high ceiling, at least three stories with hundreds of tiny windows lining its walls. Arches crisscrossed the ceiling and hung down some twenty feet at their lowest points. Statues of monsters and strange beasts jutted out from several locations on each wall. To Tom, the place looked like a cross between a cathedral and a haunted castle, kinda gave him the creeps. But what most caught his attention though, were the books that floated about, apparently of their own accord. Tom saw people reading, their books hovering in mid-air. The pages even turned themselves, somehow knowing when the reader had finished the page.

Suddenly, one of the floating books fell to the floor for no apparent reason. Max ran over, pawed and sniffed it. Then another book fell. Unfortunately, this one landed on the foot of a passerby. That unleashed a disastrous series of events: first the fellow cried out at the unexpected pain and grabbed his foot, hopping around on one leg. Max ran over to him. A look of complete terror crossed the man's face at the sight of a huge furry creature galloping straight for him. Scrambling back, he bumped into a woman who sat casually sipping her tea. This caused her to spill the hot liquid all over the manuscript she was reading. Leaping up, she screamed in surprise and frustration. Several others shushed them both. One older gentleman scowled, pointing to a sign above the woman that read "Absolutely no food or drink in the library!" Under the sign hung another, smaller sign that read "This means you!" Tom laughed. Kiran giggled. Avani shot them both a stern look.

"Kiran, go get Saint Bernard," hissed Avani. Tom winced. Kiran dashed over and grabbed Max by the collar, apologizing profusely to the man and woman, then pulled him back to where Tom and his sister were waiting for them.

Just ahead stood the librarian's desk. As they approached the counter, the librarian rose up from what he was doing and greeted them. There was something odd about this fellow, though. For one thing, Tom could see right through him. In fact, the librarian appeared to be a ghost!

Max barked at the spirit. Kiran hushed him. Max cocked his head and gave a weak whimper.

"May I help you?" asked the apparition in a sing-songy voice, ignoring Max's outburst.

Tom glanced sidelong at Avani who gave him a reassuring nod, so he took a deep breath and asked, "Um, do you have any books on magic?"

The ghost stared at Tom in apparent disbelief as he absently tapped his finger on the desk. The effort, of course, made no noise.

"What is this? Some sort of a joke? Do I look like the kind of spirit that could conjure up a book out of thin air?"

"Well..." began Tom, thinking he looked exactly like that kind of spirit.

"Everyone knows there haven't been any books on magic since the great library in Nalanda was burned to the ground! That was almost a hundred years ago, during the War of the Wizards. Perhaps you've heard of it?" The sarcasm seemed to crackle in the air around Tom.

The apparition leaned forward to within a foot of Tom. Tom—leaned—back.

"Is this some kind of childish prank?" In a high whiny voice the spirit continued, "Oh it's, *let's pull the ghost's leg day*, is it? Hey—that's a good one. Pull the ghost's leg, ha! Like to see you try it!"

"Anyway, run along," said the spirit, regaining his composure. "I have serious patrons to service! Shoo, run along now, I say."

"He's not from around here," began Kiran, standing up for Tom. "His name's Thomas Holland. He's from another world!"

The ghost stopped moving, as did all the books floating about the library. In fact, the whole library fell deathly silent.

"Did—you—say—Thomas Holland?" asked the spirit in a quiet, reserved tone.

"That's right!" said Kiran.

The books resumed floating and people started talking in whispers. Everyone in the library was looking in Tom's direction; everyone—except the ghost, that is. The librarian now stared down at his desk, apparently finished with them. "Sorry, I can't help you. I could try an interlibrary search, if you like, but the results would be the same."

"No thanks." Tom could tell this conversation was getting nowhere. He glanced at Avani and she turned and led them all from the building.

* * *

Once they'd left the library the specter raised his right hand. Moments later, from high up in a secret reserved section of the library, protected by strong magic and a sign that read "For Kings and Philosophers' eyes only; must be accompanied by a ghost!", a large, dusty tome floated out of its place on the shelf, then along the aisle and over the balcony. Lazily drifting down three stories to the ground floor, it floated over to the librarian's desk and stopped. The book was titled *The Prophecy of Elfhaven*. It was handwritten by the ancient prophet Earstradamus. The librarian waved his hand across the book. A small cloud of dust drifted in all directions as it opened to a chapter entitled: "Thomas Holland." The ghost raised his gaze once more, his hollow eyes staring off in the direction that the children had gone.

* * *

As they strode down the library steps, Avani asked, "You obviously noticed the book that fell on that poor person's foot?"

"That was awesome!" began Kiran. "He cried out, then leapt back when Saint Bernard ran at him, and he spilled the woman's tea. Then everyone shushed them. It was great!"

Ignoring her brother, Avani continued, "More evidence of the magic failing. That would never have happened a yara ago."

"That was the weirdest and coolest library I've ever seen," said Tom reverently. "The building itself was bizarre, but the librarian!"

"It used to be a Cimoan monastery. They were an ancient order of monks. Very devout holy men, and masters of martial arts," explained Avani.

"Like Shaolin priests or kung fu masters, huh? Sick! I've seen all the Jackie Chan movies. Twice! Well—at least the ones that were translated into English, that is," admitted Tom. "What happened to em?"

"They were all wiped out during the War of the Wizards." broke in Kiran.

"The librarian mentioned the War of the Wizards," said Tom.

Avani nodded, then walked briskly down the street. Tom hurried to catch up. "Come on, there's one more place I want to show you," she said. "It's called the Citadel."

On their way, Tom noticed a tall clock tower. Only it seemed odd, somehow. It leaned slightly to the left and its top was wider than its base. Constructed from gray stone, it had a sort of wizard's cap sitting on top, pointing off to the right. Another strange thing: it was covered in characters similar to Egyptian hieroglyphs. But the most striking feature was the fact that it had three clock dials on each face, stacked one above the other. The uppermost dial went from one to fourteen, but the numbers were backwards from what Tom was used to. The middle clock looked normal, one through twelve. The bottom dial, however, went in the usual direction, but it ran from one through twenty-eight, with strange symbols every four hours.

"What's that?" asked Tom.

"That's our clock tower. You can see the time from anywhere in the city," answered Avani.

"What do those symbols mean? The ones all over the sides?"

Avani gazed up at the tower. "I'm not sure. There are legends, but they contradict each other. It was built long ago."

Tom paused thoughtfully. "Why are there three clocks?"

"The top one is elven time; the time here in Elfhaven. The other two, no one knows, or remembers anyway."

Out of force-of-habit, Tom glanced down at his wristwatch, then quickly up at the tower, then back at his watch. "The second clock is on Earth time," Tom blurted excitedly. "Central time to be exact. See!" Tom held his digital fitness wrist watch out for Avani and Kiran to see.

That's amazing! But how would it know Earth time? Unless...

"Wow!" began Avani, "if the top two clocks are the time on our two worlds, in two different universes—then that would imply—"

"That the third clock shows the time on a third world—in a third universe..." finished Tom. They both just stared at each other.

Apparently unimpressed by the implication, Kiran continued to play with Max. Avani and Tom, however, excitedly chattered away as they walked down the street, taking a left at the next corner.

This road was not as well kept up as the previous streets. Nor was it made of sunbaked clay, but instead was constructed of cobblestones with long blades of grass growing between the stones. At the end of the street, another hundred paces ahead, stood a shallow dome of a building. So shallow, in fact, that it gave the appearance of the top part of a giant ball sprouting up from the ground.

The structure was a soft cream color, and as far as Tom could see, it had no windows or doors. Suddenly, they heard a commotion behind them. As they turned, a strange creature came bounding around the corner. Black in color, it stood about a foot and a half tall, with high, pointed ears and large, brown intelligent-looking eyes. Its long fur glistened as it screeched to a halt in front of them, its eyes clearly pleading for help. The sound of clanking swords and running feet grew near.

"Quick," urged Avani, "hide behind us."

The creature sprang behind them and lay down, putting its hands over its head, as if that would hide it. Max tipped his head, staring intently at the creature, then cautiously stuck out his snout and sniffed. Tom's friends huddled close together. "Max, look at me," said Kiran. Max glanced up, taking his eyes off the creature.

As an afterthought, Avani threw her cloak over the critter then breathed a deep, calming sigh.

Tom smelled a strange odor—an odor somewhat reminiscent of— skunk!

Moments later, two elven guards dashed around the building from the direction the creature had come, and screeched to a halt ten paces away.

"Have you seen a gremlin?" asked a breathless guard.

"What did it do?" asked Avani nonchalantly.

"It picked the lock at the royal stable, then opened the stall doors on the king's prize horses and shooed them out. The horses took off at a full gallop. We still haven't caught all of them. Did you see a gremlin?" repeated the guard.

"Ah—yes, yes I did," said Avani vaguely.

"Which way did it go?"

After absently rubbing her chin for a moment she said, "Umm, I believe—he may have gone—that way." She pointed down the street, past the Citadel.

"Thanks!" said the guard as they turned and raced off down the street.

Tom stared at Avani in shock. "You lied to the guards!"

"I didn't exactly lie," she said innocently. "After all, I did say I'd seen a gremlin, which was the truth." Her large, soft, almond-shaped eyes radiated honesty as she continued, "I said it *might* have gone in that direction. I didn't say it actually *went* in that direction."

Tom continued to stare at her. Avani just shrugged.

As soon as the guards were out of sight she removed her cloak. "It's okay, they're gone. You're safe now."

The gremlin stood up, put a paw on Avani's calf and cautiously peeked around her leg. Satisfied the guards were truly gone, the gremlin stepped out. It gazed up, straight into Avani's eyes, then smiled and winked. A distinct patch of white fur marked the right side of the gremlin's head.

The creature seemed to notice Max for the first time. Cautiously, keeping its eyes fixed on Max, it scurried right up to him. Max drew back slightly, his fur rising around his neck. The gremlin leaned forward nose to nose with Max, then sniffed. Instantly it jerked back, its eyes intently studying Max's face. After a moment, it smiled, then suddenly turned and bolted off back the way it had come. Max started to give chase, but Kiran grabbed his collar.

"Wow," said Tom, "that was weird. Was that really a gremlin?"

"In the flesh," squeaked Kiran, slowly being dragged down the street by Max, still trying to chase the gremlin.

Still facing Avani, Tom said absently, "Max, stop!" At Tom's command Max abruptly stopped, causing Kiran to fall backward, landing hard on his rear end.

"It's unusual to see one during the daylight, and I've never had one seek my help before," said Avani thoughtfully.

"Ouch," moaned Kiran.

Tom asked, "He had a patch of white fur on his head. Do all gremlins have one?"

She shook her head no, staring off down the street.

Tom, following a hunch, asked, "Are you still carrying those magic crystals?"

Avani jiggled her satchel. It made a soft tinkling sound.

"Could they have had something to do with him trusting you?" reasoned Tom.

She considered. "I don't know—perhaps."

Kiran got to his feet and rubbed his backside. The three continued on their way, following the round building as it curved off to their right. About a quarter of the way around, there was an indentation in the wall. It was a perfect cube with each side measuring about twice Tom's height. The walls were smooth and made of the same strange material as the building itself. Noticing an odd dark patch, he walked up to the far wall, shielding his eyes to get a better look. An indentation in the building's surface, about a half an inch deep, came into view. It was in the shape of a five pointed star. Above it was a familiar drawing.

"This looks like the same symbol as the one on your box back home, the one your father gave you," said Tom.

"Yes, I've known that for years, but I haven't been able to figure out the connection."

"What is this place anyway?"

"It's called 'The Citadel,'" said Avani. "It was built eons ago, even before the time of the wizards and the Cimoan monks. Legend has it that inside is stored a magical artifact that keeps the barrier up and amplifies the magic all over our world. As the king mentioned, his advisors believe it's failing. That's why not all magical devices work anymore, and why the barrier is getting weaker. They're afraid that it may fail altogether soon; if so, we'll be 'sitting parrots' for the troll army to pick us off." They walked out of the alcove and stopped beside the building.

Sitting parrots? wondered Tom. He ignored the comment. "You said it seems to be failing. How is it then, that you can still use magic?"

"Not many can. There are a few of us, mostly the young, who have the gift, although there are some old-timers who still remember the odd incantation or potion or such, but it seems to be a dying art. Anyway, some of us have a natural ability, but we don't really know what we're doing."

"Come on, let's go. I'm starving," said Kiran.

Avani laughed. "It has been a long day, let's head home. Nanni and Nadda must be worried."

It was getting dark, so Tom reached into a belt pocket and retrieved his LED headlamp. He turned it on and pulled the elastic strap around his head, using it like a miner's lamp.

Kiran and Avani seemed transfixed, staring at the magical device perched atop Tom's head.

"What?" said Tom.

The siblings glanced at each other, then back at the light.

"Oh, my headlamp. It runs on electricity." The two just stared at him. Tom scratched his head. "I think I'll save my lecture on electricity for another day." He started walking away. Kiran and Avani followed without saying a word.

As they walked, Tom's thoughts returned to the Citadel and to the matching symbol on Avani's cube.

"I bet there's a key inside your box back home; a key to the Citadel. If we could just figure out how to open it, maybe we could enter the Citadel and see what's wrong."

"Perhaps. I've wondered that myself but—as I've said, we've tried everything. Elven scholars and dwarf master smiths tried to open it. If they couldn't do it, I don't see how we can."

"It belonged to your father, right? And he intended it to be yours one day, so surely he left you a clue," reasoned Tom.

Avani looked skeptical. "Maybe, we'll talk more when we get home."

"Sure, but do you mind if I meet you guys there?" said Tom.

"Where are you going?" asked Kiran.

"I've thought of a couple of questions to ask the librarian."

Avani and Kiran stared at each other.

"I can go with you," offered Kiran, "and show you the way home."

"No, I remember. Oh, but Kiran, could you take Max home with you?"

Kiran's eyes lit up, "Sure!"

* * *

A short while later, Tom climbed the library steps for the second time that day. Removing his headlamp, he turned it off and stuffed it into his shirt pocket. Opening the heavy door, he walked straight up to the

114

librarian's desk, but the librarian wasn't there. There was, however, a small sign suspended above a tiny bell. The sign read "Ring bell for service." Tom reached over and flicked the bell with his finger, but nothing happened. He glanced back at the sign, which had changed. It now read "Are you sure you need service?"

"Yes," said Tom a little too loud. He reached over and flicked the tiny bell again. Still no sound. Scowling, he glanced once more at the sign, which now read "You really need to be serious about asking for help before ringing the bell, you know." With that Tom flicked the bell as hard as he could, and a huge, deep reverberating gong blasted throughout the building. Books fell from shelves and people grabbed their tables to keep them from bouncing around. From across the vast library many eyes glared at Tom. The eyes, and their corresponding faces, did not look happy.

"Sorry," said Tom sheepishly.

A moment later, there was a whooshing sound, and in a blur the ghost flew down from an alcove high above, making a fast, well-executed "S" curve, stopping abruptly at his desk.

"Oh," said the apparition flatly, "I should have known it would be you, making such a racket."

"Sorry, I didn't know," said Tom, embarrassed.

"Haven't you ever been to a library before? Oh—don't answer that. You're from another universe, right? One without libraries, no doubt! Anyway, now that everyone in the place has been disturbed, *how* may I help you?" The spirit absentmindedly tapped his finger on the desk again, and as before, it still made no noise. Tom shifted his weight uneasily from foot to foot.

"Yes," began Tom, "well, you see—the last time I was here, earlier today, I mean—"

"Yes, yes, get on with it," huffed the librarian.

"You mentioned the War of the Wizards, as if everyone knew about it.

Well—since I am from another universe, you see, I actually don't know about it. I thought maybe you could tell me the history behind it," Tom quickly leaned back in case the librarian threw another tantrum.

The ghost glared at him for a long moment, then finally drew himself up to his full height and pretended to inhale in a deep breath. Then in a droning monotone voice, said:

"The War of the Wizards began in the year—"

"Sorry," said Tom, interrupting him, "but what events led up to the war? What was life like before the war? What did the wizards do, on a day-to-day basis, before the war began?"

The ghost resumed attempting to tap his finger on the table. Finally, he rolled his eyes and began again:

"During the *reign* of the wizards, which *preceded* the War of the Wizards," said the spirit, in the same dry tone, "the wizards founded large schools and universities, all over the land. Their charter was to teach children and young adults how to use magic for the betterment of all."

"How many wizards were there?" asked Tom.

"Thousands; every village had at least one WIR," answered the librarian matter-of-factly.

Tom raised his brow. "WIR?"

"Wizard In Residence!" spat the ghost in annoyance. "May I continue?"

Tom nodded.

"The wizards formed a Wizards' Council consisting of over a hundred wizards. In all major decisions, the kings of old would consult with the Wizards' Counsel before deciding which course of action to take."

"What happened to the wizards?" asked Tom.

"Finally we get around to your original question on the War of the Wizards. Will there be any further interruptions or may I get on with my tale?" huffed the librarian. Tom made a motion like pulling a zipper closed across his mouth.

The spirit glared at Tom for a moment, then leaned back. A glazed, faraway look crossed his eyes—or where his eyes should have been that is, and once more his voice droned on in a monotone:

"The enormous influence and power of the Wizards' Council proved too much for some. Those wizards became corrupt, hungry for ever more power. The few started spreading discontent amongst the ranks. Eventually a powerful leader of those dark wizards arose. His name was Naagesh. The Wizards' Council became embroiled in loud, heated debates, lasting well into each night. Urgent matters were swept aside by way of petty bickering and pompous political posturing. The deep partisanship caused the council's effectiveness to grind to a halt.

"At that point in history Larraj was the head of the council. Some say he was the brightest, wisest and most gifted wizard of all time. He tried to persuade the other wizards to remain calm; to stay level-headed. He hoped this would provide them with much-needed time so that their rational minds might surface once again, and end this petty bickering amongst themselves. But Naagesh would have none of it, and spurred his followers to gather still others to their cause. Giddy with their rapidly growing numbers, and power, the dissenters called for Larraj's resignation and threatened to take over the Wizards' Council, by force, if Larraj did not step down.

"Fearing for the very survival of the council itself, Larraj decided that it would be best for him to leave. By doing so, he hoped that it would diffuse the tensions and allow things, once again, to return to normal. So Larraj stepped down from the council and left the order entirely, and was never heard from again. In any case, sadly, his effort to restore peace failed and the tensions continued to escalate. Eventually the wizards formed strong alliances within their own order, and finally war broke out. It was wizard against wizard. All the elves were afraid. The wizard's powerful, magical blasts could be seen, heard, and felt for several kiloters around. They were destroying the lands, and everything in them. It was rumored that each time Naagesh killed a wizard, he would first painfully drain them of their magical powers, much like a vampire drains its victim's blood, adding their power to his own. Anyway, eventually the wizards ended up killing themselves off; although mysteriously, Naagesh's body was never found."

"Thanks," said Tom, yawning from the long monotone speech. "One last question. What happened to the magic schools once the War of the Wizards was over?"

"All those institutions of magical learning rapidly fell into disrepair and finally closed altogether, soon after the wizards were gone." Confirming what he had already heard from the king.

Tom turned as if to leave, then turned back, "Oh, the last—very last question, I promise."

The ghost gazed at him skeptically. "Yes?"

"I overheard someone mention a prophecy—a prophecy that I'm somehow involved in. Do you know anything about it?"

"Sorry," said the librarian, suddenly busy polishing his desk, "but I'm afraid I have no recollection of any prophecy."

"That's alright," said Tom. He turned and walked toward the door. "Thanks again. You've been a big help."

* * *

The spirit raised an eyebrow, saying, "Oh, *it's what I live for*, Master Tom. Huh—*what I live for*? Ha! Sometimes my jokes just *kill me. Kill me*?" The spirit's laughter lingered long in the air. Finally realizing that Tom was no longer there, the smile abruptly disappeared from the ghost's face as he sheepishly glanced left and right to make sure no one had noticed.

Chapter 14: Magic or bust?

The next day was rainy and dreary. However, Avani's face lit up each time someone mentioned magic school. Even though it was only 3:45 AM, Elvin time, she was flitting around like a hummingbird loaded up with nectar. Tom had mixed feelings, though. He'd never believed in magic before, although he knew many of his friends did. There was no scientific proof that magic existed back on Earth, but he certainly had proof that it existed here. So he was excited to see if he could actually do something magical, but he was also a little worried. His new friends here had all grown up around magic. What if he were totally inept at it? What if he made a fool of himself? Would the others laugh at him? Tom had been called a nerd and a wimp and been laughed at in school, back on Earth. He shivered.

Tom was about to put on his adventurer's belt, then he decided that he probably wouldn't be having any adventures cleaning stables, or at magic school, so he stashed it behind the front door.

Kiran, was apparently disgusted with the idea of having to go to magic school. But Tom wasn't buying it. Last night on his way to bed, he'd walked past Kiran's room. The door had been slightly ajar and he'd seen Kiran dressed in a hooded, floor-length robe, holding a stick like a magic wand, playing Wizards and Dragons with Max.

None of them, however, were looking forward to cleaning the stables. That was hard, hot and dusty work. Avani's grandparents packed three canvas satchels containing paper and writing utensils for school. Plus, they gave them each a separate sack with a jug of water and a hearty lunch inside.

"It's nearly 4:00 AM. You don't want to be late for your first day of work," said Nadda.

"But I haven't had seconds of eggs and horned-lizard sausage yet," complained Kiran.

"You should've thought of that before you went outside the barrier after dark," scolded Nanni.

Nadda glanced at Nanni and said, "I'm sure that'll be the last time they ever break the rules, dear." Nanni's eyes spun around to regard Nadda. They both laughed.

"Come on, off with you three. You don't wanna be in worse trouble than you're already in," said Nanni. She handed her grandchildren their satchels, and sack lunches, then kissed each of them on the cheek as they walked out the door. Lastly, she handed Tom his supplies. "Thank you for volunteering to do the work with Avani and Kiran. I know it means a lot to them, and it shows great integrity and loyalty on your part. Nadda and I are very proud of you." Nanni patted his back and pushed him out the door before Tom could respond.

"Bye, Max, you be a good—" but the door closed before Tom could finish saying goodbye. Tom just blinked.

It was raining. "Come on, we've got to get going or we'll be late," said Avani. Pulling the hood of her cloak over her head to block the rain, she hurried off down the street toward the castle, Kiran right beside her.

Tom flipped up the hood on his hoodie, and ran to catch up. "You're sure it's okay, leaving Max with your grandparents?"

"He'll be fine," said Avani distractedly. "Maybe we can bring him along tomorrow."

"It feels strange leaving without him, that's all," said Tom. Avani didn't answer.

It took them only fifteen minutes to walk the ten blocks or so to the castle's main gate. Just before they entered, a hooded figure passed by, walking the other way. As he did so, he glanced over at Tom. His eyes glowed yellow.

That's the same guy I saw with Lorin. The one with the sword. Tom took a couple more steps before glancing back over his shoulder. The man was nowhere to be seen. Tom shuddered and picked up his pace.

Once inside the main gates, the stables were just off to their left. As they arrived, they saw Prince Devraj and Lorin conversing in the courtyard.

Leaning toward Kiran, Tom asked, "Is that Lorin? Does he work at the stables?"

"Ah huh, he's the stable master," replied Kiran, then yelled, "Ho, Lorin!"

Lorin turned from the prince and nodded at Kiran. "There you are. It's time I put you all to work."

As they entered the stables they shook off their wet cloaks and hung them on high pegs on the rough, darkly stained wooden wall, just to the right of the entryway. Lorin gave them a quick tour of the stables, pointing out where the grain, water, and straw were kept. Tools were stored in a shed out back, plus he showed them where to dispose of the manure once the rickety old wooden wheelbarrow was filled.

Lorin leaned on his hoe and eyed his new "work crew" skeptically. One by one he looked each of them in the eyes. His gaze paused for several seconds on Tom. Tom began to fidget.

"I'm going to assign you all chores for the day. Each day I will rotate these chores." Lorin glanced at Kiran. "There will be no leniency for age." Then his gaze shifted to Devraj. "No special treatment for status or title." Moving on to Tom. "That includes individuals of—unique origins." The stable master's eyes shrewdly studied Tom's strange facial features. Finally his gaze fell to Avani. "And lastly, I will tolerate no cheating, using magic to accomplish your chores. Do I make myself clear?" Avani glanced at her friends, then nodded.

"Today Devraj and Kiran are assigned a *shovel-ready project*. You will shovel up the horse manure and place it in the wheelbarrow. Once it's full, take it around back and shovel it into the dung wagon." Devraj shot

Lorin a look that could kill, but if Lorin noticed, he didn't show it.

"Avani, you groom the horses and check their hooves for cracks. I'll teach you how to file the hooves with the correct roll to the edge another day. For now just let me know if you find any sharp edges or cracks."

Lorin turned and walked toward Tom. "For each stall, you will replace the old straw with new. Then fill all the horses' food and water bins, understood?" Tom nodded.

Although his hood was still up, as Lorin stood over him Tom could see more of his face. A grizzled white beard peeked out below the hood. Tom couldn't quite make out his eyes, still, from what little Tom could see of him, Lorin looked much older than Tom had first thought.

"You all know your jobs. Put your satchels by the door and get to work." As Tom sat his satchel down he noticed that someone had roughly carved his initials, T. H. into the wooden handle. Tom smiled, then glanced over at Avani's and Kiran's bags. Sure enough, each of them also had their initials carved into them. As he turned, he noticed Prince Devraj's bag. It was made from finely tanned leather with a marble handle and a brass plaque that had the prince's initials elegantly engraved into its surface. Tom smiled to himself again, then walked to the first stall to begin the day's work. He saw what needed to be done and glanced around for tools. Lorin's hoe leaned on a nearby wall. Tom walked over and reached for the hoe.

"Stop!" yelled Lorin. Tom froze, as did everyone. All eyes were on Lorin.

Now, in a voice barely louder than a whisper, Lorin said, "Use—the—rake, in the corner. It's the right tool for the job." Lorin grabbed his hoe and strode briskly outside into the still-pouring rain. Tom glanced at Avani. She gazed back at him, her brow raised.

A while later, Avani stood grooming the horse in the second stall as Tom finished replacing the first stall's straw. He moved into her stall and began raking around the horse.

"Too bad you can't use magic to do your chores," said Tom. "Back home I own a great Disney flick called 'The Wizard's Apprentice.' It's about a wizard who gave his apprentice the job of cleaning up their place, then the wizard left for the day. It was hard work, so the apprentice decided to use a spell to do the job. It worked well at first, but eventually it got out of control and the apprentice couldn't stop it. The kid was in big trouble when the wizard came home!"

"What's a *flick?*" asked Avani.

"A film; a movie. Oh—never mind."

Her eyes lit up. "So there is magic in your world?"

"No," said Tom. "That's just make-believe. There's no *real* magic. At least—none that I've ever seen."

"That's sad. I can't imagine a world without magic. How do your people survive against ogres and demons?"

Tom chuckled, "There're no ogres or demons on Earth." His face turned serious. "But there are evil men; men ruled by greed and power. There's also war; which is often fought to gain power, or riches, though leaders always claim it's for some other reason. But wars back home are fought with high-tech weapons and technology, not with magic."

"Strange. It seems so—alien. Your world must truly be a cold and lonely place without magic." Avani shivered.

"I don't know. I never had anything to compare it to, I guess."

"Get back to work, you two," said Lorin sternly. "The king sentenced you to work, not to talk." They quickly resumed their assigned tasks.

About an hour into their workday, Kiran was struggling with a particularly stubborn piece of dung when it suddenly broke free. Flying through the air, it hit the prince squarely on his bottom. Some fell off in clumps; most remained on his britches. Kiran inhaled involuntarily and slapped his hand over his mouth, to keep from laughing. The prince spun around and scowled. Tom had seen what had happened and broke up laughing, until the prince focused his fury onto Tom. The smile immediately disappeared from Tom's face, and he quickly resumed raking up straw from the floor. A few minutes later there was a small pile of manure in the next stall, and Tom called for Kiran to come clean it up. Kiran was busy working on his own mess so Devraj came over.

"Where is it?" hissed the prince.

"Right there," said Tom pointing to a fragrant brown mound near the back of the stall.

"I don't see anything," said the prince coldly. Tom leaned over, away from the prince, pointing directly at the muck pile. Devraj glanced around, then kicked Tom hard in his rear end. Tom landed face first in the dung. He jumped up and spat twice, screamed, clenched his fists and ran straight for the prince. Somehow, miraculously, Lorin materialized out of nowhere, stepping between them and holding Tom back. The prince sneered at Tom, as if daring him to try something.

In a calm voice Lorin asked, "What happened?" Tom spat once more, and scowled at Devraj. Avani and Kiran stopped what they were doing and watched.

"Nothing," began Tom, slowly letting out a deep breath. "I—I tripped and fell, that's all." Tom's eyes burned as he glared at Devraj.

"Go clean yourself up," said Lorin. "There's a washroom in the back of the stables." Lorin's gaze shifted to the Prince as he called over his shoulder. "And be more careful next time. These—stalls can get rather—slippery." Under Lorin's stern stare, Devraj dropped his sneer but his eyes remained locked in battle with Lorin's. After a brief pause the prince pivoted and strode briskly across the room. Avani and Kiran stared at him.

"What?" spat Devraj.

Kiran hurriedly resumed working, but Avani continued to stare at the prince. After a moment, Devraj stormed away. The last hour of work seemed to drag on forever.

Finally Lorin spoke. "That's enough work for your first day." Then he added, "Believe me, you'll be sore tomorrow. There's fresh drinking water over there in that bucket. Use the tin cup hanging on the wall. After you've had your fill, you can clean up in the washroom. At least you can remove some of the stench before you head to school."

Tom lifted the beat-up old tarnished tin cup. Dark stains and pock marks covered its surface. He sniffed it cautiously before dipping it into the water-bucket. Despite the cup's gross appearance, the water tasted sweet and fresh. After the others had done the same, they each took turns in the small, cramped, dingy washroom. *I guess this is part of the punishment.* For the second time this morning, Tom glanced around at the grey, roughhewn boards with cobwebs in the rafters; heavily stained water basin; and rusty toilet bucket.

Once they'd all freshened up, they picked up their things and left the stables.

By now the rain had stopped and the sun was peeking out from behind the clouds, just above the horizon.

Lorin was waiting for them outside. "Thanks, see you all tomorrow. Oh, and try a slugwort poultice for your sore arms and legs; works every time." As they waved goodbye, Tom thought he heard Lorin chuckling, but when he glanced over his shoulder, Lorin wasn't there.

Walking through the castle gates, they turned left down a roughly tiled street, less well-maintained than most of the others Tom had seen. Continuing for a couple of blocks, they found a stone bench beneath a large tree and sat down. Too tired even to speak, they just sat there sipping their water in silence.

After a half hour or so, it was time to be on their way. Kiran moaned as he got up. They all knew how he felt, but the others kept quiet, though

125

they moved rather stiffly. Even at this slow pace it took them only a few minutes to reach the granary.

As they gazed up at the structure, they were a bit disappointed. It looked just like the same old dilapidated, abandoned building as before; a tall cylindrical structure perhaps four or five stories tall, it was made of wood with paint peeling off it in many places. Some of the boards were pulling away from the walls, and there were no visible windows.

On one side of the building, they found a door that was propped open by a stone statue. From pictures he'd seen, Tom thought the statue looked like a gargoyle. It had wings for ears, big hollow eyes and a mouth carved into a perpetual frown. They pushed the door open all the way and walked in. Tom was the last to enter and as he did so, he glanced back. The statue's eyes had followed them and it was now smiling.

Tom turned and shouted. "Hey guys, the statue moved."

The others stopped and glanced back, but the statue looked the same as before. The others laughed and kept walking.

"No, really…" said Tom weakly. Every few seconds Tom spun back around, but the statue never moved again. Finally, Tom gave up and sprinted to catch up.

Darkness engulfed the lower floor, but they could see a faint light coming from the far end of a hallway, off to their right. Tom heard no sounds so he figured they must be early for class.

"Hello," called Avani tentatively, "is anybody there?" Her voice echoed around them. No one answered.

"This is creepy," said Kiran.

The prince's hand rested uneasily on the hilt of his dagger, strapped to his waist. Tom noticed the prince's stance, so he instinctively reached for the pouch on his belt that contained his Swiss army knife. Unfortunately, he didn't have his adventurer's belt. *Oh that's right; I left my belt at home. As if my little knife would protect me, anyway.* Tom forced a nervous smile.

They walked slowly toward the light. When they were about halfway there Avani called out again, still no answer.

"Is there more than one old granary?" asked Tom. "Could we be at the wrong one?"

"No, this is it," she said.

As they approached the source of the light, they saw a rickety stairway bolted to the inside wall of the granary. As one, their gaze rose. The stairway curved up and around the building. About halfway up, maybe three stories above them, a landing jutted out from the wall with a small room beyond that.

"The stairway was always here," whispered Kiran, "but the room is new."

Another dim light shone from an old oil lantern on the landing at the top of the stairs. As they crept up the stairway, a board creaked loudly underfoot. They all froze. Tom held his breath. The sound echoed in the empty silo for several seconds before it finally died away. There was no response, so Tom let out his breath. They resumed their climb until they made it safely to the landing. A door stood slightly ajar on the tiny, newly constructed room.

The room appeared square. Tom estimated it to be about twice as wide as he was tall. There were no windows and as far as they could see, only one door.

"This can't be it. The room is way too small," said Devraj.

"Perhaps it's a small class—a very small class," laughed Kiran nervously.

They cautiously entered the room but immediately stopped, shocked looks on their faces. The inside of the room was enormous! It was the size of Tom's middle school auditorium back home. Tom gasped as he realized the walls and ceiling were transparent. Only he wasn't looking at the inside of the building, he was seeing things outside the granary. They were three stories up, and were gazing out at rooftops, treetops, and the distant horizon. Smoke curled up lazily from several nearby chimneys.

Between the homes, the tops of crimson, orange and yellow trees dotted the landscape, swaying slightly in the breeze. Glancing up, Tom saw clouds drifting slowly across the morning sky. Out of the corner of his eye he spotted two birds flying off toward Elfhaven castle. At least he thought they were birds. They had heads like small monkeys and four wings each with tiny hands in the middle of their forward wings, and long kangaroo legs that trailed behind them as they flew.

For several seconds everyone just stood there.

After the initial shock wore off, they shifted their attention to the center of the auditorium. Several others had already arrived and were seated in a semicircle around a small, raised platform. A simple desk and chair occupied the center of the stage and to the left of the desk stood a modest wooden lectern.

Kiran elbowed Tom and pointed at the platform. "Look at that plant." Shifting his gaze, Tom studied the weird plant. Rooted in a dark earthen clay pot, it stood about six feet tall. Its leaves had olive and rust-colored spots on them with long spikes jutting out from its spindly branches.

"Gives me the creeps," said Tom. "What are those things on the desk?"

Avani replied, "The bottles are probably potions, or ingredients for making potions, as are the herbs, feathers and stones. To the left, that's a crystal ball, for seeing the future or observing things far away."

Tom noticed a rack of test tubes and a stone bowl with a matching stone post. "That looks like a mortar and pestle. In the old days they used to use those for grinding medicines back on Earth."

"Awesome, look!" said Kiran, gesturing to the right. Cages of live animals stood stacked beside the desk. Some of the creatures reminded Tom of rabbits, plus some rats—except they had longer ears and were hairless. There were also frogs—but with sparse, spiky blue hair on their heads, and big-eyed chickens, all in separate cages. Tom noticed that each time the frog croaked, a miniature fog horn sound, they would disappear from one cage and reappear in another. Likewise, when the chickens clucked, their eyes blossomed into huge orbs.

"I hope the animals won't be hurt," said Tom staring intently at the bizarre frogs.

Just then an elven girl walked up from behind. She had a twinkle in her eye and a wry smile on her face. Winking at Tom, she said, "Hey, maybe we'll get to dissect them," then she walked on to find a seat.

Avani and Kiran looked a little pale and Tom felt a tad queasy himself.

"Who was that?" asked Tom.

Avani scowled and said flatly, "Her name's Tara." Tom stared after her.

"Let's go sit with the others," said the prince. Avani brightened at that and took off, practically running over Kiran.

Tom hurried to keep up as she raced down the aisle. The prince, however, walked at a more dignified pace. By the time Tom got there, Avani was already seated right up front. Tom sat down beside her. Kiran chose to sit back in the fourth row, just behind a group of younger kids.

Soon after he sat down, Tom began to hear his name whispered by those sitting near him. Glancing up, he noticed several of the other students gawking at him. Most, but not all, looked away when Tom returned their gaze.

Tom leaned toward Avani and whispered, "Why are they all staring at me?"

Avani glanced around. "Well, you have to admit you're somewhat unique here in Elfhaven. You're actually getting to be quite famous."

Shocked, Tom opened his mouth to speak, but no words came out. Tom wasn't the only one to notice his new found notoriety. As Prince Devraj walked up, his eyes paused on each of the kids that were watching Tom. The prince stopped abruptly in front of him and scowled.

"You're sitting in my seat," the prince said coldly.

Tom glanced at Avani, then back at Devraj. "I am?" Hesitating, Tom stood up and moved to the other side of Avani, then sat back down. The prince continued to glare at him. Slowly Tom rose once more.

Chapter Fourteen

"Ah—perhaps I'll just go sit with Kiran." Tom shared a quick look with Avani, then turned and hurried up the aisle. As he did, several students' eyes followed him. Avani glared at Devraj.

Tom spotted Kiran a few rows up, off to his left. No other kids were sitting in that row. Sliding sideways, he sat down just beyond Kiran. Once seated, Tom scanned the room. There were three large lab benches scattered about the room, one in the row directly behind them. Several small vials were neatly arranged on each bench along with a cage with one of the odd rabbit creatures in it.

Another group of students now entered the hall. Tom spotted Malak and Chatur among them. He waved as they passed by. The two friends waved back, grinning from ear to ear.

"Hey, Tom waved at me, lizard breath," said Malak.

"No he wasn't, maggot brain," replied Chatur. "He was clearly lookin' at me."

Malak punched Chatur in the arm as they sat down in the middle of the hall. Baring his teeth, Chatur rubbed his arm and growled. Tom glanced at Kiran and they both shook their heads.

Finally, in walked Goban, everyone watched as the bulky dwarf made an obvious show of sauntering down the aisle. When he spotted Tom, he smiled and headed down their row. As he squeezed past Kiran, he nearly knocked him over. Seeing this, Tom grabbed the arms of his chair for dear life and barely avoided the same fate as Goban squeezed by. Finally, Goban plopped down in the chair beside Tom.

"Holla dawg! Had to Floss for my peeps, figured you'd come through, though." Goban pulled out a gigantic foot-long sandwich from his tunic and slapped it on his lap.

"Yeah, about this hip-hop speak." Began Tom. "See, I'm not too good at it. Do you know how to speak, ah—regular?"

As Goban eagerly unwrapped his sandwich his eyes darted left, then right. Leaning close he whispered, "Sure, but don't tell anyone. I've got appearances to keep up, ya know?" Goban gulped down a gigantic bite.

"I gots your bizzle, dawg," replied Tom.

Goban snorted, sending food all over the girl in the row below. She leapt up, frowning disgustedly, dusted herself off, then moved a couple of chairs father away.

Quickly swallowing, Goban's face took on a look of surprise. "Thought you said you couldn't speak hip-hop."

Tom smiled. "That's about the only words I know."

Dropping the sandwich in his lap, Goban made a fist and thrust it toward Tom. Doing the same, Tom sent his fist heading straight for Goban's but at the last second it dove below then rose up behind Goban's. Tom's first two fingers sprung up and apart, then wiggled, like two eye stalks of a snail, staring right at Goban. Goban's eyes popped wide for an instant, then they both broke up laughing.

At that moment, a ruckus erupted up front. One of the older boys sat arguing with the girl beside him. As she faced the boy, Tom recognized her. It was Tara.

"Why do we have to come to this stupid class, anyway?" spat the boy. "I already know all the magic I need."

"Oh, is that so," barked Tara, "Then how precisely do you change a toad into a boy?"

"Well—I don't know how, but I don't care because I don't need to know."

"Good, then when I turn you into a toad, you won't be able to turn yourself back." Scowling at him, Tara raised her hand menacingly. Her fingers began to glow bright red. Instinctively the boy threw up his hands in a feeble attempt to shield himself. A faint green light flickered around his hands.

Just then there was a rumble from the stage. All eyes stared, as the large potted plant began to rattle. The rattle turned into a shake. The floor, beneath the kids' feet, started vibrating in time with the shaking plant.

Tom and Goban glanced at each other, then back at the stage. Next, the plant began to smoke. Worried looks crossed the student's faces. Suddenly there was an explosion of light and a thunderous boom. A dense cloud of greasy, stinky-smelling smoke billowed from the spot where the plant had been, covering everyone in the first two rows. Several kids jumped up coughing and ran for the exit. Slowly, through the haze, the dark outline of a person emerged. As the smoke cleared, a tall, regal, elderly elf stood precisely where the plant had been moments ago. Gasps burst forth from some. The ones that had run, stopped. Still others merely stared, open mouthed.

Beady hawk eyes, sharp cheekbones, and a strong jaw characterized the man's face, while short neatly cropped hair, greying at the temples, finished off his head. He wore a long-sleeved shiny black doublet that buttoned up the front via many loops on one side, fastened around oblong bone buttons on the other side. The top of his jacket had a high straight collar. Below, he wore tight black pants that disappeared into tall, black lace-up leather boots extending up nearly to his knees. A dark half-cape, its hood thrown back, lay draped across the elf's back and shoulders, Quiet murmurs filled the room.

The person strode forcefully to the front of the stage, then abruptly stopped. Scowling, his beady eyes swept the hall. "Who was it that said this was a stupid class?"

No one spoke or raised a hand, but many of the students glanced at the boy in the front row. The green light quickly faded from the boy's hands, as did the red glow from Tara's fingers. They both stared up in surprise at the plant turned elf.

"Ah, you must be the culprit. What's your name, boy?" the adult demanded.

"Daaruk," replied the boy nervously.

"If that pathetic attempt at protecting yourself is any indication of your—magical prowess, then it's clear you desperately need this class.

Hmmm—how can I change your mind, help you to see the usefulness of magic? I know! Perhaps double homework for the next two weeks. I'm sure that will do the trick," hissed the adult.

"And who was the young lady that nearly turned you into a toad? You perhaps, the one holding her arm in the air like a gnarly old slither tree branch?"

Spatters of hesitant laughter rang out.

"Yes, ah—well, I just wanted him to shut up, that's all," said Tara, her jaw tightly clenched.

"Sadly to say, if you had turned him into a toad, I'd be obligated to turn him back." A few more students chuckled, cut short when the elf's steely gaze lanced out at them. The hall fell silent.

"And what's your name?" asked the adult, softening his tone.

"My name's Tara, sir," she replied.

The elf smiled ingenuously at her and leaning toward her said, "A pleasure—to meet you Tara." As he turned away he added, "Oh, and you can lower your hand any time now."

Blushing, Tara hastily lowered her arm. Snickers sounded.

The figure rose back up to his full height. "As you've probably deduced by now, I'm your new magic instructor. My name is Snehal Khanna but you may call me Professor Snehal, or Master Khanna, or just Master, understood?" Snehal scowled as his eyes rapidly swept the hall. No one spoke so he continued. "For those of you who were afraid and bolted for the exit like a flock of startled zaptar chicks, you may return to your seats. I won't bite—hard, anyway." This time no one laughed. Those still standing darted for their seats.

"That *was* a joke," said the professor. Nervous laughter ensued.

At that moment, another flock of the strange monkey-headed birds flew past. The students' eyes tracked the birds' path across the sky.

"Perhaps this room is too much of a distraction for you," said Snehal coldly, and in one fast, fluid motion his arms swept up and around, his cape billowing in the wake of his arms. There was a loud "crack" and the room seemed to shift. Where an instant before clear sky filled their view, now stood only roughhewn wooden walls and a high and equally rough wooden ceiling. No longer able to see outside, the students murmured their disappointment.

Snehal smirked. "Perhaps if you all get perfect scores on tomorrow's quiz, I will consider putting the room back the way it was."

Goban leaned toward Tom and whispered, "I think I liked him better as a plant." Tom snorted involuntarily.

"What was that?" bellowed the professor, glowering as his eyes slowly scanned the room. Goban and Tom stared straight ahead, stone-faced. After a moment, Snehal seemed to give up his search and strode to his lectern, picked up a large stack of papers, then walked to the front of the platform once more.

"Here's a copy of the course syllabus along with what I intend to cover in today's lesson." Gazing glumly out at his class, he handed Tara the stack of papers. "Please pass these around." Tara smiled, her hazel eyes twinkling as she accepted them. Bouncing swiftly around the hall, she passed them out crisply and efficiently.

"Today, for your first lesson, I'll teach you the four basic elements of magic. Tomorrow you'll learn what the three methods of implementing them are. Can anyone tell me one of the four elements of magic?"

Avani's hand shot up.

Snehal's steely eyes focused on her. "Name?"

"Avani."

"That's Avani, sir," corrected Snehal. "You aren't by chance Avani Dutta are you? Last of the Keepers of the Light?"

Avani glanced nervously at the prince. Just beyond Devraj she noticed Tara glaring at her. Avani smiled and turned back to the teacher. "Yes—ah, yes, sir, I am."

"Welcome to my classroom, Avani Dutta. And what element of magic were you going to enlighten the class with today, Avani?"

"Altering matter, sir," said Avani confidently.

"Correct," stated the teacher flatly. Raising his arm, he snapped his fingers, and a blackboard appeared behind him. With a quick wave of his hand, a small piece of chalk rose and quickly wrote the words "Altering Matter" on the board with a large number one preceding it.

Without looking back at the blackboard he continued in a monotone, "But what does *altering matter* really mean? Can you give us an example?"

"Um—creating something from nothing—ah, sir," Avani replied.

The professor seemed bored as his gaze drifted across his class. "Good! However, there's a popular misconception about creating *something from nothing*, as you put it. Although it does appear that we're making objects out of nothing at all, we're actually creating them from the molecules of air, water and soil that surround us; rearranging those molecules into something useful. Any other ways to alter matter?" His focus returned to Avani.

"Changing something into something else?" she said hesitantly.

"Also correct; the caveat here is that you can make an object appear to be something else, which is really just making the observers believe the object has changed, without really altering matter. Then there's actually changing the object into something else, which is truly altering matter. Any other examples?"

Avani shook her head.

The professor leaned toward her and his smile morphed into a frown. "Destroying—matter…" There was a pause. The whole class collectively held their breath. Finally, Snehal stood back up and started pacing about the stage.

"And just like creating matter uses the existing elements or molecules to make an object, destroying matter changes that object from a complex thing into its basic building blocks of elements and molecules. When this happens you might see what appears to be a puff of smoke, for instance, but that's just a release of these basic molecules back into the air."

"OK, can someone else tell us another basic element of magic?" asked Snehal, unsuccessfully stifling a yawn.

A young boy in the fourth row slowly raised his hand.

"Name?" said Snehal.

"I'm Gopi, ah—sir," said the boy.

"Very well, Gopi, what's another element of magic?"

"Ah—Is—making an object float, one?" he asked timidly.

"If you mean float on water, no." Several students snickered. "If you mean float in the air, or to levitate, you'd be correct." Once again Snehal snapped his fingers and the chalk wrote the words "2: Making Objects Fly," on the blackboard, just below the first element.

"Can you give us an example of this type of magic?"

Gopi scratched his head for a second. "A flying carpet?"

"Yes, anything else?"

"How about making a friend float up into a tree, and pick a fruit for you?" replied Gopi.

"Good, somewhat self-serving perhaps, but good. When we make an object hover in mid-air, or fly from here to there, that's using the second element of magic. Does anyone know another element of magic?"

Malak raised his hand.

"Name?"

"Malak, my name's Malak, sir."

"OK, 'my-name's-Malak', what's another element of magic then?"

"Weapons," said Malak with a grin.

"Excellent," hissed Snehal, and with a snap the words "3: Weaponry" appeared on the board behind him. The professor's voice, now steely hard said, "Offensive and defensive applications are a powerful and very dangerous form of magic. Can you name something that uses this type of magic?"

"A shield, like Daaruk tried to use against Tara," said Malak confidently.

"Yes, a magical shield—if done properly," Snehal sneered and glanced sidelong at Daaruk, "can either deflect or absorb offensive magic. What else?"

"A magical blast to knock someone unconscious," replied Malak, glancing at Chatur and smiling. Chatur frowned.

"Good, anything else?" asked the professor.

Malak, obviously emboldened by his two consecutive successes smiled broadly. "Ah—a magical bomb; one big enough to wipe out a whole legion of trolls."

Snehal slammed his fist down hard onto the lectern, his eyes locking onto Malak's. "Now you're talking! With thinking like that, you're on the path to becoming an evil warlord." The smile immediately fell from Malak's face. Nervous laughter sounded.

"That was not meant—to be funny," said Snehal, scowling. The room fell silent.

Striding briskly back across the stage, Snehal asked the class, "And what's the last type? Does anyone know what the last category of magic is?"

The teacher's beady eyes darted around the room like a bird of prey searching for its next meal. No one raised their hand so he continued, "The last element is: magic that causes changes in behavior. Would anyone like to know what kinds of behavior can be modified?" Complete silence.

"No? Well I'm going to tell you anyway. There are potions that give one courage, and others that make someone fall asleep. There are even potions that can make people fall in love." Several students giggled. Ignoring them, he turned toward the blackboard and snapped his fingers one final time. The words "4: Behavior Modification" appeared below the first three elements.

"Excuse me, sir, but are potions the only way to change behavior?"

asked Tara.

"A very astute question." Professor Snehal gave her a broad smile. Tom visualized the professor as a snake just before its tongue leapt out and swallowed a frog—whole.

"No, I'll go over the three implementation methods at tomorrow's lecture. Suffice it to say that potions are only one way of changing behavior; there are others."

"How long do the effects last?" asked Prince Devraj.

"Excellent question, your Highness," responded Snehal, bowing slightly. "For potions, you will find that the effects vary, depending on the dosage given and the quality of the ingredients used, plus the skill of the practitioner who created the potion, of course. But, in general, the effects can last anywhere from a few myntars to a few oorts."

Roughly a few minutes to a few hours. I should find out the exact conversion factor sometime. Tom frowned. *And I noticed the teacher didn't ask the prince to call him sir.*

Snehal gazed out at the sea of mostly bored faces staring up at him. "I think it's time we move on to the lab."

Out of the corner of his eye Tom saw Malak reach over and grab Chatur's ear and twist it.

At that same instant the teacher began speaking. "Before we move on, however, are there any questions about the four elements of—" Chatur's cry of pain interrupted him.

"What's—going—on?" spat the professor, annoyance dripping off each syllable.

"My apologies, sir," began Malak, "but Chatur here just pulled my ear—and for no good reason."

"That's not true!" yelled Chatur. "It was him! Malak pulled my ear." At that, Chatur reached his arm around Malak's neck, putting him in a choke hold, all the while cursing furiously at Malak. The teacher first raised an eyebrow, then casually raised his hand. Leaning forward, he mumbled something beneath his breath. Chatur immediately stopped choking Malak and put his hands to his lips, or more exactly, to where his lips had been, just moments ago. But now his lower face was smooth—his mouth gone. Chatur's eyes bosomed into a look of sheer panic. Malak, however, broke up laughing. The teacher's hand rose once more, and an instant later Malak's mouth had disappeared as well. The same panicked look shone on Malak's face. Kiran began to giggle. Once again the teacher raised his hand, searching for the one who dared laugh. Kiran shut up instantly and slouched down in his chair. Tom remained perfectly still. He could feel an unsettling chill as the teacher's gaze first crossed Goban, himself, Kiran, then slowly moved on. At last the professor lowered his arm and leaned back.

"Anyone else care to interrupt?" asked Snehal, as his eyes ratcheted from one student to the next. "No? A wise choice—now where was I…"

Tom realized he'd been holding his breath so he slowly let it out. As he looked around the hall he could see others doing the same thing. Finally, his gaze fell on Malak and Chatur, who still looked panicked, but they were staying put. Tom glanced sidelong at Goban, whose eyes showed the same mix of fear and relief that Tom felt.

"Oh yes, today's lab," said Snehal, as if nothing had happened. "Tomorrow, I'll lecture in depth on the three implementation methods of magic, but first, let me just mention their names: One - Potions, two - Incantations or Spells, and three - Mind Control. For today's lab, it's important to know that these three methods exist."

Tara raised her hand. "Yes, Tara," said the professor warmly.

"Can an element of magic be implemented by more than one method?"

"Oh, yes," he replied. "This is actually a broader version of the question you asked earlier about different ways to change behavior and as I said before, I'll explain this all in more detail tomorrow."

"Sorry, sir…" began Tara apologetically.

The professor leaned toward her and smiled. "Oh no, not a problem, not a problem at all." Tara blushed, sat up tall and smiled back at the professor.

The smile evaporated from his face as he rose once more and strode across the platform, "This is actually an excellent question, since it dovetails perfectly into today's lab. So here's a brief explanation: usually there are several types of magic that can accomplish the same result. For instance." The professor reached inside a cage, pulled out one of the rabbits and sat it on the desk beside him. Snehal waved his hands dramatically over the creature while at the same time in a slow, monotone voice he uttered the words "Defluo Tibi Turbatus Lepus." Immediately the rabbit disappeared, accompanied by gasps from several of the students. Professor Snehal smiled at this, gazing with obvious joy at the startled looks on his students' faces. Suddenly his arm shot straight up, twisting his wrist and spreading his fingers far apart flamboyantly. At the same time he uttered the word "Recreo." The rabbit reappeared. Several students clapped while others murmured excitedly amongst themselves.

"Wow, that was cool!" said Tom. "I wish mom could've seen it. She'd freak." Tom's eyes adopted a faraway look. Goban glanced at him sidelong, but said nothing.

"Now we will, once again, make a rabbit disappear; only this time, we'll do it with a potion." The teacher tipped his head forward and droned the words: "So I don't have to do all the work, and have all the fun, we'll do this exercise as a lab." He smiled unconvincingly.

Snehal had the students divide up in groups of three or four. Each group was assigned a separate lab bench. On each bench sat a cage with a rabbit inside, and several small vials of a dark liquid, capped with a cork stopper. Tom, Goban and Kiran chose the workbench behind them. Kiran grabbed one of the vials and removed its stopper, then sniffed its contents. His head jerked back and he wrinkled his nose.

"Ugh, that smells awful!" said Kiran, quickly replacing the lid. The other two chuckled.

"Sir, how do we use this potion?" asked Tara.

"Well, Tara," began the teacher, "there are two ways a potion can be administered. You can pour it on the rabbit, but if you do, the reaction will be slow and will require a large quantity of potion to be effective. Getting the rabbit to drink a few drops usually works better. But, by way of example, why don't we let Avani's group put a few drops of potion on their rabbit?"

At the prince's table, Devraj pulled the stopper off one of the vials and handed it to Avani. She carefully lowered the bottle to just over the cage and dripped three drops across the rabbit's back. Within moments the fur began to disappear; then the skin. As the process continued you could see the muscles and tendons, the blood vessels, and soon, some of the animal's vital organs. Several girls squealed, made faces and turned away. Many of the boys laughed. Tom, however, thought he might be sick.

The teacher smiled and said, "Now, let's try something different, shall we? Please select one person from each of your lab tables. Have that person put a couple of drops on their finger and place it in front of the creature's nose. If it won't take it then just rub it on its mouth and it'll lick it off. Careful! If you take too long, your fingers will disappear."

Kiran pulled the stopper off one of the bottles and handed it to Tom. Goban leaned over to get a closer look. Tom put a few drops on his finger and stuck it through the cage, directly in front of the rabbit's face. It sniffed his finger a couple of times, then licked it three or four times. By the third lick they could see right through the creature, and within seconds it was totally invisible. Murmurs of awe and squeals of laughter echoed through the hall, the other lab stations having had similar results. Tom glanced down at his finger, muscles and tendons clearly visible beneath his now-invisible skin. A feeling of panic came over him, and he shook his finger vigorously. Kiran and Goban both laughed.

"Professor Snehal, how long does the effect last?" asked Avani.

"This particular potion should last about five myntars, plus or minus, depending on how many drops you gave your animal."

Sure enough, a few minutes later several of the animals started to reappear. They looked eerily like ghost rabbits at first, but soon they were solid once more. After all the animals had reappeared, Snehal had the students trade off, giving each a chance to experiment with the invisibility potion. Glancing down, Tom noticed his finger had returned to normal. He breathed a deep sigh of relief.

After everyone had taken their turn and all the animals were once again visible, the teacher said this was a good stopping point for the first day.

"Your homework assignment: memorize the four elements of magic. We'll have a short quiz first thing tomorrow morning."

"A quiz? Uhhggg!" exclaimed Kiran. Tom glanced at Goban. They both smiled.

As they were leaving Kiran picked up a couple of vials of the invisibility potion and put them in his pocket. Tom stared at him.

"Homework," said Kiran innocently.

Tom lifted a vial and rolled it around in his fingers. After a moment's thought, Tom decided it would be wrong to take it without asking, so he replaced the vial on the lab bench. As he did so he noticed Malak and Chatur standing in front of the teacher, their heads lowered, their shoulders slumped forward dejectedly.

Snehal glared down at them. "Have you two learned your lesson?" Malak and Chatur nodded in unison.

"And you won't cause a disturbance in my class ever again?" They shook their heads.

Muttering something the teacher snapped his fingers and suddenly Malak and Chatur were restored to normal, mouths and all.

"Ah, too bad," said Kiran. "He could have waited a day or two before fixing them."

Tom chuckled, then turned to his new friend. "Goban, before you go, back home I have a book on medieval weaponry with a design for a crossbow in it. It might prove useful in the upcoming war."

As Kiran headed off toward his sister, Goban replied, "Sick." By this time most of the kids had gone, but even so, Tom and Goban moved away from the others, up near the top of the auditorium.

On the way there Tom asked, "Have you heard news about the troll army?"

"Yeah," began Goban, "I overheard my father and King Dakshi talking this morning. Several hundred trolls set up camp near where you were captured. With several thousand more on their way. Even worse, a couple thousand ogre troops were spotted leaving the Icebain Mountains, also heading this way. Ogres and trolls usually hate each other, but my dad thinks the ogres must be in league with the trolls."

"How many elven soldiers do we have?"

"About three thousand. Unfortunately, the trolls have about twice that many, and the ogres just make matters worse," said Goban gravely. "Our only hope is that the magic barrier holds. But I've heard, in places, the barrier has started to fade in and out."

"We've gotta find a way into the Citadel," murmured Tom.

"The Citadel?" asked Goban.

"It's a long story. Avani believes that inside the Citadel there's a magical artifact that keeps the barrier up. She's got a locked metal box, left to her by her father, which I bet contains the key to the Citadel."

"I've heard of that box. Some of the dwarf masters tried to open it once, unsuccessfully."

"We've gotta figure a way to get into it," said Tom.

"Hmm, you said you had something to talk about, something that might help the war effort," Goban reminded Tom.

Tom stopped thinking about the mystery of the Citadel, and began explaining to Goban what he had in mind. Pulling out a sheet of parchment and a quill and ink, he started drawing the plans for a crossbow. First the stock that would hold all the parts, then the bow, also called a prod.

Tom pointed at the prod. "This is where all the power comes from, so the bow needs to be made of metal or several layers of laminated wood."

Goban nodded, intently studying Tom's drawing. "We could make it from iron wood with metal supports."

Tom next drew the string that would launch the arrow. "You haven't yet invented tough synthetic fibers, so you'll have to make the string out of animal gut so it's super strong, just like they used to do on Earth in olden times." Tom continued to draw. "The bolt or arrow is short, sharp and tough with prongs on the tip and feathers on the back end so it'll fly straight, just like a regular arrow, only shorter and stockier."

Goban's eyes glowed with excitement. "We can have the feathers twist slightly, front to back, which will make the arrow spin through the air, flying straighter. We do that with our regular arrows."

"Good idea," said Tom. "This next item is the most important and touchiest piece of the whole thing." Tom drew the cocking mechanism that held the string, and the trigger release lever that pulled the clasp down inside the stock, releasing the string.

"That's all that's needed in a basic crossbow design. However, I'll show you a cranking mechanism that'll make it a whole lot easier to use." Tom sketched out a hook that would grab the string, and a bar that the hook was mounted on. Notches were cut in the side of the bar. Farther back on the stock Tom drew a gear with a handle on it that he called a cranequin. The teeth in the gear meshed with the notches on the bar.

"When you crank the handle it rotates the gear causing the bar with the hook on it to be drawn back, like so. Understand?" Tom stabbed his finger to the page.

Goban nodded, studying the page closely.

"The concept is called leverage," explained Tom. "You turn the handle a large distance and it only moves the gear a small distance, but it's much easier to turn."

Tom pointed to the cocking mechanism. "As the bar is drawn back, the hook pulls the string, flexing the bow. When the bar hits this point, it pushes on the lever that pivots a post up in front of the string. Now you can crank the lever back slightly, allowing the string to be held by the post instead of the hook. Then just swing the hook out of the way. The crossbow is now loaded. To fire it, you just pull the trigger here, and it'll pivot the post forward, releasing the string. Simple, huh?"

Tom gazed over at his friend. Goban paused, still staring at the drawing, then his face sprang up, a look of excitement blazing in his eyes.

"This leverage idea will change everything!" blurted Goban. "We could use that cranking device on all sorts of tools. It could allow one dwarf to do the work of ten!"

Tom smiled. "Wait 'til you see what I give you next time." But Goban wasn't listening.

"Oh, and there's one more enhancement you might consider making for the crossbow," said Tom.

This brought Goban back. "Yes?"

"It's my own idea," began Tom. "If you mount two crossbows on a wooden board, then hook a rope across both triggers, one person could pull the rope and fire both crossbows at once, all by himself. It could effectively turn one warrior into two."

Goban's eyes grew wider, if that were possible. Grabbing the plans from Tom, he rushed from the room, without even thanking him.

Tom blinked a couple of times, then sighed. *What changes did I just unleash on this poor unsuspecting world?*

145

Chapter 15: Out of the frying pan...

When Juanita awoke, she wasn't sure how much time had elapsed. She tried to stand up, but her ankles were bound together with a heavy rope and her hands were tied behind her back. She surveyed her surroundings. She lay on a rough dirt floor in some sort of tent with crates stacked high around her. Sitting up, she peered over one of the boxes. In the center of the space stood a low table with rough brown papers scattered across its surface. Off to her right, on a nearby wooden crate, sat a crudely made clay water jug. Beside the jug were several badly bent and tarnished tin mugs. Voices sounded from outside.

"Ready yet?" growled a voice, growing louder as it approached.

"Da troll army mostly here. Some ogres too," grunted another. "Da rest be here soon."

"Kain't take dis waitin'. Should attack now."

"We kill elves soon enough. First we wait for da Wizard. Rumors say, he got some magic talisman. Supposed ta open da barrier."

"Humph," spat the other, as they continued on their way. Soon their voices were too faint to hear.

A war with the elves. Juanita paused. *Those guards I saw, near the wall, they must've been elves, and that wall probably surrounds the elven city. If the trolls can be believed, that's where the elves are holding Tom. And those blue sparks that surrounded my hand, that must be the barrier they mentioned. Interesting though, the barrier, if that's what it was, didn't stop me...*

She frowned. *I've got to find a way to escape.* Scanning her surroundings once more, her gaze fell upon the crockery jug sitting near the edge of the crate. The crate was about five feet from where she lay. With her arms bound behind her and her legs tied together at the ankles, she had to lie on her back, placing all her weight on her forearms. Raising her bottom, she scooted an inch toward the crate, then shifting her weight to her rear,

146

she moved her arms forward an inch. The effort was exhausting, plus the rough ropes dug into her skin each time she put weight on her forearms.

Wish I'd worn jeans, she lamented. *I dressed for Tom's birthday party. Had I known I'd be trekking around some bizarre alien world, I'd have worn jeans, a parka, and sneakers, instead of this stupid party dress and these useless shoes.* Glancing down, her once-beautiful dress was now filthy and torn in several places, plus her three-inch heels, now heelless, with their thin, tasteful gold straps, were scratched and covered in mud. Juanita shook her head as she scooted.

It took several minutes to inch her way over to the crate with the jug. Every so often, she'd stop and raise her head up to check her progress. The effort brought the hem of her dress up around her thighs, and she could feel a breeze where she'd caught and torn her pantyhose on the rough dirt floor.

Laying on her back for a moment, Juanita tried to catch her breath. *Not very ladylike, I guess. Though, as a child I was more of a brainy tom-boy then a girly-girl.* Now within range, so she took a deep breath, pulled her knees back, and kicked the crate hard with both feet. The jug shook only slightly, so she scooted a little closer and pulled her knees farther back, then kicked once more. This time the pot rocked back and forth precariously, but finally settled down, although a tad closer to the edge. Pulling her legs back as far as she could, she kicked with all her might. The jug tipped, hovering at the edge for what seemed like an eternity, then finally crashed to the floor, shards flying in all directions.

Chapter 16: Magic squared?

When the kids arrived for their second day of work at the stables, they were still tired and sore from the previous day. As they entered the building they set down their satchels and lunch sacks just inside the stable's main doorway, off to one side. Today's task list had Tom and Avani working on cleaning up the manure piles. Prince Devraj was assigned the task of replacing all the straw, while Kiran got to groom the horses. Kiran grinned ear-to-ear.

"This place smells even worse today than yesterday, if that's possible," said Tom. Avani wrinkled up her nose and nodded in agreement.

After working awhile in silence, Avani asked, "Tom, yesterday you talked about your home world. When the war is over, assuming we survive," she paused, glancing down at her feet. "Will you go back home? Will you leave Elfhaven?"

"I hafta go back. Mom's there, plus Uncle Carlos and my best friend James. That is—if I can ever find a way..." Tom leaned on his shovel, considering. "But, if I do find a way, would you like to come visit my world?"

Without even glancing his way, Avani responded, "Ugh, no way! If it doesn't have magic, I'm not interested." Tom watched her work for several seconds, then picked up his shovel and helped her.

Before they knew it, the two of them had cleaned three stalls and most of the main floor. Somehow the work seemed a little easier today. As he exited the stall Tom saw Lorin holding his satchel.

As if sensing Tom's presence, Lorin faced him. "I was just moving it out of the way." Lorin placed the satchel behind Avani's and Kiran's.

Walking into the next stall, Tom glanced back, then resumed his poop patrol.

Before they knew it, the work day was over. After a fairly unsuccessful attempt at cleaning themselves up, they walked down the street, sat on the same bench as yesterday, and sipped their water. A short while later they headed off to school. It could've been Tom's imagination, but everyone seemed a little less stiff and sore after the day's work than before they'd started.

Tom made his way up beside Avani. "I didn't get to ask you before. What do you think of our magic teacher?"

Avani glanced sidelong at Tom as they walked. "He's great! If you like grumpy old elves who think highly of themselves, and drool over pretty girls like Tara."

Tom chuckled. "Don't sugar-coat it, tell me how you really feel." Avani's eyes popped up, intently studying his face. Tom smiled. She hesitated. They both laughed.

After a few minutes they arrived at school. As they sat down in the classroom, the other kids nearby immediately got up and moved a few chairs farther away from them. Apparently today's "cleanup" hadn't been sufficient. Tom sniffed his shirt.

Hoping to talk with Goban before class, Tom glanced back toward the door. As if on cue, Goban sauntered in with his usual exaggerated gait. When he spotted Tom, his eyes lit up, although he continued his slow, casual pace until he finally plopped down beside him.

"Whoa, you two are ripe! Did someone move the latrine in the middle of the night, and you guys fell in the hole?" Goban scrunched up his eyes and held his nose.

"Very funny," said Kiran. "You think we smell bad now, you should have smelled us before we cleaned up!"

"No, thanks, I think I'll just go sit over there." Goban started to stand up but Tom grabbed his arm. Goban, glared at Tom's hand, but slowly sat back down.

"Any more news?" asked Tom.

Goban sighed. "I overheard the palace guards say that the first thousand trolls joined the others. King Dakshi and my father were discussing what to do if the barrier fails entirely. After they spoke, dad left for home to try and convince the dwarf high council to send soldiers to help the elves.

"Oh, and I gave the plans for the crossbows to Dad. He promised to get his best master smiths on the project as soon as he arrives home. They should have prototypes here in a few days. Probably have a hundred or so more within the week, another three hundred by the end of the month; that is—if we have that long…" Goban's eyes met Tom's. Neither of them spoke.

After a moment Goban went on, "There's more." He gazed down sadly at his feet. "Father says, with the war about to start, I hafta leave as soon as the first shipment of crossbows arrive, probably within the week."

Tom glanced at Kiran, then lowered his voice, "Wow, if it's that dangerous, shouldn't you leave now?"

"I don't wanna leave. Besides, the trolls aren't at war with the dwarves. Not yet anyway."

Tom thought for a moment, then said, "We've got to get into the Citadel." But Goban wasn't listening; he was looking toward the center of the hall, so Tom followed his gaze. Professor Snehal had just entered the classroom, a little less dramatically than yesterday. Tom spotted Avani sitting up front beside the Prince and he noticed that no one was sitting beside them, either. Tom smiled.

"I hope you've all studied for today's quiz," said Snehal flatly. "As you know, this test will cover the four elements of magic."

Murmurs of complaints echoed throughout the hall. Snehal handed Tara a stack of quizzes and asked her to pass them out. Jumping up, she brushed a curl from her face and smiled, then swiftly handed out the tests. From where Tom sat he could see Avani's eyes following Tara. Avani was scowling.

"If you all studied as I told you to, this quiz should take you only ten myntars to complete. And so, after exactly ten myntars, the tests will be collected. Wait until everyone has a copy of the quiz. I'll give you the go-ahead when it's time to begin."

A few moments later Snehal continued, "All right, has everyone got a quiz? There's to be no cheating, which includes looking at your neighbor's papers or using any type of magic to find the answers. Have I made myself perfectly clear?" The professor's beady eyes swept the room for any objections. Glancing around, Tom saw lots of unhappy faces.

"Good, then let's begin." Sitting at his desk, Professor Snehal pulled out a scroll and began studying it. Tom imagined it was an ancient spell for turning students into rodents, he smiled at the thought. As if reading his mind, the professor's eyes rose and he glared directly at Tom, and just as quickly, Tom's gaze fell to his quiz.

After a couple of minutes, Tom cautiously sneaked a peek. Once again, the professor's attention was fixed on his scroll so Tom idly glanced around the room. Several students wrote slowly, while others absently scratched their heads with their quills. Tom noticed Avani furiously writing something, a confident look on her face. The prince, however, did not look too happy. Tom grinned, and went back to his test.

At exactly ten myntars, Professor Snehal said time was up. The papers from everyone's desk magically floated straight up into the air, then turned sideways and glided over to his lectern, where they neatly stacked themselves into a large pile. Even before the process was complete, Snehal began his lecture. The topic was titled: *The benefits of one element of magic over another*. The lecture droned on and on over tiny differences that Tom thought trivial. To relieve the boredom he and Goban passed notes, discussing news of the upcoming war, careful not to be spotted by Professor Snehal.

A note from Goban read, "I also heard a small group of ogres have arrived. They've set up camp near the main troll headquarters." The note continued, "Plus, the barrier failed a couple more times. One hole was big enough to allow a dozen trolls through before it closed again. The elves fought hard for several myntars before they drove the trolls back beyond the barrier. Two elves were badly injured in the skirmish. One may not survive."

"We've gotta figure out a way into the Citadel," Tom wrote back. "After class let's ask Avani to review the poem her father gave her. Maybe we can solve the riddle and open the box."

"Poem?" asked Goban.

"Oh, that's right. You weren't there. I'll explain later," scribbled Tom.

"You really think there's a key to the Citadel inside?"

"Makes sense, plus—what other hope do we have?"

Goban lowered his gaze, thinking.

Finally, the professor finished droning on and progressed to the next part of the day's lesson.

"All right," began Snehal, "yesterday I promised I'd go over the three implementation methods of magic, in depth. As I mentioned before, they are: First: Potions, which we used in yesterday's lab; Second: Incantations or Spells; and Third: Mind Control."

Shuffling some parchment papers on his lectern, the professor continued, "Potions are a combination of chemistry, alchemy, and magic; part art and part science, and they're always made from natural ingredients. Plants such as liverwort or pine thistle are commonly used along with animal parts like black spiked toad livers or dragon's tears."

One of the students said, "Dragon tears are tough to get, I'll bet." Scattered snickers sounded. Professor Snehal glowered at the class.

Avani raised her hand.

"Yes, Avani?"

"Sir, are exact measurements important?"

"Good question, Avani. The answer may seem a bit—vague, though. It depends on the potion. Some potions are much more tolerant of—discrepancies in exact amounts of ingredients, relying more on magic to infuse the necessary characteristics into the liquid. But most potions need exact quantities of ingredients to work properly. Sometimes errors will cause the potion not to work at all. Other times—it can lead to disaster."

"Can you give us an example, sir?" asked Gopi.

"Certainly," replied the professor, cocking his head. "For instance, the ingredients for a potion to make beautiful, long, silky blond hair are the same ingredients for creating a swarm of bees. Only the exact amounts are different." Horrified looks appeared on the faces of several of the girls in the classroom. Tom spied Malak talking excitedly with Chatur.

"Yesterday Prince Devraj astutely asked how long a potion's effects last." Snehal acknowledged the prince with a slight nod. Devraj tipped his head a fraction, in response.

"One way to increase the length of time a potion lasts is by adding rocks and minerals which often help stabilize the potion. Things such as green fairy coral or powdered Ogham stones work particularly well.

"Our second implementation method is: incantations or spells. This type is a very powerful magic and requires much study and practice to perfect. You must first memorize the exact wording of the spell. Then relax completely, blank your mind and think only of the result you wish to achieve. Visualize the event as if it had already happened."

"Like in hoop ball," blurted someone in the second row. Laughter ensued. Once the ruckus died down, the professor continued.

"Exactly right, and just like in hoop ball, the follow-through is critical. You must keep chanting and concentrating on the desired result until the magic has completed its course; otherwise it may fade away or worse yet, backfire on you." Several students glanced nervously at one another.

"The last implementation method is: Mind Control. This is the most difficult form of magic to master, but if you can, you'll find it both useful and powerful. Properly done, it'll allow you to control weaker beings by directly taking over their minds."

Chatur glanced sidelong at Malak and blurted out, "Some people are so dumb, you don't even need magic to control their minds." Malak leaned over and bared his teeth at Chatur. Professor Snehal glared at them both.

Immediately they both clapped their hands over their mouths, slowly sinking deep into their chairs. The professor continued to glare at them for several more sectars, then returned to his lecture.

"Okay," he began, "we'll move on to the *fun part* of today's lesson, *the lab*. For this we'll be working with the first basic element of magic and implementing it via an incantation. By the way, that's the first implementation method, for those of you who missed it on the quiz." Some of the students glanced at each other. "Please move to the lab benches and take a seat." Everyone stood and shuffled to their benches.

"First, you'll notice several bowls of water with a few vials of ingredients beside them. For each group, have someone pour the entire contents of the vials into a bowl. By the way, this'll be the last time I'll premeasure the ingredients for you. Once you've combined the vials, stir the mixture vigorously. When everything has dissolved, you'll have a thick, colorless, odorless liquid. Basically it's just a glorified salt brine. Since this is a beginning class in magic, we'll start with something simple, turning this soup into green slime. If done correctly, it should rise up about three inches above the edge of the bowl, and then solidify. Let me know when everyone has mixed up their starter batches."

After a couple of minutes, everyone put down their stirring spoons and gazed up expectantly at the teacher.

"Good," said Snehal. "Now I'm going to write the incantation on the board. You can read it in your mind but don't say it out loud yet. Not until I give the command. Does everyone understand?" The professor's face looked deadly serious as he intently scanned the room. No one spoke, but several students nodded. Snehal moved over to the blackboard and scribbled some words. To Tom they made no sense but in his mind he read the words phonetically, *in-ber er-ga lim-us.*

"Now, class," began the professor, "as I said earlier, the key to using an incantation correctly is to focus your mind. Visualize the end result, in this case—green slime. Keep all other thoughts out of your head. Think only of green slime, then speak the words, slowly and deliberately. Say them with equal volume and equal pitch. If you do it correctly, you should see your brine start to bubble, then ooze, and finally change color and expand. Once it has stopped expanding—and make sure it has stopped completely—visualize it hardening in your mind. Any questions?" asked Snehal. "OK, then let's have one person at each table try it first."

Goban furrowed his brow, concentrating hard, then quietly spoke the words. The bowl did vibrate slightly, and a hint of green formed in the soup, but that was all. A kid at the next workbench stared at Goban's results and laughed, but as Tom's gaze drifted around the room he saw several experiments that had gone slightly awry. Some had changed color, and a couple had oozed over the lip of the bowl. One was just steaming. Only two had worked perfectly. Avani sat back smugly, as did Tara; both had a nicely shaped green mass that stuck up about three inches above the top of the bowl. They were obviously green slime masters.

At Tom's lab station Kiran went next. His experiment turned out almost perfect except for a slight dip on one side. It reminded Tom of one of his mom's egg soufflés that had fallen. Nonetheless, Kiran grinned ear-to-ear. The rest of the class seemed to have had similar results to the first go-around.

The last to try from their group was Tom. Once the teacher gave the go-ahead, Tom focused his mind on the bowl, visualizing the container bubbling, then shaking, then turning green and pushing upward beyond the bowl's lip. Reciting the words several times in his mind, "inber erga limus, inber erga limus," he prepared to speak the words out loud, his face a mask of total concentration.

In a slow, deep monotone voice the words boomed from Tom's lips, as if they had a will of their own, "INBER ERGA LIMUS." At first nothing happened, then the bowl began to vibrate, then to steam. It turned a faint green color, then got darker and darker, rising steadily upward toward the top of the bowl. Tom smiled. But once it reached the top, instead of rising a few inches and stopping, it began oozing over the edge. Tom's smile vanished as the green glob kept growing. Soon it covered the whole bench, then started dripping off the table in several places. Other kids took notice; some laughed and pointed. Soon the whole class was laughing. But once the green slime hit the floor, it started to hiss and smoke and expand even faster.

Tom, Goban, and Kiran glanced nervously at each other, then jumped up onto their chairs, trying to keep away from the steaming mess. This set the class into uproarious fits of laughter, until the ooze kept growing and expanding and began covering the entire floor, including where the other students sat. Now everyone jumped up onto their chairs. No one was laughing any more.

The bubbling, steaming ooze continued to grow at an alarming rate. What's worse, it began to smell strongly of rotten eggs. As it flowed around people's chairs, the chair legs began to smoke. Panicked looks filled the student's eyes. Soon there would be nowhere left on the floor that was free of the slime, except for up on the platform where Professor Snehal stood watching the circus unfold before him.

The hint of a smile crossed the professor's face. Suddenly, he raised his arms and made huge, sweeping circles parallel to the floor, first with his right arm, then with his left. At the same time, he droned the words "Caesum actutum limus!" There was a loud howl as winds rushed in from all directions, followed immediately by a wave of flames that rapidly spread across the floor. Screams rang out from several frightened students. But the flames lasted only a few moments, then quickly fizzled and were replaced by a thick, foul-smelling smoke. When the smoke finally cleared, there was no sign of the green slime. Carefully at first, a few of the bravest students stepped off their chairs and onto the floor. Slowly the others followed suit.

Tom realized he'd been holding his breath. Letting it out slowly, he meekly glanced around the room. All the students were staring at him. Tom's face went beet-red.

"Tom, your hands," said Goban anxiously.

Tom glanced down at his hands. Tiny blue sparks danced between his fingers for a few seconds, then slowly faded away. Tom looked questioningly at Goban, then up at the professor.

Snehal had been staring at Tom's hands also. Slowly his gaze moved up to regard Tom's face. Snehal whispered the words, "The prophecy." Then he narrowed his eyes, which seemed to bore right through Tom. At the same time the professor absently tapped his finger on the podium. Once, twice, then one final and particularly loud "tap."

Snehal's eyes left Tom and gazed out over his class. "This, I think—will end today's session, before we get into any further trouble."

Malak laughed. Kids stared at him. His smile disappeared.

As they stood up to leave, Tom glanced at Goban, who raised an eyebrow, the hint of a smile forming on his face.

"Wow, that was awesome!" said Kiran excitedly. "How did you do that? Can you teach me?"

Though shaken, Tom managed a half-hearted chuckle. As they walked toward the exit, Tom glanced over his shoulder. Avani just stood there, staring at him, her face chalk-white. Tom hoped he hadn't frightened her, although he found it hard to imagine anything that would frighten Avani. He glanced back once more, but he'd lost her in the crowd of students pushing hard to leave. Tom did notice, however, Prince Devraj speaking with Professor Snehal. The pair stood motionless, staring at him.

Chapter 17: Intrigue, Deceit, and Betrayal

The slap of Devraj's boots echoed down the long, dimly lit hallway.

Why did I not wear moccasins? A bead of sweat trickled down his left cheek. He'd taken the long way around, but the entrance to the war-room lay just ahead. The slap of his boots seemed to get louder as he neared the door. Unconsciously, he held his breath for the last few steps. Finally reaching the doorway he glanced both directions, then placed one hand on the handle and the other on the door itself, to mute any noise. In one swift motion, he opened the door and slipped inside, then closed the door using both hands, as before. Devraj breathed a deep sigh.

What am I doing sneaking around? After all, I'm the prince. I can go anywhere I please. No one would dare challenge me! So why am I so nervous?

He wiped sweat off his brow and glanced around the room. It was dimly lit by a candle chandelier hanging from the ceiling, high above the center of the room. Directly below the chandelier stood a large oval table with ten sturdy leather chairs surrounding it. At the head of the table stood a larger ornately carved chair, the one where his father sat when the war council was in session. On top of the table, in front of the king's chair, lay several large yellowed parchments. A quick glance confirmed they were the elven defense plans for the upcoming war.

Devraj considered, *these plans have everything in them: Where the elven troops will be stationed and how many troops are at each location; where the weaknesses in the barrier have occurred so far, and where they're likely to occur in the future; plus when and where the troops will retreat to should the barrier fail entirely.* The prince reached for the document, but his hand froze just inches from the parchment. He hesitated, then slowly withdrew his hand. Sighing, he turned and strode toward the door. A foot from the exit he stopped, his outstretched hand hovering above the door handle.

Devraj scowled. *What's wrong with me? Am I truly so petty that I would let my jealousy of Tom cause me to commit treason? What is it about him that infuriates me so? Is it the knowledge he has that I don't possess? Is it Avani's affections toward him? No, I failed my mother. The servant was obviously a hired assassin. I could have saved her life, had I acted sooner. I will someday be king. I mustn't fail my people ever again.* Glancing back at the table, he continued his line of reasoning. *It's for Tom's own good. He's not an elf. He shouldn't be experimenting with things beyond his comprehension. It's my duty as prince to protect the other students, to protect the elven people, to protect Avani...* With that, he whirled around and strode briskly to the table. Grabbing the plans, he rolled them up and placed them inside his tunic. Then he walked to the door and slowly opened it, carefully peering down the hall. No one was there. Slipping out quickly, he closed the door without making a sound. Breathing a deep sigh, he raised himself to his full height and began walking down the hallway.

"Prince Devraj," said a voice from behind.

The prince froze, then slowly turned.

"Oh, Tappus," said the prince nonchalantly.

Tappus bowed low. "Your highness, I've been looking all over for you. Your father is going ahead with the solstice feast this evening. He suggests you attend."

"Celebrating, when we're on the verge of war?" scoffed the prince.

"The king believes it'll help take people's minds off the upcoming war."

The prince grimaced. "Fine, tell my father I'll be there within the oort."

"Very well, your Highness." Tappus bowed once more. But as he did so, his eyes darted to a bulge in the prince's tunic. Standing back upright, he took a step backwards, pivoted smartly and walked away. Devraj watched him go for a few sectars, then continued on his way.

* * *

Juanita had struggled for hours trying to cut the thick, tough ropes binding her hands, but the broken shard was hard to work with, especially with her hands tied behind her back. Making matters worse, her wrists bled from several small cuts where she'd slipped on the rope and slashed herself. The shard was getting slippery from blood and sweat, making it hard to hold. If she dropped it, she'd have to find another. Even so, it felt like she was almost through. Only a few more minutes and she'd be free. At that moment she heard voices coming her way. As quickly as she could she scooted back over to where she'd originally awoken, and pretended to be unconscious.

The tent flap slapped open and she heard several beings enter the tent. "It rainin' harder. Have da meeting in here," growled a deep voice. "Bellchar, see if da prisoner's awake yet." Juanita tried not to breathe, clamping down hard on the shard in her right fist. Footsteps approached. A rough hand grabbed her shoulder and shook her violently.

"No, she still out," laughed Bellchar.

"Good. Gag her mouth. Cover her head. If she wake up, she kain't yell or see notin'." A moment later, a foul-tasting rag was thrust into her mouth and a stinking sack pulled down over her head. She fought hard not to gag. Soon, several others entered the tent and began speaking amongst themselves. She redoubled her efforts to cut the ropes.

* * *

The rain came down relentlessly and it was pitch black as the hooded figure entered the troll encampment. He moved silently among the tents like a panther searching for its next meal; if a panther would hunt in hellacious weather like this, that is. Once he'd found the tent he was searching for, he threw open the flap and strode in boldly. Several trolls and ogres sprang to their feet. The trolls bared their teeth and drew their weapons; green sparks lanced around the intruder's hands as he reached

160

up and drew back his hood.

"Naagesh," said Sliembut. "Bellchar, Fowlbreth, lower your weapons, fools!"

What passed for a smile slowly crossed Sliembut's rock-strewn face.

"Naagesh, let me introduce you to two of our greatest allies. This is Lardas, Supreme Commander of da ogre forces, and his lieutenant, Dumerre." Lardas was tall, for an ogre, nearly as tall as a troll. And like most ogres he was fat, though large ropy muscles adorned his arms and legs. He wore typical ogre battle dress, a leather kilt and leather leggings, and forearm armor with long bones sown lengthwise into the leather to shield against sword strikes. Atop his head sat a leather battle headdress with long devilish horns attached. His small beady eyes, deeply inset under large bushy eyebrows, jutted out from his head. His chin seemed as if it had been shoved up into his face, giving him a ferocious perpetual scowl. Lastly, his ears appeared to be falling sideways, as if some warped, flat mushroom had chosen the sides of his head to sprout forth from. All of this was typical of ogres, of course, yet what set him apart was the fact that he wore a large necklace strung with twenty razor-sharp Zhanderbeast claws. In his right hand he held a huge club, the top of which had jagged, broken gnarly roots protruding from it, as if he'd just pulled a good-sized tree out of the ground to use as a weapon. Which indeed he had…

The wizard Naagesh tipped his head forward ever so slightly.

Sliembut stood apart from the other trolls. He wore a feather headdress and a large green amulet hung suspended around his neck by a gold chain. A tall muscular troll, he seemed smarter than the others. Gesturing toward Naagesh he said, "And this be Naagesh, last of da great wizards, here to help us rid the world of elven kind."

"Forgive me, but—you don' look much like da old drawings I've seen. Why is dat?" asked Lardas, a suspicious look crossing his smooth green face.

161

"After the War of the Wizards I knew I had to disappear into society, to bide my time until the right moment came to return. So I used magic to change my appearance. I took on a new identity," explained Naagesh.

Lardas bowed low. "Ah, of course. We be honored to share our humble tent wid you."

Naagesh smiled, bowing his head a fraction. In so doing he noticed a figure in the shadows. The person lay behind some crates, by the side wall of the tent, with a rough woven sack covering their head. "Who's your guest?"

With a grunt and a nod from Lardas, Dumerre rose, turned around, grabbed the sack and violently ripped it off the prisoner's head. Then he pulled the gag from her mouth. A tall human female whipped her long auburn hair from her face. Her eyes shot daggers around the room, finally fixing their hateful glare on Lardas.

"So, awake now, be you?" said Lardas.

"Why're you keeping me prisoner? I've told you everything I know. You have no right to hold me, especially all tied up like—like—some animal bound for slaughter!" yelled the woman.

"Interesting," said Naagesh, smiling. Juanita's eyes whipped from Lardas to Naagesh. The wizard slowly looked her up and down, his gaze finally coming to rest on her face. "Could you please take her outside for a moment? We have some—sensitive business to discuss."

She seemed to recognize Naagesh was the one in charge. "Are you afraid to talk about me to my face? What do you think I'm going to do, scream you to death?" shouted the woman. She struggled furiously against the iron grip of Dumerre, but her feet were bound, so Dumerre just grabbed her by her hair and dragged her from the room, cursing him all the way.

"Sorry for da—disturbance," hissed Sliembut.

Naagesh ignored the apology and instead raised an eyebrow, staring expectantly at Lardas.

Lardas grimaced, glancing first at Sliembut, he began, "A couple of days ago, I sent my emissaries to meet with da trolls here in Elfhaven Valley to offer our support in da upcoming war. Apparently, da trolls had captured her but she proved too much for the six of dem, and she got away." Lardas gave Sliembut a wry grin, then continued, "My lieutenants, Dumerre, caught her and brought her here."

Naagesh tipped his head sideways and muttered, "The prophecy doesn't mention anyone else..."

"What?" said Lardas and Sliembut in unison.

"Just thinking out loud," replied the wizard. "I'm sure you're aware of the human child that entered our world a few days ago, Thomas Holland," Naagesh said it more as a statement-of-fact than as a question.

Sliembut shot a dirty look at Fowlbreth then said, "You've heard of him? My men captured da boy, but he also escape."

"With da help of some elven brats," added Bellchar indignantly.

"Enough excuses!" yelled Sliembut, smacking Bellchar upside the head with the back of his hand.

"Ouch," muttered Bellchar.

"Anyway," continued Naagesh, "I believe this is no coincidence. I think this woman's connected to the boy, somehow."

"Yes—" began Sliembut, shooting Lardas a knowing look, "she said she's da boy's mother."

Lardas snorted, "She keeps jabbering on about parallel worlds, or someting. I tink da creature mad! She say she just wants ta find da boy. Take him home."

"Hmm—no matter," said Naagesh, changing the subject. "The reason I'm here this evening..." He paused, letting the suspense build, "is that the elven plans for the defense of Elfhaven, including their current strengths and weaknesses, just so happen to have fallen into my hands." With a flourish, Naagesh unrolled the plans on one of the crates. The others leaned forward eagerly.

"By the way, as I promised, I've created a magical battering ram that will allow your troops to punch a hole in the elven barrier, large enough for ten or twenty soldiers at a time to get through. I'm sure you've noticed how the barrier seems to be acting—erratic at times."

"Go on," said Sliembut anxiously.

"The elven scholars and sages believe that the magic power behind the barrier is failing. They believe the barrier may only last a few more days, a week at the most. And as an added bonus, my battering ram should speed the barrier's collapse." At that point Naagesh smiled broadly. Lardas and Sliembut followed suit.

"When do you need dis document back?" asked Sliembut.

"I made a copy; this one's yours to keep. I have plans—for the original…" Naagesh walked to the doorway. With a nod he opened the flap and disappeared into the desolate night.

* * *

Standing outside in the pouring rain, Juanita was completely drenched by the time she finally freed her hands. Hurriedly untying her feet, she prepared to run. But before she could move, she heard the tent flap open, and Naagesh stepped out. Quickly hiding behind a tree, she peered around the trunk to watch. The wizard threw his hood over his head, shielding himself from the torrential rain, grabbed a walking stick that stood leaning against the tent and ran off into the night. She waited a couple of seconds, then ran after him. The darkness and the rain made it hard to see, but every few seconds she caught a glimpse of his dark form striding off in the distance. She ran on.

A few minutes later she arrived at the spot where she'd last seen Naagesh. There was no sign of him. Squinting in the dim moonlight, she wiped the rain from her eyes, then searched the ground for footprints. The rain had washed them away.

Her wrists hurt. Glancing down, blood dripped from several small cuts where she'd slipped with the pottery shard while cutting her bonds. Rain mixed with the blood, made them bleed even more. Gazing at her sleeve which had nearly torn free, she ripped it off the rest of the way, and tied it tightly around her wrist to stop the bleeding. At that moment, she heard something off in the distance ahead. Taking a deep breath, she ran toward the sound.

After a time she came upon a stream to her right. Stopping, she listened carefully once more, but all she heard was the gentle babble of the brook beside her. Slowly she turned completely around. By now the rain had mostly stopped, but it had been replaced by a strange fog which chilled her to the bone, making it difficult to see.

What's that, up ahead? Something's moving. As silently as she could manage, she crept toward the movement.

There he is! I found him. The hooded figure walked with the aid of a tall walking stick. Juanita followed him, keeping a safe distance, so as not to be heard, but not so far back that she'd lose him again.

A few minutes later that same strange blue aura highlighted the person's body.

That's odd. His walking stick is actually a hoe. Suddenly the figure turned around, gazing straight at her. She froze, then slowly sank down to her knees, until her eyes lay just above the thick layer of mist. After a moment the wizard whirled around, striding swiftly to the elven city's outer wall. Voices sounded off to her right. There, about thirty feet away, two of the elven guards stood talking beside an open gate in the wall. The hooded figure raised his right hand. A scream burst out from the forest farther down the wall. The guards bolted off toward the noise. The figure walked to the gateway and slipped silently inside. Juanita glanced in the direction the guards had gone. They were nowhere in sight. She sprinted for the open gate, sparkling for a moment as she passed through the barrier, then slipped inside.

* * *

It had started to rain, but Tara was only a block from her goal. She shivered, then pulled her hood over her head, partially because of the chill rain and partially so no one would recognize her.

Tara continued to war with her demons within. *What am I doing? This is wrong! How did I get wrapped up in this?* As she continued walking, her footsteps made splashing sounds which echoed off the homes beside her. She could sense the buildings watching her, judging her. Their presence felt unusually strong tonight. Tara shivered once more.

Passing a dark alley, she glanced over to her left. She took a few more steps, then suddenly froze. Slowly she turned and silently tiptoed back toward the alley. With her back pressed hard against a building, she took a deep breath then quickly glanced around the corner. There was no one there, only an old garden hoe leaning against the alley wall, rain dripping off its well-worn handle. Shaking her head she sighed, turned back and continued on her way.

Soon she came to a darkened house, the home of Avani's grandparents; the one she'd been searching for. Walking up the front steps, she looked both ways before slowly turning the handle. The door swung silently inward. Glancing around once more, she quickly disappeared inside.

Down the block in the alley she'd just passed, a hooded figure leaned against a hoe and watched her from the shadows.

Chapter 18: Jail house rock

The next day, the group arrived a little early to class. Still carrying his satchel, Tom sauntered over to the lab bench, gazing at all the things laid out for today's lab. There were polished stones that gleamed brightly, pulsing as if alive. Powders of several different colors and textures filled small, flat pottery dishes. Tom sniffed an orange-colored one and his eyes nearly closed from the foul stench. Off to one side sat a darkly stained wooden wand. Tom felt drawn to it as if it called to him. As he approached, ornate runes along its handle began to materialize, glowing bright yellow. He reached for it. Suddenly, red sparks leapt from the wand and zapped his hand. Tom leapt back, sheepishly glancing around to make sure no one had seen him, then hurried away, shaking his hand.

I hope this lab goes better than yesterday's. Tom shuddered, just thinking about it. At that moment he heard voices coming from the entrance to the hall. As he looked that direction he saw Goban talking with some students just inside the doorway. Rushing up the aisle Tom stopped beside his friend. The two walked a few feet away from the others where Goban gave Tom his daily briefing on the status of the upcoming war. Apparently, about half the trolls and a third of the ogre troops were now camped a few kiloters northwest of Elfhaven. The barrier had again failed in several places, but luckily there had been no trolls or ogres near the barrier when it collapsed. Tom had been thinking a lot about the failing barrier, the Citadel, and Avani's silver cube. He knew they were all connected somehow.

"We've got to get into the Citadel, find out what's wrong." Tom paused. "How about if we all meet there this evening, just after dark?"

Goban nodded. "Have you asked Avani?"

"No, let's talk to her after class. We'll make sure she brings her father's cube. Maybe we can figure out a way to open it."

Chapter Eighteen

At that moment, Professor Snehal strode briskly into the lecture hall and directly to the lectern.

Tom motioned for them to take their seats. As they headed for their usual row, Tara passed them in the aisle.

"Good morning, Tara," said Tom pleasantly. She immediately stopped, her eyes darting to his satchel, then quickly up to his face. She paused, then without a word, hurried off to her seat.

Tom frowned as he watched her go.

"What's wrong?" asked Goban.

"There's something strange going on," began Tom. "Yesterday, at the stable, I caught Lorin moving my satchel, which seemed odd. Now I just saw Tara glance at it then look away like it had burned her."

"Maybe Avani's grandparents packed some special treat in it?" joked Goban.

Tom chuckled halfheartedly. "Maybe..." Sidestepping along their row, they took their seats. Tom set his satchel down beside him.

"Today's lecture and its accompanying lab will be on making a person appear to be someone else; whether another person, or an animal, or even an inanimate object. He or she will not actually be changed, as in *altering matter*, but to others they will appear to be someone, or something else. This time we'll create this illusion by using an incantation," began the professor.

As Goban listened to the lecture, Tom glanced over at his satchel. After a moment he picked it up, sat it on his lap and reached for the clasp.

"As you all know, and as with any of the four elements of magic—" But before Professor Snehal could finish his statement, in marched five royal guards with their weapons drawn. Everyone glanced up in surprise.

"What is the meaning of this?" bellowed Snehal. "You have no right!"

"We have every right," snapped Sanuu. "There's a traitor in your midst. Yesterday, the defense plans were stolen from the war room."

Sanuu and Tappus quickly scanned the room, then rushed directly to

Tom. "Is this your satchel?"

"Yes, but…" began Tom.

Sanuu grabbed the bag, flipped open the clasp, reached in and lifted a sheaf of parchments high into the air. "The missing defense plans. Take him away!"

Tappus grabbed Tom's arm and jerked him to his feet. Sanuu handed the document to another guard, then grasped Tom's other arm. Together they dragged him from the hall.

"Wait!" cried Tom, "there's been a mistake. I didn't take any plans. I'm not a traitor! I don't even know where the war room is."

Tom locked eyes with Avani, desperately pleading his innocence. Her gaze darted from Tom to the prince. Devraj's face seemed oddly calm and unreadable. Hesitating only an instant, she jumped to her feet and ran after Tom.

"Stop!" commanded Snehal, freezing Avani in her tracks. "Take your seat, Avani."

She whirled around to face the professor. "But Tom—where are they taking him? What will they do to him? He's innocent, I know he's innocent." Avani looked to the prince for support but Devraj remained silent.

Tom glanced back at her one last time before being dragged through the doorway.

* * *

The guards wouldn't answer Tom's questions. Even worse, they held his arms so tightly they began to go to sleep. Upon entering the castle gate, the guards turned right, walking down a long, narrow hallway, then entered a stairway on their left that led steeply down. Tom's feet barely touched the steps as the guards mostly carried him along. The deeper they went, the darker and colder it got. The walls, ceiling, and floor were made of roughhewn stone. Every hundred paces or so, iron racks were mounted on the uneven walls. In the racks sat large flaming torches, but they were so far apart, Tom could only see a few feet ahead before it was dark again. As they descended still further, a foul stench added to the depressing feel of the place. Tom heard water dripping in the distance and some sort of animal squeaking and rustling about, but so far he hadn't seen anything.

Deeper and deeper they went. Finally the stairs made a left-hand turn and abruptly ended at a massive wooden door. There was a slot in the door at about the height of an adult elf's eyes. A guard stood by the door, a set of keys dangling on a large loop from his belt. He was muscular with broad shoulders, although he had a bit of a pot belly, something Tom hadn't seen on many elves. A dagger stuck out prominently from his belt and a massive broadsword lay strapped across his back. He glared at Tom with obvious disgust. Still watching Tom suspiciously, he twisted his head and spat.

At a nod from Sanuu, the guard turned and said something through the slot, then his keys jingled as he unlocked the door. With a strong push from the guard the massive door swung inward with a loud creak that echoed up the stairwell. Inside stood another guard, armed just like the first. A hallway stretched out ahead of them as far as Tom could see in the dim light. Tom's captors dragged him down the narrow hall; the guard with the keys followed them. Tom thought the stairway couldn't have smelled any worse, but he was wrong. Rows of locked doors stood on either side of the hallway. Someone moaned. Someone else yelled obscenities. As he passed a cell on his right, Tom heard a growl. The hairs on the back of his neck stood out. Glancing up at a tiny hole in the cell door, Tom got a glimpse of hideous blood-shot eyes staring back at him. Tom shivered, and it wasn't from the cold.

At the next cell on the left the jailer stopped and unlocked a dark, rough wooden door, then jerked it open. A damp cold poured forth from the room, accompanied by a musty, moldy smell.

The jailer spun Tom around, looking him over carefully. He patted down Tom's arms and legs, down to his ankles. *Probably searching for concealed weapons*, thought Tom. For the first time since he'd arrived, the guard spoke.

"Here's your new home, traitor. Hope you enjoy it. Oh, and let me know if there's anything I can do for you. Anything at all." The guard gave a deep, edgy laugh and pushed Tom forcefully into the cell.

"No wait!" cried Tom. "I'm innocent!" The door slammed shut, Keys clanked as they turned in the lock. The room was pitch black. Tom felt chilled already. He wrapped his arms around himself and shivered. The sound of dripping water echoed all around him as he plopped down on the cold rock floor.

How did this happen? How did I get into this mess? And how am I going to get out of it?

There was a rustling noise from inside his cell. His heart raced. The rustling turned into a scratching sound. Tom scooted backwards, away from the noise, until his back bumped up against the cold, rough, solid rock wall of his cell. He shook all over. The scratching sound grew closer. Tom instinctively reached for his adventurer's belt. Then he remembered he'd left it at Avani's grandparent's house. He patted himself down and felt something small in his right front shirt pocket. Reaching in, he found his LED headlamp.

That's right! I put it in my pocket at the library. Would the guard have taken it if he'd found it? He wouldn't know what it was, and it doesn't look like a weapon. Tom pulled out the light, his fingers shaking as he fumbled to find the on switch. Suddenly light leapt from his hands. He moved the beam back and forth, freezing on a small creature in the center of the room. The creature looked similar to a rat, but a little thinner, with enormous bulging eyes and a short, spiky tail. The animal stopped advancing once the light hit him. Tom breathed a small sigh of relief.

171

Chapter Eighteen

"Aren't you a cute little critter," said Tom, hoping to calm the animal, and himself. Instead, it drew back its lips, exposing long, sharp teeth and hissed.

Where's Max when I need him? Tom was petrified. Keeping the light beam firmly on the animal, he nervously glanced around his cell. The walls were hand-hewn rock, making it look more like a cave than a cell.

Glancing up, Tom saw the ceiling high overhead. There were no windows, except for a slot in the door at eye level and another slot near the bottom, presumably for plates of food to enter and empty plates to exit. There was a rack on the wall to hold a torch, but there was no torch in it. In one corner stood a tin bucket with a stack of dry, rough leaves beside it. In another corner lay a pile of straw. *My bed?* he wondered.

There were no other entrances or exits, so Tom deduced that the lower slot must be how the animal had gotten in. Keeping his back to the wall and the beam of light on the animal, Tom slowly inched his way around the cell, trying to keep the animal between him and the door.

"Shoo, go on shoo," said Tom, as fiercely as he could manage. The creature made a chittering noise then bared his teeth once more. Tom tried to remember how many hours the small watch battery could power the lantern.

Wish I had my flare gun. Although, the guards would have probably taken it, anyway. In any case, it wouldn't be too smart to fire a flare gun off in a cell. For one thing, Uncle Carlos would throw a fit. Tom smiled at the thought, in spite of being cold, damp and scared spit-less. Actually, Tom realized after a few moments, thinking about his uncle only made him feel all the more alone.

* * *

Tom's friends were frustrated, magic school seemed to drag on forever. Avani, Kiran, Goban, Malak, and Chatur agreed to meet in the park after class to discuss Tom's plight. Once school finally ended, they all took different routes to the park, no longer sure who they could trust.

When they'd all arrived, Kiran said, "Shouldn't we ask Prince Devraj for help? He could talk to his father; tell him Tom didn't do it."

"Don't be stupid, Kiran," said Chatur sharply. "Didn't you see the smug look on Devraj's face when the guards burst in, as if he knew this would happen? I think the prince may be involved."

"Are you saying you think Devraj stole the plans?" asked Avani, a shocked look on her face.

"I'm not saying he did—I'm not saying he didn't," replied Chatur flatly. "But I bet he'd be happy if Tom took the blame, that's all I'm saying."

"Why would he want to falsely accuse Tom?" asked Avani.

Malak and Chatur glanced at each other and rolled their eyes.

"What?" she said, scowling.

"Girls can be so naive," said Chatur matter-of-factly. Malak just nodded.

"Stop insulting me like I'm not even here. What do you mean? Get to the point!"

"OK, plain and simple," began Chatur. "The prince has the hots for you and he thinks you've got a crush on Tom." Malak and Chatur nodded at each other knowingly.

"What? Are you crazy?" said Avani. She looked at Goban for support but he just shrugged. She began again, "It's true, Prince Devraj and I have discussed marriage, but that's more like a business contract, to unite the Keepers of the Light with the royal family. It has nothing to do with— love. Besides, we aren't even officially engaged yet, not really, and even if we were, it'll be years before we're actually married."

"I'm just saying—" said Chatur with a shrug.

"Girls, they're always so dense when it comes to matters of the heart," said Malak, shaking his head. Goban snorted.

"That's enough!" yelled Avani. They all just stared at her.

"Well," she sighed, glancing first at Chatur, then at Malak, "I suppose I have been showing some interest in Tom. He's new, he's a friend, he's more my own age and he's from another world!" For a moment Avani seemed lost in thought, then she squared her shoulders and went on.

"Okay, for now anyway, we leave the prince out of this. Our number-one priority is to get inside the Citadel, before the barrier fails altogether. For that, we need Tom's help. We've got to find a way to break him out of the dungeon," said Avani. The others continued to stare at her.

Avani looked from blank face to blank face and sighed. "You call yourselves a rescue party? Poor Tom—Poor, poor, poor, Tom..." Now it was Avani's turn to shake her head.

Chapter 19: Unlikely heroes

Tom wasn't sure how much time had elapsed since he'd finally persuaded the rat from you-know-where to leave his cell. It could've been a day, perhaps two or three. Without daylight, it was difficult to tell when one day ended, and the next began. In that time he'd been served two or three awful-tasting meals and slept on the pile of straw in the corner. And he was still cold.

From the moment he'd been locked in his cell, he'd proclaimed his innocence, almost constantly. He'd demanded to speak with the king, or at least Prince Devraj, but the guards ignored his requests. Tom began to lose hope, afraid he'd be locked in this dungeon forever…

Lying on his straw bed, Tom awakened from a fitful sleep at the sound of voices nearby. He couldn't make out what was being said, but a moment later he heard the main prison door open, down the hall. This had happened several times since he'd been here, but so far no one had come to see him. This time, however, he heard feet shuffle up to his cell door, keys rattle, the lock turn. Slowly the door swung open with a creak.

Someone stood in front of the guard, holding a torch. Tom had to shield his eyes from the unaccustomed light. The person holding the torch said something to the guard, who turned and walked back into the hall, closing and locking the cell door behind him. Footsteps slowly receded down the hallway. The person who remained placed the torch in the holder on the wall and turned around. Still partially covering his eyes, Tom squinted up at the newcomer's face.

"Who's there? Show yourself," said Tom, trying to sound brave.

"Yo dawg," replied a familiar voice.

"Goban, Goban is that you?" said Tom, hardly believing his ears.

Goban stepped into the torchlight and smiled. "At your service."

"Wow, how did you get in here?"

"I've got my connections. I am a prince myself, you know?"

"Oh, I guess you are. I never really thought about it. Your father is king of the dwarves, after all, so that would make you..."

Goban swung his arms out wide, smiling broadly. "Like I said, I gots connections."

"Wow," said Tom, "it's getting knee deep in princes around here."

Goban chuckled.

Tom got up and hobbled unsteadily over to his friend, grabbing him by his vest with both hands he pleaded, "Goban, I didn't do it! You've gotta believe me. I was framed!"

Goban leaned back, trying to pull away from Tom's fierce grip. "I know."

"I keep telling the guards that, but they won't listen. I've asked to see the king, or at least Devraj, a hundred times, but the guards just keep ignoring me. I've gotta get out of here!"

Goban finally succeeded in prying himself free from Tom's death-grip. "That's why I'm here bro. I keep trying to tell ya, but—"

"It's cold and damp in here. There's no light, except from my LED headlamp, and I'm not sure how much longer the batteries'll last, so I'm using them sparingly."

Goban raised an eyebrow. "Wow, slow down. Have they been feeding you cafftea berries? You're as hyper as a gremlin."

"The bed is just a pile of straw and it itches something awful. Plus, there's this ugly rat creature that keeps sneaking into my cell when I'm asleep, and curling up beside me, probably just trying to keep warm."

"If you'll just let me finish, I think I can help."

Tom took a deep breath and began pacing back and forth. "But enough of my complaining. Goban, I'm glad you're here. I've had plenty of time to think and I've got an idea that might help the war effort. It came to me last night. It's from a book called the *Iliad* and it's about the Trojan War. The wicked cool part was when Odysseus had his men build a giant wooden horse. They left it just outside the Trojan's main gate with a few soldiers hidden inside. Then the Greek ships pretended to sail away. Seeing this, the Trojans cheered, thinking the war was over, thinking they'd won. They ended up partying late into the night."

"Ah—that's a terrific story Tom, I'm sure, but—"

"Then once the Trojans had all passed out, the Greek warriors slipped out of the horse and opened the main gates, letting in the Greek army.".

Goban frowned. "How nice for them, but we don't really have time for—"

"I figure we could do something similar," said Tom. "Only—instead of a horse, you could build a wooden dragon, with slits cut out of its sides, disguised along the edge of the scales, so your archers could shoot arrows from inside."

Goban raised an eyebrow. "Go on."

"Do the dwarves use any kind of flammable liquid or gas?" asked Tom excitedly.

"We use swamp gas when we need extra hot fires for our forges."

"Perfect!" said Tom. "We could put that under pressure, I'll explain how to do that later, then they can shoot flames out the dragon's nose. It's called a flame-thrower, actually. What do you think?"

Goban's eyes lit up and now he began pacing around saying, "It would need to be on wheels, so the troops can move it easily. And the wheels would have to be on the inside so they can't be seen from the outside."

"Okay, enough about this," said Tom. "You said that's not why you're here. Don't keep me waiting, what was the real reason you came?"

Goban blinked. "Oh—oh yeah; I'm here to rescue you," he said. "Come on, we don't have much time."

Tom looked Goban over skeptically. "And just how do you expect to do that? You don't seem to have any weapons on you?"

Goban grinned. "We've got a plan!"

"We?" said Tom hesitantly.

"Avani, Kiran, Chatur, Malak, and myself, of course."

Tom frowned. "Something tells me I'm not going to like this—plan."

Goban rummaged around in his pocket and produced a small glass vial. "It just so happens, Kiran had a couple of vials of that invisibility potion. You remember—the one from class? All you need to do is drink this and then you and I will just walk on out of here. Right under the guard's very noses," said Goban, beaming with pride.

Tom backed away. "Oh no—you're not getting me to drink that stuff."

"Come on, it worked for the rabbits. You saw for yourself."

Tom stepped forward, tentatively. He took the vial and shook it, then held it up to the torchlight. "Is this stuff safe?"

"Hardly any of the rabbits died," stated Goban flatly. Beads of sweat began to form on Tom's brow.

"Just kidding!" chuckled Goban. "None of the animals died... Well, not right away, that is."

"OK, stop!" yelled Tom, then he froze, listening carefully to make sure the guards hadn't heard him. After a moment without hearing any footsteps, he let out a sigh. "Is there enough potion?"

"Only one way to find out," said Goban. "Bottoms up!"

Tom removed the stopper and sniffed the vial. His head shot back, his eyes nearly closing as he wrinkled up his nose.

"This smells awful!"

"Who cares? Drink up. We don't have all night, ya know." Goban grabbed Tom's arm and raised his elbow, forcing the liquid toward his lips.

"OK, OK," hissed Tom, "I can do it myself!" He stared at the vial for an instant, then held his nose and swallowed its contents in a single gulp.

"Yuck!" spat Tom. "That tastes worse than it smells." He coughed a couple of times, then rasped out the words, "Is—it—working—yet?"

"Not yet, you're still as ugly as ever."

"Ha, ha. That's not very fun..." Tom stopped talking as he noticed his hands begin to fade. When he was about halfway invisible, the process seemed to stop. Tom held his breath and glanced at Goban with a horrified expression on his face... Finally he started fading again, and at last he was totally invisible.

"It worked!" cried Tom excitedly.

"There's just—one—small—problem," said Goban, "which we failed to anticipate, I might add. It's—your clothes. They're still visible."

"My clothes..." began Tom, glancing down, he realized his clothes were just hanging around in space, without a body. When he moved his arm, his sleeve moved, but there was no hand visible in it.

"Ah—this is—er, only a slight snag," began Goban, "and ah—quite easy to fix, really." Goban scratched his head, then his eyes lit up. "Just take off your clothes."

"Take off my clothes?" croaked Tom, in disbelief.

"No one can see you," reasoned Goban. "We can stuff some straw in your clothes, and it'll look like you're asleep in the corner. Perfect, huh?"

"No, it's not perfect! What if I turn visible before we're outside, or before we can get me some clothes?"

Goban gazed at the cell floor for a moment, his brow furrowed in thought. Then he smiled. "Don't worry, Avani's outside and she's wearing her long cloak. You can cover yourself with that, just until we can get ya some clothes, trust me! Now hurry up and strip and fill your clothes with straw. We don't have much time."

Goban called the guard as Tom frantically got out of his clothes and stuffed straw into them. He tried to make it look as if he was curled up asleep. But to Tom, it looked more like a poorly built scarecrow that had just fallen over. Once the guard arrived, Goban called through the slit in the door and said he was ready to leave. The guard opened the door, then peered past Goban, spotting the bundle of clothing on the floor.

"The prisoner was tired," said Goban matter-of-factly. "He decided to take a nap, so I might as well go."

The guard scowled suspiciously and stepped into the room. Just then there was a commotion down the hallway.

"What's that noise?" asked Goban. "Hmm, sounds like someone's fighting."

The guard paused, then turned back to listen. Clear sounds of a struggle emanated from the stairway. The guard left the room and started down the hallway.

"Don't you think you should lock the door, first? Wouldn't want the prisoner to escape, now would we?" said Goban.

The guard narrowed his eyes and clenched his teeth, but he hurried back and locked the door, then dashed off down the hall, his keys clanking with each step and with Goban in hot pursuit. When they reached the main door the guard hastily unlocked it and strode briskly through. Goban followed him. The other guard stood there trying to break up a fight at the bottom of the stairway.

"Malak, Chatur," said Goban gruffly, "what do you think you're doing?"

"Malak started it!" yelled Chatur.

To which Malak fired back, "No, I didn't, Chatur did."

"I'm so sorry," said Goban apologetically, "I take full responsibility for my two friends. Everyone knows they fight constantly. Don't worry, I'll get them out of here, right away."

Goban grabbed Chatur by the ear and with a swift kick to Malak's backside, herded the two toward the stairway. Goban glanced back at the guards. One of them nodded so Goban proceeded to haul Chatur up the stairs. Malak scrambled to stay ahead.

Once they'd rounded the first corner and the guards were out of earshot, Chatur whispered, "Goban, my ear hurts and Malak, you bloodied my lip."

Goban released Chatur's ear.

"I had to make it look real," shrugged Malak. Chatur shot him an angry look.

"What?" said Malak serenely.

"Tom, are you there?" whispered Goban, glancing all around.

"I'm right here," said a disembodied voice to his left. "I'm cold, and I feel a draft." The other three choked back laughter.

* * *

Avani and Max were waiting for them just outside the castle's main gate. Avani held a grey canvas bag. Max lowered his head and sniffed. Then he barked.

"Quiet, Max!" came Tom's voice out of thin air.

Max sniffed again, then sat back on his haunches, tipped his head and made a muffled "woof" sound.

"Why did you bring Max?" hissed Tom.

"Well, we thought he'd be glad to—er, see you," said Avani awkwardly. Max glanced from Avani to where Tom's voice was coming from, and then whined.

"Anyway, come on, we don't have much time." Avani led them around the corner into a dimly lit street of shops that were closed for the day.

Tom could see the shops went on for blocks and blocks. "Where's Kiran?" he asked.

"Nadda insisted he do some chores for him, back home. He was none too happy."

"Kiran, missing out on an adventure; I can just imagine," replied Tom.

"Ah—Tom," began Goban delicately.

"Yes?"

"You're ah—you're starting to become—visible again..." said Goban, stating the obvious.

Tom glanced down. He could vaguely make out his image, but as he watched, he got more and more solid by the second. Max came over and sniffed him again, then pawed Tom's half-visible foot.

"Avani, give me your cloak!" demanded Tom.

Avani calmly untied her cloak and slowly held it out at arm's length.

"Look the other way!" spat Tom.

"Oh, sorry," said Avani. She half-turned sideways, but her eyes kept flicking over in his general direction. Tom grabbed the cloak and threw it around himself, wrapping it tightly.

"Avani was peeking," said Malak.

"Was not!" she replied, scowling at him.

Malak fired back, "Was too!" Goban and Chatur chuckled.

Tom glared at Avani. "It's not funny! What were you doing looking at me, anyway?"

Avani shrugged. "Just checking."

"Checking? Checking what?" he cried.

"I was just checking to see if you're built the same as elven boys."

"What?" exclaimed Tom. Everyone broke up laughing. Chatur fell down, covering his mouth. Tom's face went beet-red. He turned and stormed away.

"Where're you going?" Avani called, choking back a laugh herself.

"I'm heading to the Citadel. That's why you sprang me out of jail, wasn't it? Broke me out of the slammer, gave me a vacation from the 'big house,' had me fly the coop? All so I could help you get into the Citadel, right?" Tom paused, took a deep breath, trying to calm himself. "Did you bring your dad's silver cube?"

Avani glanced at the others. "Ah—," began Avani delicately, "yes—we need your help getting into the Citadel, but more importantly, we know you're innocent. So it was the right thing to do, helping you to ah— hammer the coop, as you said.

"Anyway, to answer your other question, yes, I brought the cube, but we need to make a slight detour first, to get you some clothes." Avani hurried up beside Tom. The others followed behind, chuckling and talking quietly amongst themselves. The pair walked for a couple of minutes along the dark road, neither Tom nor Avani saying a word.

Finally, quietly, so no one else would hear, Tom asked, "So—am I?"

"Are you what?" responded Avani innocently.

"Am I built the same as elven boys?" exclaimed Tom, louder than he'd intended.

Avani smiled and turned slightly so the others could hear. "Oh yes, pretty much the same." Everyone laughed, everyone except Tom, of course, who now turned even redder than before.

Chapter 20: Mom to king's knight four, check!

When Juanita slipped through the gateway, Naagesh was nowhere in sight. Keeping low, she followed the wall until it neared several streets lined with neat and tidy homes. On a nearby clothesline she spotted a long hooded cape that she "borrowed." Flipping the hood over her head to hide her face, she made her way toward the castle's main gate. It was still mostly dark but she saw a few people milling about. *Probably heading off on errands.*

Walking slowly, she listened to their conversations, mostly gossip and trivia, but she also heard snippets about Tom. Several people spoke in awe of the alien boy and his strange pet. But a tall slender woman spat the word "traitor" when she said his name. So far Juanita hadn't heard where he was, or if he was being held against his will.

Juanita had been up all night, she was getting hungry and her muscles were sore and tired. Earlier she'd passed by a stable. She thought that might be a good place to sleep for a while, so she started making her way back in that direction. As she approached the stable, a man dressed in the same style of hooded cloak that Naagesh had worn last night stepped out from the stable doorway. Reaching beside the doorframe he grabbed a hoe.

Naagesh. She gasped involuntarily. *It's too late to hide. He's already seen me. Just got to keep moving.* Juanita tipped her head forward slightly and continued walking past him, keeping a slow, steady pace. Unfortunately the direction she was now headed in led her straight for the castle's main entrance. She could feel the wizard's eyes watching her as she walked across the square. On either side of the castle's massive doors stood two palace guards. Boldly striding up the steps, she pretended she was headed there all along. The guards didn't challenge her so she continued, passing through a large entryway, then through another door and into a great hall. Glancing back, she saw no sign of Naagesh. Just ahead a guard stood talking with a tall, handsome, regal-looking elf. Juanita noticed the guard was armed with a broadsword in a scabbard slung loosely from his belt.

"What news have you, Sanuu?" asked the taller elf.

"Your scouts report that the bulk of the troll army has arrived and they've set up camp in Elfhaven valley. The ogre troops are not far behind, your Highness," replied Sanuu.

The guard called him "your Highness." This must be their king.

The king clasped his hands behind his back, lowered his head in thought, and walked a few paces away.

As she approached, the guard turned. "I'm sorry, but the king is not receiving visitors today, perhaps tomorrow." With a firm yet gentle motion, Sanuu raised his hand, palm outward, gesturing toward the exit.

Juanita tipped her head forward a little more, and continued to approach.

"Please, I'm sorry but I must insist you leave the hall. The king has important business to attend to," said Sanuu firmly.

When Juanita was directly in front of him her arm shot out and seized the hilt of Sanuu's sword, pivoting quickly, she drew the blade from its scabbard. An instant later, she stood a few feet away, flicking the sword's tip back and forth between the two elves. Careful to avoid the blade, Sanuu lunged sidelong at her but she skillfully whipped the sword over, pointing at his chest.

Hearing the commotion, the king whirled around, crying, "Stop!" Sanuu froze, though his eyes remained glued on Juanita.

"Who are you?" demanded King Dakshi. "Why have you threatened your king? Speak!"

A moment later, a handful of palace guards rushed in, swords drawn. The king motioned for them to stop.

"Once again," said the king, in a calmer tone, "who are you and why are you here?"

Juanita glanced at the guards surrounding her, but didn't lower her sword. Instead she slowly raised her left hand and pulled back her hood. Several guards gasped.

"My name's Juanita Holland. I'm Tom Holland's mother."

The king raised an eyebrow and glanced at Sanuu. "Go on."

"I was captured by trolls and ogres and interrogated by a wizard named Naagesh."

The king looked like he'd just seen a ghost. "Naagesh? Naagesh is alive?"

"Yes, I escaped and followed him here. I just saw him leaving the stable a few moments ago. He walks with the aid of a hoe." The king, glanced once more at Sanuu.

"Naagesh, here... Posing as Lorin." The king shook his head, obviously shaken by the news. Quickly recovering his composure, he added, "You escaped from the troll encampment unaided?" A look of surprise mixed with respect crossed the king's face.

Juanita nodded. "The troll leader said the elves had captured Tom and were holding him prisoner."

"You can't believe anything a trolls tells you. My son, Prince Devraj, and a few of his young friends rescued Tom from a troll scouting party."

"If that's true, then where's Tom now?"

The king glanced around uneasily. He cleared his throat. "Ah—well actually—at the moment he's—in the dungeon."

Juanita raised her sword and took a step toward the king. The guards leapt forward.

"Halt!" cried the king, raising his hand. Then, in a calm, quiet tone said, "Please, lower your weapon and I will explain everything."

Juanita stood firm.

"I'll grant you're handy with a sword, and if indeed you escaped from the troll encampment all by yourself, that's truly impressive, but I doubt you can best six of my men all at once. Please, lower your weapon. You have my word you won't be harmed and once I've brought you up-to-date with recent events, you and I will go visit Tom."

"And you will release him?" she demanded, pointing her blade directly at the king's heart.

The king paused, then sighed. "And I will release him."

Juanita glanced sidelong at the guards surrounding her, then back at the king. "I'll hold you to your word." Slowly, while still keeping an eye on the guards, she lowered the blade to the floor.

"Leave us," said the king sternly.

"But sire," protested Sanuu.

"Leave us," he repeated. Then he added, "Oh, and Sanuu—you seem to have misplaced your sword. See to it that doesn't happen again." The king's lip curled up into the slightest of grins.

Sanuu's face reddened. Snatching up his sword, he slammed it into its scabbard. For a moment his fiery eyes burned into Juanita's, then he stormed from the hall, the guards hurrying to keep up.

* * *

After the king told the tale of everything that had transpired since Tom had first stepped foot on their world, and Juanita had likewise told him what she'd seen and heard, including what she knew of Naagesh and his whereabouts, they strode briskly toward the dungeon.

"I'm sorry your son was detained. All the evidence initially pointed to him—as being the traitor. But I've come to learn that Tom was framed. Still, I had hoped that by keeping him locked away, the real traitor, believing that he'd fooled us, would make a mistake and expose himself. But the point's moot. Thanks to you, we now know that the traitor is Naagesh and that he's been posing as our stable-hand Lorin. After we free Tom, I'll send my men to capture him."

187

Chapter Twenty

They walked the rest of the way down the long stairway to the dungeon in silence. Several times Juanita stole a quick glance at the king. As they approached the dungeon's massive door, the guard's brow rose at the unexpected sight of the king and his alien companion. With a nod from King Dakshi, the guard quickly unlocked the door, swung it open and snapped to attention. Inside, the other guard led them briskly down the dank hallway, their boots echoing hollowly off its stone walls, until they arrived at Tom's cell.

The guard grabbed a flaming torch from its wall hanger and handed it to the king. His keys jingled as he awkwardly fumbled for the right one. A moment later there was a loud creak and the door swung open. King Dakshi raised his arm toward the cell, gesturing for Juanita to enter. She glanced at the jailer, then shook her head no. The king sighed, then walked in first. Juanita went next, followed by the guard. There, lying in the corner, now exposed in the flickering torchlight, lay an obvious straw dummy. The guard rushed forward, glanced down at the dummy, then up at the king, a horrified look on his face.

Juanita bent down, studying the dummy in the dim torchlight. "These are Tom's clothes." Standing up, she glared at the king. "Where is he?"

King Dakshi glanced from the straw dummy to the guard, then back to Juanita, "It appears—your son has escaped."

Chapter 21: Key to the Citadel

On the way to the Citadel, they made a quick trip home for some clothes for Tom. While there, he grabbed his adventurer's belt from behind the door, and strapped it on. Kiran had finished his chores and eagerly accompanied them as they made their way to the Citadel. When Tom stepped out into the street, he was surprised at how bright it was.

Gazing up into the night sky, Tom realized once again how different this planet was from Earth. "Wow, I never noticed before. You've got an asteroid belt."

Glancing up himself, Malak replied, "The Ring of Turin. Sure, don't you have one back home?"

"No. We've just got a moon." Facing Goban, Tom noticed a small battle axe strapped across his back. Tom raised an eyebrow.

"I stashed it here earlier," Goban said, answering Tom's unasked question. "I thought a little—security might come in handy." He smiled.

Avani spoke up, "We have the cover of nightfall on our side, but there may be a traitor in Elfhaven. If so, we don't want them to know what we're up to."

"Then we'd better get there quick," said Tom, turning and taking off running. The others hurried to catch up.

They'd only gone a short distance when Tom rounded a corner and froze in his tracks. A couple of blocks ahead, a group of palace guards with torches in their hands, were headed their way. Tom hastily retreated back around the corner and stopped the others. Kiran got down on all fours and cautiously stuck his head around the corner, then immediately pulled back.

"They're searching all the shops. They must've discovered you escaped."

"That was quick. I hoped they wouldn't figure it out, at least until morning," said Goban.

"Hmm, and I thought the straw-filled dummy looked so realistic, too," said Tom..

"Quick, the voices are getting louder," urged Avani. "They're coming this way. Hurry!" They took off running back the way they'd come. Around the first corner there was an alley off to their right, so they turned into it. The alleyway led them straight for fifty paces or so and then curved to the left. Suddenly it came to a dead end. The alley had been boarded up with a tall wooden fence. It was too high with no hand or footholds, so they couldn't climb over it. There was no way out.

"We're trapped and the voices are getting closer," moaned Chatur. "They'll be here any myntar."

Just then, Max whimpered and pawed at the fence. Kiran ran over. "Looks like a small gate. I don't see a handle or latch, but there's a seam running all around it."

"Avani, can you open it with magic?" asked Goban nervously.

"Ah, I don't know. I—I can try." Avani relaxed, closing her eyes as she touched her satchel. The crystals glowed, spilling light out from under the flap. Kiran pushed on the gate but it didn't budge.

"The voices are getting louder. I think they're in the alley," cried Chatur.

Beads of sweat began to form on Avani's brow. Tom pulled out his Swiss army knife and ran to the gate. Flipping out the screwdriver tool, he pushed the blade into the opening near the bottom, then began sliding it up.

"Hurry, they're almost here," hissed Chatur.

On the second side there was a soft "click" noise. Kiran fell through the fence as the gate swung inward, hinged from above.

"Hurry, everyone inside," urged Tom. They all piled in and Tom quickly swung the gate closed. Footsteps approached as the latch softly clicked into place. Tom held his breath.

"What was that noise?" came a voice.

"I didn't hear anything. What did it sound like?" said another.

"Not sure. Like a 'tap' or something."

"You probably just kicked a pebble. Come on, it's a dead end. We've plenty more places to search. The traitor's not here."

Footsteps approached the fence. Someone began tapping on it. The fence creaked as it flexed inward slightly. Someone was pushing it. It flexed again, farther this time, looking as if it might break any moment.

Before anyone could stop him Max pawed the fence. Kiran grabbed his collar. Max glanced forlornly at Tom. Everyone held their breath.

"Did you hear that? Hey, it looks like there's a gate at the bottom. Here, come help me push."

The fence flexed inward. It couldn't hold much longer. Suddenly, a trumpet blared in the distance, from the direction of the castle.

"That's the signal. The war's begun."

"The enemy must've broken through the barrier, but how?"

"I don't know. Come on, let's go."

There was a pause, then the sound of running footsteps quickly receding into the distance. Kiran let out a huge sigh and released Max. Max whimpered, then pawed the fence once more.

Another trumpet blared, accompanied by the sound of hundreds of running feet, presumably troops heading off to battle.

Even in the dim light, Tom could see the worried look on Avani's face.

"The war's begun. We're too late…" she said, as she slowly sank to the ground.

"We don't know for sure the barrier's failed completely," said Tom. "It could just be a momentary flutter, like's been happening for the last few days. Anyway, we've got to try."

They all stared at one another. Avani slowly nodded and got to her feet.

The alley was too narrow for the moonlight to reach the ground, so

Avani whispered an incantation and a dim yellow light ignited on her open palm. She raised her hand and blew. The small ball of light gently rose and flew toward Kiran. As it did, however, Max leapt and caught it in his mouth. Light seeped out from between his teeth, and his gums began to glow a dull red.

"No, Max, drop the magic light thingy," whispered Tom, patting him on the head. Max turned his big playful eyes toward him but didn't release the light.

"Max—" repeated Tom, bending over and frowning. Kiran grabbed a stick and threw it down the alley. Max let go of the light and ran after the stick. The light lazily drifted up, zigzagging as if disoriented, until it hovered just in front of Kiran.

Avani said, "Kiran, you lead." Her brother smiled, turned, and took off down the alley. Max returned the stick to him, but wouldn't let go of it, so Kiran led the way half-pulling Max along with him. The light floated just ahead, dimly illuminating the path beyond.

Several empty crates of various sizes stood open, stacked haphazardly along the walls. Rusted tools and wagon parts lay scattered upon the ground. Grass and weeds pushed their way up between the cobblestones at odd angles. Noises of nocturnal birds or small rodents, sounded all around them. Something skittered by, just beyond the floating light's range.

"What was that?" asked Malak anxiously.

"I don't know, but it seems to be afraid of the light," said Goban. "Keep moving we don't have much time."

Malak glanced over at Chatur and swallowed hard.

"Looks like this alley's been abandoned for some time," said Tom, picking up the pace.

Avani responded, "It was probably closed off during the last troll war. They were shifting a lot of the shop district over to make wagons, tools and weapons for the war effort. Once the war ended, this whole district shut down. They've just recently started opening up some of the shops again as bakeries and textile mills. There's even a brewery."

As they hurried on, twice more they saw something skittering away into the shadows, but still weren't able to see what it was.

Tom ran over to Goban. "Have you heard any more news?"

"I heard King Dakshi sent one of his fastest messengers on horseback to his cousin King Bharat, king of the lake elves, pleading with him once again to send troops. He gave the messenger your flare-launcher. Once he's on his way back, either by himself or accompanied by the lake elven army, he's to send up a flare, when he's within range. White means they're sending help, red…" Goban left the words unspoken.

Tom knew exactly what red meant, he sighed. "Hopefully they'll send help, and soon."

"I wouldn't halt your breathing," said Goban.

Hold your breath, wondered Tom.

The alley soon ended at another fence, just like the one they'd entered from. Tom flipped the latch, raised the gate and cautiously peered out. There were sounds of intense fighting off in the distance. Tom started to crawl out but Goban pulled him back. A moment later several hundred troops dressed in full battle gear ran by. Once the thundering footsteps died down, they crawled out and ran across the street to the next fence. Once again, Tom tripped the latch and they quickly entered the alley. This alleyway was similar to the last one, so it didn't take them long to navigate their way through. When they left the second alley, they were only a couple of blocks from the Citadel.

"It's just around the corner," said Kiran excitedly. He ran off, Max still in tow tugging on the stick. The others hurried after them.

As they cleared the last corner, the round dome of the Citadel stood dark and silent to their right. There were no signs of guards so they ran to the place where the symbol on the wall matched the one on Avani's box.

"Is that the cube?" asked Tom, pointing at the grey canvas bag that

Avani carried.

By way of answer, Avani set the bag down and slid the cloth sides to the ground. The dull silver cube lay exposed before them, faint colored lights glowing from the buttons.

"Look," said Tom, pointing to the symbol on the cube. It shone with a faint golden hue.

"And that," added Goban gesturing to the matching symbol on the wall of the Citadel. It too glowed golden yellow.

"Whoa," said Malak and Chatur in unison.

Max sniffed the box.

"I think we're on the right track," said Tom. "Avani, what was that poem your dad used to tell you?"

Avani paused, concentrating.

"Add the colors of life, to point the way;

Up, up I say, the levers shall sway;

Just when you thought, the riddle be solved;

Out pops another, to test your resolve;

Of nicknames past, the key to a key;

Sweetness springs release, as known were thee."

Tom said, "Well, it's obvious the first two lines refer to the lights and levers on the box." Goban bent over and tried moving the levers. They were frozen in position.

"The second line mentions the levers. 'Up, up I say, the levers shall sway.' I bet that means the levers need to point up," reasoned Tom.

Goban frowned. "Yes, but they won't budge."

"The first line said, 'Add the colors of life, to point the way.' What could that mean?" asked Tom, thinking out loud. He paused. "Perhaps the colored buttons have something to do with releasing the levers."

Just then they heard a skittering noise, like toenails clicking over cobblestones. Tom smelled a faint odor of skunk. Avani put the cube behind her. Everyone jumped back against the wall and froze. A heartbeat later, a gremlin bolted around the corner and stopped right in front of them. It blinked, then looked Avani in the eye and smiled. Max walked up to the creature and sniffed. This time the gremlin stood still, his eyes studying Max's face, but it did not run. Instead, it leaned forward and cautiously sniffed Max back.

"Max, come," whispered Kiran, shaking the stick he still carried from the alley. Max walked over to Kiran, and sat down, his mouth open, his tongue hanging out to one side. Kiran petted him.

"Look, it's the same one that we saved the other day," said Avani, pointing to the white patch on the right side of the creature's head.

The gremlin leaned sideways, craning its neck, trying to peer around Avani at the cube.

Avani opened her mouth, glancing first at Tom, then back at the gremlin. "We can't open it. Do—you—want—to—try?"

By way of answer, the gremlin stood up and walked toward her. Avani set down the cube and stepped out of the way. The critter glanced at the others, then sat on his haunches beside the object. He craned his neck, then touched one of the levers. There was a slight spark and his tiny hand shot back. Tom remembered the small electrical current that he'd felt when he first touched the cube.

The gremlin carefully touched it again, this time leaving his hand on the first lever. He tried turning it, then moved on to the next one until he had tried them all.

"We think the levers somehow all need to face up," said Avani. The animal gazed up at her.

Malak shook his head. "You're talking to a gremlin, Avani."

She grimaced, sticking her tongue out at Malak, then turned back to the gremlin. "We also think the colored buttons may unlock the levers. The poem said:

"Add the colors of life, to point the way;

Up, up I say, the levers shall sway..."

The gremlin blinked at her a couple of times, then started pressing buttons while trying to turn the levers at the same time. Nothing happened, so he began pressing multiple buttons with his right hand, as he turned levers with his left. Abruptly the creature sped up, his tiny hands flashing with lightning speed, testing every possible combination. Suddenly one of the levers moved, pointing straight up with a firm 'click.' The gremlin paused; his sharp eyes studying the pattern of buttons he'd just been holding. For the first time, the critter looked straight at Tom, his eyes darting back and forth, as if summing him up. Finally, he winked at Tom then reached for the buttons once more. He pressed two buttons and another lever flipped upright, clicking into position. There was only one more lever.

Suddenly another trumpet blast sounded. A moment later, they heard running feet heading their way. The kids leapt back into the shadows of the Citadel's entryway. Avani grabbed the magical floating light and put it behind her, wrapping her hands tightly around it. The gremlin let out a squeal and ran off into the night.

"NO!" cried Avani, about to run after him, but Goban grabbed her arm and held her back.

An instant later row upon row of troops ran by, dressed for battle. The kids held their collective breath.

Once they'd passed by, Chatur asked, "Do you think they saw us?"

"I don't think so, they weren't looking for us, anyway," said Malak, peering cautiously around the corner. "I think they've gone."

Avani released her hands, and the light drifted back up above them. She slumped forward. "We were so close, he almost had it!"

But Goban wasn't listening to her. He was staring intently at the cube. "The two buttons he just pressed were the red and the green ones, and that released the yellow lever."

"Did you see which two buttons he pressed before, to get the first lever to move?" asked Tom.

"No," began Goban, concentrating, "but the lever that released first was the magenta one."

"Does anyone remember what color buttons the gremlin pressed to release that first lever?" Tom's eyes ratcheted from Malak, to Chatur, to Avani, to Kiran, to Max. They all shook their heads, except Max, who just drooled.

"Doesn't matter," began Tom. "I think we have enough information to solve the problem. Do they teach you guys story problems in math class here?" They all just stared at him.

"You know, like: 'Two trains leave New York at the exact same time. The first train travels at fifty miles per hour heading northeast, while the second train travels at thirty miles per hour heading south-west?" More blank stares.

"Is an hour the same as an oort?" asked Kiran.

"Yes, well sort of," said Tom.

Malak said, "What's a New York?"

"Is there an Old York?" chimed in Chatur.

"Never mind," said Tom, scowling, as he gazed intently at the cube. "We know that when he pressed the red and green buttons, he could move the yellow lever. We know when he pressed the first two buttons—we're not sure which ones—that he was able to get the magenta lever to move. We have only one lever left, that's the cyan-colored one. You guys don't know story problems, how about mixing paints?" The others glanced at each other, uncertainly.

Tom continued, "If you mix magenta and yellow paints you get red. If you add magenta to cyan you get blue. Similarly if you mix cyan and yellow you get green."

"Oh, I remember," said Goban excitedly. But then he frowned. "But—this doesn't work out right. The gremlin pressed the red and green buttons to get the yellow lever to move."

"Oh—right," said Tom. He squinted at the box and absently rubbed his chin.

Suddenly his eyes brightened. "I've got it! We've been looking at these colors like they were paint but they're lights." Tom was rewarded by more blank stares. "Mixing paints is called the subtractive color model because you're removing colors. For example, if you mix the three primary colors of paints, magenta, yellow and cyan, you get black! No color! What we need is the additive color model. With light, you're adding colors. If you add the three additive primary colors, red, blue and green, you get white, which is all colors combined." Goban furrowed his brow, concentrating. The others continued to stare at each other blankly.

"The important thing is this: with light, when you mix red and green, you get yellow. Just like here, when the gremlin pressed the red and green lighted buttons, the yellow lever released."

"Oh, I get it!" said Goban excitedly. "So all we have to do is remember what colors of light gives us magenta, when we mixed them together. Ah—red and blue?"

"Exactomundo!" cried Tom smiling. The others just stared at him, "You look like a bunch of zombies straight out of 'Shaun of the Dead'," he said. Still no reaction. Tom shook his head, then pressed the red and blue light buttons. Next he reached over and moved the magenta lever around freely. Then he brought it back, pointing straight up, and released the buttons. It clicked firmly into position once more.

"See? We only have one color lever left, cyan. So what two colors of light make up cyan?" asked Tom.

Goban just smiled. "We don't even need to know color schemes. We've already used red and green, and red and blue. The only combination left is green and blue."

"Very good, Goban! Give the dwarf a gold star," said Tom beaming. Goban glanced at Avani. She shook her head and shrugged.

Goban leaned forward and pressed the green and blue buttons. Tom slowly moved the cyan lever. When it pointed straight up, there was a satisfying "click" as it locked into position. For an instant, nothing happened, then there was a loud hiss and one side of the cube popped open. A cold mist poured forth and the lights on the cube faded. They all held their breaths as Avani cautiously reached inside the cube. A horrified look crossed her face and she screamed. Everyone jumped back.

"Just kidding," she said, smiling. The others scowled at her. Slowly she withdrew her hand, pulling out a long, cream-colored, cylindrical tube from the box. She glanced up at the star-shaped indentation in the Citadel wall. Then, turning the cylinder over slowly in her hands, she frowned.

"May I have a look?" asked Tom, holding out his hand.

Avani handed him the tube. It was surprisingly heavy and Tom nearly dropped it. Goban leaned over to have a look. Along its length were ten dials that ran clear around the tube. Each dial had letters on it; one letter per position on the dial. A straight red line ran between them, lengthwise across the whole cylinder.

"It looks like a combination lock," said Tom thoughtfully. He turned to Goban. "Are you familiar with combination locks?" Goban shook his head.

"With a combination lock, you rotate each of these dials until they line up with this line. Often times the combination is just a series of numbers, but in this case they're letters. They probably spell something—some word or name that makes sense to the owner. That's the combination that will unlock it," explained Tom.

"I think I understand," said Goban uncertainly.

"Avani, what was the rest of the poem, again?"

"Um," she began.

"Just when you thought, the riddle be solved;

Out pops another, to test your resolve;

Of nicknames past, the key to a key;

Sweetness springs release, as known were thee."

"Well, it's clear what the first two lines mean: this cylinder is the second puzzle," said Goban.

"And the next line," began Tom, "'Of nicknames past, the key to a key.' Clearly if we find the combination that opens this lock, the key to the Citadel should be inside. But what does 'Of nicknames past' mean?"

Kiran blurted out, "It's got to be a nickname for dad."

"Maybe it's a nickname your dad used to call you, Avani," offered Chatur.

Squinting sidelong at his friend, Malak said, "Uh oh, Chatur's trying to get smart on us now." Chatur punched Malak on the shoulder.

Choosing to ignore the fighting imbeciles, she replied, "I don't know, perhaps."

"Were there any nicknames you used to call your dad?" asked Tom.

"Um, Dadums, or scritchy face,"

Tom raised an eyebrow at the latter.

"What? He had a beard," said Avani, defensively.

"Well, in any case, neither of those are ten letters long. How about nicknames your dad called you?"

Avani squinted, "Um, whistle blat, prickle melon, pixy shade."

Goban glanced at Tom. They both tried hard not to crack up. Chatur and Malak didn't have as much luck. Avani scowled at them all.

Tom cleared his throat. "Ah, 'pixy shade' is ten characters long, if you count the space between the words, that is."

Goban spun one of the dials around. "There isn't a space character."

Tom tapped his cheek, thoughtfully. "That eliminates multiple-word nicknames, then."

"I've got an idea," said Kiran.

An explosion sounded. A moment later the ground shook. Off in the distance there were screams and the sounds of fighting. They all glanced at each other in horror.

Tom wiped sweat from his forehead. "Were there any other names your dad called you?"

Kiran jumped up and waved his hands. "Hey, I'm over here. I've got the solution."

"The last line of the poem," said Tom, concentrating. "'Sweetness springs release, as known were thee,' implies that the name describes something sweet."

Hurrying over, Kiran thrust a small vial in front of Tom's face.

"What's this?" asked Tom.

"It's the other vial of that invisibility potion I 'borrowed' from class the other day." Kiran glanced sidelong at his sister. She scowled but said nothing.

"So?" said Tom.

"Don't you remember when Professor Snehal had Avani put a couple drops on that rabbit?" said Kiran, sounding frustrated.

"It exposed its insides..." began Avani tentatively.

Goban's eyes lit up. "I get it! If we use just a few drops on the cylinder, it should reveal the mechanism inside. If so, we might be able to figure out what the combination is."

"Took you long enough," said Kiran smugly.

Tom grabbed the vial from Kiran and removed the stopper. "Goban, watch carefully. If I put on too much potion, it may become totally invisible before we can figure out how the mechanism works." Tom held the vial above the tube and slowly tipped it on its side. Everyone's heads tipped along with it. He put one drop on each end of the cylinder and another in the middle. A moment later the outside of the tube began to fade.

"See that bar at the bottom of the dials?" said Goban excitedly. "It looks as if it's blocking the hasp from releasing the door mechanism. The rod is resting on the inside of the dials. And look, each dial has a notch cut out of it—" Goban pointed to the notches.

"—so if we turn the cylinder so the rod is exactly at the bottom—"

Tom returned Goban's serve.

Goban volleyed back, "—and if we line up all the notches underneath the rod—"

Tom closed with, "—I bet the rod'll fall into the notches, open the hasp and unlock the door." Tom rotated the cylinder until the rod was at the bottom, resting on the inside of each dial. That put the red line squarely on top. Then Goban rotated the first dial until the notch lined up beneath the bar.

"OK, try the next one," urged Tom. Goban turned the second dial until its notch also lined up right below the bar.

"Put another drop of the potion between the other drops," said Goban.

Tom moved his hand over the cylinder and carefully put a drop on either side of the middle drop. Within moments, the rest of the "guts" became visible. "Hurry, Goban, the effect won't last much longer."

Goban began to sweat, as he quickly turned each dial until the notches lined up below the rod. When the last one was in place, sure enough, the rod dropped a small distance down, into the notches, and that was enough to release the latch. There was a tiny 'click' and the end sprung open.

Tom glanced at the dials and read, "Stinkberry?" He raised his brow and looked at Avani.

"Oh, I forgot. Nanni used to make stinkberry tarts. Ah—they're really quite sweet," explained Avani, blushing.

Tom continued to stare at her.

Avani sighed, "I loved them so much Dad used to say 'if you eat too many you'll turn into a stinkberry yourself, someday.' After that, the nickname just sort of stuck."

Tom blinked at her.

Avani's face turned totally red. "I don't wanna talk about it."

"Fine, care to do the honors?" Tom held the open cylinder toward her. "After all, you are the Keeper of the Light."

"We'll both do it," she said, holding her hands out together, palms up. Tom tipped the cylinder and a dull black, star-shaped object slid from the tube into Avani's outstretched hands. It was so dark, in fact, Tom found it hard to focus on it.

"Looks like it matches the indentation in the wall. Why don't you take this puppy for a spin?" suggested Tom, smiling.

Avani raised her eyebrows and stared at the others. Kiran glanced at Max, then back at Tom. Avani shrugged, then hurried over to the wall. Holding the black star beside the indentation, they matched perfectly.

She took a deep breath and placed the star in the indentation. Instantly a bright white light shot from the star and from the surrounding wall. Tom felt, more than heard, a soft hum that seemed to originate deep beneath their feet. A moment later, a large section of the wall just vanished. Avani leapt back, inadvertently removing the star from the wall. The light faded, from both the star and the wall, but the doorway remained open...

Chapter 22: Into the belly of the beast

"Where's Tom? You said your men would find him and bring him here!" demanded Juanita. She was dressed in a plain rough muslin jerkin, a knee-length skirt, and sandals that the king's servants had found for her. Apparently elven women didn't wear jeans. Over that she wore the same cloak she'd *borrowed* when she first arrived in Elfhaven.

The king glanced over the parapet at the war unfolding in the distance. Then he focused his gaze steadily on her. "I did as I promised. I've sent out search parties. My guards have spoken with Avani and Kiran's grandparents; he's not there but they suspect he's with their grandchildren. I'm sure he's fine. We'll find him soon."

"You realize I'm not going to rest until he's safely back in the castle," she said firmly.

King Dakshi sighed. "Understood. But you must also realize that I'm doing all I can, and as important as the safe return of your son is to you, my first priority is winning this war. If we fail at that, we'll all be dead..." His voice trailed off but his steely eyes remained fastened tightly onto hers. She nodded almost imperceptibly, so he turned to speak with his military advisors.

"Um, there's one more thing," began Juanita tentatively.

The king turned back to face her, scowling. "Yes?"

"I'm somewhat of a scholar on ancient military tactics—perhaps I could help with your war effort."

The king glanced at his advisors. He paused. "I'm sure you are, but our worlds are quite different. Our weapons are quite different. You haven't fought trolls or ogres before. You haven't used magic or fought against it before, I have. And up 'til now, I have not lost a war, and I don't intend to lose this one. Now if you please, I must get back to my battle strategy." King Dakshi whipped around and began discussing tactics with his advisors.

Juanita gazed off into the distance. At this point the battle was contained near the main gate of the outer defensive wall. The elven army held their own, but they weren't able to make much headway against the steadily swelling troll ranks.

"Sorry to interrupt again," she said, unable to stop herself. "Just give me two minutes. If you find my logic faulty, I will not say another word. I promise." She made a motion as if zipping her lips closed.

The king sighed. He and his aides, turned to face her. They did not look happy.

"Please, I promise you won't be disappointed."

The king glanced hurriedly at the battlegrounds, then said, "OK, two myntars, but please be brief, then not another word, unless I request it. Do we have an agreement?"

"We do."

"Then what tactic might you suggest, Miss War Strategist?" he said tartly. No one laughed.

Juanita cleared her throat, "Well, first off, an observation: I see that the trolls are only able to get a few soldiers through the barrier at a time, and thus they're wisely fighting near their entry point, protecting those behind, giving their comrades time to get through. I believe they will continue this tactic until their numbers have swollen sufficiently to break through your defenses."

The king glanced at his advisors, who were murmuring amongst themselves. "Go on."

She took a deep breath and pointed at their battle map. "Put a platoon here and here on each side of the troll forces. Then disrupt the trolls' strategy by having your forward guard appear to retreat. I'm betting the trolls won't be able to resist the temptation and will charge the retreating elves. When they're far enough away from the barrier you can close the door behind them by having the other two platoons rush in and cut them off. Once the trolls are completely surrounded, your forward guard can reverse direction and your archers can wipe them out. If all goes well, you should be able to repeat this tactic several times before the enemy catches on to what you're doing."

One of the king's advisors spoke, "Sire, her logic is sound. I believe her plan may work."

Several other advisors grudgingly nodded agreement. The king paused, then picked up one of the walkie-talkies that Tom had lent him. "General Kanak, are you there?" Static blared from the radio for a moment, then a voice sprang forth. "Kanak here."

He glanced sidelong at Juanita. "There's been a change of plan."

* * *

Avani slapped her hands onto her little brother's shoulders and peered deep into his eyes. "OK, Kiran, you wait here. If anything goes wrong, run for help."

Kiran stood up tall, leaned forward, and stared defiantly back at his sister. "You're not leaving me here while you guys go off on an adventure."

"Ummm—," began Malak awkwardly, "how 'bout if Chatur and I stay here on guard duty? We can shout into the Citadel if anyone comes. And if you yell for help, we'll go get some." Chatur vigorously nodded his agreement. Avani glowered at Chatur, then Malak, then back at Kiran.

Her face turned an angry red as she whirled around and stormed through the Citadel's dark doorway muttering, "Great! Kiran never does what I say, and Malak and Chatur are about as brave as a pair of baby stirblatz lizards." Goban chuckled as he sauntered past Tom, following Avani inside. Lastly, Kiran and Max entered the Citadel.

Tom stared at Malak and Chatur. They both just stared at their feet. "You were brave enough to break me out of the dungeon, but you're afraid to go into the Citadel?" Tom continued to stare, in disbelief.

206

Chatur glanced at Malak, then swallowed. "In the dungeon we knew what we were getting into. We don't know what might be waiting for us inside the Citadel."

Tom shook his head, turned and followed his friends through the entryway.

They hadn't gone far when there was a loud hum and the floor shook. Spinning around, the doorway had disappeared. Turning back, they gazed ahead into the dim light emanating from somewhere above. Deep shadows covered the walls, ceiling and floor, all of which appeared roughly chiseled out of solid rock. Just ahead the cavern floor sloped down slightly.

"Shall we go on?" asked Tom, in a hushed tone.

Avani gazed off down the passageway. "What other choice do we have?" Glancing at the others, they each slowly nodded, so she sent the magical floating light out a few feet in front of them. Max started forward but suddenly spun around, barking frantically.

Tom walked up and knelt beside him. "What is it boy, what's wrong?" Max stood at a spot just before the floor sloped away. Facing down the tunnel, he barked once more. Tom reached out and felt the floor. It was cold and hard, as he'd expected. Inching his hand forward out onto the part that sloped away—his hand suddenly went through the floor. The others gasped.

"We're trapped," said Tom.

"What do we do now?" asked Goban. "We can't go forward, and we can't go back."

"I have an idea." Avani tipped her head and relaxed her shoulders. Her muscles seemed to melt into total relaxation, yet her eyes remained sharp and focused. She opened her hands, palms upward, and began to chant, "Veritatem revelare, veritatem revelare, veritatem revelare!" At first nothing happened, then suddenly light spilled forth from the satchel containing her magic crystals and the walls, ceiling, and floor began to shimmer. An instant later, everything had changed: the walls and ceiling were now a smooth, polished metal. The floor had a narrow winding path that led forward and downward. On either side of the path a deep pit fell off out of sight below. The path itself was only about a foot wide and looked paper-thin.

Tom stood up slowly. "Avani, what did you do?"

"I figured there must be an illusion spell at work. I did a counter-spell. I made it reveal the truth."

"What do we do now?" Tom gulped, staring uneasily at the thin, narrow path.

In one smooth motion Goban unslung his battle axe from his shoulder as he knelt by the pathway and slammed the axe handle down hard onto the path. There was a loud "boom" that echoed down the hallway, but the pathway remained solid.

Goban stood once more, smiling. "Dwarves are at home in caves. I'm not afraid. I'll go first." Before the others could say a word, Goban stepped out onto the pathway. Tom gasped, but the path held. Goban glanced over his shoulder, smiled and waved, then continued on down the path as if he were just going out for an afternoon jaunt in the park.

"Elves are brave too," said Kiran, leaping onto the path before Avani could stop him.

Tom glanced at Avani and swallowed hard. Sweat began to form on his forehead.

"What's wrong?" she asked.

"I'm scared of heights."

Avani stared at him, a concerned look on her face.

Tom let out a deep breath. "For as long as I can remember, I've always been afraid of heights. When I was two years old my family went on vacation to Yellowstone National Park. One day we were at the miniature Grand Canyon of Yellowstone. Being only two, I waddled right under the guardrail and up to the edge. In my mind I can see the toes of my right foot hanging over the cliff. It was a long way down. The next thing I remember, Mom grabbed me and jerked me clear up over the guard rail and into her arms. I'm not sure if I really remember it, or if it's just because I've heard Mom tell the story so many times, but the scene is vivid in my mind."

Avani smiled and put her hand on his shoulder. "It's okay, I'll go; you and Max can wait here." Avani stepped onto the walkway.

"No—no, I'm coming." Tom took a tentative step toward the path. In so doing, his foot kicked a pebble over the edge. It hit the wall a few feet below with a resounding "tap." Tom froze, listening intently for the sound of it hitting the bottom, but it never came. Taking a deep breath he stepped out onto the path. *So far so good.* He sighed. There was a whimper behind him. Ever so slowly, Tom turned his head.

"It's okay boy; you wanna wait here?" Max barked. "If that's a no, then you'd better hurry up." Max put his head down and walked to the edge of the cliff. He sniffed the path and pawed it with his foot. Whining, he slowly stepped out onto the walkway. "That's a good boy," said Tom, as he carefully continued edging forward.

Tom had to pay attention because the path curved every so often, but after ten minutes of gut-wrenching fear, he saw that the others had safely reached a solid platform on the far side. By now, sweat was dripping off Tom's face and his hands had begun to shake. *Only twenty more feet, you can do it.* Gazing up at the others he forced a weak smile. Avani smiled back. At that moment the path made a slight angle to the left. Tom felt his right foot come down—on nothing. A panicked look crossed his face and those of his friends. Tom's arms flailed wildly. Falling, his chest hit the path but his legs and hips hung below. Desperately his hands flew out but he couldn't reach the other side of the path. Slowly he started slipping over the edge. Max darted up, grabbed his sleeve in his mouth, hunkered down, and pulled back with all he had. Though slower now, Tom kept sliding. An instant later Goban was there grabbing Tom's other arm and with a loud grunt jerked Tom back up onto the walkway. Goban leaned forward, hands on his knees, trying hard to catch his breath. For several seconds no one moved, except Max who licked Tom's face. Finally Tom pushed him away. Goban hurried back to the platform, Tom crawling slowly behind. Once there, he collapsed, arms outstretched as if trying to hug the ground. *And I was disgusted with Malak and Chatur for being afraid,* Tom chided himself.

Max trotted up to Tom and licked his face several more times. "I'm okay boy" said Tom. "Stop! You're okay; I'm okay, right Max?" Max lifted his paw. They all laughed. Tom reached up and shook Max's paw, then unsteadily got to his feet.

"The next part looks easier," said Avani, sighing as she glanced sidelong at Goban. A solid floor stretched out before them. The walls and ceiling shone soft white. "Shall we go?" she asked. They began walking.

Here the hallway widened enough for them to walk side-by-side. Tom, feeling a little giddy from surviving his ordeal, smiled. *We probably look like we're straight from the Wizard of Oz. Avani is Dorothy, Max is Toto, and Goban is the Tin Woodsman. That just leaves Kiran and me. One of us is the Scarecrow, and the other, the Cowardly Lion. But which? Probably, after my performance on the path, they'd all say I was the Cowardly Lion. Oh, well.* Tom skipped and began to sing, "We're off to see the—"

"Shhhh!" said Goban. "I think I hear something." Suddenly the floor, walls and ceiling lit up in a two-foot-wide swath. As they walked through the glowing area, another section lit up a few paces ahead of them. This pattern continued each time they crossed a new patch of floor. After a few minutes, Kiran stopped and pointed ahead. There, fifty feet in front of them, stood the entrance to a large chamber. Once there, they peered cautiously into the room.

The circular chamber had a high, domed ceiling with dim light emanating from a huge saucer, high above. High-tech instruments lined the walls, but the focal point of the room was a gigantic center console that housed several holographic displays and hundreds of multi-colored crystals sticking out of the console at odd angles. Tom wasn't sure what to make of all this strange stuff. It certainly didn't look like it had been made by elves. But what most caught his attention was a small screen off to his right with a red flashing display. From that general direction came a deep sound which quickly rose in pitch, then suddenly would drop, starting over again.

Sounds like an alarm. Tom took a couple of steps into the room and the others followed. Suddenly, beams of red light shot out in a crisscross pattern, directly in front of them. They spun around, but where the doorway had been, there was now a solid wall.

"Careful!" cried Tom. "I think the beams are lasers. If so, they're deadly." He patted his pockets. "Does anyone have something I could use to test em?"

Kiran blurted, "I've still got the stick. The one I used to play tug-of-war with Saint Bernard. Would that work?"

Tom nodded.

Kiran handed him the stick. Tom slowly stuck it out in front of them until it touched one of the red beams. A puff of smoke curled up, followed by a soft "clack" as the tip of the stick hit the floor.

"Yup, lasers. Don't touch the red beams," cautioned Tom.

Avani cupped her hands around her mouth and yelled, "Hello—is anybody there?" Tom, Goban, Kiran and Max all just stared at her.

"What?" she said. "We've gotta do something."

Presently they heard a hum, and then the sound of a door opening off to their left. A moment later, in walked an ogre in full battle armor carrying the largest axe Tom had ever seen. However, there was something strange about this ogre; Tom could see through him.

"Why have you disturbed the sanctity of the sacred Citadel?" boomed a voice from all around them.

Gasping, Avani and Kiran stepped back. Goban drew his own axe and took a small step back. Max barked ferociously as Tom held him by his collar. Tom stood his ground.

"Look," said Tom, in a matter-of-fact tone, "I can see right through you, so you're either a ghost, or a hologram. Judging from the look of this place, I'd say the latter." Tom glanced around the room. "Um—in here, I think you'd be more convincing as an Imperial Storm Trooper, though."

The crackling sound of static filled the circular room and the visage before them flickered, faded, then reappeared in full, bright white body armor, brandishing a brilliant blue laser sword.

Avani, Kiran, and Goban all leaned back.

"Impressive!" said Tom, casually taking a step forward. "But—Imperial Storm Troopers don't use light sabers. They use blasters. Jedi knights use light sabers."

"Silence!" boomed the armor clad visage. Avani and Kiran glanced at each other and shivered. But a moment later they again heard static and the image of the laser sword flickered and was replaced by that of a space pistol.

Wow, we are in the Wizard of Oz, and this guy's the crazy wizard!

Max growled. Tom glanced back at Kiran, who timidly stepped forward, grabbed Max's collar and quickly pulled him back.

Careful not to cross the line of the lasers, Tom took another step toward the image, "Hey, how is it that you know what a storm trooper looks like, anyway?"

"How is it that you know?" repeated the visage, cocking its helmet covered head.

Tom raised his brow. "I know because I'm Thomas Holland, from the planet Earth."

"Thomas Holland? From the planet Earth?"

"What are you, a parrot?" said Tom, his confidence increasing. But the scene reminded him of his mom. *She'd love this. I wish she were here to see it.* Tom blinked back an unexpected tear.

"Star Wars is my mom's favorite movie. Mine too, I guess... But once again, how do you know things about Earth?"

"I have many functions. One is to listen to voices—voices from other universes. If things seem particularly—interesting, I might even open a portal to the other world."

"You opened the portal that brought us here?" Tom's jaw fell.

"Unfortunately, the day you crossed over my power levels had dropped below the minimum required to open a portal; unless—of course—I had help from the other side."

"The detection grid!" exclaimed Tom.

"You're a bright one, aren't you." Then, as if speaking to himself, the visage murmured, "But of course he is. He's Thomas Holland, the boy from the prophecy."

"The prophecy? No one will tell me anything about it! What is it, and how am I involved?"

The visage shifted once more and took on the guise of a wise old Obi-Wan Kenobi. "These aren't the droids you're looking for. Move along, move along," said the hologram, absently waving his hand before him.

Whatever this thing is, it's completely insane. Tom paused. *I'm getting nowhere, let's try another tack.* "This is my friend Avani. Her father left her a box with a cylinder inside, and in that cylinder was a key; a key to this Citadel."

"What is your father's name, child?"

"My father's name was Pavak, Pavak Dutta," she replied.

"And where is your father now?"

"He died a year ago, during the last troll uprising."

"Pavak, dead? That explains a lot..." Instantly the laser beams vanished and the doorway reappeared. A moment later the image flickered and was replaced by that of Avani and Kiran's father.

Kiran yelled, "Dabi!" and ran toward his father's image.

"Kiran, wait!" urged Tom, but it was too late. Kiran was already there.

He tried to wrap his arms around his father but they passed right through the visage. Goban re-slung his axe across his back.

Tom gazed at Avani sadly. "I tried to warn him." A tear trickled down her cheek, the corner of her mouth began to quiver.

Tom walked over and wiped the tear from her cheek. "It's just an illusion."

"I know," she said.

Kiran ran back and hugged his sister. Avani held him tight, they both began to sob quietly. Tom averted his gaze, awkwardly shifting his weight from one foot to the other, finally focusing on the visage of their father.

When no one spoke, Tom asked, "Look, I need to get back home—to Earth—can you help me? And don't tell me you've got a hot air balloon that will do the trick."

The image flickered. "I'm sorry, but it took nearly all my power to open the last portal, even with your mother's help. I cannot open another one without a new power source."

Several seconds had passed when finally Avani stood up tall, squared her shoulders and wiped the last tears from her eyes. "The reason we're here," she began, gaining strength, "is because the barrier is failing. It may have failed altogether. The troll and ogre armies are attacking as we speak. Is the source of the barrier's magic power here in the Citadel?"

Her father's image raised its head slightly. "You are Avani Dutta? Pavak's daughter? If so, and if Pavak is truly dead, then that makes you the Keeper of the Light."

"Yes, I guess so." Avani repeated her question, "Is the source of the barrier's magic power here in the Citadel?"

"Yes and no," stated the hologram.

"Please, can you be more specific, ah—Father."

"Yes, the Citadel is the source of the barrier's power. And no, it is not magical."

"Not magical?" began Tom. "What is it then, a force field? What's

214

wrong with it? How can we fix it?"

The image raised its head to regard Tom. "The Citadel houses a machine—a machine that amplifies the magic that naturally exists in this world—in this universe. It also creates a protective barrier to keep the elven people, and the Citadel itself, safe. And yes, you could call it a force field."

"Has the barrier failed completely, then?" asked Tom.

"No, not yet. But soon, very soon."

"So what's wrong with it? Why is it failing?"

"See that display over there?" The hologram's arm gestured in the direction of the small console with the red flashing display. Tom and Goban walked over to the console, their steps echoing in the cavernous chamber.

"Yes, what is it?" Tom asked.

"That vertical bar is the readout for the main power supply's energy."

Tom frowned. "It looks empty."

"That is correct. We are now running on emergency backup power, and that is nearly depleted."

"We thought it had failed entirely, cause the elves blew the battle horn. The troops rushed off to war."

"My sensors detected a breach in the barrier, caused by some magical force. That same force is holding open a hole for trolls and ogres to pass through."

Avani's jaw dropped. "Only a wizard could wield such power."

"I thought all the wizards were dead?" said Tom.

Avani just stared blankly into space.

Tom asked, "How do we fix the power source?"

"This installation was built a thousand years ago. Its power supply was meant to last just a thousand years. Last year, a space ship was sent from the universe that built it, with a new power source, but it crash landed a hundred kiloters from here in the Icebain Mountains. I suspect evil wizardry was to blame. Your father, Pavak, intended to lead an expedition to recover the energy source, and thus restore the Citadel's power. Apparently he was killed before he had the chance."

Avani glanced from Tom to the visage. "The Icebain Mountains are at least a month's journey from here. There are high cliffs covered with ice along the way. Torrential rainfall this time of year causes rivers to overflow their banks, producing thunderous rapids and gigantic waterfalls. Not to mention the haunted forests we'd have to hike through, inhabited by ravenous beasts, magical creatures, cutthroat thieves and scheming gypsies. Oh, and did I forget to mention the ogre nation, itself? Even if we could avoid being killed on the way there, and somehow sneak past all the ogre forces, it would still be a two- to three-month journey, there and back."

"Oh, piece-a-cake then," said Tom, shaking his head.

"Perhaps the dwarves could help. Our people live closer to the Icebain Mountains," offered Goban.

"That might buy us a week or so," reasoned Avani. "But that still wouldn't be enough time."

"Maybe we could get a dragon to help us? It could fly us there," said Kiran hopefully.

The others just stared at him.

"What? I read it in a book once," he said defensively. They all continued to stare at him. Kiran looked away, not saying another word.

Tom sighed, turning back to the hologram. "What should we call you?"

"I am called—the Guardian." The image shifted once more and became that of a tall, grey-robed figure with a long beard, holding a thorny, wooden staff. "Is this more appropriate?"

Tom scratched his head. "Very nice. Your 'Gandalf the Grey' impersonation, I presume..." He stared blankly ahead. *Hmm—we need a power source. I'm stuck in a primitive culture on an alien world that hasn't invented electricity yet, let alone a power storage device. If we were back on Earth we could just use a battery charger, or get a jump from a battery.*

"That's it!" cried Tom. Now everyone stared at him.

"Chloe!" he exclaimed. They continued to stare.

Tom turned excitedly to the image. "Ah, Computer—" but he was cut off.

"I prefer—the Guardian, or just—Guardian."

"Fine, whatever." Tom grinned. "What if I could get you an almost-new, 12-volt car battery? Could we adapt it to charge your power source?"

"Manufactured on the planet Earth, I presume?"

"Yes."

"Due to the difference in the physics between the two universes, electrical energy created in your universe is 1000 times more potent than if it had been generated here. How many Amp Hours?"

"It's a 100 Amp-Hour battery."

The Guardian's voice sped up, almost too fast for Tom to understand him, "Hmm, an Earth-style battery with 100 amp hours of capacity, would be—just give me a moment—that would be—about—12 Volts times 100 amp hours equals 1200 kilowatt hours. Converting to Joules: 1200 kilowatts times 3.6 million Joules per kilowatt equals—4.32 billion joules! Taking into consideration the charging losses—that should keep the barrier up at full power for about—1.1579 months, give or take," finished the Guardian, with a giant, mock inhale of breath.

Tom spun around to face his friends. "All we hafta do is get Chloe, my robot, and bring her back here."

"And just where did you leave her?" asked Avani skeptically.

"Well, the last time I actually saw her, she was in that glade, you know—the one where you rescued me from the trolls."

"Ah—you mean the glade that's right now, as we speak, in the very heart of the enemy encampment?"

Tom cleared his throat. "Um—that would be the place." The others stared at each other in shock.

Tom asked the Guardian, "Computer, er—Guardian, on our way out, could you make that bottomless pit thingy go away, and open the front door for us? Oh and, one last thing: if we do make it back here alive, could we do without all the Indiana Jones-style trap junk next time?"

The visage grimaced and replied in a cold, dry voice, "The 'front door,' as you so—quaintly put it, will open automatically when you leave. When you return, just state your names as you enter the Citadel. Assuming they don't keep punching holes in the barrier, you have 1.25 days of power left before it collapses altogether. Good luck—and have a nice day!"

Chapter 23: A romp in the "troll" park

"Ok, to pull this off we're gonna need the prince's help," said Tom, standing outside the Citadel. He watched as Malak and Chatur ran off to warn their parents about the failing barrier.

"Are you crazy?" said Goban. "Rumor has it Devraj may be the one that set you up. In any case, you're an escaped prisoner. The prince will be obligated to turn you in."

Tom shook his head. "We have no choice. Devraj is the only one who can safely lead us through the enemy lines and back again."

Tom narrowed his eyes, thinking fast. "Avani, go find the prince and bring him to that park, the one with the dead fountain in it. You know—the one by the Library? Don't tell him you've seen me, or that I'll be there."

Avani sighed. "What with the war going on, he may have his hands full."

"Do whatever it takes, just have him there in an hour, ah—in an oort. Goban, get any information you can on where the troll forces are camped, and the location of their sentries."

Goban frowned. "The guards are probably searching for me, too. Since I was the last to see you, I'm sure they suspect I helped you escape. But hopefully they're more concerned about the war right now than on finding us. I have contacts at the castle that are loyal to me. I'll see what I can find out."

Tom nodded. "Kiran, can you take Max? Leave him with your grandparents. Oh, and warn them about the failing barrier. They'll need to get to the castle soon."

Kiran smiled and bent down to pet Max. "Come on Saint Bernard, you're coming with me."

"What'll you be doing?" asked Avani.

Tom had a strange faraway look in his eyes. "I'm going to do a little—research myself."

They all sprinted off in three different directions. Max passed Kiran and it looked as if Kiran was having trouble keeping up.

* * *

The librarian raised its spectral head from its desk. "You! Aren't you an escaped prisoner? One who's wanted for the crime of high treason, I might add."

"Um—you see—that was sort of a misunderstanding," said Tom, matter-of-factly. Glancing around the empty library, he asked, "Where is everybody?"

The ghost raised an eyebrow. "Perhaps you haven't heard, but there's a war going on. Prudent people head home, in times such as these, so that they can kiss their fat little bottoms good-bye in private. I should turn you in, you know. I could scream for help," warned the spirit, a look of mock fear in his eyes.

The librarian raised his hands and in a feeble voice cried, "Help! Help!"

Tom just stared at him. "I don't think anyone can hear you. They're all too busy fighting a war, as you pointed out. But why scream for help? Can't you just go for help? Can't you leave the library?"

The librarian raised his nose, crossed his arms and turned away slightly. "I choose—to stay here. I don't exactly—fit in, most places. Only on rare and special occasions have I been known to—venture forth from the library."

"Why not?"

The ghost scowled. "Well, if you must know, I'm actually agoraphobic."

"What?" said Tom, in disbelief.

"It means a fear of open or crowded spaces," explained the ghost condescendingly.

"I know what it means, but a ghost who's afraid? That's ridiculous. What are you afraid of, dying?"

Still looking away, the spirit raised its nose higher.

"Anyway," Tom continued on, "the reason I'm here is to ask some more questions."

The ghost didn't move or speak.

"Okay, I'm sorry," said Tom flatly. The spectral form remained silent.

"Look, I said I was sorry. What more do you want?"

"Say pretty please."

"You're joking, right?" blurted Tom, but the spirit's lips remained sealed.

Tom sighed. "Okay, *pretty please*—may I ask you some questions?"

The ghost turned back part way and raised one eyebrow.

Tom shook his head. "The Guardian said that some type of magic was creating a hole in the barrier, allowing trolls to come through. Avani said that only a wizard could wield such power. But you said earlier that all the wizards died during the War of the Wizards."

"Who is this Guardian fellow?" asked the librarian curiously.

"The Guardian lives in the Citadel and protects It, and this city."

"Is he nice?"

"What? I don't know!" spat Tom. "Come to think of it, you two have a lot in common. For one thing, I can see right through you both."

"The Guardian's a ghost, too?"

"No, he's a… Never mind. I just need to know if any wizards could have survived the War of the Wizards."

"Well, you don't have to get all snooty about it," spat the librarian. Then, idly tapping his finger on his cheek he said, "Let me think. Hmm, there was an old fairy tale I read, once upon a time. But like most fairy tales, its ending was rather Grimm."

Tom scowled. "Just tell me the story."

As before, the same faraway look appeared in the ghost's eyes. *Uh oh, I hope this isn't going to be another long, boring monologue, like last time.*

The spirit cleared its throat. "The story goes like this: on the last day of the War of the Wizards, there were only two wizards left alive. The good wizard Larraj and the evil wizard Naagesh were seen battling during a terrible storm near the edge of an enormous crevasse. Titanic blasts of green and blue magical energy lit the sky for several kiloters around. As the story goes, in the end they both tumbled over the cliff, each trying desperately to strangle the other, all the way to their death."

Tom scratched his head. "If that were true, it's not too likely either wizard survived."

"I said it was a fairy tale."

Tom turned to leave, paused, and then turned back. "How long can a wizard live, anyway?"

"On this planet the elves' and dwarves' average lifespans are about two hundred yaras. Wizards, however, with the aid of powerful potions and magical spells, can easily live five hundred yaras. There are even legends of wizards who lived to be over a thousand."

"Thanks," said Tom, stepping toward the door.

"One more thing," said the librarian.

"Yes?"

"If one of the wizards did survive, and I'm not saying he did, mind you, and if he's the one creating a hole in the barrier to let the trolls in, I'd put my money on it being the evil wizard Naagesh." The spirit laughed. "If I had any money, that is."

"Thanks again." Tom called, as he walked out the door.

"And if I could actually pick the money up..." said the librarian wistfully.

* * *

222

Hiding behind a tree in the park, Tom stretched his neck, trying to relieve the stiffness from sleeping with only a bit of straw between him and the cold hard dungeon floor.

Tom's stomach growled. *I should've asked Avani to bring me something to eat. Anything would do, anything except those foul smelling slither-toad pastries that Nadda makes.* Tom shivered just thinking about them. Glancing at his watch he wondered, *Where are they?* A minute later Goban came running up the road and across the park.

What? Goban's running, instead of his usual swagger. The guards must be looking for him, too.

Tom stepped from behind the tree. "There you are," Tom said, with mild annoyance.

"Thanks, I wondered where I was," replied Goban, panting heavily. "I wanted to talk with Avani, to make sure Prince Devraj was coming. I hid in the bushes just outside the castle's side entrance, but they didn't come out that way. I hoped they'd already be here."

"Think she's having trouble convincing Devraj to come?" asked Tom, concern in his voice.

"Don't worry. Devraj would follow Avani anywhere. They'll be here."

Tom paused, staring off down the street. "Haven't heard any sounds of war for a while."

"The troll army withdrew. The elves believe they're regrouping, waiting for the rest of the ogre army to arrive, then they'll attack full force in the morning."

Since they had to wait for the others anyway, Tom asked, "What did you learn in class, while I was—away?"

"Today we learned how to make an object float in midair. But yesterday, the day you were hauled off to the dungeon, we learned how to make someone look like something else. Kiran turned me into a gremlin."

Tom looked Goban up and down. "Too bad he couldn't turn you back."

"Very funny," rasped Goban.

Tom smiled, visualizing Goban as a gremlin. "Did you really look like one?"

"The professor said that it was all in our minds, but even I thought I was a gremlin."

"Awesome!" replied Tom. Then he changed the subject. "So did you find out anything about me?"

"At this point, you're still considered an escaped prisoner. The king's men have been searching everywhere for you. At least—they were before the war broke out."

Tom grimaced. "What else did you learn?"

"The troll armies' main base camp is set up in Elfhaven Valley. Half the ogres' forces arrived this afternoon. They're expecting the other half tonight. The trolls haven't posted many sentries, except right at the outskirts of their headquarters. I overheard a couple of palace guards say it's because the trolls are arrogant. But I think they're just stupid.

"Oh, and there's one more thing..." began Goban, watching Tom closely. "I heard that another stranger from your world arrived in Elfhaven yesterday."

"Someone from Earth? How, who?"

"I haven't confirmed the rumors, yet. I didn't actually see her for myself—"

"Her? Stop stalling and tell me who's here!"

"Ah—it's—it's your mom."

"What?" Tom sank to the ground, in shock.

"Like I said, it's just a rumor. I don't know for sure..."

Tom stared up at his friend. "No, she's here. It makes sense. Somehow I can sense she's here. But why did she wait so long? Why didn't she follow me through the portal immediately?"

Goban didn't answer.

Tom jumped to his feet. "I've gotta find her."

Goban grabbed his arm. "But the guards—you're an escaped prisoner, remember? Before you can reach her they'll just throw you in the dungeon again. Besides, we need your help! We can't find or control your machine without you, and even if we could, we'd never be able to figure out how to fix the barrier. We need you!"

Tom stared blankly at his friend. "I've got to find her. She's my mom. Don't you understand?" Goban just stared back, but at that moment they heard a noise. The two quickly hid behind a tree. Tom peered around its trunk. Avani and Devraj were heading this way. Once they were close, Tom stepped out.

"You!" spat the prince.

"Ah, did you miss me?" said Tom. "Rumor has it that you may be the one who set me up, if so, I should be mad at you." Goban stepped from behind the tree.

The prince's eyes shifted from Tom to Goban. His scowl deepened.

"Anyway, we need your help," said Tom.

The prince laughed. "Help you? It's my duty to turn you in. Besides, we're at war, I have more important things to do." Devraj glanced over at Goban. "I should turn you both in." He paused. "Why did you think I would help you, anyway?"

Tom faced Avani. "Tell him what we learned last night."

She nodded, then told the prince how they'd solved the mystery of the cube and unlocked the cylinder, finding the key within. Once they'd opened the Citadel, she skipped to the part about the Guardian, and what he'd said about their remaining time. As she spoke, Tom noticed an odd expression on Devraj's face. Was it surprise mixed with—respect?

"Tom's 'rob-it' is our only hope. The Guardian said it would buy us a months' time. Perhaps time enough to find the magical replacement power source, before the barrier fails all together."

"It's a robot," corrected Tom, "not rob-it, and her name's Chloe." As usual, no one was listening.

Chapter Twenty-Three

Still scowling, Devraj stared at each of them in turn. "So what do you want from me?"

Tom walked right up nose to nose with the prince. "You can lead us into the troll encampment, help us find Chloe, and bring us all back safely."

Devraj laughed. "Are you crazy? We're at war! Besides, you know the trouble we got in last time, going beyond the barrier after dark. This would be far worse. Before, we barely avoided being captured by six trolls. This time there would be thousands of trolls and ogres, all armed to the teeth."

"Yes, but last time they knew we were there. This time they won't suspect that anyone would be stupid enough to break into their own camp," reasoned Tom. "Besides, as you said, right now you're in hot water with your father. But if you could save the kingdom by—say—restoring the barrier, you would be a hero. Might go a long way toward finally getting some respect and admiration from your father. Hey, they may even write songs about your heroic deeds."

The prince scowled at him. "I know what you are trying to do. You think I'm vain. You think you can use my ego to get me to help you."

Tom leaned back on his heels with his thumbs in his belt. "Yup!"

The prince's jaw muscles flexed. For several long seconds, no one moved. Finally, the prince rasped, "No! You have judged me wrong. This is a fool's errand and you're nothing but a bunch of fools."

"Fine!" spat Avani angrily. "We don't need your stupid help anyway. We can do this all by ourselves."

"Avani, no!" commanded the prince. "I order you to stay. Let Tom and Goban get themselves killed. Besides, it's too dangerous for a—girl."

"What?" she shouted. "Come on guys, Devraj is obviously too scared and we don't need his help anyway." Whirling around, she strode off briskly, Goban close behind. Tom stared hard at the prince a moment longer, then turned and followed his friends.

Once out of earshot, Goban asked, "Think he'll turn us in?"

"I don't think so, he knows how important this is. But we should be on our guard," hissed Avani, her eyes still burning with anger.

"There's one small hitch—" began Tom, uncertainly. "It's my mom. I need to go find my mom."

"What?" said Avani, sounding confused. "The Guardian said there was no way you could get back to Earth. Not without finding another power source."

"His mom—," began Goban. "She followed him here. She's in the castle."

Avani's mouth fell open. She stared at Tom.

"I've gotta go to her. She'll be worried."

"But we can't do this without you," pleaded Avani. "It's your plan. It's your machine. We don't even know what it looks like, let alone where it's at and how to control it."

"I know—it's just that… We need the prince's help. It's useless without him." Tom's gaze dropped to his feet.

"We can do it without the prince. I know we can," said Avani firmly. Then her tone softened. "But we can't do it without you. Don't abandon us. Not when we need you most."

Tom took a deep breath, He glancing from Avani to Goban and back. Slowly, he let out his breath and nodded. The other two grinned ear-to-ear.

"Okay," he began, "since the battle has stopped, for the moment at least, we should be able to sneak through the enemy lines fairly easily. We just need to be back before the battle resumes in the morning. Where shall we meet?"

"How about by the east gate?" offered Goban.

"Good." Tom's eyes glanced at Avani's waist. "Where's your magic crystals?"

"At home."

"Okay, you go get em. Goban and I'll head to the east gate and scope out the situation. Have your grandparents get a message to my mom. Say I'm OK. But don't tell them where we are, or what we're doing. Mom'd just worry too much."

"I need to pick up a couple of things first," said Goban.

"OK, meet me at the east gate once you're done. Oh, and Avani?"

"Yes?"

"Could you bring me something to eat? They only served me one horrible meal a day, in the dungeon. You guys broke me out before I got to eat today. I'm starving."

Avani's eyes ballooned. "Oh, sure. I should have thought of that. I'll bring you some food."

"Great, let's meet at the east gate in—," Tom glanced at his watch, "half an oort."

* * *

Goban and Tom hide in the shadows near the east gate as Avani crept up. High above on the rampart that capped the outer shield wall, several elven sentries strode briskly by. Every so often one would peer outward, over the parapet, watching for any sign of enemy activity. Tom had timed the sentries' rounds. They went by exactly every ten minutes. It was nearly dark and a cold fog had drifted in, making it hard to see.

"Where's Kiran?" Tom asked.

"I told him it was too dangerous. So he had to stay home."

Tom raised an eyebrow.

"You don't see him here, do you?" Avani said defensively. Tom decided to let it go.

"Oh, here," she said. Reaching into her cloak she pulled out a bundle and unwrapped it. Smiling, she held the contents out to Tom. "I brought you two of those slither-toad pastries you like so much."

Tom sniffed them cautiously. "Thanks—ah—these smell—delicious." Fighting hard not to gag, he took a small bite, chewed, swallowed stiffly, then forced a smile. Gingerly, he took another tiny bite, then re-wrapped it.

Goban glanced at the sandwich wistfully, "Aren't you gonna eat that?"

Avani stood looking the other way so Tom quickly handed the pastries to Goban. Goban took a big bite, then rolled up the remainder and stuffed it in his pocket. "For later," he said, foul smelling crumbs flying from his mouth as he spoke.

Tom shivered. "I see you still have your axe. Good, we may need it."

"She's my sweetheart!" Goban lovingly patted the axe handle poking up behind his shoulder. "Her name's Aileen. She's sharp as a dwarf girl's wit, and she loves to play tag with trolls."

Avani giggled.

Tom spotted a coil of rope slung over Goban's other shoulder. "Sweet. What's the rope for?"

"We may need it to pull your machine."

"Good idea." Tom grasped the East gate's handle with his right hand and staring at the others said, "It's now or never." Smiling, he turned back and pulled. Nothing happened. He pulled again. Goban came over and they both pulled but it still didn't budge. They stared at each other. A sinking feeling came over Tom.

"It's locked," said Goban, stating the obvious.

Avani looked shocked. "They never lock this gate."

Tom sighed. "Must be cause a the war."

"What'll we do now?" she asked. "The main gate's too well-guarded. We could never get through—"

Tom grabbed Avani's arm and put his forefinger to his lips. Someone was approaching, running close along the wall. It was too dark to see who. The three shrank down into the shadows and the mist. Suddenly, Prince Devraj appeared beside them.

"I thought you weren't coming," said Tom.

"You wouldn't have a chance without me," stated Devraj flatly. Avani scowled but said nothing.

"And you wouldn't get very far without this," Prince Devraj pulled a key from his tunic.

"How did you know where we'd be?" asked Goban.

"When you left, I followed you. I overheard your conversation about meeting at the east gate. I knew the gate was locked so I went to get the key."

Tom smiled. "Great. It's almost dark, why don't we get going. First, let's head—"

"NO!" spat the prince. "If I'm coming, I'm in charge. What's more, all my decisions are final, you will follow my orders to—the—letter. Do I make myself clear?"

Avani and Goban glanced at each other, then slowly nodded.

"Completely," said Tom, the hint of a smile crossing his face. *I knew he'd show up. I was counting on it.*

"Everyone ready?" whispered Devraj, unlocking the gate with his key.

"Ready to rock 'n' roll," replied Tom. Devraj glanced at Goban uncertainly. Goban shrugged. The prince looked up at the sentries, now far down the parapet. "Okay, let's go. The guards are still heading the other way."

"Wait, what's your plan?" Goban grabbed Devraj's arm.

The prince stared at Goban's hand. Goban quickly removed it.

"My plan—is based on the fact that trolls don't like water, so there should be less trolls camped by the stream, the same stream where Avani found her magic crystals. So we will head there, then follow the creek upstream. It passes very near the clearing where we found Tom. Once there, we shall get his rob-it and bring it back here."

Tom winced. "What if something goes wrong?"

"Avani can use her magic. If that fails, I have my sword, Goban his axe."

Goban smiled and tapped his battle axe's handle. "Aileen'll get to come out and play."

Avani and Tom chuckled nervously.

Devraj stared at Tom. "Where is your weapon? You did bring a weapon with you, right?"

Tom hesitated, then reached into his belt and pulled out his Swiss army knife, flipping open the main blade.

Devraj stared at the tiny blade in amusement.

"What?" Tom held the knife so they could see. "It's multi-functional, with 33 different tools."

The prince rolled his eyes, turned and strode through the gate, followed closely by Avani and Goban.

"No really," said Tom weakly. But by then they were gone. Tom stuffed his knife in his belt and hurried to catch up.

The ground was littered with fallen troll warriors. And there were more bodies far off to their right where the wall curved toward the main gate. Prince Devraj led them in single file, choosing to walk around, rather than over, the dead soldiers. After they passed through the barrier, there were no more bodies.

Keeping low, they crept from tree to tree. The farther into the woods they ventured, the thicker the mist.

Tom swallowed hard. *The fog is probably to our advantage.*

They froze at the sound of running feet. Devraj drew his sword, Goban his axe, Tom his Swiss army knife. Crouching low, they squinted ahead through the fog. Within seconds they realized the footsteps were coming from behind. As they swiveled around, Kiran almost ran over them.

"Kiran!" hissed Avani. "I told you to stay home."

"And you thought I would obey you this time—because...?"

Chapter Twenty-Three

Avani slapped her hands on her hips, leaned forward and bared her teeth at her brother. "Kiran, you go home this instant!"

Kiran just smiled. Avani shuddered with rage, then faced the prince.

Devraj glanced from Avani to her brother. He cleared his throat. "Kiran, I agree with Avani, it's too dangerous. You should go home."

Kiran crossed his arms and scowled.

"Come on, let's go." Spat Avani angrily. "Kiran's obviously going to tag along, no matter what we say." Grimacing at her brother, she whirled around and strode briskly off. Devraj and Goban put away their weapons, then the prince ran after Avani. As Kiran walked by he smiled at Tom. Goban was close behind.

Tom sighed, folded up his knife and followed them.

A couple minutes later they came to that same brook where Avani had originally found her magic crystals. Turning right, they followed it upstream. As they rounded the first bend, Tom got a glimpse of something through the mist, on the other side of the creek, maybe thirty feet away. It appeared to be—a mist wraith. In the dark, Tom fumbled with his belt, then pulled out his infrared night goggles, flipping the power switch as he quickly slipped them on. A quiet yet satisfying hum sounded and everything took on various intensities of green.

Tom adjusted the focus. Sure enough, it was a mist wraith, like the one they'd seen the night he'd been rescued. What's more, there was a person standing beside it. Tom reached up and adjusted the resolution on his goggles. The scene jumped into bright, magnified clarity. The person wore a hood and used a hoe as a walking staff.

Someone's in trouble. But before Tom could cry out to his friends, he noticed that the hooded figure seemed to be talking to the wraith. Tom froze. As if sensing his presence, the hooded figure turned toward him. *There's a beard peeking out from under the hood of his cloak; and the hoe... It's Lorin!* Tom realized in shock. Shaking, he sprinted off after the others.

"Hey guys," whispered Tom, thrusting his goggles up onto his forehead. "Guys!"

"Quiet!" hissed Devraj.

"But I just saw—"

"Silence!" The prince shot Tom a look that could kill an ogre. Devraj spread his hand out flat and pumped his palm down twice. They all immediately crouched down low. Voices sounded from up ahead. Tom pulled out his knife, fumbling for the main blade in the dark. The voices grew louder.

"Phawta," spat a troll, "why we stand guard duty? Da Elves cowards. Dey not attack us, not wid da whole troll army here."

"Hmm, I tink you right, Fowlbreth," huffed Phawta. "Have patience doe, da wizard's magic batt'rin ram worked. First ting tomorrow, once da rest of da ogre's arrive, we punch more holes in da barrier and attack full force. Wizard say it should speed da barrier's collapse."

The trolls walked by, passing within ten feet of Tom and the others. The beasts continued talking, but their conversation soon became too faint to hear.

Devraj and Goban released their death grips on their weapons. Glancing down, Tom noticed he'd opened the spoon instead of the knife blade. Sheepishly glancing around, he quickly put it away.

"They said they would open more holes in the barrier and attack first thing in the morning. We've got to send someone back to tell my father," Devraj stared intently at Kiran.

Avani glowered at her brother. "Who would we send? We can't trust Kiran to go back, and anyway, it's too dangerous to send him alone. And we can't afford to send anyone with him to *babysit* him." He stuck out his tongue at her.

Goban added. "We may need all of us to pull this off."

Kiran grinned. "Avani's right. I'm not leaving. All the fun's still to come."

"You know we got in big trouble last time for not rushing back with vital information," stated the prince. The others stared at him.

Devraj scowled. "Ok, how about if we tell my father that we learned this information on the way back, not on the way there?"

Tom's eyes fastened hard onto the prince's. "If you lie to your father, I won't challenge you, but I won't lie to him either. If he asks me what happened, I'll tell him the truth." For several tense seconds their eyes stood locked in battle.

"Children, could we get going?" said Avani. "We have to get back before dawn, remember?"

The prince's eyes finally broke free from Tom's. To Avani, he said, "Okay. Against my better judgment we move ahead." Standing, they continued on their way.

In all the excitement with the trolls Tom had forgotten about seeing Lorin and the mist wraith. When he finally remembered, he decided he'd keep it to himself, at least for now.

They hadn't spotted any more trolls in the last ten minutes, so they were able to move fairly quickly. As the fog thickened still further, voices sounded off to their right. They slowed their pace when suddenly, out of the fog, they spotted a group of trolls huddled around a campfire. Several of those rat creatures, like the one from Tom's cell, stood roasting on sticks over the fire. The trolls passed around a large brown jug. Taking turns, each downed several gulps, rubbed the back of their rough forearms across their lips, then passed it on.

A loud, raucous conversation was going on. It was deep and guttural with lots of grunts and growls. Tom couldn't make out many of the words. They sounded like bawdy, off-color jokes, like the ones he'd heard his uncle's male friends tell late at night, when they thought he was asleep. Strangely, this made Tom realize, yet again, how much he missed his uncle; almost as much as he missed his mom...

They continued slowly onward, hunched over, past the troll camp, but soon another one appeared, also off to their right. The creek was now just to their left. There were several campfires, but none near the stream. Apparently Devraj was right about the trolls not liking water.

"How much farther?" whispered Kiran.

The prince pointed up ahead. "Almost there, only another hundred paces or so." At this point the creek veered off to their left. It would no longer provide them "safe passage."

Peering through the mist, it looked as if they would have to walk right between four troll camps, two on each side.

"We can't go that way," whispered Goban. "There's too many of em and the camps are too close together. They'll spot us for sure."

"No other choice," replied the prince, equally quiet. "We could try going way around, but we would probably be faced with the same problem at some point."

Devraj drew his sword, Goban his axe. Tom slid his night goggles back down, adjusting the focus. Devraj led the way with Goban bringing up the rear. Hunching over, where the fog was the densest, they carefully crept on. Most of the trolls were passed out, or at least enjoying themselves a little too much. They made it past the first two groups without incident, although they had to stop and drop to the ground a couple of times, when someone looked in their direction.

We're more than halfway there. Tom shivered slightly. Suddenly one of the trolls stood up and began walking straight toward them. They dropped to the ground and held their breath. The troll stopped a couple of paces away and nearly "watered" them.

"Hey, it colder den a ogre's mother out here, 'way from da fire," yelled the troll over his shoulder. The others snorted with laughter.

"If you drink less, you pee less," wheezed a voice. More hoots.

"Funny!" said the first one. "Tomorrow I kill me some elves. I need notches on my spear, for better grip."

"If you aim better, you get plenty notches," came a response. The others laughed uproariously. Pulling up his britches, the troll wandered back to the fire.

Once he'd gone, the kids rose and resumed walking. As they neared the last campfire, just off to their left, Tom stepped on a twig. It made a loud crack. They all froze.

A troll punched the one beside him and snorted, "Hey, what dat noise?"

"It notin'. Here, 'ave another swig," grunted the other as he reached up to hand his friend the jug.

The first troll pushed the bottle away, rose, and headed straight for them. The other troll just chuckled.

"Do something," hissed Tom.

Kiran grabbed a rock and threw it over the troll encampment. It landed with a heavy "thud" on the other side.

"Hey, I heard it too. It came from over der," said a voice. Several trolls jumped to their feet and grabbed their weapons, staring in the direction the "thud" had come from. The first troll slowed, but kept heading toward them.

"Avani," urged the prince. "Any time now…"

But she was already in a relaxed position, her eyes closed, her right arm resting softly across the satchel with the singing crystals inside. Suddenly, a blood-curdling scream, as if from a possessed demon, sounded from the other side of the enemy encampment. One of the trolls kicked a passed-out warrior, but he only groaned. The others raised their weapons and crept cautiously toward the sound. The troll that had been heading their way stopped, then turned and hurried back toward the noise.

"Good job," whispered the prince, nodding first to Avani, and then to her brother, "quickly now." Devraj rose and they scampered off, leaving the last camp behind. Within minutes, they were at the spot where Tom had been tied to a tree.

"Where's your pet device?" asked the prince.

Tom glanced around, trying to get his bearings in the fog and the dark. "Are you sure this is the place?"

The prince glowered, pointing to a tree in the small clearing. "That's where you were tied up."

"Oh, right," said Tom. "Then she should be just around the corner." Everyone followed as he ran through a gap in the trees.

Tom took a couple of tentative steps into the second, smaller clearing. "Okay, then, Chloe would be—right about—there," Tom's arm shot out, pointing at a tree about ten feet to his right. Striding briskly over, he stopped a few feet from the tree. "She's—she's not here..."

His eyes searched the clearing, looking for any sign of her. "I could have sworn..."

"If you've brought us this far into enemy territory, for no reason!" snarled the prince.

"Look," whispered Kiran, pointing to the ground a few paces from the tree where Tom was standing. The others gathered around.

"Strange tracks, like no animal I've ever seen," said Avani.

Tom adjusted his night goggles and blurted out excitedly, "Those aren't animal tracks. Someone dragged Chloe off in that direction. She has caterpillar tracks, but if you drag her, she'd make these two thick lines, because the motors aren't running." Devraj, Avani, and Kiran stared blankly at him, but after a moment, Goban nodded.

"All we have to do," said Tom eagerly, "is follow the tracks. They'll lead us right to where they've taken Chloe." Everyone except Kiran looked skeptical.

Kiran smiled then turned and ran off in the direction that the tracks led.

"Kiran, stop!" hissed the prince. Avani glanced at Devraj, then ran after her brother. Goban hefted his battle axe and swung it around a couple of times in a wide arc. Grinning at Devraj, he dashed off after the others.

Tom stood waiting for the prince.

"See, this is what I was talking about. No one listens to me. I'm just a lowly prince, I guess. They said they would follow my orders, but NOOOO!" The prince clenched his teeth, drew his sword and dashed off after them. Tom choked back a laugh as he fell in line behind him.

* * *

The tracks led through a dense section of woods. Soon they came to the edge of a large clearing. Several tents stood around the glade.

With Tom's night goggles he could easily see through the fog to study all the various-sized tents. They were well laid out in military precision. "This looks like a temporary command headquarters."

"I agree," whispered Goban. "What do you think, Devraj?"

The prince breathed a deep sigh. The night had gotten colder, so his breath froze immediately, drifting away in the chill night air. "I concur. The other groups were just soldiers, sitting around campfires. This is the first time we've seen actual tents."

"Look, the tracks lead to that small one over there on the right," whispered Kiran. A cluster of tents stood straight ahead. A couple of them were illuminated. Strange at this late hour. But Kiran was right. The tracks led to a smaller, darkened tent which stood just a few paces off from the biggest, well-lit one.

The prince stared straight ahead for a moment. "OK, I don't see any guards. Tom, Goban, and I will approach the tent. Once we are there, Tom and Goban will enter. I will stand guard outside. Assuming Tom's pet is in there, he and Goban will carry it here, to relative safety, and then we can figure out how to bring it back with us. Avani, you and Kiran wait here. If anyone approaches, create a diversion." The prince glanced at Tom and Goban. They both nodded.

As they began to stand, the prince put a hand on Tom's arm, stopping him. A troll wandered around the corner of the tent. He was weaving slightly and sang a strange guttural song. Tom was pretty sure the tune was way off key.

"I think he's sampled the ale a bit," said Kiran, grinning.

"I believe that's the one they call Bellchar," said Tom, removing his goggles and stashing them in his belt. "He seems to be—a little—slow."

"How can you tell it's him?" asked the prince.

"I don't know, it's that long scar above his right eye, I guess."

The prince sat back and thought for a moment. "Any ideas?"

Avani spoke, "Remember the spell we learned in class yesterday, the one where we made people believe that someone was something else?"

"Hmmm, I wasn't there that day," said Tom. "Where was I? Oh yeah, I remember! I was in the dungeon," Tom glared at the prince. The prince glared back.

Finally the prince turned to Avani. "Go on."

"I'll make Tom appear to be a troll. That should distract—Bellchar, was it? Long enough for you to sneak up behind him and club him over the head with the butt of your sword."

"You think you learned the spell well enough?" said the prince skeptically.

Avani just smiled and patted her satchel.

"OK, let's do it," said Devraj.

"Don't I have a say in this?" said Tom. "Why does it have to be me? I think Goban would make an excellent troll." Goban glowered at him in the dim light.

"Come on, let's go!" Devraj grabbed Tom by the arm and lifted him to his feet. Bellchar had stopped beside the tent, facing the other way. The prince nodded to Avani.

She relaxed. Avani seemed to be tapping into the magic quicker the more she used it. As she closed her eyes, Tom could see she was mouthing something. After waiting for several seconds, without feeling anything happening, Tom decided she must have failed. Glancing over at the others, he noticed they all had shocked looks on their faces. Tom glanced down and saw that not only did he appear to be taller, he also looked rather scaly. Rock-hard formations jutted out from his chest, arms, and legs. His clothes had also morphed into a couple of well-placed rags. In shock, Tom realized he now stood there before them—as a troll.

Unable to resist the urge, Tom leaned toward his friends and quietly said "Boo!" The others rocked back slightly but continued to stare.

"Come on," said Devraj, pulling Tom, the troll, toward the clearing. "Walk up to Bellchar and distract him. Then I'll club him over the head and knock him out. By the look of him, it won't take much."

Tom took a deep breath and as he did, his chest rose up and down in a large stony arc. *I didn't sign up for this. This wasn't in my contract.* Tom smiled. *That's what my uncle might have said, if he were in my shoes.*

Tom crept slowly toward Bellchar. Out of the corner of his eye, he could see Devraj sneaking up just beyond the trees to his right.

Breathe, calm down. I wish I'd taken those acting classes Mom tried to get me to take. Tom stopped about five feet from Bellchar. Suddenly Tom's lips fluffed up and became red and juicy. Next his chest popped out. He had stony boobs! A moment later they popped out again, even larger. Tom spun around and glared at Avani. It was hard to see, without his night goggles on, but he could've sworn she was grinning. Bellchar coughed, cinched up his belt, then turned toward Tom. Tom whipped back around, smiling warmly at Bellchar. Bellchar's rocky brow rose in surprise. Tom vamped it up, wiggling his hips.

"Huh," said Bellchar, as his dull eyes wobbled around, trying hard to focus.

Remembering a scene from a movie, Tom turned his head slightly and smiled. Batting his long eyelashes, he placed one hand on his hip and beckoned with his forefinger. "Come here, big boy."

Bellchar's eyes popped open. The troll walked right up to Tom, who kept glancing nervously over his shoulder. *Where's Devraj?*

Standing before him, Bellchar swayed slightly, then gave Tom a giant 'troll hug.' Then he planted a big, wet, slobbery kiss square on Tom's mouth. Tom's eyes blossomed and he frantically tried to push away.

"Devraj, now!" Tom tried to say, but it came out more like, "Dev—ugh ra—j, no—ugh w!" Tom struggled a moment longer, then there was a solid "thud." Bellchar released his passionate grip and gazed at Tom with an odd, faraway sort of look, then fell over sideways. Goban waved from up in a tree, directly behind Bellchar.

Avani released her spell. Tom instantly reverted back to his old self. Tom spat, wiping his mouth frantically, then coughed a couple of times. Devraj walked up, chuckling quietly.

"Why didn't you hit him?" hissed Tom, in exasperation.

"I was—savoring the moment," began the prince, but he had to cover his mouth and turn away, to keep from laughing.

Goban let go from the tree, landing with a thud. "I saw what was happening, so I came to the damsel's rescue." Goban smiled broadly. "By the way, I hit the troll with the side of my axe. If I'd killed him, they'd be alerted to our presence. This way they'll think he just passed out."

Tom spat a couple more times. "Come on, let's go." He shot first Avani, then Devraj a dirty look, then turned and stormed the last few feet to the tent where the tracks ended at the doorway. Cautiously pulling back the tent flap he peered inside. It was dark, but he could barely make out piles of swords, axes, clubs, and maces. Tom put his goggles back on. There, in the center of the tent, stood Chloe. He waved for Goban to come over. They glanced around to make sure no one else was coming. Devraj, now apparently back to his old self, walked up, turned around and held his sword across his chest, then he nodded to Tom. Slipping quietly inside the tent, he and Goban ran to his robot. Smiling, Tom knelt beside her.

"Chloe, we found you!"

"If the family reunion is over, we need to get her out of here," urged Goban.

Reluctantly Tom stood up and nodded to his friend. With one on both sides, they bent down, grabbing Chloe underneath her frame, and strained to lift her.

"Wow, she's heavy. Have you told her she should lose some weight?"

Tom wrinkled his nose at Goban. "Very funny. All these sensors make her heavy. But it's the battery, mostly. It weighs a good forty pounds all by itself." Suddenly, there was a commotion in the large, well-lit tent, just beyond the one they were in. Goban and Tom stared at each other. Tom's eyes glanced to the floor and then back up. Goban nodded and they slowly lowered Chloe to the ground. But as they did, Tom's foot caught the edge of one of the swords and it tipped and started to fall. Goban reached out and grabbed it, just before it hit the sword beside it. The two stared at each other, both afraid to breathe.

"Naagesh, took you long enough," said a guttural troll voice.

"Nice to see you, too, Sliembut. I was—delayed along the way. There were mist wraiths about. No matter, I see the magical battering ram I gave you did the trick," said the other voice, apparently Naagesh.

"Yes, it took four trolls to wield it. When it neared da barrier, it glowed bright orange. When it touch da barrier, it turned blood red. Den da barrier dissolved, for several paces around, just like you said it would," replied Sliembut. "We attack at dawn. Dis time wid several holes and wid the combined might of da troll and ogre forces, da elves'll be no more." Several trolls chuckled.

"Phawta, have da guards wake da troops. Start 'em moving toward da city. We attack at dawn," said Sliembut.

Tom heard someone rush from the tent behind them.

"Where's your—guest?" asked Naagesh.

"Um—she—escape."

No one said a word.

Tom glanced at Goban, then down at Chloe. Goban quickly placed the sword back upright, then they bent down to pick up the robot. Struggling, they slowly lifted the heavy machine. Out of the corner of his eye, Tom saw the sword start to slide sideways. It hit the blade beside it and three swords ended up falling to the floor with a clatter. The two friends stared at each other in horror.

"Did you hear something? Sounded like it came from behind the tent," said Naagesh.

"I didn't hear notin'," replied Sliembut.

"Something's going on here. I can sense it... Sliembut, have someone investigate," commanded Naagesh.

"Fowlbreth, go check it out."

Chapter 24: A little help?

Juanita climbed the last few steps of the winding stone stairway leading to the castle's parapet. A chill wind had begun to blow so she wrapped her cloak tightly around herself. Far below, fog covered the courtyard and the fields beyond, stretching clear to the outer defensive wall off to the northeast. Walking along the parapet, she stopped beside the low stone railing and gazed upward. From this height she was well above the fog, and the sky overhead was crystal clear. Stars shone brightly and the asteroid belt that formed the Ring of Turin twinkled from a million tiny points of light. *Like diamonds tossed outward by God herself. If I wasn't so worried about Tom, the view would've taken my breath away.*

Where is he? Why hasn't he shown up? I got his message saying he was all right, so I know he knows I'm here. What could be so important that he didn't immediately come to me? She walked to the end of the parapet and up the last few steps that led to the main tower. From there, she could see beyond the outer defensive wall. The forest lay shrouded in darkness. Several miles away, she could just make out hundreds of flickering points of light.

Campfires. The troll and ogre armies, waiting for morning to attack. How beautiful and deceptively peaceful the night looks. Yet what horrors will the morning bring? Her thoughts returned to her son.

Tom, where are you? Don't worry, she told herself. *He's probably just off on a make-believe adventure. Playing some elven game he's learned from his new friends. Unless he's doing something stupid. Trying to be a hero. Trying to save Elfhaven.* She shivered for a moment, then a smile slowly crept over her face. *No, Tom hasn't a brave bone in his body. He's even afraid of heights. He'd run and hide long before he'd ever do something courageous.* She stood up tall and sighed. Then she began to laugh uncontrollably. A lone tear trickled down her cheek.

A little help?

* * *

Fowlbreth threw open the tent flap and peered inside. From behind him, Prince Devraj raised his sword, ready to strike. At that same instant, Kiran threw a rock and hit the fallen Bellchar in the head.

"Owww," moaned Bellchar. Fowlbreth released the tent flap and stomped over to his comrade. Devraj slipped silently back into the woods.

"Bellchar, vut happ'n?" asked Fowlbreth, shaking his friend roughly.

Bellchar gazed above him dizzily, then his eyes rolled up into his head and he collapsed once more. Fowlbreth bent over his friend and sniffed.

"Drunk again," muttered Fowlbreth in disgust. Grabbing Bellchar's arm, he dragged him back toward the main tent.

After holding their breath for several seconds, Goban and Tom cautiously crept out from behind some crates.

"Come on, let's go," whispered Goban. Bending down, and as quietly as they could, they lifted Chloe and carried her out of the tent, awkwardly hobbling over to where Avani and Kiran waited, groaning all the way. Devraj appeared from behind the trees and followed them, his eyes sweeping the area as they went.

Carefully setting Chloe down behind a clump of trees, the others joined them.

Collectively, Tom's friends let out a long-held breath.

"We heard the trolls talking with someone named Naagesh. Apparently he's helping them," said Tom.

Avani gasped. "The evil wizard? But he's supposed to be dead. I knew it would take a wizard to create a hole in the barrier."

Goban nodded. "Apparently Naagesh gave em a magical battering ram, the one we heard the sentries talking about earlier. That's what punched the hole through the barrier, and they intend to punch more holes and attack full force at daybreak. They sent someone to wake the troops,"

"Then there is no time to lose," said the prince. "We must reach Elfhaven before they do, or the city will fall."

"Your device is too heavy for two of us to carry that far," said Goban, focusing on the task at hand.

Kiran spoke up, "I thought your robot could move on its own."

"It can, but it's loud, the trolls would hear it. Besides, it would use up too much battery power. We need all its energy to recharge the barrier."

The prince glanced around nervously. "We've got to hurry. How about tying Goban's rope on it and dragging it?"

"No, it's too heavy, the tracks are locked in position when it's not running, so we'd be fighting it all the way," said Tom.

"What about tying four ropes to it, one on each corner? Then each of us could take a rope and lift it," suggested Goban.

"Maybe…" said Tom uncertainly, but Kiran interrupted by swinging his arms vigorously. For once everyone turned toward him.

"That thing we learned in class, you know—how to make things float." No one moved. "Oh, just watch," he said in frustration. Waving his hands over Chloe, he muttered an incantation. She shook slightly, then one side of her began to rise. A moment later the other side started up, but then slowly sank back down. Beads of sweat began to form on Kiran's forehead. Tom's eyes found Avani's. She nodded, relaxed and closed her eyes. A moment later, a soft yellow glow flowed from her satchel and Chloe rose back up once more, hovering a couple of feet off the ground. She wobbled for a second, then stabilized.

"I did it!" whispered Kiran, triumph sparkling in his eyes. Tom winked at Avani. Her lip curled up into just the slightest hint of a smile.

"Quickly now, tie your rope around the thing and let's be off, before that troll comes to," urged the prince.

Goban tied a bowline knot around Chloe, and the prince hurriedly led them back the way they'd come, Chloe floating along behind.

A little help?

As they approached the same troll camps they'd gone by earlier, trolls were now awake and groggily picking up maces, spears, shields and clubs, throwing some over their shoulders while tying others around their waists. A few stomped out still smoldering campfires. Luckily the trolls were making quite a racket. Even so, twice the kids had to suddenly drop to the ground as a troll thundered by. A few moments later another troll ran toward them. Tom and Goban pulled Chloe down, once more. This time her mast, holding up the platform with the sensors and LEDs, stuck up slightly above the mist. She was sure to be spotted. The troll was heading straight for them. Panicked looks crossed their faces. At the last moment, Kiran threw his cloak over Chloe and the troll ran right by. Tom and Goban stared at each other, swallowing hard.

Taking off once more, Devraj frantically picked up the pace with Tom in the rear, pulling Chloe behind him. With Kiran's cloak still over her, she looked like ET bobbing and weaving, side to side, as she floated along. Soon they neared the relative safety of the stream. But the closer they got to the barrier, the more trolls they encountered. Each time trolls ran by they had to stop and duck down into the mist, and there were more trolls every minute. To make matters worse, the forest was very dense at this point and each time Tom got too close to a tree, the twigs would wrap themselves firmly around his arm, so he had to stop and jerk his arm free. The others seemed to shake off the twigs almost without noticing them. Tom shuddered.

Even with Devraj's near-panicked retreat, because of these delays, it took them almost an hour to get back to the edge of the forest. Hundreds of trolls were now assembled off to their right, near the main gate, and more were arriving every minute. Dozens of ogres stood directly in front of them, blocking their way to the east gate. The enemy army seemed eager to fight.

"What do we do now?" asked Kiran nervously.

"I don't know. We're trapped," said Devraj, his shoulders slumping forward. For the first time ever, Tom saw a look of despair in the prince's eyes.

"Is there another way in?" asked Tom.

Devraj hesitated. "All the gates will be locked. I only brought a key for the east gate."

There was a moment of awkward silence. Suddenly the first rays of sunshine began to filter through the trees, causing the fog to swirl and start to evaporate.

Goban frowned at Devraj. He grabbed his battle axe and swung it off his shoulder. "Well, we've got to do something. The fog's lifting; it'll be daylight soon and the battle's about to begin. Come on, there's fewer trolls to our left. Maybe one of the other gates will be open or perhaps we can sneak through the barrier and call for help." Hunching over, Goban hurried off to their left, running parallel to the wall. Kiran and Avani ran after him. Devraj slowly raised his head and met Tom's eyes.

This isn't like Devraj. "Come on, let's go," urged Tom. Slowly Devraj nodded. Tom ran off after the others, pulling Chloe behind him. Devraj drew his sword, took a deep breath, then followed.

They ran for several minutes, till they found a break in the enemy lines. Goban took advantage of the situation to cross through the barrier. They hurried along the shield wall for several minutes. More and more rays of sunlight broke through, lighting up the ground around them, causing the fog to completely disappear. Suddenly they came to a corner in the outer defensive wall. Around the corner a large pile of stones were mounded up against the wall. Behind the stones, they could just make out the outline of a tiny door.

"What's that?" asked Goban.

"For thousands of years, wood sprites used to trade with our people. In the early days, an elven king built a special entrance for them, more to honor them than anything. It requires special fairy magic to open the door. When the magic started weakening the wood sprites left, moving high up into the mountains. No one's seen one in at least a hundred years," answered Prince Devraj dully.

At that moment the barrier flickered. Battle cries rang out, followed immediately by the sound of intense fighting. A few seconds later, the barrier flickered again. The sounds of fighting grew nearer.

"They're punching holes in the barrier. The battle's begun," cried Avani.

Goban began tossing rocks like mad. "What are you waiting for, come on, help me clear these rocks." Everyone except Devraj ran over, stooped down and began frantically throwing rocks left and right.

"Devraj, get yer sorry elven hide over here and help us!" screamed Goban. But the prince didn't move.

Suddenly a group of ogres ran up, cursed, then swung their massive clubs. Just before the weapons smashed into them there was a loud "whomp" and blue sparks flew in every direction, lighting up the forest around them and sending the beast's clubs flying backwards with tremendous force. The creatures screamed once more.

"The ogres have found us!" cried Kiran.

By now most of the stones were gone. Goban grabbed the ancient gnarled bone handle and pushed, but nothing happened. He slammed his shoulder against the door. "Come on, don't just stand there, help me."

This is strange. Tom turned around slowly. *It's like a déjà vu. Like I've been here before...*

The others ran up and began pushing frantically on the door.

"Tom, not you, too? Help us!" cried Goban in frustration.

"Goban, This is weird. I've been here before—in a dream. At least I thought it was a dream. And you were all here with me. It's happening just like before..."

"Well you're not dreaming now. Help!" yelled Goban.

Tom shook his head then ran over and helped push, but the door still wouldn't budge.

Devraj spoke flatly, "It's no use. I told you. It's sealed with fairy magic."

The ogres beat their clubs on the barrier and yelled to their comrades.

The prince turned to face the ogres, squared his shoulders, pointed his sword at the nearest one, and let out a long, deep sigh.

"Avani, try your magic," screamed Goban.

"I'll try, Goban." Lowering her head and relaxing her shoulders, a familiar glow sprang forth from her satchel.

The ogres screamed once more. A moment later several trolls rushed up holding a strange blunt rod. The troll's eyes, though dark as night, seethed with anger. The rod they were carrying had skulls for handles and slowly pulsed with a dark orange glow.

"Hurry, Avani. The trolls have arrived and they've got the magic battering ram. It's only a matter of time 'til they break through the barrier," urged Goban.

She chanted something beneath her breath, sweat forming on her brow. The light from the satchel glowed brighter, tendrils of magical energy arced and twisted, then reached out and touched the door, but still the door stood fast.

Trolls slammed the battering ram against the barrier, causing it to flicker once more. There was a crackling, sizzling sound, accompanied by a bitter smelling smoke that burned Tom's eyes and nose. The spot where the sinister device touched the barrier began to glow a deep blood-red. The barrier was steadily being melted away.

Glancing back at the trolls, Tom tipped his head sideways and squinted. *There's someone—a hooded figure, behind the trolls, hiding in the shadows...* Tom took a couple of steps toward the barrier, trying to get a better look.

Suddenly there was a crackling sound behind him. Turning, he saw the door glowing brightly. A moment later it swung violently inward with a loud creak. The glow faded. Tom spun around but the hooded figure was gone. However, there was a rippling, like a mirage ahead of him, outlining a small hole in the barrier directly in front of him. Suddenly a huge green ogre arm reached through the now-smoking hole and grabbed him by the throat. The ogre began to squeeze. Tom frantically tried to pull the arm off him but the beast was too strong. Tom grew weak. His vision began to fade. Suddenly a sword lashed out at the ogre's arm. The beast let out a terrible scream and released his death-grip on Tom's throat. Tom gasped for air as he glanced over at Devraj, still holding his bloody sword before him. The prince nodded slightly, his eyes now clear.

Goban helped Avani to her feet saying, "Nice job, Avani!"

She looked shaken. "I didn't do it. At least—I don't think I did."

"Go, go, go!" cried Goban, pushing her toward the doorway. She scrambled through the tiny opening, followed immediately by Kiran.

"Come on," yelled Goban to Tom and the prince. Tom grabbed Chloe's rope and pulled her through, with no room to spare.

Then Goban ran for the doorway himself. He got part way in, but he couldn't make it and had to back up. Taking off his axe, he tossed it through the opening. Then he stepped back and launched himself head first, arms forward, like Superman, and he got stuck halfway through. Tom and Kiran scrambled back, grabbed Goban's arms and pulled desperately. From behind Prince Devraj walked up, raised his foot high and kicked Goban firmly on his backside. Goban catapulted out of the doorway, landing squarely on top of Tom. Devraj leapt through the doorway just as the first trolls and ogres rushed through the barrier. Running to the tiny opening, the beasts stuck their spears through, but couldn't reach them. The beasts screamed with frustration.

Goban picked himself up, then easily pulled Tom to his feet. Tom gasped, trying to recover from having the wind just knocked out of him. They hurried away from the open door, and the angry trolls. Kiran retrieved his cloak from Chloe, threw it around himself and shivered.

A moment later Devraj ran up. Glancing first at Tom, then at Goban, the prince said, "I'm sorry."

Goban stared at him for an instant, then said, "Sorry for what?" Devraj slowly smiled, then nodded his thanks. The prince turned and dashed off toward the castle, the others hurrying behind. Tom took one more deep breath, then ran after them.

"Shouldn't we try to close the door?" asked Avani, as they ran.

"It's too small for trolls or ogres to get through," Devraj shouted over his shoulder. "Besides, there isn't time."

Pride beamed brightly in Kiran eyes as he addressed his sister. "That was awesome, Avani! You opened the door right at the last myntar."

Still looking shaken, she replied, "I—I don't think it was me..."

"I thought I saw someone standing in the shadows," rasped Tom, still trying to catch his breath, "behind the trolls, just before the door opened. But when I looked back, no one was there."

"Say, what happened to you back there?" asked Goban. "You looked like you'd seen a ghost."

"I don't know. It was like I was reliving a scene from my past, or like I was watching myself from afar. Somehow I knew what would happen next, but I couldn't change it." Tom shook his head. "I can't really describe it."

Devraj slowed, then stopped, allowing the others to catch up. "Ok, I will go tell my father what we have learned."

"Be sure to tell him about Naagesh" blurted Tom, "and the magical battering ram. And don't forget to tell him about our plans to recharge the barrier."

Devraj grimaced, "Yes, yes, I will. Look, it will be fastest if we split up. Tom you take your machine and go directly to the Citadel. Avani, you and Kiran run home and get the key, then meet Tom there." Staring directly at Tom, Devraj continued, "Start recharging the barrier as soon as possible. Goban, you come with me. It'll be best if Father hears this tale from the two of us."

"What about our punishment? We're supposed to be at the stables at four in the morning," asked Kiran.

The prince gave a thin smile. "Don't worry, my father will be too busy with the war, and besides, when he hears what we have learned and what we have done—well, if we can fix the barrier, let's just say, we won't have to do any more chores for a while."

Kiran grinned.

"What about me?" asked Tom. "I'm still an escaped prisoner. One wanted for treason, remember?"

The prince paused, staring hard at Tom. "I will see what I can do to get the charges dropped." He turned to the others. "Good luck, all. The fate of Elfhaven rests in your hands. You must get the barrier's magic recharged, before the trolls destroy the city."

Devraj's eyes fell on Tom once more. They stared at each other for several long seconds. Finally, the prince gave him a tiny nod. Tom, his eyes still firmly fixed on Devraj, nodded back.

Chapter 25: One for all and all for war

"Your tactic worked well," said King Dakshi, glancing at Juanita. "Three times the trolls fell for our little trap. But the battle has now escalated. I fear the time for subtle tactics has passed. We must use all our might to hold back the enemy forces."

From where she stood, beside the king on the castle's main turret, Juanita could see the barrier flicker in the distance. A moment later, it flickered again. She nodded absently. "Still no word from Tom? Can you send more guards to search for him?"

"Just the message from Avani's grandparents, saying he was all right." The king sighed. "I'm sorry, but I can't afford to send any more guards. At this point I need every soldier I've got." His eyes met hers, lingered a moment, then his gaze shifted to the battlefield.

"Then I must go search for him myself."

"I understand." King Dakshi gazed at her once more, his eyes scanning her face as if to memorize every feature of it. Juanita turned to go.

"Thanks, Juanita Holland. Thanks and good luck."

She gave the king a thin smile, then ran off down the stairs, taking them two at a time.

* * *

The sun now fully up over the horizon, three separate holes had breached the barrier. Several hundred trolls had managed to rush through so far, and the number was rising.

"Tom!" yelled Goban, running across the courtyard, with a new crossbow in his hands and a big smile on his face. "Look, the first crossbows, they arrived last night, while we were out on our treasure hunt." Goban slowed, then stopped beside his friend, breathing hard.

"So I see," Tom began. "I'm shocked! You're running in public again. Whatever will your fans think?"

Goban glanced around sheepishly, "No one's about. Don't tell anyone, promise?"

Tom chuckled, then stared at the device in Goban's hands. "Hey, that's similar to my idea of having two crossbows on a single beam."

"I improved upon your idea," said Goban, beaming. "Instead of them being side by side, I had the builders put one on top of the other. This way it's more compact."

"Sweet!" said Tom.

Goban glanced around. "Where's Avani and Kiran?"

"I went to the Citadel but they weren't there. I left Chloe and ran back to find you. Say—I thought once the crossbows arrived, you were supposed to leave with the dwarves that delivered them, supposed to go home, weren't you?"

"Yeah, but it's kind of too late, what with the war having already started and all. Besides, the trolls aren't officially at war with the dwarves, not yet anyway, though I wouldn't put it past them to kill us if we tried to leave Elfhaven. Anyway, I told my father's men I had to train the elven archers on the new crossbows and I said you needed my help recharging the barrier. Then, just for good measure, I took off running before they could say no." Goban winked.

"Well, I can always use your help. But won't your dad be royally pissed?"

"Royally pissed, that's a good one!" Goban slapped Tom heartily on the back, then stared down at his feet. "Probably."

Tom studied his friend's face intently for a moment, then they both smiled. "How many crossbows do we have? Where are they?"

Goban patted the one he held. "I was only expecting a handful, but the dwarf smiths worked night and day. They delivered a hundred. I showed Devraj how to use em. His father put him in charge of a whole battery of archers. He's off training em, as we speak."

Tom's eyes widened. "Wow, has Devraj ever led soldiers into battle before?"

"Nah. Guess his father feels he needs the experience. Or maybe he's testing him."

"Do ya know if the king is angry with us for—" Suddenly, many deep-throated horns blared forth from the castle's main tower.

"What's happening?" asked Tom.

"Probably another hole in the barrier."

Tom winced. "If this continues, the barrier's going to collapse before we can recharge the power supply. Come on, we've gotta get into the Citadel." He turned and ran.

* * *

Once Juanita cleared the stairs, she picked up speed, sprinting toward the main gate. As she bolted through the central square she found it in turmoil. Townsfolk ran into the castle, bringing what few precious belongings they could carry. Guards dashed to and fro, many of them heading from the armory back to the battlefield.

Rapidly scanning the area around her she spotted a stack of long poles propped against the wall to her left. Picking up the nearest one she hefted it for balance, sighted down its length, and ran her hand across its smooth surface. With a grim look of determination on her face she wove her way through the mad onrush of townsfolk and out the castle gate, her staff pointed straight ahead, balanced perfectly on her shoulder.

* * *

By now the morning sun cast deep shadows around all the buildings as Tom, followed closely behind by Goban, ran around the last corner and up to the Citadel's entryway. Avani, Kiran, and Max stood waiting for them. Avani held Chloe's rope as the robot hovered beside her.

"Hurry, open the Citadel," urged Tom, "we're out of time!"

"What's wrong?" asked Avani worriedly. "What else has happened?"

"The trolls are opening more holes in the barrier. It's gonna collapse at any moment. Come on, open the door!"

Her face as white as a ghost, Avani ran to the wall and placed the key in the indentation. The doorway hummed open as before. Upon entering the Citadel, they called out their names, as the Guardian had instructed. The lights flickered twice, then one by one, they slowly lit up down the hallway.

Tom grabbed Chloe's rope and took off running. As the Guardian promised, there were no bottomless pits, lasers, or other hidden dangers that might cause their untimely death. Within moments, they sprinted into the control room and came to an abrupt stop.

"We're back," yelled Tom, impatiently pacing around the room. A second later, the Guardian's image appeared before them, this time looking more like Friar Tuck from Robin Hood.

"Ah, I'm glad to see you're back. To be honest, I didn't expect to ever see you again."

"We've gotta hurry," cried Tom. "The enemy has some kind of magical battering ram, and it's punching holes in the barrier."

"Yes, I know. My sensors detected the disturbances. It's requiring precious extra power to try and repair the damage. If this continues, the barrier will collapse at any moment."

"Quick, let's start charging the power supply. That'll keep it from collapsing, right?" blurted Tom.

The Guardian leaned toward them and his face changed to that of a kindly old schoolteacher, smile wrinkles surrounding his sparkling eyes. "I am afraid not. We cannot charge the same power cell that the system is using. Currently it is running off the tiny backup cell. We will need to charge the main power unit. Once it's charged, with whatever power we can quickly extract from your battery, we will need to switch from the backup cell to the main unit."

"Can we hot-swap it, ah—switch it over instantly?" Tom asked.

The Guardian shook his head sadly. "I'm afraid that won't work either. No, we must shut the whole system down, then reboot."

"Reboot!" cried Tom. "How long will that take?"

"Ten myntars," stated the Guardian.

"Ten myntars!" exclaimed Avani, horrified. "You mean the barrier will be down and we'll be totally defenseless for ten myntars?"

"How long will it take to charge the main power source?" asked Tom, shaking his head.

"Approximately one Earth hour, if your battery is indeed fully charged, and assuming my calculations are correct, which they always are, of course."

Tom gave a deep sigh. "OK, let's get started. Avani, ah—Kiran, could you set Chloe down please?" Tom glanced at Avani and she nodded almost imperceptibly. Facing the robot, Kiran scratched his head, then began waving his arms over Chloe. Slowly she settled to the floor. Kiran beamed at the others. Avani winked at Tom.

Next, the Guardian told them where to find some cables in a cabinet against the far wall. Tom ran over, threw open the cabinet doors, and removed the cables. They had giant metal clips on one end, like jumper cables, but the other ends had strange connectors on them. With a wave from the Guardian's hand, which was probably just for show, an access panel opened on the right side of the main console. Tom dashed over to the exposed panel. Pulling his robot's controller from his belt, he pointed it at Chloe, and fired her up.

Once her diagnostics had completed, Chloe's platform rotated until her LEDs faced Tom, as if watching him. She made a cheerful chirp.

Tom glanced at his friends. *That was weird. I didn't command Chloe to do that.... Could the magic be affecting her?* A bit shaken, he maneuvered Chloe beside the console's access panel, then turned her off, setting the controller down beside her.

From his belt, Tom pulled out a screwdriver and opened the side cover on his robot, exposing the battery.

"Do I need to remove the battery from Chloe first?" asked Tom.

The Guardian's voice resonated all around them. "No, we can charge it from there. Just clip the red lead onto your battery's positive terminal, and the black one onto the negative. Then, on the other end of the cable, there are two small connectors. One is triangular, the other square. Can you see them?"

"Of course," shouted Tom.

"Patience, we must do this carefully, or it could blow the whole system."

"Okay, just get on with it, will ya?" huffed Tom. Avani stared at him strangely.

"These connectors have powerful magnetic couplers in them. Line the triangular one up first. Slowly, *carefully*, move it toward the matching triangular indentation on the panel. Use both hands, the magnets are very strong. And, whatever you do, do not let the connector short across the two terminals!"

Tom set down the square-shaped connector and, using both hands, grabbed the triangular one. Trying to match the indent in the panel, he lined it up so that one peak pointed straight up. He moved it slowly forward. At about six inches from the panel, the cable jerked out of his hands and into the socket.

"Careful!" scolded the Guardian. "I told you the magnets were strong. If that had shorted across both terminals you could have destroyed the power source, possibly taking the whole Citadel and more importantly, *ME*—with it!" The Guardian pretended to exhale deeply. "Okay, try the next one, only THIS TIME, hold on tight!"

Chapter Twenty-Five

"Now you tell me!" sighed Tom, beads of sweat rolling down his forehead. Absently wiping off the sweat with his left hand, he picked up the remaining wire with his right. Tom sat down carefully, this time placing his feet on either side of the panel. Then he grabbed the wire with both hands, just behind the square connector. Bending his knees, he slowly inched himself forward, one cheek at a time. Taking a last deep breath he extended his arms until he felt a slight tug on the cable. Leaning back, he tightened his muscles and allowed his arms to move forward, slightly. Suddenly his arms went taut. Strain evident on his face, his hands began to shake.

"You can do it!" yelled Kiran. Max barked. Avani and Goban held their breath.

Tom bent his knees a little more and leaned farther back. The wire started whipping wildly back and forth, getting dangerously close to the triangular connector.

"No!" cried the three of them, in unison. Goban leapt forward and grabbed Tom's hand. Together they stopped it from whipping around, then slowly moved it away from the triangular connector and toward the square one. When it was about three inches directly in front of the receptacle, they couldn't hold it any longer, and the wire flew from their hands, snapping into place. No one moved.

"Well, is it working?" gasped Tom, finally remembering to breathe.

For a moment, there was no response, then the Guardian said, "Connection is positive, current flow at optimum." Everyone cheered.

"It appears as if your energy source is compatible, and it is indeed fully charged. I'm afraid your battery cannot transfer energy as quickly as I'd hoped, though. Your battery technology is quite primitive. I must limit the current flow to prevent your battery from overheating. The process will take about three Earth hours."

"Three hours! We don't have three hours," cried Tom.

"I can push it and extract exactly 92% of the available energy in just under an hour, but the battery might be damaged."

"Would that be enough to bring the barrier up at full strength?"

"Yes."

"Fine," said Tom. "Go for it!"

"Wait for our signal before you—ah, re-shoe…" said Avani.

"Reboot," corrected Tom.

"Ah—right. Wait for our signal before you—reboot." She turned to the others. "We need to inform Devraj and his father, so they know how long this will take, and that the barrier will be completely down for ten myntars while it reboots."

Goban and Tom nodded. Kiran glanced up from petting Max.

"Okay," began Tom hurriedly, "Avani, you, Kiran and Max go search for the prince. Let him know what we've learned. Goban and I will try to find the king. I don't know if the guards will let me near him, but Goban should be able to speak to him."

* * *

"There, up on the tower." Goban pointed upward, toward the east tower. By this time the two had climbed a back stairway on the curtain wall, and were walking along the rampart. A low stone railing stuck up on either side of them, even so Tom felt queasy. From there they could see all the way to the city's main fortifications. Tom shifted his gaze to where Goban pointed.

"I see several palace guards. I don't see my mom—oh, but I just got a glimpse of the king," agreed Tom. "How do we get up there?"

"Follow me." Goban took off running along the rampart. Tom nervously tried to keep up.

The tower was round and located on the castle's far corner. They sprinted toward the tower then into a tunnel which ran straight through it. On the other side stood a narrow stone staircase which curved,

261

winding around the outside of the tower, all the way to the top. There were no rails on the stairway. Tom edged up slowly, hugging the inside wall, trying not to look down. As they neared the top, several guards, facing the other way, blocked the way forward.

Glancing down at the sheer drop-off beside him Tom swallowed hard then slowly leaned out beyond the step, craning his neck around the round tower, trying to see the battlefield in the distance. Suddenly his foot slipped on the slick well-worn step. Tom began to flail wildly, but just before he plunged to his death Goban grabbed his arm and pulled him back.

Goban frowned. "You're starting to make a habit of this."

Tom let out a huge sigh then gave Goban a sheepish grin. "Thanks," he said. Grabbing Goban's arm firmly for support he took a deep breath and leaned back out once more. Off in the distance he could just make out a ferocious battle scene, beyond the city's main gates. Even at this distance, Tom could hear the battle cries of the triumphant, and the screams of the fallen. Occasionally, he could even hear the faint clicks of sword against sword and sword against mace.

Standing back upright he shuddered, then stared up toward the top of the stairs.

At that moment one of the guards turned around. It was Sanuu. His eyes narrowed and his jaw tightened as he reached out and grabbed Tom by his hoodie.

"You!" spat Sanuu. "The traitor!"

"We've gotta speak to the king, it's urgent," said Goban.

Sanuu's scowl deepened. "Not before this one's thrown back in the dungeon."

Goban raised himself up tall—well, as tall as any twelve-year-old dwarf lad could, and scowled back. His voice rang out, "I am Prince Goban, heir to the throne of the sovereign nation of the dwarves. Prince Devraj assured us that all charges would be dropped. And this news is urgent!"

Sanuu, caught somewhat off-guard by this unusual display from Goban, glanced uneasily over his shoulder up at the king. "Ah—I'm sorry Prince Goban, but as you are undoubtedly aware, the king is rather busy right now."

"But the barrier's about to collapse, there isn't much time!" pleaded Goban.

"If you give me the information, I promise I will pass it on to the king at the next opportune moment."

Tom could hear the king speaking to his military advisors above him.

"We're sustaining heavy losses," said an aide. "For each troll we kill, we're losing three elven warriors. The results are only slightly better against the ogre troops."

"Do we know for sure that it was Naagesh who gave the enemy the magical battering ram?"

"No, your Highness. But if Naagesh is truly alive, and helping our enemies, we may not survive this war…"

Sanuu scowled once more at Tom, then called to his guards, "Take this traitor to the dungeon." Sanuu glanced suspiciously at Goban. "And make sure he doesn't escape this time." Two guards stepped down on either side of Tom but before they could grab him, Tom cupped his hands around his mouth, and yelled, "What about the prophecy of Elfhaven, King Dakshi?" Everyone fell silent. A moment later, footsteps slapped the flagstones of the tower floor above. Then the king appeared, gazing down at them. For what seemed like an eternity, no one spoke or moved.

Finally, the king said, "Send them up, Sanuu."

"Where's my mother? What've you done with her?" demanded Tom.

"Like mother, like son," muttered the king, with a hint of a smile. "She's fine, at least she was the last time I saw her. However, I'm afraid she went out onto the battlefield, looking for you."

The king gazed deeply into Tom's eyes. "You know of the prophecy?"

263

"Well, not exactly, sire—ah—people mention it when they first meet me, but no one'll tell me what it means. I know it somehow involves me, though." Tom swallowed hard and stared at the king. King Dakshi, however, seemed lost in thought, so Tom hurried on, "But that's not important right now. What is important is that we're recharging the barrier's power supply. In less than an oort it will be charged and ready to repel the attacking army completely. However—there's one small hitch."

"Go on," said the king, his attention now riveted on Tom.

"To switch to the new power source, I have to turn off the barrier and reboot it. That'll mean the barrier will be completely down for ten myntars."

The king rose to his full height. His gaze drifted to the battle scene, off in the distance. Letting out a deep sigh, he asked, "And when the barrier comes back up, will it be as strong as it was in years past?"

"It will, your Highness."

The king faced them once more. "Thank you Tom, Goban. I will send a messenger when I'm ready for you to—ah—reboot, was it? Wait for my messenger outside the Citadel."

Turning to Sanuu, the king said, "Sanuu, I should have told you sooner. Tom is not the traitor. He is hereby pardoned. Give him any aid he may require."

Sanuu raised his brow but said nothing.

"Oh, and your Highness?"

"Yes, Tom?"

"If you see my mom, tell her I've gone to the Citadel and I'll be right back once the barrier's restored."

The king nodded, then faced his advisors. "Prepare the men to retreat inside the castle. Fortify the castle's gates and have archers man the forward ramparts. Send word to my son to move his crossbow brigade to a spot just east of the main gate, to protect the army's retreat. Just before I send Tom the signal to restart the barrier, I'll give you the go-ahead to bring the troops back inside the castle. Spread the word. Have the troops ready and, oh—send a few criers around immediately. Make sure all the townsfolk are safely inside the castle." Sanuu glanced at Tom as he dashed past, followed quickly by several more guards.

Tom grabbed Goban. "I need Avani's key to the Citadel. See if you can find her and Kiran. Tell em what's going on. I'll meet you all at the Citadel." Goban nodded and ran off down the stairs; Tom took a deep breath, then followed, leaning against the turret wall, slowly taking one step at a time.

* * *

The hour is nearly up and still no sign of Goban or Avani. I can't get into the Citadel without her key. Tom glanced anxiously at his watch. He'd been waiting outside the Citadel's entrance for the last fifteen minutes. Pacing back and forth, he glanced down the street for the hundredth time. A moment later he heard running footsteps. Suddenly Sanuu came bursting around the corner. He slowed, then stopped beside Tom.

"Where are the others?" asked Sanuu.

"I sent Goban to find Avani, but they're still not here."

"I saw Goban speaking with Prince Devraj. His troops are stationed near the main gate. About a hundred trolls managed to scale the city's outer wall. There's heavy fighting going on. I haven't seen Avani."

"Thanks," said Tom. "Any news from King Dakshi?"

"Yes, the king said to reset the barrier in fifteen myntars. He will call a full retreat to the castle, just before then."

"Okay, but I hafta find Avani. She's got the key to the Citadel."

"I'll see if I can find her. Good luck." Sanuu whipped around and sped off, running back the way he'd come.

Five minutes passed when Avani finally ran around the corner.

"Sorry," she croaked, bending over to catch her breath. "Sanuu found Kiran and me. We hadn't found Devraj, yet."

"Goban must not have found you either?" said Tom. Avani shook her head.

"Where's Kiran and Max?"

"Sanuu is taking them to Devraj."

"Good. Quick, open the Citadel." Tom glanced at his watch. "We've less than ten minutes." Still gasping for breath, Avani handed Tom the key.

Opening the door, they ran through, yelled their names, and took off running down the hallway at full speed. The lights flickered on, slower this time, and they were running so fast, the lights had trouble keeping up with them. When they reached the Citadel's control room, the Guardian stood waiting for them.

"OK," began Tom, breathing heavily. "Is the primary power source fully charged?"

"I have extracted 92% of the energy from your battery. As you said, we don't have time to extract the rest. Please remove the charging cables. The reboot process could cause a power surge back into your robot, possibly exploding her battery."

Still gasping for breath Tom ran over, disconnected the cables, and quickly screwed Chloe's access panel back on.

"Do ya have enough charge to bring up the barrier at full power?" wheezed Tom, tightening Chloe's last screw.

"We do," confirmed the Guardian.

"Excellent! Then reboot in exactly—" Tom glanced at his watch once more, "nine minutes' time."

"Earth minutes or Elfhaven myntars?"

"Arg!" hissed Tom in frustration. He furrowed his brow and glanced at his watch once more. "Ah—let's see—" *There were fourteen hours on the elven clock tower to Earth's twelve.* "Avani, are there fourteen hours in your

266

elven day, or twenty-eight?"

"Fourteen."

"Ok, fourteen divided by twenty-four is roughly 2/3, times nine earth minutes equals—just under six elven myntars," said Tom frantically. "Reboot in six elven myntars."

"You could have just told me it was Earth minutes, I could have done the conversion," replied the visage dryly.

Tom clenched his jaw.

The Guardian began to giggle. "One one thousand, two one thousand, three one thou—"

"What are you doing?" shouted Tom.

"Just adding to the suspense."

"We have plenty of suspense, thank you!" cried Tom. The Guardian folded his arms, turned his head and scowled, as if pouting.

Tom leaned toward Avani and whispered, "I think he's too low on power. His circuits are acting crazy." Tom's hand made a circular motion in the air around his ear.

"I saw that!" huffed the Guardian, pretending to turn farther away.

"I hope he has enough power left to handle the—re—reboot," she said solemnly.

"He's got to…"

"Oh, look! A cute little critter," said the Guardian. The two turned to see what he was looking at. There, half-hidden behind the center console was a gremlin. In fact, it was the same gremlin as before, the one with the white patch on the side of its head. Avani smiled at it and it smiled back. Then it winked at Tom. The gremlin's gaze fell to Chloe's controller.

Tom just blinked at the creature, and then to Avani, said, "Come on, let's go. We don't have time for pets. We've gotta find Goban and Kiran." Turning, they raced from the Citadel.

* * *

"There, over by those archers." Avani pointed to the right of the main gate. "That's the prince standing beside them."

"And Kiran and Goban are behind him," added Tom.

Avani waved and yelled and they waved back. Goban ran toward them, closely followed by Kiran and Max. Tom happened to glance off to his left, where Lorin and his strange sword carrying friend stood in a small grove of trees, deep in a heated debate.

Kiran ran up. "Look it's Malak and Chatur," he said, pointing off to their right. There, a hundred feet away, about halfway to the outer wall, their friends were once again fighting—not the enemy, of course, but each other. They were rolling around in the dirt. Malak had Chatur's arm behind his back and Chatur didn't seem too happy. At that moment, a group of trolls scaled the city's outer wall, throwing several elven archers off the rampart, screaming as they fell. Scrambling down some nearby steps, the trolls fanned out. They were behind the prince's troops and hadn't yet been spotted. One of them was running straight for their two friends.

"Malak, Chatur, look out!" cried Tom, running at full speed toward them, followed closely by Goban, loading his crossbow as he ran.

Malak glanced up just in time and rolled out of the way. Chatur was a second too late. The troll grabbed Chatur's leg, raising him high in the air. An instant later, the beast slammed him down hard onto the ground. Chatur didn't move. The troll stepped over Chatur's inert body and swung his club off his back. Grasping it with both hands, he raised the club over his head, about to deliver the fatal blow. Goban, still a ways away, raised the crossbow, trying desperately to aim as he ran. Suddenly, Malak jumped up on the troll's back and wrapped his arms around its neck, putting the troll in a choke-hold. The beast thrashed around violently, trying to throw the small elf off its back. Goban stopped a few feet away, but he couldn't get a clear shot without risking hitting Malak.

The troll started moving to the left, then whipped back to the right. This proved too much for Malak, sending him flying. Goban fired twice, once from the upper crossbow, and once from the lower. He hurriedly began to reload, but before he'd finished, the troll wobbled, then fell over backwards. Goban raised his weapon again, but the troll didn't even twitch. Malak crawled to Chatur, as Avani and Kiran ran up.

"Chatur, speak to me! Don't be dead. Please don't be dead," cried Malak, a tear running down his cheek. Kiran turned away, and Avani held her brother close. Just then, Chatur coughed.

"Why didn't you push me out of the way?" wheezed Chatur. Everyone sighed.

"You gave us all a fright, you dolt." Malak turned away and wiped the tear from his cheek.

"We'd better get him out of the way. Let's drag him over toward the castle, see if you can get a guard to help us," urged Tom. Goban and Malak each grabbed one of Chatur's legs and began dragging him in the direction of the castle.

"Ouch, ouch!" complained Chatur. "Can you be any rougher? I think you missed a rock. Better go back and make sure I hit em all."

Tom smiled. Glancing toward the rampart, elven troops had surrounded the remaining trolls that had scaled the wall. He looked right. Lorin was nowhere to be seen. As he turned to follow his friends, something caught his attention. There, near a large tree, stood Professor Snehal and Tara. They were arguing. Tom squinted, raising his hand over his brow to see clearer. He ran toward them.

"Professor Snehal. Is everything all right?" called Tom.

The two turned to face him.

Snehal replied in a flat monotone voice, "No, Tom, everything's not all right. Please come and help us," The professor held a gnarled walking stick. As Tom approached, Snehal smiled at him, then leaned toward Tara and whispered something in her ear. She glanced at Tom, then shook her head. The professor yelled at her. She cringed. Once again he whispered something in her ear, this time moving his hands in a circular pattern in front of her. Slowly she turned toward Tom once more. Her eyes seemed to cloud over as she raised her arms. Red fire began to encircle her hands. Tom stopped, then took a step backwards.

Cocking his head to one side he said, "Tara?"

Suddenly a bolt of crimson flame leapt forth, scorching the ground to his left. Tom leapt back, shouting, "Tara no! What're you doing?" A second blaze erupted, narrowly missing him on his right side. He jumped again.

"Do as I say!" commanded Snehal. "Kill him now."

Tara squinted, shaking her head. She appeared to be fighting with herself.

After a moment, her eyes began to clear and she lowered her arms. "I—I can't."

The professor slapped her hard with the back of his hand. Flying backwards, she hit her head on the tree trunk, then slid to the ground, unmoving.

"No!" cried Tom, taking a step forward.

Snehal sneered as he faced him. Motioning with his hand, a troll stepped out from behind a tree. The professor said something to the troll, then pointed at Tom. Tom's jaw dropped as he scrambled to back away, his eyes locked on the troll. Suddenly the beast raised its club and stomped straight for him, its lips curled up ferociously, exposing brown, rotting teeth. Tom frantically tried to escape but he tripped over a stone, falling on his back, the troll almost upon him. Instinctively he raised his arms above himself, as if that would protect him. The troll let out a blood-curdling scream and swung his club high up into the air. Tom closed his eyes…

Chapter 26: Last call

"Why aren't the troops back yet?" demanded King Dakshi, scowling at an aide. "I gave the order. The troops should be safely inside the main gates by now, but they haven't even begun their retreat. The barrier will collapse any myntar."

"The troops were informed, sire," said the aide nervously. "They should be here by now."

The king grabbed Tom's walkie-talkie. "General Kanak... General Kanak, are you there?"

After a moment's static, the walkie-talkie squawked, "General Kanak here."

"Why haven't your men retreated, as I ordered?"

"The fighting has gotten more intense. The holes in the barrier have widened. We cannot do an orderly retreat."

"In a couple of myntars there will not be a barrier. Make a run for it. That's a royal order, General."

"Yes, sire!"

The king slammed the radio onto his command table. "Sanuu?"

"Your Majesty?"

"As General Kanak brings his troops back to safety, have my son's archers guard their retreat, then follow them in. As soon as Devraj's men are safely within the castle walls, close the gate."

"Yes, your Highness." Sanuu dashed off down the stairs.

Tappus cleared his throat. "Forgive me, sire, but—"

"Yes, Tappus?" snapped the king.

"What about the Earth woman, and her son—and the other children?"

King Dakshi sighed, gazing off at the distant battle. "We can only hope they make it back in time."

* * *

271

Pockets of fighting were all around Juanita. *Where should I go? I've no idea where Tom might be.* Up ahead a couple of elven warriors were fighting off an ogre, and two trolls were headed straight for them.

"Look out!" she yelled, running to help. "Behind you!" One of the elves turned, just in time. Juanita dove forward, thrusting her staff between the first troll's legs. The staff flexed but held. The troll tripped, landing face down. The elven warrior dispatched him immediately. The second troll faced Juanita and swung its mace. She rolled out of the way as it crashed into the ground beside her, bouncing her up into the air from the force of the blow. Juanita spun the staff around, smacking the troll upside the head. It roared with rage. As she leapt to her feet, the staff accelerated toward the troll once more. But just before her staff connected, the troll staggered. Glancing down dully, an arrow stuck out of his chest. A moment later, a second arrow joined the first. The troll staggered once more, then fell. Juanita glanced at the elven warrior as he lowered his bow.

"Thanks," she said, nodding slightly, "but I could've handled him myself."

Noticing her strange human facial features, the elf froze in shock.

Obviously never seen an Earth woman fight before, probably making a mental note never to piss one off in an elven pub.

"Have you seen my son, Tom? Thomas Holland?"

The elf slowly shook his head.

At that moment Juanita noticed someone far off to her left. The figure was hooded. He slowly turned toward her. He was holding a hoe. *Naagesh!* She grimaced, swinging her staff around in a tight arc, she snapped it smartly against her side, then ran toward the wizard.

* * *

The battle raged all around them. The prince's troops fought valiantly with swords and knives, their crossbows uselessly slung over their shoulders—no time to reload. They were only a hundred elven warriors against thousands of trolls and ogres. Devraj's eyes swept the plain for any sign of hope. But everywhere he looked, more and more trolls were pouring through the outer gates and over the outer wall. Like fighting red ants after someone disturbed their nest, the enemy poured forth. By now the elven troops were in complete disarray. Here and there, pockets of soldiers made a run for the castle. General Kanak's brigade, however, was more organized. They had formed a large, inverted "V" shape and were slowly making their way toward the castle's main gate.

At that moment, Sanuu ran up. "Prince Devraj, your father ordered General Kanak to bring back his troops at once. You are to guard their flank, then follow them into the castle."

"Understood," said the prince. Leaning toward his second-in-command, Devraj yelled over the battle noise, "Lieutenant, we're to protect the General's retreat. As his troops pass in front of us, have our men reload their crossbows, then form a 'V' like General Kanak's troops, and start moving toward the castle, keeping us between his troops and the troll army."

Facing Sanuu he said, "Thank you, Sanuu. Tell my father we are on our way." Sanuu sprinted off.

* * *

There was a high-pitched scream of motors and gears, then a deep "thud." Over Tom's head the troll cursed. Pulleys whirred and wheels spun. The troll cried out once more. Tom opened one eye and meekly peered out beyond his upraised arm. His mouth fell open at the bizarre sight. Chloe was attacking the troll! She ran over the beast's foot at full speed, then reversed direction, spinning around and ramming his other

273

leg. The troll was holding his foot, swinging his club, and cursing a blue streak all at the same time. Tom hurriedly inched back then leapt to his feet. Heroically darting in, Chloe rammed the troll, then darting out, spinning around and charging back in for yet another strike. The troll swung his club downward, crashing into the ground, narrowly missing the robot.

What? How? Tom glanced side to side as he backed away still further. Then he spotted it, twenty feet away, behind the body of a fallen troll warrior, sat their gremlin friend, leaning back on its haunches, holding Chloe's controller. It swung the unit around, wildly jerking the joystick left and right, as if playing a video game. The gremlin winked at Tom as he slowly reached out and pressed the controller's red button, then sat the controller down beside him.

Tom's jaw fell open. *No way!* He couldn't take his eyes off the bizarre battle. Chloe spun around smartly, facing off with the giant troll. Motors screamed, but Chloe stayed put, her LEDs flashing brightly. The troll yelled and raised its club once more. Dirt flew in a huge fishtail behind Chloe as she tore off straight for the troll. At the last moment, the troll jumped to one side. Chloe turned fast to catch him... a little too fast. She tipped, tried to right herself, dirt still flying from her caterpillar tracks, but unable to right herself, flipped over on her back.

Immediately the troll's massive foot came down with a crushing blow. The horrible sound of broken plastic and twisting metal rang out. Motors shrieked! Pieces flew in all directions. Chloe's "head" turned toward Tom. The LEDs slowly dimmed, then winked out.

"NO!" screamed Tom. Without knowing how or why, he raised his fists at the troll, screaming with everything he had. Suddenly, blue sparks snapped and popped and danced around Tom's fists. The sparks spread up his arms, getting brighter and brighter, then enveloped his whole body. The troll took a step toward him, grinning as he raised his club once more. The blue lightning continued to build, circling Tom faster and faster, like a dazzling blue tornado until it finally exploded in a brilliant beam and a thunderous roar...

After the smoke and dust had cleared, all that remained of the troll was a small, smoldering pile of ash. On the ground nearby, his club gently rocked side to side for a time, then stopped. Smoke lazily drifted up from the spot where the troll had been. Beside Tom's foot lay a shiny piece of metal which had once been part of Chloe. Gazing down at the scrap, Tom saw his own reflection. A part of his mind registered the fact that his eyes glowed faintly red. Tom glanced to his left. Several more trolls were coming over the wall. He began walking toward them, his jaw set, his eyes burning with fury.

Suddenly, Lorin stepped in front of him, blocking his way. Kneeling, he gently grasped Tom's shoulders in his large hands.

"Tom—Thomas Holland," said Lorin, shaking him slightly, "I'm the Wizard Larraj. Do you understand? I'll take it from here," Larraj's eyes bored deeply into Tom's, as if grasping for something to anchor to.

"Tom, it's okay, you can relax now. I can handle this," assured the wizard. Larraj spoke a few words under his breath. Golden light flowed from the wizard to Tom. Tom seemed to crumple.

"Good, now go to your friends. They'll need your help. Get them safely to the castle."

Tom nodded absently, then turned, noticing his reflection in the metal once more. His eyes no longer glowed red. Walking zombie-style toward his friends, he took a couple of steps, then straightened back up and turned once more, noticing for the first time the wizard's mysterious friend with the silver sword and the bright yellow eyes, standing behind the wizard.

"Lorin, ah—Larraj," began Tom, wobbling slightly as he glanced at his watch.

"Yes, Tom?"

"I need to give you a heads-up. Any moment now, the barrier will go down completely." Tom took a couple of deep breaths. "This is to be expected. It needs to reboot, to switch to the new power source I've been recharging."

Larraj looked puzzled. Tom continued, "The barrier will be down for twelve minutes, er—ten myntars, while it reboots. Then it'll come back up strong, and stay up."

There was a moment's hesitation, then understanding seemed to dawn on Larraj's features.

"Thanks for the head upraised, Tom Holland."

Head upraised? wondered Tom, as he headed toward his friends.

Just then there was a low-pitched sound, more felt than heard. The tone dropped lower and lower until suddenly the barrier winked out of existence. Tom glanced at his watch, memorizing the exact time the reboot started, and calculating the exact time it would come back up.

The startled trolls were caught off guard. Everything went silent. Tom held his breath as he glanced around the battlefield.

Faintly at first, a single drum sounded, pounding out a simple rhythm: boom, boom, boom. Soon it was joined by several more drums: boom, boom, boom, boom. The sound grew deafening as hundreds of drummers joined the beat: boom, boom, boom, boom. A moment later, line upon line of ogres filed through the outer gate, followed by line upon line of trolls, all in perfect lock step with the cadence of the drums. They fanned out steadily until, looking left, forward or right, all Tom could see was a gigantic wall of trolls and ogres. The drums stopped. For a heartbeat, there was absolute silence. Then, as one, the enemy raised their weapons, let out an ear-splitting cry and charged. A moment later, all the outer shield wall gates splintered at once, as hundreds more trolls and ogres exploded through.

Just moments before, three thousand elven warriors had been making a somewhat orderly retreat to the castle. Now the trolls and ogres had the elven troops running for their lives. At this rate, the enemy forces would soon have the beleaguered elves surrounded.

As Tom turned to run, Professor Snehal stood beside the same tree as before, a look of deep hatred in his eyes. Tom glanced back at Larraj, and his mysterious friend. Larraj scowled at the professor, tightening his jaw. The wizard's friend reached for his sword's hilt, but Larraj stopped him, shaking his head. Larraj once again faced Professor Snehal. The knuckles on Larraj's right hand, where they gripped his hoe, turned white from the ferocity of his grip. But Snehal just smiled, then calmly walked away. The wizard's eyes followed the retreating figure a moment longer, then Larraj seemed to make a decision and he glanced over at his friend. Together they turned to face the advancing troll and ogre army.

Tom took off running. Glancing over his shoulder, he saw Larraj slam his hoe to the ground. The hoe's surface cracked in a thousand places, white light spilling forth from each of the cracks. Larraj slammed it down again, harder this time. Wood splinters blasted off in all directions accompanied by an eerie, ear-splitting screech. Tom stopped and covered his eyes to avoid flying shards of wood. When he finally lowered his hands, he saw that where the hoe had been just moments ago, there now stood a glowing white staff, with an owl's head carved in gold at the top. Holding the staff firmly in his right hand, the intense white radiance slowly spread up the wizard's arm. Soon the wizard was entirely engulfed with white light himself, his robes gently blowing in the breeze.

Tom swiveled around and ran once more. Glancing back, Larraj stared at his staff. The head of the golden owl, sitting atop it, slowly turned toward the wizard. The owl's eyes blinked once, then its head smoothly pivoted back forward. Larraj smiled, then faced his mysterious sword carrying friend, Zhang Li, last of the famed Cimoan monks.

Still looking over his shoulder, Tom tripped over the body of a fallen troll warrior. Hastily springing to his feet, he saw Larraj nod at Zhang. Zhang threw off his cloak. His cat-shaped eyes glowed bright yellow, and his spiky, orange hair easily set him apart from all others. Beneath his cloak, he wore leather body armor covered with knives, daggers, and throwing stars. Two silver- and gold-handled swords lay strapped to his hips. He nodded back at Larraj and in a blindingly fast, yet fluid motion, drew his swords. Each sword scribed a perfect arc, then quickly came to rest, forming a giant "X" in front of his body. Slowly, the swords began to glow red.

Running once more, Tom leapt over several fallen bodies, discarded swords and clubs. The trolls were getting nearer. Making sure not to trip this time, he glanced back and saw Larraj turn to face the onrushing army. Raising his staff once more, the wizard brought it down with a crushing blow. This time the ground began to tremble, then a wave spread out from whence the staff had hit, as if the ground had become the surface of a lake. The same brilliant white light as before erupted from the staff, only this time it flew out in a solid wall straight at the enemy forces. At that same instant, Zhang took two large running steps forward and launched himself into the air. As if in slow motion his body smoothly pivoted, yet the blades hummed in a blur of red steel, cutting any and all trolls or ogres that came within their thirsty grasp.

Suddenly, out of nowhere stood a troll, directly in Tom's path. Its legs stood wide apart as it yelled a battle cry and raised its rock-embedded mace to strike. Unable to stop, Tom dove between the troll's legs, did a somersault, and came up running on the other side. Glancing back, Tom saw the troll look around, dumb-founded. Out of the corner of Tom's eye, he saw the light wave from Larraj's staff hit the first row of the enemy, throwing them back hard, as if hit by a huge, invisible hammer. These unfortunate troops crashed into the ones behind, knocking them over like dominos casually flicked by a giant's finger.

Tom zigzagged around the fallen bodies. His friends were now just a hundred paces in front of him. Off to his left stood a lone elven warrior desperately battling a troll. It was clear the elf was losing. As he drew nearer, Tom realized the elf was Sanuu. Hesitating only a second, Tom veered to his left, catching Sanuu's eye. Tom pointed behind the troll's legs, then stared back at Sanuu. Sanuu grimaced. Tom dove to the ground right behind the troll. Sanuu looked startled, but he must have understood because he yelled a curse and lunged his sword straight at the troll's chest. The troll backed up and immediately fell over Tom. Sanuu jumped over them both, his sword coming straight down through his enemy. Sanuu stood there a moment, nodded thanks to Tom, then he was gone, sprinting off toward an ogre that had an elf pinned down nearby.

"Don't—mention—it," wheezed Tom, as he struggled to crawl out from under the troll's heavy legs. Glancing left, off in the distance, Zhang landed in a crouch, head down, his arms at his sides, his swords resting serenely against his back. The blades lay parallel to one another, their tips pointed skyward. Still glowing red, they now pulsed slightly: brighter, then dimmer, giving the eerie impression the swords were breathing.

The nearest trolls and ogres alike moved back, giving Zhang a wide berth. They tried to get even farther away but thousands of warriors behind them pushed solidly forward, unaware of the danger. A look of sheer terror spread across the faces of those trying to escape.

Suddenly, Zhang's head rose. His eyes popped open, glowing bright yellow. The slightest hint of a smile crossed his lips. Then he began to hum an ancient Cimoan battle chant. Suddenly he sprang up into the sky once more, his blades flying even faster than before.

Once Tom had finally managed to crawl out from under the fallen troll, he noticed Larraj's blast had knocked out the first few hundred enemy warriors. But a thousand more climbed over the bodies of their fallen comrades and charged onward. Several rows of elven archers let off volley after volley at them, with little effect. The bulk of the elven army was hastily making its way toward the castle and Prince Devraj's archers guarded the army's retreat, as best they could. On the prince's command, the archers fired their crossbows and a hundred arrows let fly, darkening the sky. The crossbow arrows flew faster and straighter than the elven long bow arrows, and the advancing line of the enemy fell to the barrage. Cries of victory rang out from the elves. Yet even this weapon proved no match for the sheer number of trolls and ogres that kept pouring in.

A strange battle cry brought Tom's attention back to his surroundings. Glancing to his left, several trolls and ogres were headed his way. Running as fast as he could, Tom leapt over a pile of discarded razor-sharp swords, nearly landing on a club. *That would have been disastrous*. Tom swallowed hard, as he jumped over yet another fallen troll.

One last time, he glanced back at Larraj who fired several more magical blasts, scattering the enemy troops again and again, yet each time the troll army seemed to recover more quickly. They appeared to be timing their attacks. By now the bulk of the troll and ogre forces were nearly on top of the beleaguered elven troops, still trying desperately to make their way to the castle.

As his friends dragged Chatur's now limp form, a handful of trolls spotted them and headed their way. Chatur had stopped complaining—a bad sign. He had either passed out from the pain, or... Tom ran the last few steps to catch up with his friends.

"Where've you been? What've you been doing?" asked Avani worriedly.

"You wouldn't believe me if I told you." Tom inhaled deeply, trying to catch his breath. "Thought you'd be in the castle by now."

"Chatur stopped breathing," she replied. "We got him breathing again, but then he passed out. At one point I looked for you. Did I see you use magic against a troll?" Avani seemed shocked.

Tom glanced off in the distance to where the smoldering spot was still visible. "Yes—I guess I did."

Avani's eyes intently scanned his face. "How?" Malak and Kiran stared at him as well.

"I—I don't really know. He destroyed Chloe. The next thing I knew, the magic just sort of lashed out at the troll."

Avani continued to stare at him. He turned away.

"Look," cried Tom, pointing toward the castle. "The troops are heading back to the main gate. If we can get close enough we can get help with Chatur."

"Unless the trolls get here first," said Avani, pointing to her right as several trolls broke from the main group and thundered straight for them. "Watch out!" she yelled.

Chapter 27: A hero from afar

Carlos's rugged, well-worn hiking boots echoed down the brightly lit hallway as he headed toward the control room.

I swore I'd bring them back, and I will.

Forcefully swinging open the door to the main lab, he stopped. Cheng, Sashi and Leroy fell silent, gazing up expectantly at him from their workstations. Carlos glanced around the room at all the displays, equipment, and sensors. His eyes finally came to rest on the array panel housing the Temporal Field Distortion generators.

Sis used to call this room 'The Bridge" He smiled inwardly at the thought of his sister, Juanita.

One of the scientists nervously coughed.

"Have the modifications been completed?" Carlos asked.

Cheng nodded. "We've converted the power generation system to the latest switching technologies. We've also added a large bank of high energy capacitors which are now fully charged."

"How much will these changes boost our total power output?" asked Carlos.

"The new power supply should give us an increase of 150% over our old system," began Sashi, "and the capacitors will double that power."

"The energy boost from the capacitors will only last a second or two, though," qualified Cheng.

Carlos's eyes went from face to face around the room. "That should be enough time to open the portal. Hopefully the new generator will be able to sustain the portal once it's open."

"Leroy, does the latest model predict success?"

"If you're correct that we seem to be getting help from the other side, then yes. We should be able to open a portal. Whether we can sustain it—the model is unclear..." Leroy squirmed slightly under Carlos's unusually firm stare.

"Ok, let's fire her up. If we can successfully open a portal, I—and I alone, am going through to the other universe. Understood?" Carlos once again scanned the faces of his co-workers.

"Um—this operation hasn't been authorized," Sashi pointed out, nervously glancing at the others for support.

"Well then, this will have to be an—unauthorized test," said Carlos flatly.

The others nodded uneasily.

"If the capacitors are fully charged, then I no longer need your help. Why don't you all leave? That way you won't be involved, should there be trouble."

"Before you arrived we discussed this amongst ourselves," began Cheng. "We're all staying. Besides, should anything go wrong, you'll need our help." The scientists stood firm.

"Thank you. Thank you all." Carlos's jaw was tight but his eyes looked a little watery as he strode over to his workstation. Reaching underneath he pulled out a box and set it on top of his desk. From the box he grabbed a long machete and strapped it around his waist. Next he pulled out a leather flight jacket and put that on. Then he picked up a wide-brimmed leather hat. Smiling, he pulled it snugly onto his head. Lastly he reached inside and pulled out his old army service revolver.

The scientists stared at the gun, then anxiously at one another.

"You look like a certain adventure seeking archeologist in that outfit," said Sashi. The others chuckled nervously.

Carlos laughed as well. "I guess I feel a little like Indi, only instead of fame and glory, I'm just trying to rescue Tom and my sister. How hard can it be, right?" The others remained silent.

"Ok, enough stalling, let's get on with it."

Carlos strode briskly to within ten feet of the detection grid as the others hurried to their posts.

"Everyone ready?" he asked.

"Sensor array standing by," said Leroy.

"Power supply standing by," said Cheng.

"Computers monitoring, main control panel ready," said Sashi.

Carlos glanced at Cheng. "Transfer power to Sashi's control."

"Power now under Sashi's control," confirmed Cheng.

Carlos smiled. "Let's take this puppy for a spin, shall we?"

Sashi took a deep breath, then pushed the slider level up halfway. "Power levels at 50%." Nothing happened.

"Bump it up," Carlos ordered.

Sashi moved the slider once more. "Power at 75%." A slight tremor shook the building.

"Sashi, give me everything she's got!" said Carlos, a little louder than he'd intended.

Sighing, she grabbed the slider with both hands and pushed it all the way up. The building shook once more. A few green sparks flitted around the edges of the detection grid, but that was it.

"Dump the capacitors!" yelled Carlos.

Sashi glanced nervously at Cheng.

"Dump em now!"

Cheng nodded to Sashi. She reached up, her hand hovering for a second over a newly installed lever. Holding her breath, she slammed the lever forward. The lights dimmed. There was a hissing, crackling sound. Sparks leapt from several of the instruments, accompanied by the smell of burning wires. Green lightning raced around the detection grid, then spread across the whole area, and the scene began to resolve into an image. The image faded, and the green sheet dissolved, then reappeared. The image slowly stabilized. The scientists' mouths fell open at the horrific sight. The image flickered again.

Carlos raised his gun and ran for the portal.

"No! It's not stable!" cried Sashi...

* * *

As the angry trolls stormed straight for them, Goban cocked both crossbows. Malak drew a dagger and stepped in front of Chatur's body. Avani opened her satchel and withdrew her crystals, two in one hand, one in the other. The crystals glowed brightly. Avani began to glow herself. The singing in Tom's head was almost overwhelming. Tom pulled a couple of smoke bombs and a lighter from his belt.

"Lock 'n' load," he yelled. His thumb flicked the lighter and a tall flame leapt forth. Touching the flame to the fuses, he cried, "Fire in the hold!" then threw the smoke bombs toward their foes, landing just before the advancing trolls. Smoke gushed forth. The trolls slowed, bumping into one another, confused.

"That's what I'm talkin' 'bout," cried Tom.

Goban tipped his crossbow sideways and gave them both barrels. Two trolls fell.

Kiran raised his hands and muttered an incantation. Immediately two of the trolls turned into chicken-sized birds, clucking wildly and running in all directions. The other trolls just ran right over them. Tom raised an eyebrow at Kiran, who smiled back in response.

Max barked ferociously at the trolls, running at the nearest one and nipping at its heels. As Max ran by, Kiran reached out and grabbed his collar, holding him back. Max looked up at Kiran and whined.

Avani lifted the crystals in front of her. Her eyes unfocused, she seemed to shimmer slightly. Tom had to shield his eyes from the crystals' brilliant light. A moment later, a thunderous blast sounded, and now, standing directly in front of them stood a ferocious beast. Razor-sharp claws jutted from its knuckles, elbows, and shoulders, along with ten-inch-long, equally razor-sharp teeth that glistened as the monster opened its mouth and screamed. Deep crimson eyes flashed angrily. Massive muscles rippled under its dark skin, as its jaws snapped over and over again at the trolls.

The nearest trolls backed away quickly, but still others ran around the beast, surrounding Tom and his friends.

"What is that thing?" asked Tom nervously.

"Avani conjured up a Zhanderbeast," replied Kiran. Max pulled hard against Kiran's grasp, attempting to reach the beast. Kiran struggled to hold him firm.

"It's on our side, Saint Bernard," assured Kiran. Max glanced up at him, tipping his head sideways.

Tom leaned toward Avani and whispered, "We're surrounded." She twitched but didn't move. The beast snarled, then raced around the kids as they backed into a tight circle. It lunged at the trolls on either side, keeping them away. The creature reared its head and screamed once more as a blood-red liquid dripped from its fangs...

"The troops are almost back inside the castle," yelled Goban. "Devraj's archers are still guarding their retreat. At this rate they'll all be inside within a few myntars."

Tom grimaced, "We've gotta get there before they close the gates."

At that moment there was a crackling sound off to Tom's right. Glancing over, bright green motes danced around in a square pattern about twenty yards away. Tom squinted to get a better look. Suddenly there was a loud roar and a green sheet filled the area for an instant. Then it disappeared, flickered, and then reappeared. A moment later, the green faded into an unbelievable scene. A portal had opened, right here on the battlefield. It was dim and hard to see, but someone wearing a broad-brimmed hat and a well-worn leather jacket charged toward the portal, gun raised in hand, though he seemed to be moving in slow motion.

"Uncle Carlos?" said Tom, not believing his eyes.

Suddenly there was a flash of light and a deep boom, and the trolls standing directly behind them lay scattered about on the ground. Tom glanced over his shoulder. Off in the distance, Larraj's staff steamed, still pointing in their direction. Tom waved thanks, then looked back at the portal, but his uncle and the portal had disappeared.

Tom shook his head, then yelled to the others, "Hurry, make a run for the castle." He placed his mouth near Avani's ear and whispered, "Have the beast guard our retreat."

Sweat gushed from her brow but she gave a tiny nod. All but Avani grabbed Chatur's legs and arms and ran for the castle.

Did Uncle Carlos make it through before the portal collapsed? Glancing around, he couldn't see him anywhere. Tom did see, however, that the last of the main elven army had made it safely inside the gates and Prince Devraj's troops were now entering as well. Tom and his friends still had a hundred paces to go. Something had occupied the trolls, for a time, but they were once more heading this way. *We're not gonna make it.*

They were about halfway there when the last of Devraj's troops entered the castle, followed quickly by the prince himself. The gate began to lower.

"Devraj, no!" yelled Tom, over the battle noise. To his friends, "Hurry, they're closing the gates!"

As they neared the wall, sharp wooden spikes, pointing down from the bottom of the gate, stood a foot off the ground, and were still dropping.

"Devraj, its Tom. Open the gates! Chatur's hurt. We're all here, including Avani."

"Avani?" called Devraj. He dropped to the ground, peering out. "Stop, raise the gates!" commanded the prince.

"I'm sorry, your Highness" said a voice, "but the king's orders were—"

"And I'm countermanding those orders," yelled the prince. The ground shook as the gates came down entirely.

"It's too late, your Highness." replied the guard.

"Avani," said the prince, his voice breaking slightly. "I'm sorry—I'm sorry, Avani."

The Zhanderbeast faded from sight as Avani slowly walked up to the gate. She put her hand flat onto its rough surface and spoke softly.

"Devraj—please Devraj, open the gate…"

Tom thought he heard a scream, then a muffled cry.

Goban yelled, "The trolls, they're headed this way!" He stepped in front of his friends, raising his crossbow.

"The Citadel!" cried Kiran. "We can hide in the Citadel!"

"Great idea, Kiran!" yelled Tom. "Quickly, everyone to the Citadel."

Dragging the still unconscious form of Chatur with them, they ran through the city's streets and as they rounded the first corner Tom glanced over his shoulder. "Hurry, they're gaining on us."

A dozen trolls thundered behind them, closing fast. Tom's group rounded the second corner and entered a narrow street, lined with quaint little homes. Once again Tom felt the houses watching them as they raced by. A moment later, there was a commotion behind them. Glancing over his shoulder as he ran, he saw the trolls staring at the houses with panicked looks on their faces. The homes had expanded to nearly twice their usual size and were threatening to squash the beasts between the houses on either side of the street. The trolls lashed out with their clubs at the buildings.

"Hey, the homes are slowing down the trolls!" yelled Tom. Still running, everyone glanced back in wonder.

"That's awesome," said Kiran. Max barked. They picked up speed.

But further on, the street became wider and the trolls were able to run faster.

Tom glanced back. The trolls were now just fifty feet behind. "Quick, they're almost here," he screamed. Rounding the last corner, the Citadel came into view.

"We're gonna make it! Avani, get your key ready. Goban, hold em off 'til we can get inside."

Suddenly, bursting around the corner in front of them were six huge ogres who stopped directly in front of the Citadel. They were trapped.

Screeching to a halt, Tom yelled, "Avani, your Zhanderbeast!"

She lowered her head. Almost instantly the monster sprang up, roaring at the nearest ogre. The trolls stopped just beyond the Zhanderbeast's reach, then fanned out around the kids.

"We're in trouble," said Goban soberly, reloading his last round of arrows in his crossbow. He raised the weapon and fired into the surrounding trolls, then threw the useless crossbow to the ground and grabbed the handle of his battle axe, swinging it smartly off his shoulder.

He smiled as he slapped his axe's handle firmly into his left palm. "Time to party, Aileen." Malak swung his dagger fiercely each time a troll came near. The Zhanderbeast ran around them all, roaring at the enemy. Max tried to run after it but Kiran grabbed his collar. Each time the Zhanderbeast came near, the trolls leapt back.

Tom glanced at his watch. As he did, he noticed Kiran, still holding Max by his collar, awkwardly opening a small glass vial. Kiran wound up and threw it at a nearby troll. The bottle hit the troll in the leg, dumping its contents. Almost instantly, the troll's leg vanished. The troll glanced down wide-eyed, tripped, and fell face down.

Tom stared at Kiran. With a broad smile, Kiran stared back.

"You could've swallowed it and escaped," said Tom. The smile immediately vanished from Kiran's face.

As the trolls came nearer, Max broke loose from Kiran's grasp and sprang up onto the nearest troll. Startled, the troll fell backwards. Another troll bent over and swatted Max, and as if he was a mere gnat, Max flew through the air, landing hard with a "thump" beside Tom. Max whimpered but stayed put.

"Max!" cried Tom. He bent down and petted his dog. Max's eyes stared up sadly at Tom. Max licked Tom's hand. "You'll be okay, boy. You've gotta be. Just stay here, we'll protect you." A tear ran down Tom's cheek.

Tom glanced up at Avani. Suddenly her eyes cleared, her mouth fell open. She gazed down at her hands. The light from the crystals slowly faded, as did her body's glow. Tom stared at the beast that protected them. It opened its mouth to scream but instead faded, finally winking out of existence altogether.

"Tom, can you use your magic?" cried Malak.

"I—I don't know how."

"Just try," urged Goban.

Tom stood, stared at his hands and swallowed hard, then clenched his fists. His eyes nearly closed as he gritted his teeth, his face muscles knotted in fierce concentration. A faint blue spark began to dance across his hands, but slowly fizzled out. "I—I'm sorry, I can't do it."

Avani dropped her crystals, then calmly opened her right palm to her brother. Kiran gazed up at her, his jaw set, but his lips were quivering. He took her hand. Then she turned toward Tom and grasped his hand as well. Smiling at Tom, her eyes sparkling, her face relaxed, she squared her shoulders and turned to face their impending doom.

At that moment, out of the crowd stepped two giant trolls. Tom recognized Bellchar and Fowlbreth. Bellchar stopped right in front of him. The troll smiled and raised his club. Avani suddenly pulled Tom close and kissed him full on the mouth. Tom's eyes opened wide.

Chapter 28: Battles within battles...

Juanita had lost track of Naagesh. As she tried to find him again, she thought she got a glimpse of her son, along with several other kids, far off to her right heading toward the castle. Ferociously she fought her way past two ogres but by the time she arrived at the spot, the children were gone.

Where could they be? Squinting and shielding her eyes with her hand she scanned the area around her, but they were nowhere in sight. The castle's main gate now stood closed.

Maybe they made it into the castle, before they closed the gates, she hoped. *Damn it! I should have kept my eyes on him.* Desperately glancing around once more, she witnessed an amazing sight: a man dressed in white, with a long beard and a white and gold staff, fired bolt after bolt of magical energy at the troll and ogre forces.

Obviously a wizard... Naagesh? He's the same height and build but he's dressed differently, plus he's fighting the trolls. Naagesh would be helping them. It can't be him. The trolls were experiencing heavy losses, yet they kept coming for the wizard, and off to his left was the most amazing martial artist Juanita had ever seen. Launching himself high into the air, higher than any human could ever jump, he would turn in a slow spiral, yet his swords flew so fast they seemed to disappear. They might have truly disappeared, save for the fact that his enemies were falling all around him.

Maybe they can help me find Tom. What other choice do I have? She raced toward them.

* * *

Larraj lowered his staff. Letting out a deep sigh, he stared at the

291

hopeless struggle surrounding him. There were bodies of the fallen everywhere, trolls, ogres and elves alike. Discarded swords, arrows, and maces littered the field, some poking out of the soil or out of a body at odd angles. Smoke rose in gentle spirals from scorch marks where his magical blasts had struck the ground. A lone figure walked through one such veil of smoke with the aid of a gnarled walking stick. Larraj squinted, tipping his head. The individual continued to calmly walk toward him. The wizard frowned as the figure stopped in front of him.

"Naagesh, or should I call you Professor Snehal?" asked Larraj coldly. "I wondered if you'd have the courage to come back."

Naagesh smiled. "I had so hoped the trolls would've killed you by now, but no matter. If you want something done right..." Naagesh let his unfinished statement hang stiffly in the cool morning air.

"This—war is all your doing. You stirred up the trolls, blaming their troubles on the elves, didn't you? You gave them visions of grandeur, the trolls controlling the world, perhaps? With the elves as their slaves, I'll wager?"

"Very good, Larraj. You've done your homework, along with some astute deductive reasoning, no doubt."

Larraj's frown deepened. "And what do you hope to gain from all this? Is this just some pathetic attempt at revenge? To—avenge poor old daddy's death?"

"NO!" cried Naagesh angrily. "It's not just about my father. Once the trolls defeat the elves, I'll—persuade them to conquer the dwarves. Then I'll step in as their supreme leader and rule them all."

"And you think they will just hand over the reins of power to you, do you? Just like that?"

"With the invaluable help and advice that I've given them during this war, I'm sure I will be considered their most loyal, trusted and powerful ally. It won't take me long—using just a touch of magic, here and there, to—clear their feeble minds. Yes, soon they will enthusiastically hand over the 'reins of power' as you so aptly put it."

The hint of a smile crossed Larraj's face. "It's a very touching fairy tale, but aren't you forgetting something?"

Naagesh raised his brow and tipped his head to one side. "What?"

"Me," said Larraj coolly.

Naagesh calmly replied, "Oh, that..." He turned sideways, placing his hands behind his back, and began pacing back and forth. After a moment he stopped and faced Larraj once more. "You see, it's like this... It's true we were once enemies, but we're also the last two living wizards. We're kindred spirits, you and I. Perhaps we could make a deal. I'd be happy to divide up the power and responsibilities. After all, it would be a lot for one lone wizard to manage, and there's more than enough riches and power for the two of us. What do you say, partners in crime?" Smiling, Naagesh stuck out his hand, thumb up, toward his sworn enemy.

Larraj's eyes grew deathly cold. "I'm afraid I must—decline your generous offer."

The smile left Naagesh's face as he slowly lowered his hand. "Ah, well, more's the pity."

For several long sectars neither wizard spoke. Neither wizard moved. Neither wizard breathed. It was a wizards' standoff...

Finally, Naagesh broke the tension by smiling. He started to turn away, but instead, whirled back around and fired a blinding bolt of green fire at Larraj. But Larraj adeptly stepped aside, firing his own blast of blue energy, striking the ground to the right of Naagesh. The ground shook, nearly toppling the evil wizard. Immediately Larraj fired another blast, this one stronger and to Naagesh's left. The soil ripped apart, a deep chasm forming beside Naagesh. Stumbling, he dropped his gnarled staff to the ground. The staff sparked and crackled where it lay. Naagesh teetered at the edge, then fell in. Nothing happened for several sectars then finally a hand slapped hard above the rent in the battlefield, then another. Slowly Naagesh pulled himself out of the crevasse.

"Had enough?" said Larraj.

Naagesh's eyes burned with fury. "Not quite." In a blindingly fast move he fired a powerful brilliant green flame right at Larraj. Equally fast blue flames sprang from Larraj's hands to meet the onslaught. Between the wizards, fire met fire. There was a tremendous roar as the two brightly colored flames fought to overpower one another. After a tense few moments both flames suddenly stopped. The two wizards just stared at each other.

Once more green flames began to form around Naagesh's hands but at the same time Larraj's arms made a wide circular pattern as he spoke an ancient incantation. Instantly a glowing bowl of yellow energy sprang up surrounding Naagesh.

"No! What are you doing? Not again. It can't be. Stop!" cried Naagesh dropping to his knees, a look of pure horror on his face. "We're the last of the wizards. Help me, I'm too young to die!" Then Naagesh began to laugh as he reached out toward his fallen staff. Green sparks danced around its length and it began to vibrate. Suddenly it leapt into Naagesh's outstretched hand and almost instantly, four golden bolts flew away from the staff, they arced out and then sped back in, wrapping themselves tightly around Larraj's arms and legs. Larraj's staff fell uselessly to the ground and the yellow bowl vanished. Larraj struggled against his bonds.

Naagesh laughed once more as he rose to his feet and casually dusted himself off. "You fool. Did you think I'd fall for that same tired trick twice in one century?"

Larraj glanced around, his eyes falling on his friend Li. Li nodded. Larraj's gaze whipped back to Naagesh.

* * *

Well, I guess I was wrong. The wizard in white isn't Naagesh, the other wizard is. What do I do now? I see the martial arts master is circling around behind Naagesh, perhaps I can help. Juanita crept off to her right.

* * *

The evil wizard returned Larraj's glare with a grin. "You remember the conversation we were having a hundred years ago, when you'd just used that same spell on me and slowly robbed me of all my powers? You know, the one just before you let me fall to my death? As you were, no doubt, hoping I would do just now."

"Back then I tried to save you. The root let go before I could reach your hand."

Naagesh walked up face to face with Larraj. "Nonsense! I reached up for you. All you had to do was grab my hand. What's more, you left me to be torn to shreds by that giant flying raptoid that caught me in its talons as I fell."

Larraj's eyes flicked to the side where Li was circling wide. But there was someone else approaching, behind and off to Li's right. His eyes snapped back. "And did you expect me to rescue you after you'd just tried to kill me? Besides, I figured when you fell off the cliff you'd be dead already, and if not, by the time I got there you certainly would be."

"No matter," laughed Naagesh. "All's well that ends well. Now I'm going to relieve you of all your magical powers, adding them to my own. Once this procedure is complete, I will be the most powerful being that ever walked this world. Unfortunately for you, this process is quite painful and regrettably it will kill you." A crazed look came over Naagesh's face as he raised his hands high above himself.

There was a sudden whooshing noise. Naagesh lunged sideways at the last sectar. Li's sword missed his body but cut deep into his left arm. Blood flowed heavily as Naagesh grabbed his injured arm. Blindingly bright magical power surged around Naagesh's good hand as he raised it, palm outward, toward his attacker. With lightning speed Li swung his sword up again but as the blade started down, Naagesh fired a bolt of blazing green energy right at Li. At that same instant, however, a staff hit Naagesh hard on the back of his knees, throwing off his aim, and he crumpled to the ground. Still, Li was clipped by the blast and it was enough to launch him backward, spinning thirty feet in the air, landing hard on his stomach. Slowly he pushed himself up and got to one knee. He shook his head but didn't stand up immediately.

Naagesh struggled back to his feet, clamping his right hand hard against the wound to try and stem the bleeding. His teeth bared, his eyes gleamed with rage. Whirling around, he grimaced at Juanita.

"You! The accursed boy's mother," hissed Naagesh.

"And this time I'm not all tied up," she said, then in a flash she whipped the staff behind her head as her left hand rose toward the wizard, her first two fingers pointing up.

"Impressive! If a bit theatrical..." said Naagesh, then he snapped his fingers and the staff turned to dust in her hands. Her jaw dropped and she involuntarily took a step back. He smiled, raising his palm, green lightning began to spark and crackle around his hand.

"Wait!" cried Larraj.

Without lowering his hand, Naagesh glanced sidelong at his enemy, energy still popping and crackling playfully around his fingers.

At that moment, there was a deep booming sound off to their right. In the distance they could see trolls using a giant tree as a battering ram, trying to break down the castle's main gate.

Larraj closed his eyes, furrowed his brow and took a deep breath. Then, in a clear, strong voice he cried out, "Come to our aid now, oh vaporous ones. Come to our aid—and feed!" His eyes popped open. Nothing happened at first, then slowly a mist began to rise from the ground. It swirled and twisted, gently caressing the trees, the shrubs, the vines. As if blown by an unseen breeze, the grass itself began to move and sway. All across the battlefield, mist lightly curled around the trolls' legs, gently winding up their bodies, like a sensuous dance partner, patiently waiting for the music to begin. Naagesh glanced around uneasily. Trolls and ogres stood frozen in their tracks, unsure of what was happening. The mist thickened... Vague shapes began to form in the fog, indistinct at first, like an old photograph left too long in the sun. But slowly the forms grew more and more substantial until all became clear... Thousands of mist wraiths stood amongst the troll army, more than anyone had ever seen, more than legend had ever spoken of. A moment later, the trolls began to scream.

* * *

Tom blinked twice as he pulled away from Avani's embrace, but his eyes were still locked onto hers. Having heard the screams of their comrades, far off in the distance, the trolls surrounding them all froze. A look of confusion crossed their stony faces.

Bellchar and Fowlbreth's gaze slowly shifted back from the direction of the troll army, first to each other, then finally to Tom and his friends. As one, the trolls raised their clubs once more. Goban stepped forward, his axe held high, a fierce look in his eyes.

Turning abruptly, Tom threw his left arm across Goban's chest, stopping him. At the same time his right hand, palm outward, flew up in front of the trolls. "Stop!" cried Tom in a commanding voice. "You're Bellchar and Fowlbreth, right?" The trolls looked at each other dully, then back at Tom. Bellchar blinked.

Tom glanced at his watch, then back up at the trolls. "Look, I'm sorry to have to be the one to tell you this, but—this is going to leave a mark."

Bellchar raised an eyebrow and glancing sidelong at Fowlbreth, said, "Huh?"

Tom, still holding his arm out straight like a traffic cop, smiled as he calmly glanced at his watch and counted down, "3, 2, 1..." But nothing happened. He counted down once more, a little louder this time, "3, 2, 1…" Still nothing. The smile disappeared from Tom's face just as one appeared on Bellchar's.

The trolls raised their clubs once more.

Suddenly a low-pitched hum began, then dropped so low that Tom could no longer hear it. At that same instant, the trolls doubled over, clutching their ears. Max howled from where he lay. Finally, the pitch started rising again. Blue sparks danced playfully amongst the blades of grass, jutting up from the edges of the cobblestones. A moment later, the ground was covered with a sparkling, seething mass of blue lightning; then with a loud "whoomp" the barrier sprang up, launching the trolls and ogres up into the sky.

Tom saw Bellchar rise high above them, stop—as if frozen in time, then fall back down. Bellchar hit the barrier spread-eagled, directly above them, a look of total shock on his face. He cried out "OUCH!" and with another "whoomp" he was launched upward once more. This time he flew off a ways away. He ended up hitting the barrier several more times, each time farther and farther away, "OUCH, Ouch, ouch, ouch…" until finally, near the edge of the barrier, he was launched off into the forest itself.

Tom glanced at his friends. They were all just staring at him.

"Well, that was weird," he said.

The others chuckled nervously.

* * *

Four wraiths rose up from the mist, surrounding the evil wizard Naagesh. A horrified look crossed his face.

"Mind that blood," warned Larraj, pointing at Naagesh's arm. "Mist wraiths are particularly fond of blood."

Beads of sweat began to form on Naagesh's brow as he tightened his grip on his wound. The wraiths began to close in. Immediately, green energy leapt from Naagesh's left hand toward the nearest wraith but the beam passed right through it. Unaffected, they continued to advance.

"NO!" cried Naagesh, panicking. Suddenly there was a huge explosion, and as the smoke cleared, both Naagesh and the wraiths were gone. A moment later, the wraiths rose up from the mist, once more.

"Look, over there. He's getting away," yelled Larraj, nodding to his left. Swirls in the mist receded into the distance. The wraiths turned as one and floated after him. A moment later the energy bands restraining Larraj dissolved. His eyes followed the wraiths for several long sectars, then he turned to Juanita. "Thank you. We will have much to talk about soon."

"Do you know where my son Tom is? Thomas Holland?"

The wizard's eyes met hers and he paused. "Last time I saw him he was headed for the castle."

Larraj's eyes scanned her face once more, then he turned and strode off to find his friend Li.

* * *

Tom and the others cheered wildly, laughing and hugging each other. After a few seconds they turned back around. The smiles immediately dropped from their faces, however, as mist wraiths rose up from the fog all around them. They huddled close together. Goban raised his axe uncertainly. A lone wraith glided forward to within a foot of Tom and stopped. It was staring right at him. Slowly it raised its spectral hand, palm outward, toward Tom. Tom glanced at the others and swallowed hard. Shakily he raised his hand in the same manner. For several long tense seconds, nothing happened. Then slowly all the wraiths sank back into the mist, and within moments, the fog had disappeared altogether.

* * *

King Dakshi stood on the tower surrounded by his military advisors. Trolls and ogres alike were flying through the air above them, having just been launched skyward by the barrier's re-emergence.

"Well, that's a sight you don't see every day," remarked King Dakshi.

"Truly," agreed Sanuu, glancing sidelong at the king. "It's raining trolls and ogres."

As if that weren't enough, at that very instant, far off to their right, a dragon appeared. What's more, it seemed to be leading the dwarf army. Bursts of flame could be seen every myntar or so, accompanied by a loud roar.

"Is that King Abban riding the dragon?" said King Dakshi, astonished.

Holding a hand above his eyes to block the sun, an advisor said, "They're still far away, sire, but indeed, it appears to be the dwarf king."

"And look!" cried Sanuu, pointing to the southeast. Faintly visible in the late afternoon sky, a brilliant white light lit up the clouds around it.

"It's the signal!" yelled Sanuu triumphantly. "It's Tom's flare."

The king smiled. "So my cousin decided to send us troops after all. Quickly now, I don't know how or why they're helping us, but the mist wraiths have the troll forces in complete disarray. The dwarf army will attack the trolls from the north. My cousin, King Bharat, will confront them from the southwest. Have our troops reassemble, and attack the enemy forces from their flank. They will be hopelessly pinned in."

A trumpeter raised his huge bone horn and blew a mighty blast. King Dakshi grimaced, turning his head and plugging his ears. Once it was over, the king handed his walkie-talkie to an advisor, who began relaying orders to General Kanak.

The king's keen eyes slowly surveyed the scene around Elfhaven. Just beyond the barrier, the dwarf army had now met the troll and ogre forces, and were fighting ferociously, though the trolls appeared to be steering clear of the dragon. King Dakshi gazed over the recent battlefield beyond the castle walls. A lone figure, dressed in white and carrying a gold-tipped staff, walked up to a solitary mist wraith. They appeared to be conversing. After a moment, the figure in white bowed to the wraith, then turned and began walking toward the castle. The wraith stood there a moment longer, then slowly sank into the mist. In fact, as far as the king could see, all the mist wraiths were dissolving back into the fog. Within moments, the fog itself had disappeared...

Another figure walked toward the castle. Even from this distance the king recognized Juanita. As she approached, she knelt beside a large tree. A moment later she rose, holding the limp form of a young girl in her arms, then continued walking toward the castle. Without taking his eyes off her, the king said, "Sanuu, go and take that child from Juanita. If she's still alive, get her to a healer." The king spotted another figure crouching on the ground nearby. Hundreds of troll and ogre bodies lay in heaps all around him. Two swords were upraised in his hands, still smoldering, they glowed a dull red. "And bring the sorcerer and his friend, the sword-master, along as well." Sanuu bowed low and began to turn.

"Oh, and Sanuu," said King Dakshi shrewdly. Sanuu turned back.

"Ask the sword-master nicely, will you?"

Sanuu raised his brow, a shocked look of understanding slowly crept over his face. Recovering his composure quickly, he pivoted smartly on his heel, and ran off down the stairs.

* * *

Tom and his friends walked back toward the castle, still dragging Chatur's limp form behind them, while excitedly talking amongst themselves. Once they'd rounded the last corner, the battlefield stretched out before them, not a single troll or ogre in sight. Tom couldn't see any mist wraiths either. As they approached the castle, the main gate now stood open.

"Tom! Tom," cried a familiar voice.

"Mom," yelled Tom, running toward her.

Handing the limp form of Tara to Sanuu, Juanita ran to greet her son. They hugged each other tightly.

"Oh, Tom, I was so worried about you." A single tear ran down her cheek. She absently wiped it on her sleeve.

"Nothing to worry about, Mom. I'm fine! How did you get here? Why didn't you come through the portal when I did? And how are we gonna get home?"

"Easy there, one question at a time, OK?" Smiling broadly, she hugged him close.

"OK, but first, let me introduce you to my friends." Tom grabbed her hand and pulled her back to the others. He quickly made the introductions. A moment later the prince ran up, followed closely by several palace guards.

A look of relief and joy was plastered on the prince's face. "You made it! You're alive!" He ran up and hugged Avani so tightly her eyes nearly popped out of their sockets. Looking shocked, she quickly leaned back and glanced at Tom. Devraj stepped away and held her at arm's length. "I was so worried about you. I thought you were dead."

"No thanks to you," she said sharply. Devraj cringed.

She drew in a deep breath and glanced at her brother. "Kiran suggested we hide in the Citadel. So we made a run for it. We almost made it, too, but we were surrounded just before we got there."

"Then how did you survive?" asked the prince, glancing sidelong at Goban.

Avani smiled at her friends. "You mean, how did I survive, being just a girl and all, without my strong prince to protect me?"

Devraj actually blushed and stared down at his feet. "Ah, I didn't really mean—what I said before." He raised his gaze slightly and peered at her sheepishly. She glared at him for a second, then a smile slowly spread across her face. The prince smiled back.

Tom cleared his throat. "Uh—Devraj, I'd like you to meet my mom, Juanita. Mom, this is Prince Devraj, King Dakshi's son."

Devraj paused as his eyes met Tom's. Then the prince stepped up, took Juanita's hand and bowing slightly, warmly kissed it. "Pleased to make your acquaintance, my lady." Caught off guard, Juanita opened her mouth to speak, but nothing came out. Everyone laughed.

Glancing over at Devraj, Avani began, "You asked how we survived. It's kind of a long story—" but she was cut off by the distant blast of a horn.

Tom could just make out a trumpeter holding a long, curved horn, standing on the same tower where the king and his advisors stood. Turning slightly to his left, Tom saw several people running toward them from the direction of the castle. After a few moments, a messenger, followed by several guards, ran up beside the prince, breathing hard.

"The dwarf army has been spotted heading this way. They're at least five thousand strong," began the runner, pausing to catch his breath. "The odd thing is—they're being led by a fire-breathing dragon."

Tom smiled and raised his hand, palm outward, toward Goban. Goban hesitated for a second, his brow high in a questioning look. Suddenly, he smiled too and slapped his palm hard against Tom's. Tom frowned, rubbing his hand.

Just then there was a cough and a wheeze. "What does someone have to do to get a little help around here?" moaned Chatur. Everyone looked shocked. A moment later the guards rushed in, picked him up, and carried him off.

* * *

"I am in your debt," said King Dakshi. "To whom do I have the honor of addressing?"

The man in white bowed low. "I'm the wizard Larraj and your humble servant, your Majesty."

The king raised an eyebrow. "And this gentleman?"

"I'm Zhang, Zhang Li, last of the Cimoan monks." Zhang, however, did not bow to the king.

King Dakshi hesitated. "I thought all the wizards and Cimoan monks died in the War of the Wizards, some hundred yaras ago?"

"Rumors of our demise have been greatly exaggerated," stated Zhang flatly. The king seemed taken aback.

Larraj cleared his throat. "What my impertinent friend here is trying to say—" Stepping forward, he glared sidelong at Zhang, "—is that before the War of the Wizards, if you may recall, I was about to be overthrown as head of the Wizards' Council, so I stepped down. For a time, I wandered far to the northwest where I found a small village, with an even smaller Cimoan monastery in it. That's where I first met Li. Eventually, he decided to leave the monastery with me. We vowed to find a way to prevent the war from happening. But before we could implement our plan, war broke out and soon it escalated out of control. Sometime later we heard that his monastery had been called up to fight. We soon learned that all the monks from his monastery, along with those from all the other monasteries, were killed. The wizards met a similar fate. All, that is, except one, well, two actually, if you count me."

"Naagesh?" spat the king.

"Yes."

"Where is he now?"

"Last I saw him, he was injured and being chased by four mist wraiths."

"Do you think they got him?"

A faraway look crossed the wizard's eyes as he gazed thoughtfully over the battlements. "I believe so. His magical powers are useless against a mist wraith. Still, we can't know for sure…"

The king idly scratched his chin. "I heartily appreciate all the help you two have given us. Without your aid, we would not have survived this battle. But how did you know we were in trouble?"

Larraj glanced over at his friend Zhang. "We didn't, actually, not right away, that is. We came here for another reason. We were searching for Naagesh. Near the end of the War of the Wizards, I came back for him. We fought and he fell off a cliff and was captured by a vicious raptoid. I foolishly assumed him dead. No one heard from him again for years, but recently I began to hear rumors. It took Zhang and me some time to piece all the clues together. The last clue led us here. As you've probably surmised, Naagesh was the one who gave the trolls the magical battering ram, which they used to punch holes through the barrier, nearly destroying it."

"Since I didn't know you were here, you must have been hiding. Why didn't you come to me, let me know of your quest? Perhaps I could have aided you."

"Forgive me, your Highness. But I feared—if anyone knew I was here, searching for Naagesh, somehow he would find out and disappear back into hiding once more."

The king nodded. "Your reasoning is sound. So what did you do?"

"When I first arrived in Elfhaven, I took the job as your head stable-hand, assuming the name Lorin." The king shot a questioning look at Juanita, recalling that she'd said Naagesh was posing as Lorin.

She stepped forward. "I saw Naagesh at the troll command headquarters, where I was being held captive. When he left, I escaped and tried to follow him, but I lost him. Then, after a time I spotted you. I assumed I'd caught up with Naagesh again."

"Understandable," said the wizard. "I'd been following Naagesh myself. He eluded me as well. I eventually found his trail leading back toward Elfhaven. That must have been when you spotted me. Strange that I didn't sense your presence..."

Larraj faced the king and resumed his history lesson. "We were close to capturing him, just before the war broke out. Though he's changed his appearance, Naagesh was posing as Snehal, your new magic-school teacher."

The king looked shocked, then he frowned. "At first I suspected Snehal was the traitor, after interviewing my son and Tara. But when I heard what Juanita had seen, our suspicions pointed to you. Snehal was the one who convinced my son to steal the defense plans and he had Tara hide them in Tom's satchel. The professor knew of my son's petty jealousy toward Tom and used that against him. Of course Devraj never expected them to fall into enemy hands. None of us had any idea we were dealing with the evil wizard Naagesh. Still, we might have caught him, had it not been for the fact that we thought you were to blame."

"I'm sorry. Once again, that was my fault," said Juanita.

"It wasn't your fault. From what you knew, I was the likely suspect," conceded Larraj. "But through my own sources I deduced what was going on, so I followed Snehal into the woods. I believed he'd made a copy of the plans and intended to deliver them to the troll commanders. Unfortunately, he lost me on the way there, or I would've recovered the stolen plans before he got the chance to give them to your enemies."

Juanita asked, "What of the girl, Tara? She's the one that was injured, right?"

The king nodded. "She's healing quickly. She'll be fine. As I said, Snehal used her, as well as my son. Now that we know Snehal was the wizard Naagesh, I suspect he may have used a spell on both of them.

"And now, if you two will excuse me, I must get back to concluding this war." At that the king turned away, paused, then turned back, looking straight at the wizard. "I don't mean to offend, but—your face— it's covered with white hair, unusual for an elf. And your eyes, they are brown, but more round—"

Larraj threw back his hood, staring first at the king, then at Juanita. "Ah, yes—that. It's—it's because I'm not an elf. I'm human actually, from the planet Earth."

Chapter 29: Reunited we stand

Larraj walked beside Tom and his mother as they made their way to the Citadel. Juanita had her arm around her son, who idly kicked pebbles, watching them bounce off the uneven cobblestones. As they passed the park, Tom noticed the fountain worked perfectly now. Water lifted from the fountain's base and then up and out, held suspended by magic. A large blob of water began to take shape. It shifted and shimmered, adding more detail until suddenly the head of a long dead elven king came into sharp focus. The figure stared at Tom and his mouth began to move, as if talking to him, but Tom was too far away to hear what he was saying. The king's eyes however, followed Tom as he passed.

"I thought at first it was you," said Tom, still looking over his shoulder at the fountain. "I thought you were Naagesh."

The wizard glanced at Juanita. "As did your mother, but why did you suspect me?"

"First, at the stable, I saw you rummaging around in my satchel."

"Ah, that—I had heard, through my sources, that there was a conspiracy to frame you. I was trying to prevent it. What else?"

"Then I saw you outside the barrier, talking with a mist wraith."

Larraj nodded. "I was—negotiating their help in the upcoming battle."

"Negotiating? What did you have to give them in return?"

Larraj pursed his lips and adopted a faraway look. "That's a tale for another day, I'm afraid."

Tom cocked his head, then glanced up at his mother. "Were you helping us? Helping me?"

"As I said, I tried to help you when you were about to be framed."

"When else?"

"Um, let me see… I opened the wood sprite door for you. I knocked down the trolls behind you, when they had you surrounded, and I kept

307

the other trolls distracted as long as I could, to give you a head start back to the castle. I'm sorry I couldn't do more, but I was rather—preoccupied."

Tom kicked another pebble. "Mom says you're from Earth, too."

The wizard nodded.

"How's that possible?"

"As you know, the Citadel has many functions," began Larraj. "It keeps the barrier up, protecting the elves and the Citadel itself. It amplifies the magic, making it easier for elves, and all magical creatures, to use magic. But its main purpose is to open portals to other universes."

"Yes, the Guardian mentioned that. But what does that have to do with you being from Earth?"

"Wizards used to travel to other universes, searching for promising young would-be sorcerers. A few hundred years ago, the wizards noticed that Earthlings seemed to have more powerful innate magical abilities—here in Elfhaven that is—than even the elves themselves. So they began recruiting earthlings with the right—disposition."

Tom looked confused. "What do you mean the right disposition?"

"The wizards felt that many Earthlings were too—angry, greedy, selfish, power hungry. But if they chose the right candidate, chose them when they were young enough…"

"And you were one of the chosen ones?"

Larraj smiled. "Indeed, I was the first of the Earthling wizards. I was an orphan at birth, and the wizards 'negotiated' my coming here to be trained."

"If you're from Earth and you're over a hundred years old, how come you're not dead?"

Larraj laughed. "You're a blunt one, aren't you?"

"What?" said Tom. Juanita just shook her head.

"It's something about the atoms and the magic in this universe. People live much longer here than on Earth. There's no disease, and I'm told the body's cells don't mutate, possibly due to the magic. So the body ages very slowly. If one doesn't die from some accident, or get killed in battle, anyone could live here for two—or even three hundred years, maybe longer."

"And what about your friend, Zhang?" asked Tom.

"That's a similar tale. The Cimoan monks had their own—recruiting program. Only they were looking for devout holy men, who had a certain—knack, shall we say, for fighting. But when they stumbled on a planet called Zhantar, they hit the jackpot. The Zhanturians lived in a separate universe from this one, and from the one Earth occupies. The Zhanturians loved the concept of mastery. Their culture relished the process of working long and hard, concentrating on perfection. It was akin to a religious meditation. However, they were also a violent race. The Cimoan monks found that if they trained the Zhanturians from birth in the Cimoan form of religion and their own complex form of martial arts, the children took to both, like ducks to water. They became so proficient at martial arts, in fact, that eventually all that was left of the Cimoan monks were of Zhanturian origin." The wizard's lip curled up slightly. "Although, they can be a bit—quirky, at times…"

The three resumed walking toward the Citadel. Presently, they rounded the last corner and walked up to the entryway. Avani had lent Tom the key, so he placed it in its receptacle. The doorway opened immediately.

"After you," said the wizard, gesturing with his arm. Tom and his mom walked through the doorway.

"Thomas Holland," spoke Tom loudly to the empty space. He gazed up at his mom expectantly. She stared back at him for an instant, then seemed to understand.

"Juanita Holland," she said.

The wizard followed suit by stating his name and instead of slowly coming on one-by-one, as before, the lights all lit up instantly and were far brighter than in previous visits.

"I guess the power's truly back up," said Tom, striding down the sloping hallway.

Suddenly Tom remembered his most pressing question. He slowed, allowing Larraj to catch up. "Say, no one else will tell me. What is the Prophecy of Elfhaven? And how does it involve me?"

Larraj took a deep breath. "In years past, there was a legend. Many books were written about it. Unfortunately, during the War of the Wizards, all known copies were destroyed. The most famous book was written by the great blind prophet, Earstradamus. He spoke of a child that would one day come to our planet. He even went so far as to mention a name: Thomas Holland."

"What?" said Juanita, shocked.

Tom ignored her. "But what exactly is the prophecy? Is it over? Have I fulfilled it?"

"Well," began Larraj, "to answer your questions, no, I don't think it's over. In fact, I think it's just beginning."

The wizard pursed his lips and squatted down beside Tom. Looking him square in the eye for a moment, he then turned slightly and gazed up, as if reading words written in the air. "This is the Prophecy of Elfhaven, as told by the prophet Earstradamus:

In the year of the serpent, space folds;

Creature and boy, odd companions;

Magic and tools, long thought lost;

A Wizard's Mark shall confirm;

The tapestry of destiny—frays;

A heavy burden for one so young;

The Future, cast adrift in violent seas;

Pity the creature and his pet—Thomas Holland."

Tom gazed down at his feet, silent for a time. "What year is this?" he said finally.

"We have a hundred-year cycle, then the year names repeat. A hundred years ago we were in the year of the serpent. As we are now."

"That's absurd," began Juanita. "How could anyone have known about Tom? Unless—unless time works differently in this universe."

"A very astute observation. Time in fact, does work differently here, on this world, in this universe. But I suspect the Guardian can explain this better than I. In fact, I think he knows far more than he's been telling."

Tom wouldn't let go. "But what does the prophecy mean?"

"Many scholars, wizards and sages have analyzed these words ever since they were first written. Various opinions were put forth, debated. Some were rejected, some gained favor, for a time. Over the ages, these theories grew and changed. Today, none can remember the original ideas. No one knows for sure."

"But what do you think they mean?" asked Tom, staring intently at the wizard.

Larraj sighed. "It seems obvious that it refers to you and your dog, Max. It also seems likely that it's talking about your powerful gift of magic and the amazing implements and knowledge you brought with you."

"What's the line about the Wizard's Mark mean?" asked Tom.

The wizard pulled up his sleeve, exposing a tattoo. It was a simple drawing of a tall triangle beside a diagonal line with short lines radiating from its tip.

Tom bent over and peered at the shapes. "What is it?"

Larraj pointed at the tall triangle. "This is a representation of a wizard's hat. These used to be popular with wizards, long ago. They were all the rage."

"And this?" asked Tom, pointing to the diagonal line.

"That represents a wizard's wand. The lines radiating from its end signify magic flowing from the wand. I prefer a staff, myself, but many wizards used to use a wand. They felt it was easier to carry and to conceal.

Do you happen to have a birthmark or a tattoo like this?"

Tom shook his head, glancing up at his mom. "Mom wouldn't let me have a tattoo, and I think I'd remember a birthmark like that."

The wizard snorted. Juanita smiled. The three started walking again.

Tom grinned, then adopted a more serious look. "What about the rest of the prophecy?"

Larraj pursed his lips. "The rest is up to interpretation, but I believe it means that your presence can and will change this world, as indeed it already has, either for the betterment of all—or perhaps bringing about its destruction…"

Juanita scowled. "Surely this doesn't have to happen! What if we just go back to Earth or stay here in Elfhaven? What if he doesn't *do* anything?"

Larraj smiled sadly, glancing from one to the other. "It's too late, I'm afraid. The wheels of time have already been put in motion. I suspect nothing can stop your destiny from unfolding."

"Can we at least influence my destiny? Can you help me? Keep me from failing?"

"I can try, and I will," assured the wizard.

At that moment, they entered the Citadel's main chamber. Juanita's eyes lit up at the sight of the bizarre combination of high-tech 3-D displays alongside strange-looking crystals, and other devices she couldn't identify.

An instant later they heard loud static, and the image of The Guardian appeared. This time he had the look of a humble peasant, dressed in rough, brown friars' robes. His head was bald on top, with white, curly hair just above his ears and on the bottom of his chin. His hands were folded at his waist, and he was barefoot.

Tom smiled. *Ah, his Friar Tuck impersonation again.*

"Forgive me, but I believe I can better answer Tom's question," said the visage.

"Ah, you must be the Guardian," said Larraj. "Tom has told me much about you. Were you listening in on our conversation just then?"

"I was. And you must be the wizard Larraj, judging from your general appearance, your staff, and the mark of the wizard just peeking out from under your sleeve."

Larraj glanced down at his arm, raising an eyebrow.

"Plus, there's the fact that you stated your name when you entered the Citadel," admitted the Guardian, a wry grin crossing his face.

"You've never met?" said Tom, surprised.

"No, I've never actually been in the Citadel. No wizard has. Only the Keepers of the Light knew the secret of how to enter the Citadel, and what was contained therein."

"Then how did the wizards travel to other universes, to recruit new apprentices?"

"We would let our desires be known to the Keepers, then they would arrange it, when they saw fit."

Juanita stepped forward. "What is all this equipment for? Is that a power-grid monitoring screen? What do the controls do, and what are the crystals for?"

The Guardian regarded her. "I heard you state your name as Juanita Holland. I take it you are Tom's mother?"

"I am."

The visage absently scratched its head. "Hmm, I must have left the portal open a bit too long..."

"What? Are you implying that you were trying to bring Tom here? Tom, and Tom alone?"

The image stared blankly at Juanita. "Well—yes, actually. I'd been searching for many years to find him. But when I finally did, my energy levels were so low I knew I'd have only one shot at getting him here. What's worse, I no longer had the power to accurately calculate the exact date and time. My attempt opened a portal into Tom's bedroom closet, two weeks ago, Earth time."

"What?" cried Juanita, shock evident in her voice.

"My dream," muttered Tom.

"Yes, but the odd thing was, when I opened the portal I saw that Tom was already on our planet, but I hadn't brought him here yet. Time travel can be so confusing at times. However, I reasoned that this meant that I would eventually succeed at bringing him here."

"Let me get this straight," began Juanita. "You can control time, too?"

"Not control time, per se, but as our wizard friend here mentioned earlier, time works differently in this universe. As such, I can observe many points in time in your universe, on your world. All I have to do is choose the time and place that I'd like to open a portal to."

Juanita's eyes grew wide.

"Anyway, once I'd opened the portal to Tom's room, and before I could decide what to do, my energy reserves passed below the critical level and the portal shut down abruptly. This was particularly strange, as I mentioned before, I could see Tom standing near the wood sprite gate, yet I no longer had enough power to open another portal and bring him here. How could that be?"

"The detection grid," stated Tom flatly.

The Guardian smiled. "As you correctly surmised before. It was a— joint effort, so to speak."

Juanita frowned. "But why Tom?"

"I knew of the Prophecy and I needed help. Avani's father had disappeared and my power was running low. As I said, I tried unsuccessfully to bring Tom here. I thought I'd failed, yet at the same time, I knew there must indeed be a way. When I discovered that your team were working on inter-universal physics, and that you were making the area between our universes thinner, with your Temporal Field Distortion generators, it required much less energy to help you open a portal. I just gave your detection grid experiment a little nudge, and brought him here, hoping he might find a solution. Which indeed he did, although I didn't anticipate his robot coming through on my first attempt, or the critical part it would play in this drama."

Juanita scowled at the Guardian. "He could have been killed!"

The visage just shrugged.

Juanita looked furious and her jaw twitched uncontrollably. "You must return us to Earth immediately. I demand that you open a portal back to Earth right now!"

The Guardian glanced from one to the other, then back to Juanita. "True, I do have enough power to open a portal, just barely, but that would use up all my reserves. The barrier would then collapse and Elfhaven, and more importantly this citadel, would be unprotected. No, the replacement power supply must be installed first. Then I can safely open a portal so you can return home. I am afraid you will just have to wait."

"If you refuse, I'll have the king command you to open a portal."

The Guardian smiled. "I answer to no king." Then glancing at Larraj, he added, "Or wizard, for that matter."

Tom noticed his mom. *She doesn't look too happy.*

"Oh," blurted Tom, "I just remembered. A portal opened while I was on the battlefield. Uncle Carlos was about to run through. I got distracted and the portal disappeared. I don't think he made it through…"

"What?" said Juanita, sounding shocked again.

"The boy's correct," affirmed the Guardian. "I detected a portal opening while I was in the process of rebooting, but since I was powered down I was unable to help stabilize it. I don't know how they were even able to open a portal without me."

Juanita stared at her son. "What do you mean, you don't *think* he made it through? Is Carlos here or not?" Tom glanced around nervously.

"I can't be sure, since I was distracted and in the process of rebooting, but my sensors did not register anyone coming through before the portal collapsed," said the visage.

Tom quickly changed the subject. "I have another question: Why are there so many references to Earth here in Elfhaven?"

"References?" said the friar's image.

"Well, for instance, there are similarities in the building styles."

The Guardian leaned back. "That could just be a coincidence."

"What about the pictures of elephants on the castle's main doors, and the Egyptian hieroglyphs on the Library, not to mention the picture of a steam locomotive on its door."

"Okay, okay, you have a point," conceded the visage.

Gazing at Tom, the Guardian smiled. "Have you heard of the 'Wave-Particle Duality problem'?"

Tom glanced at his mother. "I've heard Mom mention it. Something about—you can observe the universe as if it's made of particles, or made of waves, but not both at the same time." Juanita smiled, despite her displeasure with the Guardian.

"Very good! Yes, that's exactly right. And the more you study the universe, or universes, from a wave perspective, the more you begin to see that everything—all matter is really made up of waves. Like those in a pond. When you toss a stone in a pond, you see waves rippling out in a perfect circle. But if you throw in two stones at once, you create two circular waves moving out from each center until the wave from one stone reaches the wave from the other. Immediately you get a complex wave pattern. Still, with careful analysis, your brain can figure out that two stones hit the water, and approximately where they hit. But, if you throw in a handful of stones all at once, the wave pattern is far too complex to figure out what actually happened, without special equipment, that is. This is exactly like a hologram. A hologram is nothing more than a complex interaction of waves, so complex in fact that the whole becomes something far greater than any of its parts. I myself

316

appear before you as one such hologram, made up of millions of individual waves."

"That's very interesting," said Tom. "But what does it have to do with things from Earth being here?"

"It turns out that not only is matter made up of waves, but so are thoughts and ideas. When I open a portal, people can cross over, but whether they do or not, there is an unseen flood of waves going back and forth through the portal, knowledge and ideas included."

Tom and his mom stared at each other in shock.

"And what's more, once a portal has been opened to another universe, it creates a small—leak, shall we say. So ever after, a small amount of data, in the form of waves, leaks through. And it's a two-way street, with data flowing both ways. We call the phenomenon 'cross talk.'"

Larraj cleared his throat impatiently. "What's the status of your power source, Guardian?"

The visage glared at the wizard, appearing miffed at the interruption. "Thanks to Tom's robot, our current power capacity is at 0.025 percent. That's enough to power the barrier for just over a month."

"Can you show me where the spaceship crashed, the one that was delivering the replacement power source?"

There was a flicker for a second, then a 3D relief map of the Icebain mountain range appeared in the air before them. A red beam highlighted a spot on the map, high in the most rugged terrain shown, on the foothills of a volcano. The red beam quickly expanded into an "X" marking the spot. Larraj walked around and then through the map, carefully studying it.

"Hmm," said the wizard thoughtfully. "A month will be cutting it close."

Tom gazed up at the Guardian. "You seem in a lot better shape today."

The image crossed its arms. "As you guessed at the time, my power was so low the last time you saw me that my programs were operating—

erratically. I'm sorry for any, ah—confusion I may have caused. Actually, it was a miracle that I had enough reserves to switch power sources, and reboot the system successfully."

Larraj stopped staring at the map. He glanced at Juanita, then smiled and put his hand on Tom's shoulder. "Come on you two, the king's throwing a special banquet this evening, in honor of the end of the war. This will be a party you won't want to miss."

Chapter 30: A feast for sore elves

"Why do I hafta wear this outfit?" complained Tom as they walked toward the castle.

"It's a royal feast! There will be kings, princes, dignitaries, even a wizard in attendance," said Avani, her eyes sparkling. "Besides, it's just for one evening."

Tom wore a fuchsia doublet with gold and bone-colored buttons, open in front, with narrow, white lapels. His pantaloons bloomed out around his thighs and were accented with gold and white vertical strips. Tall, teal-colored socks stuck up well beyond his matching—and quite uncomfortable—teal-colored pointy shoes.

"But I look totally ridiculous."

Avani smiled as she looked him up and down. "The outfit belonged to Nadda when he was your age."

"Your Granddad wore this?"

"Yes. Fuchsia and blue are our family's colors."

"Did he like it?"

Glancing first at her brother, then back to Tom, she said, "Oh yes, it was his favorite suit."

Tom glanced skeptically from Avani to Kiran and back.

Kiran snickered.

Tom glared at him. He was dressed in a similar fashion, only his outfit was blue instead of fuchsia. "You should talk."

Glancing down at himself, Kiran abruptly stopped smiling.

Max hobbled over and licked Tom's hand. Tom bent down and petted his dog. His right paw was bandaged, but the elven doctor that had worked on him said he would be "healthy as a horn-toed slitherbeast," whatever that was, within a week.

"Where's your mom, anyway?" asked Kiran.

"King Dakshi's tailors made her a new dress for the party. She ran off to put it on."

"Great!" said Avani, then she hiked up the front of her gold-colored, floor-length gown and sprinted up the palace steps. Her dress stuck out in all directions, and reminded Tom of a bright golden blowfish from the waist down. The upper half had a snug-fitting white bodice with a stiff, fuchsia-colored high collar that wrapped around her head. Huge, sheer, puffy shoulders jutted out from the bodice, with skin-tight white sleeves running all the way down to a wide set of cuffs. Alternating fuchsia and gold lace hung down in folds from the cuffs, below her wrists. Around her neck, she wore a sparking gold necklace with a sort of floral design.

Odd though, instead of each stem ending in a flower, they ended in a miniature snake head, complete with rubies for eyes. Even so, Tom thought she looked stunning. He and Kiran ran up the stairs after her; Max hobbled behind.

As they entered the great hall, Tom stopped, his eyes taking in the rich spectacle before him. Like mighty sentinels, five large marble columns stood guard along each wall. Between the columns were massive tables, covered in fresh linen. On top of each table were stacked hundreds of unusual food dishes. To Tom's left sat a roasted fowl of some sort. It smelled of butter and honey, it was golden brown, and still steaming. Tom's mouth began to water. Exotic fruit were arranged all around the bird. One such fruit was a pink spiky, lumpy pod. Each spike had a tiny eye on top. The eyes seemed to follow him as he walked by. Tom shivered, not particularly hungry anymore.

Beside each table stood a large cask with flagons of ale sitting atop it. Several people stood near each cask, laughing and hoisting large tankards.

The people behind Tom were eager to see everything, so he was forced to keep moving. Even though it was still early, he figured there were already over two hundred guests inside.

Glancing around, he noticed several palace guards dressed in their finest formal military attire, complete with polished swords and large, colorful feathers in their caps. Most stood at attention against the walls, but a few walked around greeting guests and dignitaries. Tom recognized Tappus and Sanuu standing beside King Abban, laughing. The dwarf king had an enormous tankard of ale which he drank from liberally. Sanuu's eyes fixed on Tom for a moment. Then he smiled and gave Tom a slight nod. Tom smiled back and waved. Continuing to look around, he spotted his friend Goban standing beside a large cask over by the dais. Tom hurried over.

"Hey, Goban."

"Holla, dawg," said Goban, patting Tom on his back with a hearty slap.

Goban stood eating what looked like the biggest barbequed chicken leg Tom had ever seen, and he was drinking from a small tankard of his own. "What're you drinking?"

"Ale, of course. Here, try some." Goban set down his food and snatched up a small mug with one hand while smoothly pulling the cork stopper out of the barrel with the other. Once he'd filled the mug, he slapped the cork neatly back in, then handed Tom the mug. Tom slowly raised it to his nose and sniffed cautiously.

"You're allowed to drink ale?" asked Tom, glancing around to see if his mom was watching.

"I'm a dwarf, aren't I? They start us young. But even the elf kids, once they reach the age of twelve, are allowed a nip or two, on special occasions."

Tom took a tiny sip, then his head jerked back, his eyes nearly closing. "Smooth," he croaked, remembering a word his uncle used to say when drinking with friends. Tom spied a large bowl of nuts sitting on the table beside him. "Say, who's that elf in the royal outfit over there by your father?" he asked. Goban stared in that direction. Turning quickly, Tom poured his ale into the bowl of nuts, but he gasped when he saw some of the nuts begin to float. He whipped back around.

"I don't see anyone," replied Goban, with a puzzled look.

"Oh, no matter," said Tom hastily. "Let's see who else we can find." Goban grabbed his gigantic bird leg. Tom set down his tankard and as they walked away, he glanced back nervously at the floating nuts.

Presently he spotted some of the other kids from magic school, eating heartily, laughing, and talking amongst themselves. When they saw him, they smiled and waved. Soon they found Avani and Kiran conversing with Chatur and Malak. Chatur leaned on a crutch, his left leg bandaged in two places, another large dressing wrapped around his head. Max hobbled over and lay down nearby.

"Holla, all!" cried Goban, as they approached.

"Hey, Goban, Tom," Malak smiled, vigorously shaking first Goban's hand, then Tom's.

"Looks as if Chatur is no worse for wear," remarked Goban, eyeing him up and down.

Malak smiled and put an arm around his friend. "Luckily, when the troll slammed Chatur to the ground he landed on his head, nothing there to damage."

"What do ya mean nothing there to damage? I'm twice as smart as you'll ever be." Chatur adjusted his balance onto his one good leg, then swung his crutch, smacking Malak solidly.

"Twice as smart as zero is still zero," muttered Kiran.

"What?" said Malak and Chatur in unison as they glared at Kiran. Everyone else chuckled.

There was a commotion at the entrance to the hall. Everyone turned. The wizard Larraj had just arrived, accompanied by his strange friend Zhang. Excusing himself, Tom wandered over.

"Good meeting, Larraj," said Tom, remembering what Kiran had once said.

The wizard smiled and responded in kind. "Well met, Tom."

"Quite a party, huh?" Tom glanced over at Zhang Li. "What, no swords, knives, daggers, or throwing stars?"

Li glared at his friend. "Larraj thought they would be—inappropriate at a celebration of peace." Larraj and Tom smiled. Zhang's frown deepened.

The sound of musicians tuning up caught Tom's attention. He spotted them over in the corner between two tables of food. There were three elven musicians holding instruments, plus one instrument which just floated in the air, playing itself. None of the instruments were like anything Tom had ever seen. One had several massive, round gourds with strings attached. Another looked like a V-shaped flute, and a third had several curving tubes, resembling snakes, with skins stretched tightly over one end. *Drums?* wondered Tom.

The last instrument seemed the strangest. In fact, it was not actually there... Several strings just floated in midair. A long, curving bow hovered above them. Occasionally the bow would dip down and play a note, then float back up. Instead of sounding like a violin, however, it made a sound more like a bullfrog croaking.

After a moment of tuning, the performers began to play. It was a haunting melody that seemed vaguely familiar. "Wait a minute," began Tom, astonished. "I think I've heard this before, though obviously played on different instruments. Mom used to play this song. She called it—a Bach Chorale." Tom had a puzzled look on his face as he gazed up at the wizard.

"This must be one of those—side effects of the Citadel opening portals to other universes. I was aware of the phenomenon, but I never knew exactly what was going on, not until the Guardian explained the process to us, that is. For several hundred years, even before Bach existed, many of these songs were played here in Elfhaven."

"The elves wrote Bach's songs?" said Tom, shock evident in his voice.

"Not all of them, and actually, once he began writing his own, his

323

songs were played here as well. It went back and forth—each time there was a transfer, it enhanced the beauty and depth of all of the music, enriching both our worlds."

Tom thought about this for a moment. "Is that why Goban can speak hip-hop? Did it filter down from Earth?"

"Um, perhaps. The dwarf lads started picking it up some time back, but now, even many elven kids speak it, at least when there are no adults about. It's even possible that 'hip-hop,' as you call it, was spoken here first, and then spread to Earth."

"No way!" said Tom.

A moment later there was another commotion, this time to the side of the hall. There, just entering from an anteroom, walked a beautiful woman, her hair swept up high and to one side, held there with artfully tied azure ribbons and matching azure trailers that gracefully flowed down her neck and across her shoulders. She wore a long, floor-length gown mostly in white but with powder blue panels that ran from the tight fitting waist all the way down to the floor. It had fuchsia-colored real flowers, similar to orchids, attached at the waist and shoulders as well as to two delicate wristbands. The gown was sleeveless and must have had a fair amount of yardage for its petticoat, since it occupied a good six feet of floor space.

"Mom?" said Tom in shock, as he ran to greet her. "Mom, what have they done to you?"

"It's a bit much isn't it?" she said, gazing down at her dress awkwardly.

"No, you look—beautiful! It's just that—well, I've never seen you this dressed up."

She blushed. "Well, thanks. I tried to get the tailors to tone it down, but they insisted."

"You look great, Mom! Come on, I want you to get to know my friends. We didn't have much time to talk yesterday."

"Everyone, this is my mom, Juanita. Mom, you met Malak yesterday but Chatur was out cold. They're best friends." Malak sneered at Chatur but then they both stuck out their hands, enthusiastically shaking hers. "And you met Avani and her younger brother, Kiran; I've been staying with em at their grandparents' house. They're around here, too, somewhere. I'll introduce you when I see em."

Kiran grinned ear-to-ear as he vigorously shook her hand.

Avani took Juanita's hand more gently and curtsied. "I'm honored to get to know the mother of the famous Thomas Holland." Tom raised his brow at that, but his mother smiled warmly.

Still staring strangely at Avani, Tom continued, "And this is my good friend Goban. He's a dwarf—and son of King Abban, so—so technically that makes him a prince, but he's really just one of the guys." Tom scrunched up his face.

Goban chuckled.

Juanita tipped her head. "Pleased to make your acquaintance, your Highness."

Goban snorted. "Hey, we'll have none of that, I've appearances to keep up, ya know! Just call me Goban." The others laughed.

Juanita smiled. "Goban it is, then."

At that moment, excited murmurs spread across the hall. King Dakshi and King Abban had moved up onto the dais and Dakshi now gazed out over the crowd. Off to his right stood another elf dressed in subtly different, yet equally regal garb.

Goban nudged Tom, "Come on, we don't want to miss all the fun!" Tom's friends headed for the front of the hall. He glanced up at his mom, who nodded, so he smiled and hurried after them.

Walking through the crowded hall, Tom noticed Prince Devraj had joined his friends up ahead. But before he could reach them, a girl stepped directly in his path.

"Tara!" said Tom, unable to keep the surprise from his voice. "I see

325

you're okay after that bump on the head." He winced, glancing nervously over her shoulder at his friends.

"Tom, I—I just wanted to apologize for all the trouble I caused you."

"Trouble?" Tom shifted his weight awkwardly from foot to foot.

She scowled. "You know, I helped Snehal by hiding the plans in your satchel. I don't know why I did it. He had such knowledge, he was so powerful. I wanted to be just like him." She paused. "Plus, he seemed to like me." She blushed. Tom didn't know what to say. She hurried on, "I don't actually remember putting the plans in your bag. I think Snehal—ah—Naagesh put a spell on me. But I'm not using that as an excuse. I should never have helped him. It was a dumb thing to do. And then there was—trying to kill you during the battle. I know he used magic on me again, to force me when I wasn't going to do it, but still…" She hung her head slightly.

Tom, not quite sure why he did it, reached over, placed his finger under her chin and slowly raised her head back up. "It's all right. Everything worked out okay." Tom glanced around the room and smiled. "Better than okay, I'd say."

Tara's face blossomed into a huge smile. Over her shoulder, Tom noticed Avani staring at them. She scowled and turned away.

"Ah—it's great to talk to you again, Tara. Let's do this again real soon." Stepping around her, he hurried the three short steps to stand beside Goban. *Ugh. Let's do this again real soon? That was smooth? Why am I such a dolt around girls?* Avani glanced over her shoulder at Tara and frowned. Tom shook his head.

King Dakshi cleared his throat. Throughout the hall, the chatter slowly died down. All eyes turned to the dais where the king stood waiting.

"First off, I'd like to give my heartfelt thanks to King Abban, who brought us the full might of the dwarvish army." The crowd cheered. Once the cheering had died down, the king's arm rose toward the other elf standing on the dais. "And to my cousin King Bharat, leader of his people and commander of the lake elves' army. He brought their sorely needed forces to bear, right at the perfect moment." Once again the crowd cheered.

"Without these two men, we would not be celebrating our victory here today."

"Likewise our thanks go out to the wizard Larraj and his friend the sword-master, Zhang. Their bravery and unique skills allowed us to last until the other troops arrived." More cheers rang out.

The king spotted the wizard among the crowd. Larraj gave him a slight nod. Zhang, however, stood motionless. Eventually the clamor died down enough for the king to continue.

"Lastly, I must thank Tom's mother, Juanita. Her battle tactics significantly slowed down the troll forces, giving us the time we needed for all the other diverse elements to come into play."

Juanita tipped her head toward the king and smiled. More applause.

At that point, King Dakshi stood up tall and took on a stern look. His jaw tight, his brow furrowed. "There is another reason we are here today, however." For some reason, he was glaring at Tom and his friends...

The king paused, choosing his words carefully. "I hate to cloud what should be such a joyous occasion, with the necessity of delivering harsh punishment, but I'm afraid this grave a matter cannot be delayed any longer. Considering the seriousness of these crimes, I feel it only fitting that I administer this particular punishment in public, so that all might understand the consequences of disobeying my commands." The king's eyes lanced through the crowd. "Will the following individuals come stand before me: Prince Devraj, Prince Goban, Avani Dutta." Avani glanced at Tom and for the first time ever, she looked afraid. "Kiran Dutta, Thomas Holland." Tom took a deep breath, and hurried up to join them. "Malak Dhairya, Chatur Jakarious."

The seven friends stood before the dais gazing nervously up at the king. His sharp eyes scanning from one to the next, King Dakshi's gaze

327

finally froze on Tom. The king's scowl deepened, then he moved on. Tom realized he'd been holding his breath. As he opened his mouth, a loud gasp escaped. His friends glanced at him sideways, but no one laughed.

"Avani, Kiran, Goban, Malak and Chatur; you all helped Tom escape from the dungeon while he was being held prisoner for the charge of treason. This unto itself a treasonable offense, and if you were adults, and were tried and found guilty, it could be punishable by death. Prince Devraj. You stole the defense plans then stood by and let Tom take the blame. Devraj, Avani, Kiran, Goban, and Tom: you disobeyed my orders by going out a second time, beyond the barrier, after dark, without telling anyone where you were going. Not only were you already serving a sentence for the same offense, you went out into the heart of the enemy territory, in search of something you weren't even sure still existed."

"But sire—" began Prince Devraj.

"Silence!" bellowed his father. The king glared long and hard at each of them.

"To make it clear that a royal order must be obeyed, I'm sentencing you all to five years in the dungeons!"

Gasps rang out all across the hall. Even the guards looked shocked.

"But..." began Kiran meekly. The king leaned forward and shot him a murderous look. Kiran shut up immediately. Goban looked to his father for help, but King Abban sat facing the other way, apparently more interested in his tankard of ale than in his son's plight. Tom glanced nervously over his shoulder. His mother was nowhere in sight.

Once more King Dakshi's eyes moved from person to person, boring deeply into each of them. Finally, the king stood up and relaxed his brow. "However, there seem to be some—mitigating circumstances, shall we say. For instance, the fact that you seven children solved the riddle of the Citadel, then somehow were able to sneak into the heart of the troll encampment and steal Tom's device, right from under the enemy's very noses. You then returned it here and repaired the barrier—which, without a doubt, saved the lives of all the people of Elfhaven. That feat alone was truly remarkable. Songs shall be written to commemorate this deed, mark my words." Tom glanced sidelong at the prince, but Devraj just stared straight ahead.

"And Tom, your crossbow design worked flawlessly. If the dwarves had had time to build a thousand more of them, we might have held off the trolls all by ourselves. And that wooden dragon..." The king smiled at that, glancing over at King Abban who raised his tankard of ale in salute. "Well, that's a story I'm longing to hear more about. Anyway, in consideration of these—amazing feats, I hereby suspend all of your sentences and am instead—presenting each of you with a solid gold medal of courage." The king signaled with his arm for the kids to come up onto the dais.

Still in shock, Tom and his friends walked up the stairs, and ambled over in single file to stand before the king.

Devraj silently accepted his medal with dignity, as did Avani. Kiran smiled broadly and lifted his up for all to see. The crowd cheered.

When it was Goban's turn, he accepted his medal, and then turned to the crowd, smiling. "Hey, pops bent. Yo' we busted girl. But—chillin' now, dogg. It's phat!" The kids from magic school went wild. King Abban saluted his son with his tankard of ale, then took a long swig.

When Tom received his medal, he shook the king's hand briskly and smiled at all his friends. His eyes searched the crowd until they lit upon his mom, who had a proud smile on her face. But suddenly something caught his eye. Just behind the farthest pillar stood the ghost from the library. He smiled at Tom and gave him a thumbs-up. Tom shook his head, rubbed his eyes, then looked again, but the ghost was nowhere to be seen. *Did I imagine him?*

"Tom?" said the king quietly. "Tom, are you there?" Tom shook his head once more, then turned to face the king.

"Ah—yes, your Highness?"

"The use of your magical communication devices, and the 'flare launcher,' proved invaluable during the war. Thank you. Oh—and there's one more thing." The king frowned, pursed his lips, and lowered his voice. "Ah, I—I must apologize to you," whispered the king. "Tappus had seen my son leave the war room with something hidden beneath his tunic. I knew you weren't the one that stole the defense plans, but I also knew that someone was manipulating my son and trying to set you up. I felt that if I played along, the traitor might expose himself."

Tom thought back to his time in the dungeon and shivered. "That's okay, I understand."

The king smiled down at him but there was a sad look in his eye. "Thank you, Tom. We owe you more than you know." The king stood back up and then in his full deep voice said, "Oh, and Tom, could you bring up Saint Bernard?"

Tom grimaced, saying, "His name's not—" but everyone started laughing, including the king. Tom glanced over at his mom, who was trying unsuccessfully to keep a straight face. Tom blushed and turned around. "Max, come here, boy."

Max hobbled over to the stairs, gazed up at Tom and whined. Hesitating only a second, Kiran and Malak bolted down the stairs and together they were able to carry Max up onto the dais. Max hobbled over to the king, then raised his right paw. The room fell silent. For a moment, the king just stared at him, but then taking the hint, he bent over and shook Max's paw firmly. Max barked. Everyone laughed. Next, the king put a matching medal around Max's neck, after which he reached behind his throne and produced a gigantic bone. Tom didn't know what kind of animal it had come from, and he wasn't sure he wanted to know, either. Max eagerly took the bone from the king's hand. Then he sat down, putting one of his large paws on the end of it, and chewed heartily.

The king handed out the last two medals to Malak and Chatur, each of whom beamed proudly at their friends.

Avani turned to leave, then suddenly stuck a finger in each side of her mouth, and let out a loud, high-pitched whistle. A moment later, there was yet another commotion at the back of the hall. Tappus and Sanuu burst around the corner in hot pursuit of a gremlin. The king raised his hand, palm outward, stopping the guards. The gremlin screeched to a halt as well, wide-eyed. Again the room fell silent. The critter glanced around until he spotted Avani, then galloped across the hall, up the stairs and launched himself into the air, landing precisely in Avani's arms. She stumbled back a few steps, a stunned look on her face.

"Ah—your Highness," began Avani, "this gremlin—sire, we would not have been able to open the Citadel without his help. Plus, he saved Tom's life…"

The king appeared shocked, but then leaned forward and studied the creature. Finally, he stood up and smiled. Snapping his fingers, he whispered something to an aide. A few moments later, another slightly smaller medal was placed in his hand. Bending forward, the king put the ribbon around the gremlin's neck. The gremlin smiled up at Avani, then, grabbing the metal with both hands, bit into it. He glared at the medal. Uneasy laughter sounded from the hall. The king quickly signaled a servant who rushed up with an odd-looking orange-colored fruit. King Dakshi carefully handed the fruit to the gremlin who immediately bit into it, juice flying in all directions. The creature gazed up and smiled, causing the kids to laugh once more, then they all made their way down off the dais, all except Tom.

After the others had left, the king asked, "Yes, Tom?"

"Ah, your Highness, I'd really like to help find the Citadel's missing power source—go on the mission to find it."

The king glanced at Juanita, standing in the middle of the hall. She shook her head, no. King Dakshi cleared his throat, pausing. "You've certainly proved yourself worthy and have bought us needed time, but I think, in this case, the adults should be able to take it from here. Besides

331

we can't afford to lose you. We need your help to switch out the old power source and—re-boot was it?—the new one, once we have it."

"Mom can do that part, if I'm—delayed."

The king choked back a laugh, then he glanced once more at Juanita. "When the time comes, and I assure you it will come soon, we can discuss the matter further. In any case, I think your mother should have the final say."

"What if Mom came with us?" blurted Tom. The king laughed and rested his hand on Tom's shoulder. "Enough of such talk. This is a day meant for celebration, so let's celebrate!" The king gestured to the party below. Tom glanced across the hall and spotted his mom heading his way. Together he and King Dakshi ambled down into the crowd. A moment later, his mother walked up.

"Juanita, you look ravishing in your new gown," said the king. "Do you like it?"

She brushed her hand idly across the dress's pleats and smiled. "It's not exactly my usual style but—yes, it's beautiful, thank you."

The king smiled warmly, and with a sparkle in his eye replied, "My pleasure, my lady."

Juanita blushed.

"Tom, may I borrow your mother for a few myntars? I'd like to introduce her to some of my guests."

"Sure! Have fun, Mom."

The king signaled for the band to play and extended his right elbow toward Juanita. She hesitated an instant then smiled, taking his proffered arm in hers. Together they strode off talking and laughing.

Tom watched them go, thinking to himself, *hmm, maybe we'll get to stay awhile after all!*

At that, he turned and hurried off to find his friends. As he did so, he passed many adults enjoying themselves, smiling, talking and laughing loudly, especially King Abban, who had acquired quite a following of older elven women. The king smiled and flirted, and they followed suit by laughing heartily at his bad jokes. As the musicians began to play, several people started dancing. Tom spotted Avani across the hall talking with her grandparents, so he headed over.

"Oh hello, Tom," said Nanni. "Nadda and I would like you to know that we are so very proud of you and Avani." She beamed a gigantic smile at them both.

"And we're proud of Kiran, too," piped in Nadda.

"Yes," agreed Nanni. Though she now adopted a stern look and shook her finger at them. "And don't you ever do that again. You nearly scared the dickens out of us! Thank goodness we didn't hear about it until after you were back home safe and sound."

"Nadda," began Tom, changing the subject. "I hear this outfit was once yours, when you were a boy."

"Yes, that's true."

Tom hesitated, "I also heard you liked to wear it?"

Nadda snorted. "I hated it! It was scratchy, and made me look ridiculous." Tom scowled at Avani. She just giggled.

"May I have this dance?" Nadda offered his hand to Nanni.

"Why certainly, kind sir, I'd love to," she replied, smiling up at her husband as she took his hand. And at that they danced off handsomely around the floor.

The dance reminded Tom vaguely of a waltz.

"They dance beautifully," he remarked, watching as the grandparents pivoted smoothly, freezing for an instant, then their forward feet slowly drew back as one. Changing direction, they glided off once more.

"Care to give it a try?" asked Avani, smiling as she offered Tom her hand.

A horrified look crossed his face. "What, me—dance? I couldn't—I—I don't know how..." She giggled. At that moment Prince Devraj walked up and took her outstretched hand.

"If Tom won't dance with you, would you do me the honor?" The prince bowed deeply.

"I would love to, your Highness," Avani replied, elegantly curtseying, then stepping smoothly into his outstretched arms. She glanced sidelong at Tom and winked. Then they were off, gracefully gliding around the floor, as if they'd been born dancing.

"Blew your chance," said Goban, putting an arm around his friend's shoulder. Tom laughed nervously. The pair stood there for a few minutes, watching Avani and the prince glide by.

Finally, Tom sighed and faced Goban. "What're your plans?"

"Well, my father's heading back to our own lands in a few days. I asked him if I could stay and go to magic school, learn from Larraj this time."

Tom raised an eyebrow. "Larraj is re-opening magic school? Wow, that's great! But—I'm surprised you're interested. You didn't seem all that excited last time."

"I know, my dad was shocked too, but it was a hoot, and besides I wouldn't want you to learn more than me."

Tom chuckled. "That's great. It'll be fun to do some real magic for a change. I think I've had enough of making green slime." Goban snorted, then laughed, slapping Tom hard on his back, nearly knocking him off his feet.

Tom winced. "I hope Mom'll let me stay. She wants to get us back home, to Earth, as soon as possible."

* * *

"Ah, your highness," began Juanita.

"Must we be so formal? After all we've been through? Call me Dakshi," he replied with a grin.

She continued awkwardly. "Hmm—okay, Dakshi then. There's one small matter that's been bothering me."

"Are your accommodations not to your liking? Have any of my servants offended you?" asked the king, concern evident in his voice.

"No, no, nothing like that. You'll probably think it silly, but when I first arrived, I borrowed a cloak to hide my identity. It was hanging on a line with some other clothes, drying in the breeze. I found it at the first house I came to after entering Elfhaven. I feel I must return it."

King Dakshi laughed and snapped his fingers. An aide rushed over. The king whispered something in the aide's ear, and the servant ran off.

"Done. Lay your conscience to rest," said the king, chuckling as he led her over to a short, portly gentleman holding a huge tankard of ale.

"Juanita, I'd like you to meet my best friend King Abban, Supreme Leader of the Dwarf Nation."

King Abban laughed and removed his right arm from around a plump, giggling elfish woman.

"Don't be absurd. Call me Abby," said the dwarf, reaching out and warmly kissing Juanita's hand.

She tipped her head slightly and smiled. "I'm honored, your Highness—er, Abby," she replied.

"Care to lift a pint with your new best friend? I think these lovelies can make room for one more, especially for someone as exquisitely beautiful as yourself," said the dwarf king, grinning as he again put his arms around two of the nearest ladies, squeezing them tight.

"Oh, but it would be rude of me to drink you under the table, wouldn't it?" Juanita replied with a grin of her own.

King Abban laughed heartily.

A sad look crossed King Dakshi's face as he addressed Abban. "I'm sorry, my dear friend, but I haven't yet finished introducing Juanita to all my other guests."

King Abban tipped his head and winked at Juanita.

Nodding back, she replied, "Later, perhaps." Then she turned and strode off, King Dakshi by her side.

The king gazed sidelong at her as they walked. "I must apologize for my friend, Abban. During celebrations such as these, he tends to favor the ale a bit."

Juanita glanced back over her shoulder. The dwarf king toasted her with his tankard. She nodded, then turning her attention once again to King Dakshi, she gave him a wry grin. "I've been to bars. I can handle myself just fine around drunken men."

King Dakshi chuckled. "I'll bet you can, at that!"

Hmm, this guy's all right. I always imagined royalty to be—stuffy and boring. She smiled to herself. As they approached another regally dressed elven gentleman, she tightened her grip around the king's arm slightly. *Perhaps I could get used to this place, after all...*

* * *

Avani and the prince approached Tom.

"Had a nice dance?" asked Tom.

"It was wonderful, you should try it some time," said Avani, grinning.

The prince faced Tom. The two stared at each other for several long, awkward seconds. Finally Devraj stuck out his hand toward Tom. Hesitating only an instant, Tom grasped the prince's hand firmly.

"I feel obligated to thank you for saving my people. I was wrong about you. I—I was jealous, I suppose..." The prince glanced at Avani, then sped on, "jealous about your strange knowledge that I do not possess. Plus, all the attention you receive from your connection with the Prophecy."

"And the fact that I'm from another world? I understand," said Tom, looking deeply into the prince's eyes. They stared at each other a moment longer, then the prince released Tom's hand and to Avani said, "Excuse me, but I must attend to our guests." He pivoted on his heel then strode off toward his uncle, King Bharat, who was conversing with his father and Tom's mom.

Avani glanced first at Tom, then at Goban. She took a deep breath. "Tom, there's something, ah—could I speak to you for a moment, in private?" She glanced at Goban.

"I can take a hint," said Goban, bowing low as he backed up, nearly colliding with a couple of dancers. Tom snickered, but when he glanced at Avani, she looked deadly serious. Avani led them over to the side of the hall, where Max lay watching all the festivities. They were alone. Tom bent down, absently petting his dog.

"I've been wanting to talk to you for some time," she began, "but I just couldn't find the right moment." She let out a deep sigh.

"Yes?"

"Ah—it's—it's about that kiss," she said.

"Kiss?" he replied innocently.

She scowled. "You know very well what kiss I'm talking about."

"Oh, you mean when the trolls were just about to smash us to smithereens and you kissed me full on the lips? That kiss?"

"Yes, that kiss!" snapped Avani, louder than she intended. She glanced around to make sure no one had heard her. Still frowning, she squirmed, pulling nervously on her dress. "It's just that—well—I thought we were about to be killed and—"

"You don't need to say another word. I understand completely," he reassured her.

Relaxing her shoulders, she let out a colossal sigh. "Thanks, Tom, I knew you'd understand."

Tom smiled. "Of course, I understand—you've got the hots for me." Avani gasped, turning beet red. Max looked up and drooled.

Epilogue: Still hope?

Several hideous faces hovered over him in the bright light. Carlos squinted, trying to make out what manner of beasts had him trapped. He blinked, then blinked again. Slowly the monsters came into focus.

Carlos coughed. "Oh, it's you."

"Who were you expecting?" asked Sashi, letting out a deep sigh.

Carlos glanced from Cheng to Leroy to Sashi. He coughed once more. "At first I thought you were monsters. Monsters like we saw a moment ago." His cohorts stared at each other strangely.

Sashi spoke. "You've been out for over ten minutes. We called the staff nurse. She said you've probably had a concussion. She's on her way over."

Carlos tried to sit up but immediately collapsed.

"She also said not to let you sit up until she arrives," said Cheng flatly.

"What happened?" asked Carlos, wincing as his fingers touched a large knot on his forehead.

"The portal collapsed just before you got there. You ran headlong into the wall at full speed," replied Leroy.

"Not again," moaned Carlos.

"What's more, your gun went off. You shot a hole in the ceiling. I was hit in the head by a chunk of falling plaster," lamented Cheng, rubbing his head.

Sashi shot Cheng an angry look, then turned back to Carlos. "If you'd gotten to the portal a second sooner, you might have been cut in half—or worse…"

"Come on, help me up. We've got to try again," groaned Carlos.

"We can't," said Cheng. "Dumping the capacitors' power instantly like that overloaded our circuits. It'll take weeks to repair the damage."

Carlos sighed. "We need more power. How can we get more power?"

The others just stared down at him blankly.

"Come on. You're supposed to be brilliant scientists. So think of something brilliant." There was a pause.

"Um, well—the Main Injector loop in Fermilab's Accelerator Complex is down for maintenance. Its superconducting power supply is a thousand times more powerful than ours," said Leroy tentatively.

"We'd have to move our equipment over to the Main Injector facility," said Sashi. "There's no way to pipe that much energy all the way over here."

"And we'd have to beef up the detection grid to be able to handle that much power," added Leroy.

Sashi sighed. "We're all dreaming. They'd never let us near the thing."

"Leave that to me," said Cheng. "My sister is engaged to the director of that lab."

A thin smile spread across Carlos's face...

— §§§ —

For a taste of the sequel and the 1st Place winner of Writer's Digest 25th annual book awards titled "Thomas Holland in the Realm of the Ogres" turn the page.

Thomas Holland in the Realm of the Ogres

Chapter 1: Treachery! So it begins...

Tom ducked as a book magically floated by, narrowly missing his head. "Anything you wanna look for while we're in the library?" he asked Avani.

The Elfhaven library had the usual dry musty smell of old parchment and leather, but an unusual chill surrounded them.

Tom rubbed his hands together vigorously, then placed them into the pocket of his Chicago Cubs hoodie. He gazed at the ceiling high above them. For the hundredth time he stared in awe at the massive crisscross wooden beams that capped the warehouse sized room. The dark ceiling stood in stark contrast to the gigantic windows whose light cast eerie shadows everywhere.

Statues of monsters and strange beasts adorned alcoves along the walls, each looking poised to leap from their pedestals.

"Shush," whispered Avani, brushing a lock of her long golden hair from her face, exposing a tall pointed elven ear. "I want to find a book of maps so we can trace the route the king's expedition is taking."

"The Guardian of the Citadel could show us a 3-D holographic map," suggested Tom.

"I want a book of real maps. One you can touch, feel the roughness of the parchment, hear the crackle as you turn the pages."

Tom shrugged.

A few people sat quietly here and there, though it was late and the library was mostly deserted. Rows of bookshelves towered high above them, but posed no problem for library patrons. All they had to do was ask the librarian for a book and it magically floated to their desk, opened to wherever they'd left off, and even turned the pages for them.

Avani carefully scanned the elvish runes at the head of each aisle. "Where's Goban?"

"He went to the castle to talk to Prince Devraj." Tom still marveled at the fact that just two weeks ago, he'd been in his room in the suburbs of Chicago, putting the final touches on his robot Chloe. He'd always been a nerd and he definitely didn't believe in magic. Well, at least until he went through the portal at Mom's lab and ended up in Elfhaven. Now, only two weeks later, his best friends were Goban, the bright twelve year old son of King Abban, the leader of the dwarf nation, and Avani, an equally bright, magically gifted thirteen-year-old elven girl. Avani was not only the last Keeper of the Light, but also The Chosen One by the Magic Crystals. This would have been totally unbelievable two weeks ago. Now it seemed normal. "Amazing!" he said out loud.

"What?" asked Avani.

"Oh, nothing. Just thinking."

As they turned down a narrow aisle between two tall rows of shelves, a book floated off the stack right in front of Tom. Stopping abruptly, he leaned back doing his best to avoid getting hit. Still, as it passed by the book brushed his nose then pivoted sideways in mid-air and smacked his ear. It was headed in the direction of the librarian's desk. Tom spun around and glared at the ghost who called himself "*The Librarian*." The spirit's gaze immediately dropped to his desk, busying himself with his work. *Did the apparition just smirk?* Tom's frown deepened.

"Come on," said Avani. "What are you waiting for?"

Tom watched the ghost suspiciously for a moment longer, then followed her. "We should've waited for your little brother. He likes the library."

"Kiran isn't interested in maps. He'd much rather be with the adults, searching for the lost magical artifact," she replied.

"So would I," muttered Tom. He paused, then added, "Technically it's not lost. And it's not magic, for that matter. We know where the power source is."

"Yeah, deep in the Realm of the Ogres."

"Hmmm. So where's Kiran, anyway?" asked Tom.

"At home, playing with your pet."

"Kiran and Max sure have taken a liking to each other."

As they strode down the dark aisle, the bookshelves towering above them, Tom reached out and let his fingers flap across the spines of several ancient leather-bound books embossed with ornate gold lettering. The leather felt dry and gave off a faint musty smell.

"I can't read these titles," said Tom. "Isn't the magic supposed to translate the words?"

"Just spoken languages. Many old elvish scripts and runes exist, plus all the dwarvish dialects. I can read five or six. Grandfather claims he can read twelve, but I think he's lying."

"Nadda, lie?" said Tom. "No way."

Avani shrugged.

Tom paused. "So where is this book of maps? I thought you said you could read these signs."

"I can," she said, craning her neck to see down the aisle.

"Why don't you just ask The Librarian?"

"I can find it myself," she said sharply. "Besides, you know how tiresome that ghost can be. Oh, there it is." Avani headed briskly down the row. Tom watched her go.

Two more books flew off the shelves in rapid fire, one on each side of Tom. This time he managed to miss getting slapped in the face by both of them. Tom glanced over his shoulder at The Librarian, but he was talking with someone, looking the other way.

As Tom turned to follow Avani he heard voices in the next aisle. Normally, he would have ignored them, but he thought he heard one of the voices whisper 'the artifact.' Tom stopped and looked around. No one was watching, so he slid a book off the shelf, leaned casually against the bookcase and pretended to read.

"Did they leave?" said a sinister voice.

"Yes."

"When?"

"This afternoon."

Two voices were speaking, but Tom could barely hear them. A small gap between two large books stood off to his left. Tom scooted over.

"Has *He* been notified?"

"Yes."

"Then the trap is set."

By now Avani was down at the far end of the aisle holding a book and gazing at it intently. Tom tried to catch her attention. *"Pssst,"* he said, waving his own book frantically. She didn't respond. Tom frowned, then leaned against the bookshelf and pretended to read once more.

"We're to meet *Him* tonight," the sinister voice continued.

"Where?"

"The old granary."

"When?"

"Half past midnight."

Tom waved both hands at Avani. *"Pssst,"* he said, a little louder this time. She still didn't notice.

"Did you hear something?" the voice hissed.

"No."

Someone moved in the other aisle. Books were thrown. Suddenly a huge eye peeked through the bookshelf. Tom whipped around, his back to the bookcase. A giant hand thrust through the shelf right beside Tom's head. A ring in the shape of a skull adorned one of the fingers. The skull's eyes began to glow a deep blood red. Books crashed to the floor as the hand thrashed around beside him. Another hand burst through the bookshelf on Tom's other side, scattering still more books. Grabbing

Chapter One

Tom's hood in its fist the hand jerked back, slamming Tom hard against the cabinet.

"I've got him!" cried the voice.

"Avani," hissed Tom, his hoodie now tight about his throat. He couldn't breathe. Tom got a glimpse of her but she was still intently studying her book.

The sound of fabric tearing filled his ears. Glancing up in horror, Tom's hoodie tore as the out-thrust fist pulled harder...